THE MAD MAN'S HOPE

THE COMMUNE'S CURSE: BOOK 2

LUCY A. MCLAREN

For Nan—

For always asking how the writing was going.
Love you forever.

CONTENT WARNING FOR THE READER—

Thank you so much for picking up *The Mad Man's Hope*, the second book in my dark fantasy series, *The Commune's Curse*. It truly means the world to me. So you're aware, I tend to explore some of the darker aspects of the human experience within my characters. As such, this book contains some difficult and potentially upsetting subject matter, including: sexual assault, violence, descriptions of injuries, mild gore, religious oppression, sexism, racism, and homophobia. Take care of yourselves, my friends. Your mental health is more important than any story, so put this book aside if you feel any of these aspects could be difficult for you to read right now.

THE KINGDOM OF SEPTIMA
THE ISLES OF SCREE
THALLIES' ISLANDS
ALPINSIDE MOUNTAINS
ALPIN
THALLION STRAIT
COLD STREAM
LAETIUS RANGE
LAETIUS FOREST
HESSION
LAETIUS
THE ABANDONED ISLES
HESSION HEIGHTS
BARREN MOUNTAINS
HESSION'S END
CRYSTAL MOUNTAINS
SCALE RANGE
THISTLETON
VERITAS
BOAT
LITTLE HAVEN
OLD OAK WOODS
OAK INN (RUINS)
HAVEN'S COVE
HAVEN FOREST
BESSIE'S TAVERN
CASTLETON
NOOK PASS
NOOK TOWN
MONARCH'S OCEAN
LAKE OF KINGS
HAVEN'S END
MONARCH'S GARDEN
NOOK FLOW
TASKAN FOREST
AMBLE HILLS
CRAG'S EDGE LAKE
TORRANT ESTATE
TASKAN
AMBLESIDE
CRAGSIDE
WOLF COVE
THE COMMUNE
THE CRAGS
TASKAN BAY
THE GREAT SEA

The Noman Islands
The Great Sea
Docks
Temple
Village
Isle of Veritarra
Bay of Veritarra
Straits of Ezzarah
Docks
Ezzarah's Isle
Old Temple (Ruins)
Samalah's Isle
A'laha'a (The Sons)
Docks
Su'mula's Isle
Village
Docks

PROLOGUE
EIRIK

The young man inhaled deeply, drinking in the fresh sea air as he passed through the black, wrought-iron gates of the Commune's compound on the back of his horse. He rode a fine white gelding—a gift from the Grand Magister himself on this, his eighteenth birthday. He glanced behind him, expecting to be stopped by one of the black-hooded acolytes going about their work or red-cloaked soldiers guarding the gates, to be questioned as to his business outside the compound's thick walls. It was a rare sight to see one such as him—one of the Grand Magister's closest acolytes—passing through the gates. But no one said anything to stop him. "Master Eirik," one of the soldiers had muttered, waving him through without so much as a glance.

A thrill passed through Eirik. The Grand Magister must have sent word ahead. He really was allowed out alone, for the first time in nine years. His heart soared. He could run, couldn't he? He could go home, back to his family, back to ...

He scoffed. *No. The Torrant Estate is not my home.* The truth was, the Grand Magister had been more a father to him than his own. He was a Torrant in name only; in all else, he was loyal to the Commune

—to the Grand Magister. That he would even think of running sent a bolt of guilt down his spine.

He gave the gates and guards one final glance over his shoulder before clicking his horse into a slow trot. He had time to enjoy the ride into the city. The sun was warm on his face, even this early. The black sleeves of his shirt billowed in the cooling breeze that blew across Taskan Bay, and his black cloak flapped behind him. He felt a sense of power, that *he* of all the Grand Magister's acolytes should be given free roam as a birthday gift—for he was not the only noble child banished to the Commune by their family.

But he *was* one of the Grand Magister's chosen. He smirked down at the blood-red ruby on his right index finger. The gift was not given lightly—it was a clear badge of loyalty that he could flash to any and all who might question him in Taskan. It would buy him great influence. The Grand Magister's words from that very morning echoed through Eirik's mind.

"You will be my eyes and ears in the city, Eirik. Listen. Learn. Forge connections that will strengthen the Commune's presence in Septima. Do not disappoint me."

He pulled his horse to a stop along the cliffs that looked down at Taskan Bay. The wind was stronger here, ripping through his hair, snapping his cloak behind him, sending goose pimples across his flesh. Still, the sea air was refreshing—a welcome change to the stifling air that seemed to cling to every part of the grand manor house that sat at the centre of the Commune's compound, his home these past nine years. A sudden weight of pressure settled over him. He had no sense of joy that he'd reached eighteen summers, only a deep feeling of responsibility for the trust placed in him by the Grand Magister.

Am I worthy?

As he tried to push the uncomfortable thought away, a ship moved to dock in Taskan Harbour. He found himself curious as to who might be on board and was spurring his horse on before he could say where the compulsion came from.

Perhaps, he thought later, it was meant to be. Fate, pulling him forth. In that moment, it was, at least, an unexpected distraction from his own self-doubt.

The red-cloaked soldiers standing watch narrowed their eyes at a Commune acolyte attempting to enter Taskan without proper reason—until they saw his ruby ring. After that, their fumbling and snivelling was enough to leave a sneer of disdain on his face. *Pathetic.* He glanced down at the ring as he urged his horse onwards. *But at least I know it works.*

He could tell straightaway which ship had just arrived, for it was being secured at the docks by numerous harbour workers. He took little interest in them, instead noting the line of dark-skinned men and women waiting to leave the ship. Many were looking towards the city with wide eyes; Eirik followed their gaze, beaming with pride. The Grand Magister ensured that the capital of Septima was a sight to behold. A shame most of the immigrants would never truly be able to see it. They would each be assigned roles based on their age and skillset. Nomarran immigrants were welcomed in Septima, but there was not enough work to keep them in the city. They would be dispatched all around the kingdom, employed in towns and cities and estates where needed. Perhaps some might even be sent to the Torrant Estate, though Eirik doubted his father would welcome *outsiders* into his home. It had been years since he had seen the man, yet he recalled from his childhood the burning scorn Lord Jeremyah Torrant held for any who did not have noble blood running through their veins.

When he focused back on the ship, the men, women, and children had begun walking down the swaying wooden plank, feet landing on the boards of the dock with soft thuds. They had little by way of personal possessions, some appearing to only have the clothes on their backs. Still, he couldn't help but feel a slight niggle of envy at their freedom. Here they were, so far from their homeland. They would be provided with jobs. From there, they would make their own lives, something he could never do. His life was on a set path, and it was one he could never stray from. His loyalty to the Grand Magister ran too deep.

It was as his gaze drifted over the arriving Nomarrans that Eirik first saw him. Young, perhaps around his own age, fresh-faced, dark eyes gleaming, mouth slightly agape as he looked up at Taskan. *He's … beautiful.* His heart fluttered in his chest, and for a moment, he felt as though he might collapse from atop his horse, so weak had his knees suddenly become, so light was his head. He swallowed. He had to speak to this young man, to *know* him, to possess his adoration and attention. Before he could even think about what he was doing, he'd snapped his fingers at a nearby worker.

"You," he said, climbing from his horse's back and flashing his ring. "Hold this." He placed the reins in the confused dock worker's hand and walked toward the mysterious young man without a backward glance. As he moved closer, Eirik studied him. He seemed lost, alone, afraid. Some part of Eirik felt drawn to the young man for this very reason, drawn to the pain he knew all too well himself—but that was not a thought he could allow himself to examine too deeply.

"What's your name?" He heard his own voice before he'd even thought about speaking—anything to quiet that whisper in his mind, the reminder of hurts that had cut far too deep to ever fully heal. His voice rang across the harbour, but the young man didn't seem to hear him at first … or perhaps he simply didn't believe someone of evidently noble birth would be speaking to him. He frowned, glancing towards Eirik and then quickly away.

"What's your name?" Eirik said again, standing directly in front of the young man. This close, he could see how perfect and smooth his black skin was, with only the slightest hint of dark stubble on his jaw. The young man shuffled on the spot, fiddling with his dirty tunic, hand cupping a leather pouch secured to the belt at his waist.

"My name?" he rasped, finally looking up to meet Eirik's gaze. "It's—it's Jonasaiah, my lord."

Eirik raised an eyebrow. "Jonasaiah?" *Too much like Father's.* He said the name slowly, feeling it on his tongue, and the young man gulped. Silence hung in the air between them, dragging out until Jonasaiah looked ready to flee, his eyes wide with fear. Eirik's lips quirked into a smile. "That's quite a mouthful."

"Yes, sir, er ... m-my lord. I ..." Jonasaiah cleared his throat. "Y-you could call me Jonah for short."

"Jonah?" Eirik nodded. "Yes, I think that will suit."

Jonah bowed his head and remained silent.

"Anyway, I'm not a lord. You can call me Eirik." He looked Jonah up and down, taking in the full extent of his threadbare outfit. "We'll need to get you some new clothes."

"New clothes, my ... uh, Eirik?" Jonah peered up again, looking at Eirik through thick black eyelashes. Eirik's heart fluttered again, and he fought to conceal the quivering that threatened to take over his body.

"Yes." He glanced over his shoulder, and noting the location of the import officer, held a hand up to Jonah. "Wait here."

He turned away and walked towards the import officer, feeling rather relieved to have a moment to clear his head. He was flustered and excited all at once. This was most unlike him. He needed more time to think and couldn't risk the young man being sent away from Taskan. Something told him their meeting was ... *fated*.

As Eirik approached the rather harried-looking officer, who was working his way down a list of jobs noted on the ship's logs, he came to a decision. Eirik cleared his throat. The man frowned upwards at him, thick grey eyebrows furrowing as he opened his mouth to speak. Before he could do so, Eirik held up the ruby ring. The man's white skin paled to an unnatural shade of grey.

"Oh, uh ... how may I assist, Lord ...?"

"Torrant," said Eirik, not bothering to correct the assumption this time.

"Lord Torrant, very good." The import officer nodded. "What may I do for you, sir?"

"I am simply informing you that I shall be taking that young man"—he waved an arm lazily behind him—"as my personal guard. He will be under my employ."

"Oh." The man's lips pinched together tightly. "That's ... that's most unusual, my lord. We are clearly instructed by the Commune that each individual must be formally—"

"Are you questioning my authority?" Eirik leaned down to place a hand on the man's shoulder. "Do I need to inform the Grand Magister of your insolence?" He was using his powers before he'd even really thought about it. He watched as the man's face slackened, satisfied that his powers had grown much surer lately.

"N-no, my lord. F-forgive me." A sheen of sweat had formed on the man's bald head. "P-please."

Eirik suddenly became aware of his audience. A Nomarran woman standing behind the import officer was watching him with unbridled fear. He stood tall, slapped the man on his back, and said, "Excellent. You'll cross Jonasaiah from the ship's log and say no more about it."

The man mopped the sweat from his face with the back of his hand, gawping towards Eirik as though he wasn't sure what had just happened. "Jonasaiah, you say?" He moved a finger down the parchment laid on the table before him, tapping it when he came across the young Nomarran's name. "Yes, I see him. It will be done, Lord Torrant."

"Good man," Eirik said. "Your loyalty to the Commune is admirable."

The man nodded briskly, lips pulled downwards. "My lord."

Eirik turned away from the fool. Heading back towards Jonah, a thrill of excitement rushed through him. He held himself back briefly, watching the Nomarran who was now his. He was peering out to sea, perhaps thinking of the home he'd left behind.

Well, his home was here now. With Eirik, who now had someone all his own. A companion. Maybe more, in time. He approached Jonah and placed a firm hand on his back. For a moment, he faltered.

He felt ... *nothing*; his powers were unable to create any form of link between them, no matter how tenuous.

Curious.

When Jonah turned and raised an eyebrow at him, Eirik smiled. *He is all the more mysterious.* "Come," he said. "Clothes. I know a tailor in the city. I planned to visit him myself. And now he can clothe both of us."

"Yes, my ..." Jonah smiled, shaking his head. "Yes, Eirik."

Eirik studied Jonah's face for a moment more before retrieving his horse and leading Jonah towards Taskan's centre.

This was turning out to be a good day after all.

CHAPTER I

JONAH

13 YEARS LATER

J onah sat alone on a rotting tree stump, staring into the flickering flames of the campfire he'd so carefully constructed. The morning was cool, and the skin on his arms prickled beneath his black tunic, yet he had removed the black cloak he had slept in. Its clasp around his neck was a reminder he would rather remove, especially after he had abandoned his red commander's cloak as he had fled Lord Torrant's basement, fled from the horrors that had been revealed, fled from the true nature of the man he—

No.

I cannot think of him, not now.

Yet thinking that and banishing the pain that panged through his body with every heartbeat were two very different things.

He closed his eyes, images of that last, dreadful day flashing through his mind. Lord Torrant's forced testing of Evelyn, the pure hatred he had shown. And worse still, the skeletal presence of the young man he had visited at the brothel, Cole, broken and deformed and half-dead ...

Such pain caused by the hands of his former lover, the man he had loved for thirteen years, even through the last seven when they had been master and servant, despite his constant longing and belief that they could be together again.

He let out a shaky exhale.

He kept me waiting, promised me we could go back.

"Could it really all have been a lie?" The words, spoken aloud, drifted into the trees around him, sounding strangely hollow to his own ears.

Birdsong was his only reply.

Jonah rubbed his eyes, pushing away the pain-filled memories.

He had to focus ahead. Had to keep his mind upon the path that he had chosen, for it was all he could do to distract himself from the abyss of despair.

He would destroy the Commune. He would make the Grand Magister pay for all the pain that had been inflicted upon his fellow Nomarrans.

And for taking Eirik's love from me.

He ground his teeth, a surge of anger threatening to burst forth. He forced his breathing to slow.

For his plan to work, he had recruited the help of a young woman who had, not so long ago, been his enemy, someone he had hunted for the Commune. Why had he sought help from her, of all people? Because he had been afraid to do it alone. Because he feared he did not have the strength to see it through. Because she had been there with him in that awful place, seen Lord Torrant's abominable secrets as he had.

And perhaps because he had seen something in her in that basement. Some deep, driving need that he recognised in himself. A need to repair the wrongs he had committed in the name of the Commune.

So he would travel with Evelyn to the Noman Islands, to the home he had not seen for thirteen long years. He wondered whether he'd recognise it. Perhaps they'd recovered from the uprising of his childhood. Would his mother still be there? And if she was, what would she think of who he'd become? Of the things he had done. He exhaled. No, he was no longer the man who'd left all those years ago.

Jonah shook his head to banish the thoughts, afraid to reflect on such questions any longer. He turned his attention back to the tea he was preparing to heat in a pan above the fire and tossed dried mint herbs into the tin of boiling water. The sound of crunching leaves behind him caused him to turn, shoulders tensed. Despite knowing it would be Evelyn, he'd been unable to shake his unease ever since they'd fled the Torrant Estate.

Eirik ... Will he come for me?

Deep down, he knew the answer. He'd been shown the truth in that awful basement, his eyes opened after being blind for far too long to what was right in front of him.

I was nothing but a possession for him to mock and control. The girl has no powers. Neither of us are worth recapturing. Neither of us will gain him any favours with the Grand Magister.

Evelyn frowned as she came to kneel beside where he sat, eyeing the pan above the flames. She clasped two long, limp, auburn braids, freshly cut from her head.

"I could have helped," Jonah said, stirring the tea and preparing to pour it into two tin mugs, glad he'd been able to steal some supplies along with the horse from Lord Torrant's stables. The mindless servants on the estate had been none the wiser; such was the nature of the powers that were used to control them. They followed their daily orders and nothing more.

"No," she replied tersely. "I needed to do it myself." She touched the pommel of the sword at her waist, turning her face away from his.

"I see." He gave her an appraising look. "It will serve as a good disguise. Your hair was too distinctive. You are slim enough to pass as a boy. Your face is plain. It will do."

She shifted where she sat, crossing her arms.

"We will need luck on our side," he continued. "But we might just be able to make it to the harbour undetected. From there, I plan to find us passage on a ship south. To the Noman Islands."

Evelyn nodded, taking a mug of tea from him. They drank in silence for a time, each in their own minds, still unaccustomed to the new dynamic they found themselves in. Her quiet was a blessing. If she had pushed, had sought to ask questions about Eirik or what had happened at the Torrant Estate, he wasn't sure how he might have responded. He barely had any clear answers for himself, even as he replayed what had happened over and over again.

Why, Eirik? Why? His heart cried with each word, but he remained outwardly impassive. He would not admit his pain, least of all to someone he barely knew.

After they finished their tea and had both eaten berries and dry bread, Evelyn cleared her throat. "Comm—uh, Jonah," she said. He glanced up, unused to being addressed by his first name. For so long, he had been Commander Sulemon; the only one who had called him Jonah had been Eirik. "How long will the journey take? To your— to the Noman Islands? Is it ... is it dangerous there?"

He studied her face. It was easy to forget how young she was. A child, really, not much older than he had been when he'd first arrived in Septima, sheltered and ignorant.

Ignorant, yes. We both are.

He sighed, standing and clasping his hands behind his back. He had a sudden urge to be away from this place—from Septima, from the influence of the Commune, from Lord Torrant, whose pull was ever-present despite the hatred that burned within his chest.

Hatred, yes. But love, too. Still, after everything. It made Jonah sick to his stomach to let those words echo through his mind. He ran a hand over his face. "It will take many days. We will travel by ship. And no, it is not dangerous. The danger in the Noman Islands has long since passed. It was over when I was a child. Contained." His mind drifted back; flashes of memory returned, his mother's face at the forefront of them all. Jonah turned to find Evelyn regarding him, eyebrows raised. He couldn't tell how long the silence had dragged out. His mind was chaotic and would be until they got away from Septima, it seemed. He had to focus, forget Eirik, forget everything. Think only of their plan.

Get to the Noman Islands. Obtain enough Veritarra's Gift to take down the Commune. Return to Septima.

He almost laughed at such a ridiculous notion. *As if it is so simple.*

"We should leave." Jonah turned from Evelyn and began to pack the saddlebags. "We will enter the city today and make for the harbour. The sooner we get on a ship, the sooner we will be safe from the Commune."

Without a word, she joined him in clearing away their camp, rolling up her blanket and securing it to the horse's saddlebags. Jonah put out the fire and climbed atop the horse, pulling Evelyn up behind him. Before long, they were on the road once more. Jonah urged the horse onwards, tightness spreading across his chest. He couldn't be sure whether word of his betrayal had yet reached his fellow soldiers in Taskan; all he could do was pray to the Goddess Veritarra that they would make it through the city without hindrance.

"Let me do the talking," Jonah said to Evelyn as they arrived at Taskan. They approached a private entry gate, situated along the western wall, usually reserved for nobility and their closest advisors. To the south lay Taskan Bay, beyond which was the Great Sea, and further still, home.

Now we just need to find a ship.

Jonah prayed that Eirik hadn't yet alerted the city guard to his betrayal. Evelyn gave a curt nod as though she could sense his doubts and wanted to bolster his confidence, though her knuckles tightened upon the horse's reins.

He stood tall, drew his shoulders back, and approached the soldier. It was not someone he recognised. A new recruit, perhaps, for he was fresh-faced and clutched the hilt of his sword. As they neared, the young man swallowed audibly.

Nervous. I can take advantage of that.

He lifted his chin. "Soldier."

The young man, who had been staring steadfastly towards some spot behind Jonah's shoulder, blinked up at him, his brow furrowing. "Com-Commander Sulemon?" He fumbled to beat a half-clenched fist against his breastplate. "Oh, I am sorry, Commander. I had not realised i-it was you." He saluted again, firmer this time.

Jonah bowed his head. "I require entry, soldier. I am here under Lord Torrant's orders. I am to slip into the city unseen, hence my disguise. This ... boy here is leading me to the home of a traitorous merchant, and we need the element of surprise." The soldier's eyes flitted to Evelyn and back, mouth flapping open and shut. "I'm sure you understand the need for complete confidentiality."

The soldier nodded so hard and fast it was a wonder he didn't injure himself.

"Very good," Jonah said, eager to be away from the gate where a more adept soldier might appear at any moment. "Boy." He turned to Evelyn and summoned her forward. The soldier stepped aside and let her through, watching her without the slightest hint of suspicion on his young face. Jonah cleared his throat, drawing the soldier's gaze back to him.

"I have your word, soldier? That this will be kept between us? I don't want to have to return here and—"

"N-no, Commander Sulemon. I mean, yes, Commander. You have my word." He saluted more assuredly this time, fist clanging twice against his armour.

"Very good."

Without a backward glance, Jonah strode through the gate with a confidence that belied the thunderous hammering of his heart.

Beyond the wall, life in the city continued as usual.

Of course. Why would it not simply because my own world has been torn apart?

Evelyn looked to him expectantly, silent in the saddle.

He moved ahead of her. "This way," he muttered.

He intended to skirt along the city's western wall until they reached the harbour, avoiding Taskan's centre and, he hoped, the greatest chance of being noticed and questioned. As they walked, Jonah tried to quell the memories that Taskan threatened to awake within him. He glanced about the city streets he had once patrolled at Eirik's behest, becoming increasingly irritable, almost willing Evelyn to ask some inept question so he could snap at her. She must have sensed it, for she didn't speak a word as they walked through the streets, and Jonah was left to torment himself with recollections of years past.

When the harbour came into view, he sighed with relief. Maybe this would be easier than he'd imagined. He gave Evelyn a weak smile, which she returned, though he saw the fear that simmered beneath the surface in the nervous cast of her eyes and the way she ran her hands through her newly shortened hair.

"Do not worry. We will find a ship." He spoke the words more for his own comfort than hers and willed them to be true. He peered up at the sky—clear blue, a good omen. "Come," he said, making his way along the harbourfront, where two frigates and a galleon were docked.

Please let one of them be heading south.

He first approached the blue-sailed galleon by the name of *King Cosmo's Pride*, signalling for Evelyn to stand back with the horse, the better to keep her true identity concealed.

It didn't take him long to locate the captain—a small, grey-bearded man who was evidently eager to converse with someone new. Before long, however, Jonah had established that the ship was bound northwards to the mountain-side city of Alpin. He thanked the captain and edged away, cutting the man's enthusiastic conversation short.

He stalked towards the frigate, mood dampening and hopes sinking by the moment; the ship could only recently have docked, its crew still busy unloading their wares. They were unlikely to be setting sail for at least a few days. Upon the *Nubira*—an ode to the Grand Magister's family name—the captain approached Jonah, arms crossed over a broad chest.

"Can I help you?" he asked, dark eyes looking Jonah up and down. Evidently deciding Jonah was not worth the effort, he waved a dismissive hand. "I haven't got time for idleness. I've got another forty crates to unload and a crew itching to be away at the Goddess's Gift. Be off with you."

Jonah blanched, sure the captain mentioned the name of that particular brothel—named to mock Veritarra herself—to slight him. The man wouldn't dare have spoken to him in such a manner if he'd been wearing his red cloak.

Damn these people and their pathetic notions of power.

There must have been a flash of rage across his face, for a flicker of doubt passed across the captain's eyes. Jonah wasn't aware of Evelyn approaching him until her hand was upon his arm, drawing him back along the dock.

"Come on," she said softly. "There's another ship."

He nodded at her, strangely calmed by the gentleness of her voice. He turned his back on the captain of the *Nubira* and followed her, heading towards *Septima's Blessing,* the final ship—and their last hope—with a heavy gut.

At first, he thought the captain must be about his business in the harbour. The crew was loading a last batch of crates to the ship under the instruction of a fellow Nomarran, whose booming voice echoed across the deck.

"Be careful! Those crates are incredibly delicate!"

It was only when Jonah stopped to watch the man, saw the way the crew deferred to his command and the way he held himself with such surety, that he realised this Nomarran *was* the captain. His heart lurched, optimism blooming in his chest. He wondered what the man had done to gain such an appointment as he walked up the gangplank, once more signalling for Evelyn to wait, and approached him. The captain was finely dressed in dark grey trousers and tunic, with a fur-lined black cloak and polished leather boots.

"Veritarra's blessing to you," Jonah said in Nomarran, holding both hands upwards in greeting. The man turned to him, dark eyes narrowed. As soon as he saw the speaker, however, the suspicion melted from his face, and he moved forward with arms out. He did not return Jonah's greeting, and when he spoke, it was in the King's tongue of Septima.

"What business have you here, friend?" the captain asked, glancing towards the harbour as though expecting to see an escort. As he approached, Jonah noted the fine ruby pin glimmering on his tunic. The captain touched a hand to it. "Ah, you admire my badge."

Shit. "Is that—"

The captain beamed with pride. "From the Grand Magister. To show I am a loyal servant to the kingdom, of course. To the Commune." He gave an elaborate bow, as though he were in front of the Grand Magister himself.

Lord Torrant had one just like it, a gleaming ruby ring upon his finger, though Jonah had not thought to find one here, especially on a Nomarran ship's captain. *I must tread carefully.*

"I am sure you now understand the depth of my loyalty, Commander Sulemon."

Jonah gave a brisk nod, unsurprised that the man knew his name; he was the only Nomarran in the Commune's ranks ... or so he had thought. "Of course, Captain." He leaned in close. "But with people fawning to please the Grand Magister, we have had reports of fakes. I must be careful."

"I see." The man studied Jonah for a moment before brushing a finger across the ruby on his chest again. "Beautiful, is it not?"

"Yes, most beautiful." Jonah bowed his head, afraid his eyes would betray his wariness.

"But that is not why you are here, Commander. Is it an inspection you require? I can assure you that everything is as it should be. My crew are—"

Jonah lifted his head and narrowed his eyes. "An inspection? Nothing of the sort, Captain."

"Oh?" The captain cleared his throat. "Then please, tell me— how might I be of assistance to such a fine soldier as yourself? Lord Torrant's own man."

Jonah frowned. "Yes, that is so," he said. "But my business is elsewhere. My companion and I require passage to the Noman Islands. We were hoping your ship might provide such an opportunity."

"Companion, you say?" The captain looked towards Evelyn. "The Noman Islands? Hmm. A mission for the Grand Magister, I dare say." He nodded, clapping a hand against Jonah's back, face alight with curiosity. "The relationship has been strained between our people ... An envoy, is it?"

"It is a mission of great secrecy, Captain, so I would ask that you refrain from such questions. And that you keep it to yourself."

"Oh, you have my word, Commander." He gave Jonah a smile that didn't reach his eyes. "You are most fortunate. Our trip was delayed by ... Well, no matter. You are here, and I am in no position to deny a man who works so closely with one of the Grand Magister's own trusted agents." He again gave a flourishing bow. Jonah hesitated before responding, wondering whether the man was mocking him.

Does it matter? His ship is going where you need it to. "When do you set sail?" he finally asked.

"Why, this very day, Commander. Before the bell tolls three."

Jonah glanced up at the sky, noting the sun's position. "So soon?" he said. "That is good news. I will send my boy to stow our horse at the harbour stables and to bring our belongings aboard."

"Your boy? You have no business to attend to yourself ashore? Surely, you would like to—"

"No, Captain. That will not be necessary. My boy can see to everything."

"As you say, Commander." The captain rubbed the bristle of black hair that lined his jaw. "Well then, it seems it is set. We will find suitable accommodations for you both aboard *Septima's Blessing*. A fine ship, indeed, with room to spare. Why, I'm told that before she became mine, the Grand Magister travelled aboard our beloved *Nubira*, and so there are special cabins for guests such as yourself. The Grand Magister's guards could expect no less, hmm? So, once again, we must thank His Benevolence for the fortune that has rained upon us both." He gave the gunwale an audible slap, voice raised with fervour.

"Of course," Jonah said, backing towards the gangplank. "Thank you, Captain ...?"

"Aha, yes, my name. It is Nehemiah. But the crew calls me Nem, and you shall do the same, Commander Sulemon."

"Captain Nem. Very well." Jonah nodded.

"Now then, my friend. Send your boy on his errand and join me in my cabin. We drink—to the Grand Magister!"

Without another word, he turned and walked briskly towards the ship's stern, barking orders to his crew as he went.

ONCE EVELYN HAD BEEN GIVEN her instructions, Jonah joined Captain Nem in his richly decorated cabin. Stepping inside, Jonah was transported home. The scent of Nomarran flowers, sweet and delicate, filled the air.

Just like Eirik's beard oil. His heart skipped a beat.

Paintings on the wall depicted the Temple of Veritarra and the sunset over the beach on Samalah's Isle. All about the cabin, fire-stones—magical illuminating stones from the Noman Islands—cast their warm orange glow across the floor, walls, and ceiling. For a moment, he couldn't speak, drawn in by the unexpected scene, his breath caught in his throat by a sudden well of emotion.

"Commander?"

Jonah's attention snapped back to Captain Nem. "I'm sorry," he said. "It's just … your paintings. It's been a while. Since I was home."

"I see," Nem said. "I was asking whether you would require a cabin. Shared, I presume, with your … boy? I am not a man to question the tastes of others." He gave a conspiratorial wink.

Jonah scowled. "We will require separate cabins, Captain," he said curtly. The man's forthright comment had caught him off guard; what did he know of Jonah's past? His relationship with Lord Torrant? He cleared his throat, eager to change the subject. "You will accept payment for our passage. I don't have much, but it is the least I can do to—"

"Nonsense," Nem said, batting away Jonah's offered coin purse. "Any mission done in the Grand Magister's name is a mission I am happy to assist with." He bowed his head, touching a hand to the ruby at his chest. Then he clasped his hands together, looking at Jonah with dark, unreadable eyes. "Well, then. Separate cabins it is. There are two which would suit, reserved for Commune soldiers, as I said. They are somewhat cramped, I'm afraid, though far more than what my own crew is afforded." His lips flashed into the ghost of a smile.

"Thank you, Captain."

"Think nothing of it, Commander. It appears to be a fortunate turn of events. Really, it is as though our paths were fated to cross, is it not?"

"Mm. Perhaps that is so." Jonah gave a tight smile that mirrored Captain Nem's.

Just then, there was a brisk knock at the door.

"Enter," Nem called.

Evelyn opened the door, eyes to the ground. Before she could speak, Jonah said, "Ah, boy. That was quick. Good."

"Aha." Captain Nem clapped his hands together, and Evelyn flinched. "I shall take you to your cabins. But before we go"—his eyes darted to Evelyn's waist—"I would request that you leave *that* in your cabin. A commander must be armed, I understand, but you do not look to be a soldier."

Evelyn quickly shook her head.

"Mm. As I thought. Your sword will remain in your cabin, boy, hmm? I cannot have just anyone wielding a weapon aboard my ship."

Evelyn nodded, though Jonah was irked at the implication that they were there to cause trouble.

"Come, then." The captain led them to two adjacent cabins, each lit by a single firestone lamp, illuminating a single hammock and tiny washbasin.

"Get settled," Nem said. "We will be on our way before long."

"Thank you," said Jonah, but the man was already retreating.

"What now?" Evelyn said, standing in the doorway to his cabin. She clasped the small sack of the supplies she'd taken from the horse's saddle.

"Get some rest," he said. "Once the ship leaves the harbour, we will know we are safe. Until then, we had best stay within our cabins."

She watched him for a moment before nodding and closing his door. He heard her open the door to her own cabin, the creak of footsteps across it, the sounds of her clambering into her hammock.

Silence.

He sat on the floor with his face in his hands, memories old and new attempting to flood his mind. *No.* He gritted his teeth. *No, I will not think of him.* Eventually, he settled into his hammock and let out a long sigh. With time to let his thoughts flow freely, his worries bubbled to the surface. *Can I trust Captain Nem, truly? A man of the Grand Magister, a servant of the Commune, a blind fool as I once was.*

The reply came immediately from some part of him that was able to remain rational in the face of such anxiety. *What choice do I have?*

This is how we get to the Noman Islands as quickly as possible; we cannot risk remaining in Taskan. It won't be long before word spreads about my flight from the Commune, my betrayal ...

His breath hitched. "I am not the betrayer," he whispered into the cramped cabin. "I am not the liar, Eirik. I am not the—"

He could not say the word aloud, but it echoed through his mind nonetheless: *murderer.*

He scrunched his eyes shut and curled his hands into fists, wanting to scream.

Despite his heartache and concerns, exhaustion overcame him, and his sleeping mind took him where his waking mind would not.

To thirteen years ago.

Jonah had barely taken a dozen steps on dry land, entranced by the size and scope of the city before him, when he saw Eirik for the first time.

Impeccably dressed, clean-shaven, black hair framing his face and gleaming with an almost blue cast in the morning sun, he had an undeniable air of authority as he sat atop a great white gelding, observing the immigrants arriving in his kingdom.

Jonah had never seen anyone so beautiful.

"You ... you could call me Jonah for short."

Even now, even in his dream, he felt the burn of self-conscious-ness at introducing himself to the mysterious stranger, the young man who seemed all too interested in a simple Nomarran, a simple fool just sixteen years old and without a penny to his name.

But then he recalled turning to observe the ocean at his back, the harbour in Taskan and the bustle of people. He had been certain, in that moment, that he'd made the right decision in coming here, in fleeing the home that had been torn apart before his eyes by his own father and others possessing the powers of the cruel God Ezzarah.

In his dream, as thirteen years ago, he stared toward the horizon. Beyond Taskan Bay and the Great Sea, nestled amongst the Straits of Ezzarah, sat his homeland. His mother was still there, having chosen to remain in the lands of her ancestors rather than leave. He had not known if he would see her again though had known that departing the Noman Islands was the only choice he had. He hoped he would one day see her again—if not in this life, then in the light of Veritarra's blessing after their death.

"Jonah."

He sat up with a start, body moistened with sweat beneath his underclothes, as the familiar voice echoed through his head.

It didn't take long for his eyes to adjust to the darkness in his cabin. He made to stand, pushing the woollen blanket away from himself ... and froze, legs caught mid-swing above the floor.

At first, he thought he must be imagining the dark outline beside his bed.

Until it spoke his name once more.

"Jonah."

He shivered and reached up to touch the shape. "Eirik," he whispered, voice hoarse. "How—"

"Hush." A cool hand clasped his own, and the shadow sat beside him. Jonah swallowed the rising lump in his throat and tried to sit up, a quiet sob escaping from his lips.

"You know why I'm here." Eirik placed a hand on his cheek, fingers tracing the line of his jaw before lingering on his trembling lips.

"You came for me." Jonah closed his eyes and inhaled, drinking in Eirik's scent. He barely noticed the tears slipping down his own cheeks.

"Of course," Eirik said. He leaned down, the bristles of his close-cropped beard brushing against Jonah's face. The aroma of sweet, floral oil was almost overwhelming.

"You came to take me home."

"Home?" Jonah opened his eyes just as Eirik pulled back, his lips curled into a smile as they had been on the day they'd met. "Yes, Jonah. Home, with me." Their lips were so close that Jonah barely needed to shift his head. He could have just allowed it to happen; his entire being cried out for it. He could kiss the man he had loved these thirteen years. The man to whom he had given himself entirely.

But something held him back, and even in the dark, Jonah saw the realisation pass across Eirik's face. In the blink of an eye, his expression changed, mouth twisting into a sneer, and he clamped a hand upon Jonah's jaw, squeezing so hard that a blinding pain shot up his face and down his neck. He didn't cry out, was unable to make a sound.

"You think you can leave me?" Eirik spat. "I won't allow it. *You* do not leave *me*."

The sharp words sent a cold stab through Jonah's heart. He tried to speak then, but his mouth was held shut by Eirik's hand. He moved his free arm to stroke Eirik's face, but it was slapped away.

"You're mine. And you always will be." Eirik's hands moved to Jonah's throat, squeezing, crushing, just as Jonah had done to him in those awful final moments in the basement.

"Please," Jonah wheezed, vision blurring.

Eirik began to laugh—a cold, uncaring sound that rang through the cramped cabin and jarred against Jonah's ears. "Now you know how it feels," he whispered. "To be so betrayed by someone you *love*."

"No, no," he croaked. "No, please, Eirik. I'm sorry, I'm sorry—" His arms and legs grew slow and weak. He felt as though he were floating away from himself.

He was dying and there was nothing he could do.

"You are mine, Jonah. Mine."

As his mind slowed, some distant part of it registered someone speaking.

A girl.

Who ...

"Jonah."

He could see her face in his mind's eye, but her name escaped him.

He wasn't sure he could cling on much longer.

The fire in his throat was fading away.

Darkness was taking him.

"Jonah, wake up."

Eirik was still laughing.

His heart threatened to burst.

"Jonah!"

He cried out, eyes flying open, hands flinging out.

"Stop!"

It was Evelyn.

She was standing over him, eyes wide with fear, clasping a firestone lamp in her hand.

"I came to wake you," she said, edging towards him. "But you were, I don't know, having a night terror. You wouldn't stop moaning."

Sweat drenched his entire body as he sat up. He rubbed his eyes and blinked, taking in the room.

No lingering scent of oil.

Eirik had never been here.

He didn't come to take me home.

Jonah's stomach tightened, and he fought down the urge to vomit.

"I-I'm sorry," he whispered. He placed a hand absentmindedly to his throat, imagining he could still feel Eirik's hands clenched around it.

"Whatever you were dreaming of can't have been good," Evelyn said, frowning.

"Mm," he said, avoiding her curious gaze.

"I came to wake you," Evelyn repeated, more urgently this time. "We've set sail."

It was only then that Jonah noticed the gentle rocking of the ship, the distant sound of waves.

"I'll give you a moment to, uh, wake up properly. I've brought you a jug of water."

Jonah watched her leave, unable to bring himself to even thank her.

"Fuck." He ran his hands across his face and scalp, trying to resist the urge to scream.

By the time he'd splashed himself with cold water and taken a generous drink, his emotions were once more under control. He made his face a mask of cool determination, concealing the unceasing pain within him.

Septima was behind him. It was time to focus ahead—on his home, to seeing his mother again ...

To bringing down the Commune, once and for all.

CHAPTER 2
RAIF

The last meagre beams of sunlight were disappearing on the horizon, and with them, any measly measure of warmth they'd provided. Raif shivered atop Bert's back, pulling his cloak around his arms as heavy rain droplets began to splash against his skin. Much to his dismay, the brown wool afforded little coverage from the bitter chill that was creeping in with the dusk. He huddled down towards Bert's back, stealing some of the horse's musky heat.

Is Rose somewhere dry? Is she warm?

The hollow pit in his stomach deepened at the thought, for he doubted Avanna cared for his sister's safety; all she wanted were Rose's powers.

When he reluctantly sat up again, forcing himself to shake those thoughts away, the imposing wooden-fenced walls of their destination lay ahead. Though he knew it was Nook Town, he found himself asking, "Is that it?"

Hector grunted as he trudged beside Bert. He'd become more and more withdrawn over the past several days since they'd left the Veritas camp. To Raif's surprise, Hector pulled Bert to a halt and turned to look at him. His green eyes were underlined with shadows, his mouth twitching beneath his sodden moustache. He let out a long breath and looked toward the gates. "This is not a place we can speak freely, lad, so I'll say this now—be on your guard. I had few enough allies here when I left almost twenty years ago, and now ..." He shook his head, his wet, black hair hanging limp about his face. "Well, there're thing's've happened that make that less likely. I'm hoping to find a man called Biron still in charge. If that's the case, maybe we'll have a chance of receiving help. If not, well ..." He looked towards the town again. Raif followed his gaze. Lamps to either side of what he assumed to be the entrance sputtered in the rain.

"But we have to find Rose, don't we? We have to ask about her?"

Hector's moustache bristled as though he was chewing his lip. "Mm. We do, lad. But let's get in there first, see what we're dealing with."

More delays, more wasted time. It's not good enough. Raif exhaled, his breath a white cloud in the cold night air. He patted Bert's back, as much to give himself some form of distraction against the dread gnawing at his gut as to prevent himself from saying something he might regret.

"We'll have somewhere warm to stay tonight, at least," he muttered. Beside him, Dog let out a brief bark, bushy black tail wagging as he trotted ahead. Cara, who walked alongside Dog, glanced towards Raif with those piercing yellow eyes, her tail lashing back and forth.

"That's so, lad. That's so." Hector turned back towards Nook Town. Cara twirled around his legs, and that seemed to lend him some strength, for his back straightened and he led Bert onwards. Regardless of Hector's words of warning, Raif saw their destination as their one chance of finding Rose. *We're coming, little bug.*

Ever since Rose had been taken by Avanna, he'd been on edge; his body felt ready for a fight at any moment. Though he'd mentioned having somewhere warm to rest, he doubted he would be able to relax, no matter where they found themselves that evening. His mind was aflame with fear. How could he possibly allow himself to rest when his sister was somewhere without him, confused and afraid? And yet, with their destination in sight, his rain-soaked body trembled from exhaustion and cold.

I must sleep when I can. Rose needs me to be strong.

Their journey from the Veritas camp had been fraught with determination, eager as they'd both been to find some clue as to Avanna and Rose's whereabouts. But the trail had been cold, with no sign of either his beloved sister or the treacherous Veritas leader who had stolen her away.

So here they were, the only place they might find answers.

Assuming Avanna didn't lie to Hector. If she didn't send him down a false road.

He shivered. If Rose wasn't here, he wasn't sure what he would do.

He gritted his teeth, clenched his jaw. *No, she is here. I will find her. No matter what.* The doggedness burned within him, spurring him on, pushing through his physical and mental weariness.

When they reached the gated entrance to Nook Town, Raif dismounted and grasped for Bert's reins, allowing Hector to go ahead. The rainfall grew heavier around them as they took the final steps towards the town, and the torches at either side of the closed gate flickered as fat rain droplets hit them. In the centre of the wooden gate was a symbol Raif had never seen before; made from a gleaming golden metal that shone in the dancing firelight, it depicted two hands in a V shape, cupping the beams that shone down from a sun. He felt drawn to the symbol. A strange sense of calm settled upon him as he walked closer, the worry that weighed upon his shoulders easing, making him feel light and free for the first time in days ... weeks, even. Even the rain appeared to slow.

"Step back, lad," Hector said sharply. "It's best I speak to whoever's guarding the gate." Snapped from his reverie, Raif blinked the rain from his eyes, frowning towards the golden symbol. Before he could study it again, the gate crashed open. He leaped back to avoid being caught in its path. By the time he looked back at the gate, the curious symbol was lost from view. As he stared into the space it had occupied, a hooded figure emerged, waving an irritated fist in the air.

"Who, by Perisma's light, is knockin' on my gate at this hour?" he cried, glancing about dramatically. Then his gaze fixed on Hector. "By the light, it can't be …?" The man removed a torch from beside the gate and held it up, illuminating a deeply wrinkled face. "*Hector? Hector Haralambous? Is that you?*"

Hector let out a gentle, pained groan. "Yes," he said, moving toward the man, voice low. "It's me, Fen."

"Hector!" The man Hector called Fen smiled, holding his free arm out as if to pull Hector into a half embrace. Though the man seemed genuinely pleased to see him, Hector didn't return his merriment. "How long has it been, lad? Oh, this is a surprise, and no mistake, after the trouble we've seen …" He bustled Hector through the gate, the rest of his words indiscernible. Cara stalked through before the gate could swing shut, a white blur in the darkness, quickly disappearing into the shadows.

"I suppose we should follow," Raif said, eyeing Bert and Dog, the latter of whom whined in agreement. "I thought so." Reins in hand, Raif heaved open the gate. As he did so, he reached up to touch the golden symbol, his fingers tingling in anticipation.

Just as he was about to examine it closer, Dog jumped up at his side, giving a low growl. "It's okay, boy. I'm coming." He looked at the symbol one final time before tearing his gaze away, opening the gate fully, and entering Nook Town.

Inside, he was surprised to find golden streetlamps illuminating a cobblestoned street, shopfronts on one side, homes on the other. There was a pleasantness to the place he hadn't expected, given Hector's evident reluctance to come here.

He joined Hector, who was tapping his foot as Fen incessantly chattered. "Oh, but it is good to see you," the old man said, clapping his hands together. "I have missed your father, y'know. How long has it—"

"Fen," Hector snapped. Perhaps realising how harsh he'd been, he placed a hand on the man's shoulder and gave a tight smile. "Forgive me, but we've had a long road. We'd like to get out of this rain."

"Oh," Fen said, grinning and turning to look at Raif for the first time. "You have company. Good evening to you, lad. First time in Nook Town, hmm?" He looked as though he might say more, but Hector jumped in.

"Yes, and he's as eager to be in his bed as I," he said gruffly.

"Hmm, don't blame you. Winter's coming, that's for certain. I'd be away, too, if I weren't on guard duty!" The old man chuckled gently. Raif gave him a smile, though Hector remained stony-faced. The old man continued, unperturbed. "You'll need a stable for the horse as well. I'm thinkin' you might not know how things work 'round here since you left so long ago. We've a dedicated service for such now. Let me send for a lad to take the horse for you, hmm?" He hesitated, eyes gleaming with uncertainty.

"No, that won't be necessary," Hector said. "We would like to tend to the horse ourselves."

"You always were a stubborn one, Hector." Fen shook his head, his eyes creasing as he smiled. "Oh, you know where you should stay—"

"Yes, I know where to go, Fen. Good night to you." Hector signalled for Raif to follow and left the old man standing in the street.

"He was happy to see you," Raif noted, glancing over his shoulder to see the gatekeeper shuffling back to his hut. "Seemed friendly enough."

Hector grunted. "Don't let that fool you, lad. He's an old friend of my father's." And then, as though to himself, he muttered, "His mind must be gone if he feels so ..." He looked at Raif, eyes clouding. "No matter. Come on; this way."

More flickering torchlight lit Nook Town's streets, though there were no people to speak of. Raif thought he could hear the hum of singing coming from a great building at the north of the town. The bell tower stood at least three storeys tall, the same symbol as on the town's gate painted at its top. Hector headed towards a dark alley-way, but Raif hesitated, eyes drawn to that symbol once more, to the mysterious building and the rise and fall of harmonious voices within.

"Lad, keep up," Hector called, melting into the shadows of the alley. Raif reluctantly hurried after him, Bert and Dog in tow. They soon emerged from the end of the alleyway onto another torchlit but deserted street. In front of them stood a building with glowing windows. At the sight of it, Raif was reminded how cold he was and eagerly followed Hector. Before they could enter, a young boy ran towards them, feet splashing in the puddles rapidly forming on the muddy street.

"Can I take your horse, sir? Fen sent for me," the boy said.

"Damn it, I told him not to ..." Hector scowled. And then, as the young boy stepped closer, his face dropped. "Wait ... you—you have ... powers?"

The boy's eyes widened, his pale face flushing as though he'd been struck. "Please, sir, I'm not lookin' for any trouble. Just doing my job, that's all."

"Your *job*?" Hector croaked. "Where are your family? You're too young, lad, to be working at this hour."

The boy's gaze dropped to the ground. His clothes were drenched, clinging to his skinny frame. He couldn't have been more than seven, Raif realised—just older than Rose. His chest tightened. *Could he have seen anything? Might he know—*

"No family, sir," the boy whispered, voice barely audible. Hector glanced at Raif, his green eyes filled with some unreadable emotion.

"I'm sorry you were called for," Hector said gently, reaching into his purse and holding out a coin. "Here, take this. Go and get yourself warm, lad. Don't worry about us."

The boy hesitated, lips pinching as he looked at the coin in Hector's palm. "I'll have to take the horse, sir. Else I'll ..." He looked back over his shoulder, wringing his hands tightly. "I'll be in trouble."

Hector patted the boy's shoulder. "Okay, lad, okay. Don't worry. You can take 'im. This is Bert. He's a calm old beast; he'll not bring you any problems." He handed over a generous handful of coins and nodded for Raif to pass Bert's reins over.

"Yessir," the boy said, perking up as he pocketed the coins and took hold of Bert. He turned and led the horse away. Hector watched after him.

"Do you think he might know something?" Raif said, following Hector's gaze. "About Rose?"

"Mm. Mayhap." He turned to look at Raif. "Though I'm afraid there's somethin' going on here, somethin' I wasn't prepared for."

"Well, could we ask him? Perhaps I can go after him and—"

"No!" Hector wheezed, leaping in front of Raif as though to block his path. "No. I'm sorry, Raif, but ... I need to find out what's going on." He sighed and shook his head. "Let's get out of the rain. I know you want to find Rose, but we're here now. Let's get settled in, make a plan. I fear we cannot rush into anything, especially not now." He headed for the inn's door, leaving Raif to watch his retreating back, mouth agape.

What is he afraid of?

Inside, as in the streets, the inn was empty, though there were lit candles on every table and the fireplace was blazing. Hector seemed strangely calm as he approached the bar. Raif moved towards the crackling fire, leaving a trail of water behind him. Dog, ever curious, sniffed and snuffled all around the common room. As Raif grew accustomed to the tavern, the smell of baking bread and roasting meat reached him, and his mouth filled with saliva.

"Good evening, patrons," a booming voice said. Raif jolted to attention, turning to find a heavily bearded man entering through the kitchen door. "How might I—" His dark eyes flitted from Hector to Raif and back again, clenched fists resting upon the bar. "We don't want any trouble, Hector."

"You'll have none from us, Bernard," he said, placing his hands palm up on the bar. At the gesture, Bernard's shoulders relaxed.

"By the looks of you, you'll be wanting somewhere warm for the night," he said. "And food besides."

Hector knocked a silver coin against the bar, sending a sharp clang across the room. "We'd be grateful for it."

Bernard held his hand out for the coin, his eyes taking in Hector and Raif. At sight of Dog, he scowled. "Is that *creature*—"

"He's just a pet, Bernard," Hector said. "Nothing more."

Bernard narrowed his eyes. "Have a care, Hector. You'll find things've changed in Nook Town these past twenty years. You'd best be sure no one catches you with—"

"As I said, you'll have no trouble from us. He is a pet; no more. The lad hails from a village far from here where dogs are just that. Let him keep his dog, man."

Bernard hesitated before nodding, though his gaze lingered upon Dog. "I'll get you somethin' to eat," he muttered, moving back to the kitchen, where the clatter of plates ensued.

Raif joined Hector at the bar. Peering about the tavern, he noted a strange absence. "Where's Cara?" he said quietly; after that exchange between Hector and the tavern owner, it was all too clear that companions were not welcome in Nook Town. "And where is ... *everyone*?"

Hector leaned closer, expression stern. "Cara will be keeping to herself while we're here. For ... obvious reasons," he whispered, nodding towards the kitchen door. He cleared his throat, voice returning to a normal volume. "That's it, lad; a good meal and decent sleep is what we need after such a long journey. We'll speak properly in the morning; I promise."

Raif frowned at the forced joviality in his voice though was unable to respond before Bernard burst back into the room with a tray full of steaming food. He followed Hector and Raif to a table and laid their dinner out alongside brimming tankards of warm, honeyed ale. Raif's growling stomach took over, and he had to resist the urge to wolf everything down in vast mouthfuls. He took his time, chewing carefully, feeding scraps to Dog under the table. Hector ate slowly, seeming unable to stomach much. To Raif's relief, the dark-eyed innkeeper had returned to the kitchen so that they remained alone, though neither spoke.

Once the meal was finished, Raif became all too aware of the fire's lulling heat at his back. His eyelids drooped, and with the last of many jaw-cracking yawns, he admitted defeat. "I think I need to go to bed," he said, standing.

"You'll be sleeping upstairs," Bernard said, appearing once more from the kitchen and moving to clear the table. "First room on the left."

"Good night, lad. See you in the morning," Hector said, tapping his tankard for a refill.

"Night," Raif said, patting a leg for Dog to follow. As he crept up the stairs, voices filtered towards him, and something drove him to pause and press an ear to the wall.

"... thought to find everyone at evening worship," Hector said.

"Yes, well ..." Bernard said. There was a clatter as something was put down. "Truth be told, we've had some ... disturbances of late."

"I see." A brief pause was followed by a chair scraping against the floor. "What's happening here, Bernard?"

"That traitorous bastard the Grand Magister," Bernard said. "Sending men here, trying to convert us to his ways despite the oath that's protected us for a hundred years. Protected *our* ways."

The Commune? Raif's throat constricted. *No!*

"The Commune?" Hector said sharply, mirroring Raif's own anxiety. "What could they be doing here? Is it something to do with—"

"I wouldn't know, in truth," Bernard cut in. "Perhaps you should speak with the church elder. But I told those soldiers what I'm telling you ... We deal with those with *powers* in our own way, under Perisma's guidance. We'll be having no dealings with the likes of them." His voice held an undeniable sneer.

Deal with? Raif's heart raced. *What could that mean?* His head pounded as fear for his sister's safety forced its way back into his thoughts. When he focused again on listening, there appeared to be an extended silence hanging between Hector and Bernard. Raif began to think they wouldn't speak again. He was about to continue ascending the stairs when the innkeeper gently coughed.

"You've been gone a long time, Hector. It's not as it was when we were lads. P'rhaps you're best speakin' to the church elder, as I said." The sound of cutlery and plates clinking rang across the room. "There have been changes since you left, Hector. Be careful." Bernard let out another loud cough. "You bring powers here, you'll be expected to take it; you know that. And it's ... hrmph, no. Not for me to say. Talk to the elder, as I said."

Take it? Raif's brow furrowed. *Take* what?

There was a lot here that he did not know. With exhaustion weighing heavy on his mind and body, he promised himself he would question Hector about whatever *it* was in the morning. He let out a long, bone-weary sigh and patted Dog on the head.

"Come on, boy," he whispered, carefully making his way up the rest of the stairs and entering the small room on the left. Somehow, with Dog by his side, he felt reassured that he was connected to Rose. That as long as Dog seemed settled, she had to be safe. Some part of him told him it was true, though another part knew it could also be a lie he was telling himself so he did not go mad from grief and despair.

With thoughts of Rose filling his mind, he was asleep as soon as his head touched the feather pillow.

CHAPTER 3
EVELYN

Evelyn stood looking over the ship's rail, a pressure lifting from her shoulders. She was leaving behind what remained of Little Haven and memories of all that happened there, and she hadn't realised what a heavy hold that had over her until she was watching the shores of Septima retreat on the horizon.

Arthur. The one who had taken everything from her, who had forced her to flee Little Haven. Who had shown her that she was truly worth nothing. Was he alive or dead at the hands of the Commune? Was he one of those working at Lord Torrant's estate? Or was he taken to some unknown location to work at the Grand Magister's command? She didn't know, may never know, but one thing was certain—she was leaving behind the fear of somehow meeting him again.

Of course, she was also leaving Raif, Rose, Dog, and Hector, stuck as she was aboard a ship with a man who had hunted them for the Commune and who would likely despise her if he knew of the powers she'd felt rise up within her in Lord Torrant's home. It was hard to accept him now as someone other than Commander Sulemon. She could only hope that she could learn to trust him ...

And that he hasn't led me into some form of trap.

She sighed, regret gnawing at her heart. She glanced about to ensure she was alone before retrieving her two auburn braids from where they were tucked into her tunic. She'd held onto them rather than discarding them when she'd cut them off, some part of her strangely afraid to let them go. Aboard this ship, something had changed. She was a different person now; she had to be, else she might go mad thinking about all that had happened and the situation she now found herself in.

Yet part of her couldn't help but wonder—had her powers truly returned to her in Lord Torrant's basement? Despite her concerns, part of her longed to tell Jonah, to confide in him as she might have Raif not so long ago. But their journey had just begun, and she was reluctant to let her guard down. He would need to prove himself trustworthy, a feat she was not entirely sure he was capable of.

As the breeze lifted, she allowed the hair to unravel, watched as the braids separated, and released them into the Great Sea. She ran a hand over the short hair that remained, trying to be optimistic about Jonah's plan. *I have to believe it will work.* Despite the man he'd been, Jonah *saved* her. She couldn't ignore that. He went against his orders —he was giving her a chance to rescue Raif and Rose. Could that be enough to forget all he'd been before, all he'd done? It had to be if she wanted to see Raif and Rose again.

She stared back towards Septima. *I'll come back for you; I promise.*

Evelyn turned her back on the ocean and cast her eyes about the ship, watching as the crew went about their evening work. A cheery-faced cabin boy was moving around the deck with a lamp. Aside from his bobbing light, the only way to see anything on the ship would soon be the moon, which hovered above them like a great, glowing orb.

As she glanced up at the sky, the cabin boy passed her. "Good evening," he said. She gave a terse nod, suspicious of his attempt at friendliness. She turned towards the stern of *Septima's Blessing* where Jonah stood, black cloak whipping about as it caught the passing wind, merging with the darkness around him. Without the red cloak that marked him as a Commune soldier, he seemed smaller, less sure of himself.

When Evelyn approached, he didn't acknowledge her. His eyes remained fixed ahead, jaw clenched. He'd been more subdued than usual since she'd woken him from his fitful dream that morning, his brusqueness all the more evident. Though it was clear that a deep pain simmered just beneath the surface of his dark eyes, she wouldn't ask him to share his pain. She had secrets of her own and understood how closely such things must be guarded. The only person who'd come close to knowing the truth was Raif ...

And look how you ruined that friendship.

Evelyn bit her lip, pushing the thought away. Now was not a time for thinking of past mistakes. She needed to be able to hold onto the tiny bubble of optimism within her. As she stood beside the stoic Nomarran, however, it began to drift from her grasp. She was so unused to the feeling that she had no idea how to keep it close without breaking it altogether.

She remained still, watching Jonah from the corner of her eye.

Silence stretched between them as she struggled to find the words to start a conversation. Her mind flitted back and forth between wanting to reach out to him and wondering why *she* should be the one to make the effort to build a bridge.

Finally, Evelyn could stand her cycling inner dialogue no longer. She jutted out her chin and said, "How long has it been since you were last home?" It was the first thing she could think to ask that felt innocent enough to warrant a response without causing irritation. Jonah remained still, face an emotionless mask. When he didn't reply, she assumed she'd said something wrong. The stiff way he held himself suddenly filled her with unease. What if she had misunderstood the reason for his helping her? *Have I fallen for some trap? Trusted someone I shouldn't have* again?

There might be things at play that she could barely even fathom. The game was ongoing, her place on the board as yet undetermined.

At the back of her mind, a terrified voice whispered, *Be careful. There is danger everywhere, and on a ship, you have no chance of escape.*

A shudder ran through her. She turned, wanting to flee to her cabin, to curl up in her hammock, to conceal herself from the prying eyes of the crew and the too cheerful Captain Nem.

"Thirteen years," Jonah said, halting her in her tracks.

She returned to his side, placing her hands on the ship's rail. "Thirteen years," she repeated, staring out towards Septima once more. Though part of her relished leaving it, she couldn't imagine being away for so much time. She would return; she knew that for certain. She was tied to the place; an invisible force would pull her back, whether she willed it or not. "A long time."

Beside her, Jonah grunted. "Too long."

"Your work for the Commune kept you away." It was a statement rather than a question. Evelyn knew she was likely overstepping by speaking so bluntly but found she couldn't stop herself. *I'm done playing games.*

"The Commune," Jonah said, turning his face away. "Yes, in a way."

Now was her chance; the topic hadn't been changed or ignored. Her plan to learn more about Veritarra's Gift was forgotten for the moment; she had to learn more about those who'd caused her, Raif, and Rose so much pain and trouble. "What do you know about the powers? About why the Commune seeks them?"

Jonah shifted where he stood. "They are dangerous. Incredibly so," he said. "Those who have them ..." He narrowed his eyes at Evelyn, his face full of contempt. "They must be trained, otherwise they pose a threat to everyone and everything around them. You may not see it, but the Commune sought only to protect the kingdom."

Evelyn pursed her lips. *He still believes that.* "But they hunted down children," she said quietly. "Took them away from their families, destroyed villages. How is that right?"

Jonah exhaled. "It is as I said. You do not see it."

She scoffed. "Well, what about me? I might have powers; did you know that? Didn't you feel anything when we were in that, in Lord Torrant's ..." She closed her eyes briefly, seeing the bony figure on his stained mattress. *That poor man. What became of him?*

"Do not speak of that place," Jonah snapped. He rubbed a hand across his eyes before speaking again. "In any case, you do not pose a threat to me. My mother consumed Veritarra's Gift before I was born. Because of that, my Goddess granted me a blessing; I am immune to powers."

In the hush that followed, the rush of the ocean beneath the ship filled her ears. Parts of the story slotted into place, though not enough to allow her to understand everything. "Immune," she said. "So we, my friends and I, we never posed a threat to you."

"No, but you were a threat to the kingdom. Nomarrans are the only ones blessed with such immunity, and even then, it is ..." He trailed off with a brief shake of his head.

Evelyn clutched the ship's rail and bit her lip. Now was not the time to argue with him about such matters, to force him into giving her more answers than he was yet willing. There was no going back, anyway—she was sailing to the Noman Islands. Their plan was her focus—*had to be* her focus. They would obtain this Veritarra's Gift that Jonah had spoken of; a way to take down the Commune, he'd said.

To save Raif and Rose. To protect us all.

Jonah remained impassive, staring into the distance, mouth a tight line.

"What about Lord Torrant?" Evelyn said. "You worked for him. Doesn't he have powers? When he touched me, I—"

"Do not say his name."

Evelyn blanched at the sharpness in his voice. She frowned. "But that man in the basement. How can you *defend* him? What Lord Torrant did was—"

"You should not speak of that which you do not understand." Jonah's voice was low, quivering, almost a growl. Though his face remained impassive, his shoulders and arms were taut.

"But you—"

"No!" Jonah turned on her, eyes burning with fury. And then, seeming to remember where he was and who might overhear, he exhaled and turned back to the ship's rail. Evelyn's cheeks warmed as though she'd been slapped. Beneath Jonah's sudden rage, all her convictions were smothered. She shrank away, crossing her arms across her chest. She was acutely aware of the nearby crewmen. Part of her knew she should bite her tongue, that her words were best said when they were alone, well away from the possibility of listening ears. But she was too upset to care.

Why did you follow this man? her mind whispered. *Oh, Evelyn, Evelyn, another mistake to contend with, another path you cannot turn back from, you stupid fucking idiot.*

She blinked back tears of shame, returning Jonah's glare.

"You brought me here," she hissed, voice trembling. The desire for alcohol rose sharply up her throat. She gulped it back as best she could. "There are things I need to know, Jonah. You owe me that much."

They looked at each other for a moment longer, but Evelyn could see he was unmoved by her anger and frustration.

He hasn't changed at all.

With a sinking feeling in her gut—and earlier optimism altogether burst—Evelyn stalked away. She barely acknowledged Captain Nem as he greeted her.

She needed to be alone with a skinful of wine.

CHAPTER 4
HECTOR

I *shouldn't have come back here.* The thought cycled round and round Hector's mind, dizzying in its clarity. But what choice had there been? He had to save Rose. To try, at least.

Damn you, Avanna. Damn you for making me return to a place I never wanted to see again.

He wished Cara was close, for he longed to run his hands through her fur, feel her warm reassurance that he was doing the right thing. But, of course, she had to remain hidden whilst they were in Nook Town. If she were found—if Hector's link to her were discovered—she would be removed. That was one element of Biron's reign as church elder he'd remembered well. Animal companions were an indicator of strength in those with powers, and those with powers were enemies of the church, to be sent to the Commune.

Except me. Because my father protected me.

"*I've seen how you are with the creatures in the woods, Hector, my lad.*" *His father's eyes, green as his own, had shone with reflected firelight.* "*You must never allow anyone else to see, d'you hear? If you do, I can't protect you any longer, friendship wi' Elder Biron or no. They'll know how strong you are, and they'll not abide that in this place.*"

Father. He squeezed his eyes tight against the tears that prickled against them. He would heed his father's words, even after all these years. He couldn't risk Cara being taken from him, though that didn't stop him from pining for his dear companion.

Outside the window, birdsong filled the early morning air as the sun rose. Soon, the entire town would be rousing and making its way to first worship. Even at this time of year, when there was much to do in preparation for the yearly Reaping harvest, attendance at the Church of Perisma twice a day was compulsory. Hector had been away for eighteen years, but he would never forget that; his father had instilled it within him as a child.

"Perisma's blessing is bestowed upon us, Hector. In turn, we must show our loyalty to Him. Our gratitude that He chooses to grace us with His presence and light."

How wrong you were, Father. He did not grace us at all. He rubbed his chin, fingers brushing against stubble. "No point trying to sleep," he muttered to the empty room, a pang of sadness squeezing at his heart when Cara did not reply. He stood and glanced out the window towards the street below, wondering where she was. She was safe, he knew that much, but not so close that he could sense her thoughts. Distance, they had learned over the years, was their enemy. They were still connected through Hector's powers, yet they could not communicate effectively—perhaps a passing thought, if a lot of effort and energy was used to push it towards the other. Nevertheless, he comforted himself with the knowledge that she was likely stalking around the dark shadows of the town, searching for some hapless prey.

How he wished he could escape so easily.

Time to see Church Elder Biron again.

Hector shuffled to the washbasin and poured cold water into it from a copper jug. He splashed his face and ran a moistened hand through his hair. *Getting long,* he noted absently. Avanna had cut it for him for many years—*"I won't let you leave it like that, old man."* The memory of the Veritas leader caused him to gasp against a sudden flood of anger and grief. After all, no matter what she'd done, she'd been a good friend. In many ways, she'd saved him.

Why, Avanna ... why?

He had to accept he might never know the truth. Oh, he knew the reasons she'd given in that dreadful afternoon in her hut, when she'd drugged him and Raif and taken Rose, but he could never understand what had *driven* her to such extremes.

What changed? Why did she not come to me? He looked up and caught his own weary green eyes in the mirror, giving himself a sad smile. "Nothing to be done about it now. Let's see what today brings ... by Perisma's blessing," he muttered, unable to conceal the bitterness in his voice.

He jumped at a sudden, sharp knock on the door, almost toppling over the jug at his feet. "Yes?" he called, heart hammering.

I shouldn't have come back here.

They know about Father.

"It's Raif."

Hector had to hold back a groan of relief. He straightened his tunic, moving towards the door and opening it with an uneasy smile.

"You gave me a start, lad." He made a point of glancing towards the dim sky outside his window. "It's early yet."

Raif swallowed, peering down the empty hall, then back at Hector. "I need to speak to you."

Hector focused on him fully, noting the shadows under his grey eyes. At fourteen summers, he was already tall and broad-shoul-dered, though he held himself with an awkward air that showed he was still unused to his growing body. Raif shuffled nervously. "Of course," Hector said gently. "Come in, lad."

Raif entered his room, Dog trailing him. He shut the door and hovered beside it, twisting the hem of his tunic.

Hector nodded towards the bed. "Sit," he said. He waited for Raif to do so before joining him. "I scarce think I need to ask what troubles you."

Raif bowed his head.

Hector patted his hand. "You're worried about Rose."

Dog let out a low whine, placing his head on Raif's boot.

"We will find her, won't we?" Raif whispered.

There was a tremble in his voice, though Hector knew better than to draw attention to it. He ran a hand over his moustache, choosing his words mindfully before responding. "'Course we will, lad. It's just that ... this place, it's not as simple as just asking about her. We have to be careful who we speak to. And we cannot mention Rose's powers; that's important, you hear?"

Raif nodded, his bottom lip beginning to quiver. "I can't lose her. Not Rose. Not Rose as well as Father, as well as—as Mother." Tears rolled down his cheeks. "I'm—I'm sorry."

Hector placed a hand on Raif's shoulder. "You've nothing to apologise for, lad." As gently as he could, and despite the despair warring in his own heart and mind, he pushed comforting thoughts towards Raif. Slowly, the lad's trembling stopped, and his tears slowed. "I know we'd both hoped to have found her by now. I see your disappointment it's not been so, and I'm sorry for it. I promised you we'd find her." Hector drew himself up, looking at Raif. The lad turned his head up, eyes glistening. "You have my word. The promise remains. We will find your sister. But ..."

Raif sniffed, eyebrows raising. "But?"

Through the window, Hector glimpsed the church tower just about in view from where he sat. "This place ..." He rubbed his eyes, a long sigh escaping his lips. "We need to be cautious here. Someone here was in contact with Avanna. A Nomarran, she said, though that's unusual enough that it shouldn't be hard to find the man. Someone wanted Rose, mayhap. Led Avanna here for a reason. I ..." Hector paused. So many words and memories clashed together in his mind. He knew Raif was struggling and wondered how much the lad needed to know. Hector's past was here, and with it was a lot of pain, anger, hopelessness. He did not want to pass that onto Raif. The lad needed to retain some hope.

Raif wiped a hand across his nose. "If someone wanted Rose, that must mean there'll be answers here." He gave a nod, suddenly seeming sure of himself. "We *have* to ask around about her."

Hector saw the determination in his face. "You're right, lad. Much as it pains me to admit it, the church elder'll be our first stop. Way things are here, I'll need to make my presence known to him sooner or later. Best get it over with." He sighed. "Come on. Let's get some food and we can make a plan."

"We won't be long, will we?" Raif's impatience caused his voice to strain. "We need to get out there, Hector, we need to be searching for—"

"I know, I know, lad." Hector squeezed his shoulder. "I promise, we'll be quick. But best to keep your energy up. Look after yourself. It's been a rough few days since we left Veritas. Let's not be hasty and make mistakes now."

Raif's shoulders relaxed minutely as he nodded. Guilt stabbed at Hector. The lad trusted him completely, trusted they would find answers—find Rose.

What if we don't?

He gave his room a final glimpse before pulling the door shut, sending a thought to Cara by habit. No response came.

They made their way downstairs in silence. Dog padded ahead, his tail wagging, his nose snuffling along the ground. The tavern's common room was occupied only by a hunched old woman sitting close to the door, cupping her tea and paying them no heed as she stared out the window. Raif sat at the same table as the night before, Dog at his feet. Hector approached the bar, where he could hear the clatter of pots and pans within the kitchen.

As he waited, Hector became aware of voices speaking in hushed tones. Though the words were muffled, he sensed the urgency in the thoughts behind them.

Nothing.

It was as though his powers met a wall of resistance around every mind he attempted to touch. He pushed harder but could gain no purchase on the minds he sought. *How is this possible? It's almost as though they've been consuming—*

"Veritarra's Gift," he whispered to himself.

And then he recalled Avanna's words.

"I have been writing to a Nomarran … Elussius Muelaman … He promised he could provide all I required and more …"

Had Biron started working with this Nomarran, too? It would certainly explain the shields he detected.

We must tread even more carefully than I thought. This speaks of a deep paranoia in the church and its followers.

Pulling at his moustache, Hector strained to hear the continued conversation, regretting that Cara was not nearby. She'd always been adept at stealth and might have been able to gain entrance to the kitchen to listen.

Suddenly, the kitchen door swung open with a thud. Hector pointedly focused on his fingernails, trying to look as carefree as possible.

"… what Church Elder Orion said. It needs to be stronger, no matter the risk. There can be no arguments."

Hector froze. *Church Elder… Orion?*

Oh. Oh no.

He was distracted by his thoughts when a Nomarran man— bald-headed, black-skinned, dressed in deep burgundy robes— walked through the open kitchen door, followed closely by Bernard.

"Thank you, Elussius. I will remember—ah! Hector." Bernard gave a toothy smile, teeth starkly white against his black beard. "I didn't realise you were awake. Is your lad with you?"

Hector waved over his shoulder to where Raif and Dog sat, waiting.

"Yes, good … good. I'll see you fed." Bernard pushed his way back through the kitchen door, though not before his dark eyes flitted towards the retreating Nomarran.

Elussius. It's him. Hector watched the man leave. He would certainly need to find out more about what was going on here. This all seemed linked to Avanna's words, somehow—and, most importantly, to Rose. "Thank you, Bernard," he called. "And we'll have a tea each when—

No. No tea.

Cara? He glanced around, frowning. She was still nowhere in sight.

"What was that, Hector?" Bernard peered through the door. "Tea?"

"Oh, er, no. Ale, honeyed ale for us both, I think." Bernard raised an eyebrow but did not question the request before disappearing back into the kitchen.

Hector joined Raif, mind a-whir at the implications of what he'd just learned. The Nomarran immigrants had been part of the town since he was a boy, but it seemed their role and influence upon the church had grown, perhaps explaining the apparent consumption of Veritarra's Gift.

What could it mean? Is this why they offered to help Avanna? In any case, his wariness was increasing sharply. There were forces at play here he had not expected to face.

"So ..." Raif said, running his fingers along the grooves on the wooden table. "A plan."

"A plan." Hector nodded. "It's best that we're discreet. And you're to keep Dog with you at all times."

"Of course. But what harm could a dog—"

"Don't underestimate the superstitions here, lad," Hector snapped, then quickly bit his tongue and glanced towards the old woman by the door, who now appeared to be dozing in her seat. He exhaled before continuing in a much softer voice. "I grew up here, but I've been gone for some time. There seem to have been some ... changes. The superstitions may be *stronger*." He glanced at the kitchen door, behind which Bernard could be heard quietly bustling around. "I'll need to make my presence known. There are certain expectations that must be met. Follow my lead; that's the most important thing. And do not mention—"

"Here we are, Hector," Bernard said, appearing as if from nowhere with a tray of freshly cooked bacon, eggs, and thick-sliced bread alongside a pot of steaming tea. When he noticed Hector eyeing the teapot, he gave a chuckle. "I'll not hear of you and the boy drinking ale at this time of morning. No, a pot of this will set you right."

Because it's dosed with Veritarra's Gift, no doubt.

Hector cleared his throat and turned his gaze to the innkeeper, whose easy grin did not reach his eyes. "Yes, thank you, Bernard," he said, picking up his cutlery. "That will be all."

For a moment, the bearded man hesitated. "I ..." His eyes darted between Raif and Hector. "Let me know if you need anything else." He bowed his head and retreated to the kitchen.

Wary as he was, Hector could not ignore his grumbling stomach. He picked up some of the warm buttered bread and dipped it into his egg, allowing the yolk to spill out onto the plate. It was well-salted and delicious, and he relaxed a little despite himself. When Raif reached to pick up the teapot, however, Hector moved his arm fast as a flash, almost knocking the pot from the table.

Tea.

"No, lad," he urged. "No tea." He leaned closer, whispering, "Cara has warned me against it. I believe it may be the same as what—"

"Avanna?" Raif asked, eyes widening.

"Mm. Water will be best for us. Or ale. But no tea."

Raif gave a brisk nod. "Water." He slumped into his seat. Having evidently lost his appetite, he put his plate on the floor to allow an obliging Dog to finish his eggs.

As Hector mopped up his remaining yolk, the deep, resonating clang of bells filled his ears. Raif sat up once more while Dog let out a whine.

"Don't worry," Hector said, speaking over the ongoing peal. He leaned down to pat Dog on the head. "Church summons. Though, to be honest with you, I'd forgotten quite how loud they are. It can be a shock when you first hear 'em." He almost spoke with disdain about the beliefs held here, about the worship of Perisma and his *blessed light*. But then he glanced around and remembered where he was. Best not to draw any avoidable attention.

"Church summons?" Raif looked towards the door, chewing his lip. "I think I can still hear them." He scratched each ear vigorously, opening and closing his mouth a few times with a look of discomfort.

"You'll get used to it."

Bernard bustled in from the kitchen, wiping his hands on his apron.

"Not attending, Hector?" he called, dark eyes studying them from behind the bar. "I'll be leaving myself soon and need t' lock the front door. Wouldn't want to imprison you. Perhaps it's best you go, hmm, after all these years? Pay your dues. Church elder'll be there, too."

Hector grunted, unwilling to enter such a conversation with the innkeeper.

Raif leaned forward. "Can we go? Seems like this church elder would know about people coming into the town, wouldn't he? He'd know if—"

"Hush, boy," Hector said, cutting Raif off before he could mention Rose. He ran a hand through his hair. He couldn't avoid the church forever. Mayhap it was best to get it over with. "We'll go if it will keep you quiet."

He gave Bernard a weak smile and herded Raif and Dog towards the door. Relief filled him when the man smiled in return before walking back into the kitchen. *No suspicion from him. Not yet, anyway.*

In the street, a line of bleary-eyed men, women, and children were making their way towards the church. The sun rising behind the great building gave it an almost ethereal quality. Hector scoffed to himself, unable to quell his disdain.

I'm back, Father. After all these years, my hatred for the church you loved still burns, bright as Perisma's light itself.

As they merged into the crowd, Hector watched Raif from the corner of his eye. The boy was staring at the imposing building ahead. Ensuring no one was too near, Hector leaned close to his ear.

"I'll be the one to ask about her, when the time is right."

Raif pursed his lips and nodded, and they continued on towards the church. At the door, they joined an orderly queue. Curious eyes watched them from all sides. Clustered groups of dark-robed individuals loitered alongside the queue and whispered amongst themselves, some nodding or pointing towards Dog. *Ridiculous superstitions.* Hector ignored them, and together, he, Raif, and Dog shuffled into the building alongside the rest of the congregation.

Inside, it was much as he remembered. The stained-glass windows sitting within great, grey stone walls allowed in little light, and the church was dimmed by the heavy-scented smoke that hung in the air. Hector coughed as it caught in his throat, and he immediately craved the cool morning air outside. He was transported back to his childhood, to the mixture of dread and wonder at the inherent power that seemed contained within these walls. His eyes roved towards the raised wooden platform that sat at the front of the many rows of wooden pews. The platform was emblazoned with the same golden symbol common around the town—two hands held upwards, palms open towards the sun—which glinted with a strange luminescence even through the smoky air. To the right of the platform was a dais. Hector recalled Biron standing upon it, robed all in white, as he spoke of the goodness of Perisma, of the blessings they must all be grateful for. Behind the dais was an altar, upon which sat a domed object covered by a black cloth.

That's new. Hector narrowed his eyes, though he couldn't begin to guess what was concealed beneath the dark shroud.

"Hector," Raif said, pulling his attention away from the altar.

He turned towards the boy, quickly realising that the muttered whispers within the church had fallen silent. All around them, people sat with downcast eyes.

"Come on," Hector whispered, hurrying Raif and Dog towards the closest empty seats in the middle of the congregation.

He guided Raif to sit, a deep sense of foreboding settled upon his shoulders; his heart raced, his palms grew clammy. He cast his gaze about the gathered townsfolk, trying to find a friendly face. No one would look at him. *What's happening?*

I shouldn't have come back here.

They know what I've done; they know what I am.

He was trying to still his chaotic thoughts when a booming voice rang out.

"Hector Haralambous."

He forced his eyes up towards the dais. Steeling himself, Hector faced the speaker with all the defiance he could muster. Robed in an elaborate black and gold gown, the man looked the exact opposite as his father, Biron, had.

Orion.

Hector had known Orion since childhood, their fathers being firm friends, meaning they had spent a lot of time together when they were younger. But that did not make the man before him a friend. By the time of Hector's departure some eighteen years ago, Orion was a sullen, god-fearing young man, consumed by his fervent faith. In the years since Hector had been gone, he'd become a tall and imposing figure. He stood atop the dais, head clean-shaven and eyes framed by bushy black brows, stark against his pale, bony face.

"Orion." All eyes were on him, but Hector stared back at Orion, at eyes the colour and hardness of flint.

Orion clasped his hands in front of his chest as though in reverent prayer. He held all the confidence and flourish of a man who was assured of his position and power, of the truth of his beloved god Perisma. His lips curled into a sneer. "So, you have returned, after all this time. But do you expect Perisma to be so forgiving?" Orion's voice echoed throughout the church, clear and resounding. As he spoke, a ripple of agreement passed through the congregation. "We know you for what you are, Hector. For what you have done."

Hector ignored the townsfolk and stepped closer to the dais, palms help upwards in a desperate gesture of compliance. "Orion ... Church Elder Orion, the lad and I pose no threat, we simply need—"

"Enough. You will answer for your sins, Hector Haralambous.

Only Perisma Himself can judge you now. I suggest you pray for mercy." Orion snapped his fingers. Before Hector could move another step or say another word, he was seized by two townsmen. Raif cried out as he, too, was taken and dragged away. Almost as a reflex, Hector began searching out the minds of his captors, ready to fight at a moment's notice.

No. Save your energy. They are protected, just as Bernard and Elussius were.

Cara. He resisted the urge to search her out, even as he yearned to see her lightness within the dark shadows of that wretched place. But she would be well concealed; she understood the dangers of being caught.

He took a deep breath, attempting to calm himself. Cara was right. He would be a damned fool to attempt to use his powers here. Feeling his companion nearby gave him the strength to face his captors. He let himself be marched towards a door behind the ceremonial platform. All the while, the ever-watchful eyes of Orion and his congregation burned into his back.

I shouldn't have come back here.

CHAPTER 5
JONAH

In the cramped confines of his cabin, Jonah waited for Evelyn to awaken. Though his eyes throbbed and his whole body ached, sleep would not take him. He sighed and rubbed a hand across his face, and leaned back against the cabin wall, the wooden crate on which he sat shifting beneath him with the ship's motion. Maybe he had been too harsh on the girl, but any mention of Lord Torrant shot rage through his whole body. She had no right to ask about him; she didn't know the truth ... did she? *Perhaps she sees it clearer than I do.* Perhaps she'd tried to reach out to him in her own way, and all he'd done was shove her away.

What have I become?

Jonah's guilt got the better of him when she hadn't shown up for the evening meal. He searched high and low until he found her slumped outside their cabins, barely conscious, vomit staining her clothes. A part of him was angry that she had been so careless as to make herself so vulnerable, and that he had to step in to clean her up. He intended to have stern words with her and with whoever had supplied her with the two skinfuls of wine she'd emptied.

Silence hung heavy in the air, and his mind turned once more to thoughts of Eirik. He thought of their last kiss, desperate and full of longing. Would he ever stop wondering if he'd made the right decision that final day in Lord Torrant's home?

Does he still love me?

As I still love him.

Fucking fool.

In an attempt to distract himself, he studied Evelyn's sleeping face. She was broken, just like him—that much had become all too clear. He would need to have more care for her if they were to reach the Noman Islands without further incident.

Jonah had been so sure those whose powers were untrained by the Commune were the enemy; he'd seen in his homeland—brought about by his own father—the death and destruction caused by untempered powers. The Curse of Ezzarah, as it was known on the islands. The Commune was the solution, a way to bring those with powers into line. To place an authority over those born into noble families with powers, to create an army who could repress any attempt at an uprising from the commonfolk with powers should it ever occur again ...

But things were not so clear cut. Lord Torrant had tortured Cole, Jonah's lover, until he was near dead, purely out of jealousy. He had used his powers for such cruelty, and he worked for the Commune. Everything Jonah thought he knew, all he'd believed to be right ... It was not so simple after all. Though it never had been.

He had to admit he'd closed himself to Evelyn, not expecting their relationship to flourish beyond anything other than what was needed to complete their mission. How could it? They were too different, their views too contrasted.

He regarded her closer then, features softened by the orange glow of the firestone lamp beside the door, eyes closed rather than glaring at him with suspicion and scorn, and felt something stir within him, some feeling of camaraderie he hadn't expected. They were in this together; they wanted to achieve the same end—to destroy the Commune. If their plan was to succeed, he would need to open himself up to her. He would need to lower the wall around himself that had been present since childhood when his father had abandoned him and his mother and chosen to partake in a war against his own homeland, the defences through which he had only allowed Eirik to pass.

And look where that has brought me.

It was time to start again. Maybe befriending this girl would help him to move on, to replace the ignorance he'd allowed the Commune and Lord Torrant to instil within him. He would always remain wary of the powers, but he had to push himself to overcome all he'd been taught, all he'd lived by these past thirteen years. He might even begin to piece back together the shattered pieces of his heart.

For an unknown time, he sat at Evelyn's side. Lulled into a long-sought sense of peace by the soft flickering of the firestone, Jonah found himself in a waking dream, thinking of his home and what might await him upon their arrival. As such, he was far within the recesses of his own mind when Evelyn began to stir. By the time he noticed, she was looking at him with narrowed, amber eyes.

"What are you doing here?" she whispered, sitting up in the hammock with remarkable surety given the amount of wine she'd consumed just hours before.

Jonah glanced around the small room, then back at Evelyn. "What am I doing in my own cabin?"

Her eyes widened and her mouth dropped open. "*Your* cabin?" She shifted awkwardly, causing the hammock to swing and softly thud against the wall behind her. "Where did you, uh—what happened? Why am I in your hammock?" She looked down, and seeming to notice that she was dressed only in her underclothes, covered herself with trembling arms. "Who undressed me?" Her voice was tinged with a mixture of incredulity and unequivocal fear. "What did you *do* to me?"

"*Do* to you?"

Realisation swept over him like the great ocean that washed against the ship, so swiftly that he flinched. *Oh Jonah, you stupid man.*

He sat forward and held his hands up, attempting to soften his expression. "Evelyn, I found you outside our rooms almost blacked out. You drank a *lot* of wine. I was worried and did not want to leave you alone. I brought you here so that I might watch over you. Your clothes were covered in vomit, not fit to be worn; they were soaked and stinking. I did not think you would want to be ..." Seeing the look on her face, he knew he'd made a mistake, been far too naïve and ignorant. She would rather be covered in her own vomit than made to feel so vulnerable, so afraid. "I'm so sorry," he said weakly. "I have rinsed them for you."

Evelyn gulped, eyes darting around the cabin—to the hammock beneath her, the crumpled underclothing in which she'd slept, and the black cloak that Jonah had draped over her. Her wet clothes hung by the tiny washbasin in the corner of the cabin. She licked her lips and said, "Where did you sleep?"

"I did not sleep," he said gently. "I simply wished to make sure you were well, that you did not choke. I have seen it before, the alcohol sickness. It can be dangerous." He paused, wondering what he could say that would quell Evelyn's fears. Perhaps if she knew of what he had witnessed, the disgust he felt at the behaviours of the men he had once believed to be family and friends. He took a deep breath, coming to a decision.

It was time to be honest with this girl who, not so long ago, had been his enemy.

"I brought you to my cabin for your own protection, no other reason. I can assure you that nothing like that would ever cross my mind. When I was a child, my father led an uprising against our people. They possessed the, the—"

"Powers," Evelyn whispered.

"Yes. Ezzarah's Curse." Jonah frowned, seeing once more the flames as homes burned, the flashes of knives and swords wielded by those seeking only to oppress, the spilled blood of innocent people. *His* people. "It was terrible, truly. Men were beaten and killed, animals slaughtered, women were ... were ... raped." He croaked the word, and it sounded hollow in that tiny cabin; a word that could never truly encapsulate the horrors it described. "My mother, too. She was not the same afterwards." He shifted, the crate creaking beneath him. "My point is I would *never* hurt anyone in that way. I would never hurt you. I promise you. Any man who even considers doing such a thing is beneath contempt. Evil. Besides which, Evelyn, I brought you here. I asked you to help me. And I intend to keep you safe." He paused, looked at her face. She wore an impassive mask, apparently unmoved by his words, perhaps afraid to show what she was thinking and feeling. In that moment, something drove him to tell her more. To extend the hand of friendship, to allow her to fully *see* him. "Alongside that ..."—he looked down, unable to meet her gaze—"I would never ... I would never share my bed with a woman."

He let the words hang in the air between them, his breath caught in his chest. The silence seemed to drag on forever.

"Oh." Evelyn shifted; the hammock swayed. "I see. I mean, I think I do."

"I ..." Jonah sighed. "I did not want to tell you earlier. I couldn't. It is not common knowledge. It is not often accepted, either."

Evelyn cleared her throat. "So, you're not, um ... you're not interested in *any* women?"

"No." Jonah clasped his hands together and stared intently at the wooden floorboards. "I mean, not in *that* way."

"I see." There was another pause. "Well." She sniffed. "Do not undress me again. And thank you for sharing that. I won't say I trust you, but it's good to know you're actually human. That there are feelings behind that mask."

Jonah snorted gently. "You have no idea."

"You'd be surprised." Evelyn stood, her bare feet slapping against the wooden floorboards. "I understand now."

Jonah looked up, meeting her gaze. When he sat and she stood, their faces were at an equal height. "Understand?"

"Lord Torrant." She pursed her lips. "You were angry when I mentioned him. Defensive."

Jonah froze, knowing the connection she had made and fearing the questions it might bring. But she must have seen the fear in his expression, for she said, "I won't push you, Jonah. I won't ask about him."

"Thank you." He swallowed back the lump in his throat. "And I am sorry for how I reacted yesterday. We are together on this journey, and we must do our best to remember that."

"You're right. We have to work together," Evelyn said, giving a fleeting smile. "I don't know what to expect when we arrive at the Noman Islands. Whether they'll give us the help we need to save Raif and Rose."

"To tell you the truth, I do not know what to expect either. So many years … Perhaps all has changed; perhaps nothing. But it's true; there are things you should know before we arrive."

Mother. The candid talk of his homeland caused another pang of guilt and regret to form in his heart. Would she be able to forgive him for not returning sooner? For sending no word of his safety, of the life he'd found? There were some things he could not yet admit even to himself, let alone to Evelyn. His shame at leaving his mother was one such thing. He rubbed his eyes and yawned, exhaustion suddenly overwhelming him. He had opened up some part of himself to Evelyn, and that had relieved a burden he hadn't known he'd carried. At the same time, his mind swam with thoughts of all that lay before them.

"You must be tired," Evelyn said, shifting from one foot to another, hands crossed over her chest. "Here, you need sleep. And I need water and some food." She pulled on her tunic and trousers despite their evident dampness. She wrinkled her nose. "And some dry clothes."

Jonah chuckled, unsure as to whether sleep would truly come even if he tried. He lurched from his seat and clambered into his hammock, forcing his eyes shut, willing himself to relax.

"Jonah?"

His eyes fluttered open, focusing on Evelyn. "Yes?"

"Um ... thanks. For helping me."

The door opened and clicked shut. Jonah stared at the ceiling, at the ebbing orange light of the firestone lamp, and lost himself in thoughts of home.

Sleep did not come for many hours.

32nd Day of Flourishing
2nd year of King Arias Septimus II
20th year of Grand Magister Quilliam Nubira Antellopie III

Father,

Perhaps you are wondering why I have chosen to write after all these years.

I have word that the king is unwell. In the second year of his reign and unlikely to see a third—to live out the winter, even. His son, Cosmo, stands to inherit the throne at just fifteen years old. Such a thought ... I can barely comprehend it.

Though I hesitate to admit it, our ruler's impending death made me think of you. After Mother's death—news of which only reached me some months after—I barely spared you a thought. So why now? I myself hardly know.

I don't flatter myself that you ever wasted a moment dwelling upon my continued existence. Why should you? After you sent me away, I was no longer your concern. A shard of shame in your side that was removed to the benefit of all; a smear upon the family name erased, taken under control by the Grand Magister to be trained under his ever-benevolent gaze. I am lucky he saw such potential in me. There are others who were not so fortunate. Though I doubt you would have cared had that been my fate.

Nonetheless, I can't help but hope that there was something—a fleeting wisp of the love you never showed, pulling at your heart and making you think of your dear son, who was

But that is in the past. What of life now?

I met someone, Father.

For my eighteenth birthday, I was gifted a day of freedom. I ventured into Taskan, drawn towards the harbour by some curious force. Fate, I might say, if I believed in such nonsense.

It was then I saw him. Fresh from a ship that had ferried him from his homeland, he was wide-eyed, full of awe and innocence. And he looked at me with such wonder that I could scarce keep myself away.

Oh, how you would despise him—a commoner, not of our "noble stock," not even of this land.

Perhaps that is why I acted so rashly, taking him into my service before he could be assigned a job at a local smith or sent to the coal mines in Alpin. I convinced the Grand Magister to allow me to keep him on as my personal attendant. As I write, I cannot deny the stirring in my heart at the thought of him. I had never believed myself capable of love. After all, who did I have to learn it from?

And yet, I find myself wondering—what if he can be more to me than a simple manservant?

A foolish idea.

For well you know, Father, a Torrant man cannot weaken his honour with idiotic notions of love, especially a love that would be scorned by the nobles and royalty of Septima.

But forbidding it makes it seem all the sweeter, does it not?

If only I could see the look on your face.

I might write again, Father, for I find, with surprise, the act has lightened my mind.

Your ever hateful son,
Eirik Torrant
Loyal Servant to His Benevolence
Grand Magister Quilliam Nubira Antellopie III

CHAPTER 6
HECTOR

"Hector," Raif whispered. "What's happening?"

There was the crackling of flames in the hearth, Orion's office being all he would expect of such a man—darkened by shadows in every corner, a huge, dark-stained desk in the middle before the fire, and atop it the sacred text of Perisma. Dog whined at their feet, seeming to sense the tension within that place. Despite Raif's words, Hector remained silent, staring down at his clasped hands. He could not bring himself to answer the lad, though he dearly wanted to explain.

But how could he? How could he tell Raif that, after all the promises of protection, he'd brought them somewhere just as dangerous as Veritas had turned out to be?

"Hector, please," Raif said. "Why are we being held here?"

Finally, Hector blinked up at him. "I'm sorry, lad," he said. "I expected a man called Biron to be the church elder. This man, Orion, is his son, and ..." *He is a monster.*

"And?" Raif touched Hector's shoulder. Hector looked up to meet his gaze, finding desperation and fear on his young face. "And what, Hector? What does this mean for us? For finding Rose?"

Outside the door, the church was filled with Orion's booming voice, giving what Hector assumed to be a speech praising Perisma for bringing a traitor, a sinner, back into their beloved town for judgement. He looked away from the door. Orion would be with them before long, and he would find out for certain how much was known about all that had transpired here before he'd left.

At his side, Raif let out an exasperated huff. "You told me you'd take the lead here. That I should trust you." He leaned down, bringing his face in front of Hector's. "It's like you said—you know the people here. Know their ways. I need you. I need your help."

Hector opened his mouth to respond though found he couldn't utter a word.

How can I explain? How can I tell him the truth about this place? About me?

He took a deep breath, the incense, still heavy in the air, almost choking him. "There is power within these walls, lad. Not the powers that Rose or I possess, but a power nonetheless, and it may be far more dangerous. I cannot control it. I can scarce understand it, though I grew up under its influence. It has ... grown since then, it seems." He became aware of the strain in his voice but could do little to prevent it. His gaze drifted towards the thick, wooden door. "And now I am to answer for my sins in the eyes of Perisma."

"What? Sins? What—what does that mean? They can't hold us here, can they?" He felt Raif's stare, but his eyes were locked on the door. Orion's speech had finished, it seemed, for a tangible silence laid heavy in the church. "Hector, what do you—"

The door swung open with a loud *thud*. Orion stepped inside, eyes narrowed. Quick as a flash, some deep instinct drove Hector to stand before Raif. At the same time, Dog leaped up to stand in front of them both, hackles raised. The animal's growls filled the room, and Orion flinched. In a blink, he recovered and turned his contempt-filled gaze towards Hector.

"Keep your *creature* under control, Hector, or I will see that it is disposed of."

Hector turned to give Raif a nod, and the lad knelt to calm Dog. "Hush, boy," Raif said. "Hush, now. There's no danger here."

How I wish that were true.

"Orion." Hector stepped towards the man, looking up at the church elder. "We aren't here to cause any trouble, we just—"

"I shall be the judge of that, Hector, as Perisma's chosen," Orion said. "Sit." His self-assurance and unquestioning belief irked Hector. The man strode into the room, his black and gold gown fluttering about his lean frame. Hector sat, with Raif beside him and Dog tucked between them.

Orion regarded them over steepled fingers, thick black eyebrows creased together. "It is troubling, Hector, that you should return, at this time especially."

"At this time? I should have thought my return here would always be troubling to you, Orion." Hector forced a smile, hoping he might steer the conversation towards a lighter tone. A fool's hope, he knew, though it did not stop him from trying.

"Our fathers were friends, Hector. We might have been, too, had you chosen the right path. Though I suppose one such as you could never ..." He sniffed. "No matter. As it is, do not expect me to give you leniency." Orion brushed his hands down the front of his robe and sat taller. "Now, I hear you're staying at Bernard's inn. Has he told you of the problems we've had lately? The man has always been a shameless gossip. Has he mentioned the *traitors* coming into our midst?"

"Traitors?" Hector pursed his lips. "The Commune, you mean."

"The traitors who caused Septima to move away from worship of our beloved Perisma. To worship a false idol, a mere *man*." Orion's lip curled, and he bared his teeth.

"In that, we can at least agree," Hector said quietly.

Orion gave him a measuring stare. "Indeed."

"What of the oath? Nook Town has always been protected." Hector rubbed his stubbled chin, frowning. "Unless—"

"As well you know, Hector, the oath has protected us for many years. Yet something has changed. They think they can force their ways upon us. They are abominations to the ways of Perisma, as are all with powers." Hector cast Raif a glance, and Raif met his eyes. It seemed that Orion was speaking to himself more than them, a mad man with his foolish beliefs. Orion cleared his throat as though sensing their unspoken judgement. Hector turned to face him. "When I came into my role as church elder, I swore that I would see the powers dealt with internally in a way that my father never dared. Now we, Perisma's blessed, maintain control over our people. We found our own solution to a problem created by an ancient, uncaring god."

Dealt with? The young boy who'd taken their horse. Could that be part of this solution Orion spoke of? Anger spiked within Hector. "It seems to me, Orion, that these changes—this apparent *solution*—are the very reason the Commune have come here. Yet you seek to place the blame at my feet, somehow, despite my absence for so many years." He inhaled deeply, trying to keep his incredulity and frustration at bay. It would not do to speak harshly to this man who held Nook Town in his palm. "What I mean to say is, I hardly see how the Commune's visit has anything to do with me or the lad. Coincidence, that's all it can—"

Orion let out a barking laugh, devoid of humour. "I see, as usual, that Bernard has left out the most important detail." He laid his palms flat upon the desk and leaned forward. "It concerns *you*, Hector. Oh, it concerns you, indeed. The boy is of no consequence— or, perhaps, that remains to be seen." Orion cast the lad a scrutinising stare that Hector was all too uncomfortable with.

He leaned across Raif. "What concerns me, Orion?" he asked.

Orion's emotionless, flint-coloured eyes flitted back to him. "Isn't it obvious? They were looking for you. Well, members of your pathetic group. What is it called, Vara ... Vera ...."

"*Veritas,*" Hector snapped.

"Veritas, yes," Orion said, a satisfied gleam in his eye. Of course he had known the name; he simply wished to take control, to show

Hector how little power he held here. "You even name yourselves after the goddess of another land. Always a traitor to your own people, Hector."

"I am no longer a part of that group," Hector said, voice so low it was almost a growl. "Nor am I to answer for the Commune's actions. They have sought out members of Veritas all over Septima. Why should they not do so here, too?"

Orion snorted disdainfully. "No, Hector. They've attempted to come here before over the years. This was different. They held posters emblazoned with your face. Somehow, they knew of your roots here. They came in search of your damned group and put my people in danger. Against the word of a hundred-year-old oath—"

"Ha!" Hector scoffed. "You are hardly one to speak of an oath that you flout breaking yourself. I am shocked at your carelessness, Orion. The young man I once knew would have known better than to risk the wrath of the Grand Magister by drawing such attention to Nook Town, to his beloved church." No longer able to hold back his fury, Hector was aware that his voice was becoming louder and louder in that dark, oppressive room. "What are you doing with them, those with powers?" His lip curled. "But I think I already know. A young boy served us when we arrived here, seeming barely more than a servant to carry out menial tasks. You think you have the right to do that—to *children*?"

Orion straightened the sleeves of his robes, face a mask of cool indifference. "And here we see the truth. You care only for those with powers, your brethren. My father truly was a fool not to send you away when you were a child." The church elder placed a hand on the holy book in front of him. "As a young man, knowing that my role as church elder would soon be upon me, I prayed to our beloved Perisma. I was guided in my decision, and I remain assured that I act in this town's best interests. Perisma has shown me the way all these years."

At Hector's side, Raif suddenly sat forward. "You didn't answer his question. What are you doing to people with powers? Where are you keeping—"

"Raif, calm down," Hector said, easing him back into his seat. He calmed himself as much as he could, pushing the feeling into the lad. "I'm sorry; anger is not helpful here." He glanced at Orion, who stared at them both over his clasped hands. "Perisma, I'm sure, has guided you, Orion. But that does not give you leave to imprison people. To make children into little more than servants."

Orion snorted. "They make a choice, that is all. Stay here, in the place they are born, and have jobs that allow them a place to sleep, food, security. Or be cast out—to go where they will, be it the Commune or risking a life of poverty."

Hector sensed Raif's ire at that and pressed his hand on the lad's leg, squeezing gently. He had known what it was to flee Nook Town with nothing but the clothes on his back, and he had been a man grown when he had done so. "That is no choice, Orion. Especially for children."

The church elder studied his fingernails, giving a small shrug. "It is kinder than simply sending them to the Commune without question, is it not?" Orion looked between Hector and Raif, before saying, "In any case, I have no doubt your *Veritas* have done something to draw the Commune's attention. I know what you are involved in. How you and your little group have tried to fight against the Grand Magister. That your actions should bring their focus upon this town, should risk all I have accomplished here"—he narrowed his eyes—"is not a consequence I can so easily forgive."

Hector grunted. "I am not so sure it is that simple. You must have heard the rumours of the Grand Magister's increasing searches. His need for more children." Hector glanced at Raif, whose face was paler than usual. He must fear for his sister even more after all they had heard here. "It seems to me that a search for Veritas would be the perfect guise to allow Commune soldiers into the town. What did you tell them, Orion? No doubt you would gladly see me taken into their clutches."

"I told them the truth, of course. That you left this place years ago after your father's ... *death*," Orion said, allowing a silence to hang in the air after that word. Hector did his best not to react, though his heart galloped a fierce beat in his chest.

"In any case," Orion continued, "they departed and were told in no uncertain terms they were not welcome here again. The Formation Oath remains intact. We are protected and we pay our dues."

"That is a lie. Your choice to stop sending them those with powers will come down on you sooner or later. Their suspicions will grow, and soon."

Orion's eyes were hard and unflinching. "The light of Perisma will protect us. Besides, some *have* chosen that option for themselves. They have not received nothing from us."

Hector shook his head. "It won't be enough. The light of Perisma? You always were blinded by your idiotic faith. If the Grand Magister wants to take this town, he will do so and will not think twice about some oath created years ago."

"Speak of Perisma in such a way again and you will lose your tongue. My patience has been more than generous with you. Do not test it. I am the protector of this town, and I shall do what I believe is best for its people. It is as I said—you must answer for your sins." He stood, straightening his robes, and moved to the door, opening it silently. Outside, two men stood. The door closed, and Hector lost sight of the three of them.

Shit. What are they going to do to me? To Raif?

"Hector," Raif whispered. "When are you going to ask about Rose?"

Hector nodded. "I want to, lad, I do. It's just ... I'm not so sure it's wise just now. I've a bad feeling about where this conversation might be going. Orion is a harsher man than his father ever was. He will want to use me, I fear, to make a point. I—I should have planned for this. Fool to think that Biron was still in control here. That things had not changed in eighteen years. I fear I have led us into a trap."

"A trap?" Raif's eyes glistened with fear. "But what about—"

"Listen to me, quick now. If I am taken, you must take care of yourself. Listen to your gut, watch for Cara. Don't trust anyone, hear me? And be wary. Give them no reason to hurt you." As he spoke, he sent reassurance towards Raif, even as his own fear threatened to consume him. When the lad didn't respond, he placed a finger under Raif's chin and forced their eyes to meet. "Do you hear me, lad?"

"Oh, I ..." Raif swallowed and nodded. "Yes, I hear you, Hector." He spoke just as the door opened behind them.

CHAPTER 7
RAIF

Raif turned at the creak of the door. Orion stood with a man on either side—the two who had dragged him and Hector into this room—with a fierce look in his eyes. "Hector Haralambous, you are hereby placed under arrest for murder."

"What? No!" Raif stood, aghast. *Murder?* How could this be happening? Hector had done nothing to be arrested for. He looked to Hector, seeking reassurance that this was all a mistake, that Orion was mocking them in some way. But his green eyes were filled with sadness as he met Raif's gaze.

"Sit down, lad," he said quietly.

"As he says, boy. There is nothing that you can do to stop this. Hector has committed a grave sin in the eyes of Perisma. He has caused *great* harm."

"What? H-he would never hurt anyone!" Raif cried, refusing to back down.

This time, Hector reached over and eased him down to sit, kneeling in front of him. "Listen to me, lad. This needs to happen. Some years ago, my actions were ... I—I *did* hurt someone. But I can explain." He stood and turned to Orion. "I can explain, Orion. It was not as you think, and—"

"Did you think you could come back here and not be held accountable?" Orion's eyes were hard. "You will explain, indeed, Hector. To Perisma." He stood tall, clicking his fingers at the men beside him. They stepped forward, each grasping one of Hector's arms. As they did so, Hector gave Raif a brief nod.

"It's okay, lad," he said. Raif could only watch numbly as he was marched to the door.

"You will answer for your sins, Hector. Only Perisma may judge you now; only He may grant you forgiveness."

Orion waited for the two men to take Hector through the door before closing it. He turned to Raif. "I am sorry you had to witness that, boy. I am sure Hector has told you nothing of his past here. Of why he *must* be judged."

Raif's mouth was dry, his heart pounding. He shook his head. Orion sat behind his desk, clasping his hands atop his narrow chest. He watched Raif for a few moments and then lifted a bell on the corner of his desk, ringing it three times.

"Why have you come here?"

Raif hadn't expected the question, nor was he prepared to answer it. Hector had told him not to speak, that he must be careful, that they must not mention Rose's powers. But now Hector had been taken, and he was sitting in front of a man who seemed to be staring into his very mind. He swallowed. At his feet, Dog let out a gentle whine. He reached down to pet him before looking back at Orion. "Um, w-we came to look for someone."

Orion tilted his head. "*Someone?* I see that you are afraid to tell me the whole truth. I will give you time to understand that I mean you no harm; none here do. When you are ready to tell me your story, I will do what I can to help you. I am sorry you had to witness"—he waved his hand towards the door—"that." His lips flitted into the ghost of a smile. "Hector will not be harmed, if that is what concerns you."

Raif found himself wanting to believe that more than anything, even after Hector's words: *Don't trust anyone, hear me?*

He met Orion's steely gaze. "He won't?"

"Of course not. That is not our way." Orion steepled his fingers. "Perisma is a just god. He will judge Hector fairly for his actions."

Raif's mind was spinning. After all he had heard in this room, all that had been said about those with powers and this mysterious god, Perisma, he wished he could take a moment to himself to sort through the chaos in his mind. But that did not seem it would be an option, not now. "His actions? What did he do, exactly?"

Orion raised his eyebrows. "He did not tell you?" He tutted. "You trust a man who keeps his past so hidden from you? Well, it is not my place to share it." He leaned forward. "You may attend his trial, of course. You may learn the truth for yourself then, boy."

Just then, the door opened behind Raif. He turned numbly, still trying to process all that had happened. Through the door walked a girl of Raif's age—around fourteen or fifteen summers. He gasped, fully drawn in by her presence. Like Hector and Orion and many others in Nook Town, her skin was olive-toned, speaking of an ancestry harking back to the cursed Abandoned Isles to the west of Septima. Raif thought it perfectly complemented her gleaming blonde hair and dancing hazel eyes. All fears melted away as the girl smiled at him, and he grinned in return, feeling his face flushing.

"This is my daughter, Lebioda," Orion said.

"Lebby," said the girl, giving her father a disapproving glance. She moved to face Raif. "It's nice to meet you."

"Hello," Raif mumbled, trying to ignore the fluttering of his heart.

"Lebioda will show you the town, boy."

"She—she will?" Raif looked from Orion to Lebby and back again. It would be good to leave the stifling air of this room.

"You will be safe with my daughter." Orion bowed his head.

Don't trust anyone, whispered Hector's words at the back of his mind. But this young girl was not her father; what threat could she pose? He needed a friend, now more than ever. He stood.

Dog following at his heels, Raif allowed Lebby to lead him from the room.

As they stepped from the dim shelter of the church, Raif shielded his face against the bright morning sky. A stark chill hung in the air. In the light of day, his fears flurried back to the surface. He fought back the urge to scream.

Hector. I am alone; what am I going to do? How will I find Rose?

"Are you ready?" Lebby asked cheerfully, drawing his attention back to her.

"Oh, er, yes." Unlike with Evelyn, he felt awkward and shy around the dark-eyed, glossy-haired girl. When he plucked up the courage to make eye contact with her, his stomach did a strange sort of dance he'd never experienced before. For the briefest of moments, nothing but Lebby seemed to matter.

She held an arm up, directing them down Nook Town's main market street. "Well, then," she said, grinning at him. "Let's get going."

They walked a few steps before she paused and gave Dog a scornful look as if she had only just noticed him. "Does ... *that* need to come with us?"

"Oh, uh ..." He looked down at the guileless dog, unable to reconcile Lebby's evident disgust. "He won't cause any trouble."

The girl sighed and gave Dog an appraising look. With a nod, she began marching away. "Be sure that he doesn't. And keep him close. We don't usually allow pets in Nook Town. They tend to cause more problems. That's your first lesson."

Speeding to catch up with her, Raif almost laughed at her serious tone. "Really? What harm could a pet do?"

Her easy manner turned in an instant. "Do not speak of what you don't understand," she snapped, her tone sounding very much like her father's.

Raif froze. He had to be careful; wasn't that what Hector had said?

Don't let a pretty face get the better of you, idiot.

And yet, at the same time, a desperate part of him wanted Lebby to be his friend. Who else did he have now? A lump rose in his throat, and he swallowed it back as best he could. "I-I'm sorry."

Lebby's face softened and she stepped closer, nudging him gently with her elbow. "No, don't apologise. I-it's hard to remember sometimes. Our ways can seem unusual. We don't get many visitors, you see ... I forget myself." A smile flitted over her lips. "So, well, I suppose *I'm* sorry."

Raif nodded, smiling eagerly, glad to have her back on his side. He pointed to the closest building—a dark-windowed establishment. Atop the door was affixed a red flag, blowing gently in the breeze. "What's that place?" he asked.

"That," Lebby said, "is the brothel."

"Brothel?" Raif frowned. "What's a brothel?"

Lebby bowed her head close to his. "You know, where men go to ... relieve their *unholy urges.*"

"Unholy urges ..." Raif blinked.

"You know, if they need to ... put themselves upon a woman." Lebby's voice was becoming quieter and quieter, her eyes casting about conspiratorially.

Raif's face scrunched, understanding slowly dawning on him. A flush of heat rushed from head to toe. "Oh."

Lebby broke into a heartfelt laugh, giving him a not-so-gentle slap on the arm. Despite her amusement, Raif could only bring himself to give a weak chuckle.

"I didn't know," he said, feeling more and more half-witted by the minute. "Why is such a place so close to ..." He tilted his head towards the nearby church.

"My father thought it best to be honest about such things. 'Better to see things in the blessed light of day than keep them hidden away from Perisma's gaze,'" Lebby said, making her voice deeper and creating an uncanny impression of her father.

Raif laughed at that, embarrassment melting away. "I have a lot to learn."

"You do," Lebby said, her eyes full of sincerity. "But that's what I'm here for—to help you understand our ways. As Father says, men work for Perisma, women work for men." She shrugged. "It's a natural urge, no more. Come on."

Lebby's words sent a shiver of unease through Raif; he wasn't sure if she was joking. *Women work for men.* In Little Haven, there was no question of who was master, who was servant. Everyone was valued equally. It irked him that Lebby should be forced into a subservient role, and that she should be so accepting of it.

But he had no time to question her before she continued marching down the street, pointing out buildings and various people as they went about their business. Although his worries for Hector and his longing to find Rose constantly simmered beneath the surface of his thoughts, he allowed himself to get lost in Lebby's words. It was a pleasant reprieve not to be focused on his worries, even for a short time. Listening to his new friend, he could almost believe that Nook Town was a good place, that all would work out, that he would receive the answers and help he needed.

He could almost forget the words of warning that Hector had spoken before he'd been arrested. Though at the back of his mind, growing quieter by the minute, circled the words *Don't trust anyone.*

CHAPTER 8
EVELYN

With a bellyful of salted pork, hard bread, and water, Evelyn was beginning to feel herself again, if only the incessant throbbing in her head would stop. More wine would help, she knew from experience, but she was loath to seek out the cabin boy who enabled her to reach the abyss of intoxication she'd sought yesterday. She needed time alone. Time to allow herself to feel what she was most terrified of—that which she tried her hardest to forget. But knowing that and allowing it to happen were two entirely different things.

She shivered, a mixture of hope and dismay stirring within her. Perhaps it was time to face the memories head on ...

Am I strong enough?

Will I ever be?

She stood at the stern of *Septima's Blessing* and looked out at the endless ocean spreading towards the horizon. What tiny islands she could see in the distance were unknown to her, far from the place she called home.

Home.

Was Little Haven ever truly my home?

She let out a long, weary breath. There was no comfort to be had from such a notion, only more questions. Why had her parents left her there? Were they, as Mak suggested what seemed a lifetime ago, nobles trying to protect their child from the Commune?

Or did they simply not want me?

And why, at her time of greatest need, when she had nowhere else to turn, did the elders of Little Haven turn her aside in disbelief? After sixteen years there, the stark realisation that she was still an outsider had hit her like a bolt of lightning. The son of a village elder meant more than she ever would; he would always be believed over her, even if he lied and manipulated.

Even if he raped.

No!

She kicked the deck in frustration, for she would never receive answers or justice for what happened. True, she'd been able to fight Arthur off with the powers she hadn't known she'd possessed, but he would have recovered from those injuries long ago. She still bore the scars of what he'd done to her, was still tormented by his betrayal, by the way his abominable actions had been ignored.

Evelyn tried to comfort herself with what she did know—in the two years she'd been at the tavern, Fat Bessie offered her more of a home than she'd ever known. But that was gone now, snatched away by the Commune. Bessie and her husband, the closest she'd ever had to a family, had been murdered in cold blood. Anger and hatred spiked through her. She trembled as she fought back the urge to lash out, wanting only to punch and kick at anything she could.

On top of that, she'd let Raif and Rose down. She'd placed trust where it shouldn't have been placed—in Avanna, most of all. And the woman had betrayed her, handed her off to Jonah like nothing more than a possession.

She should never have believed help would come from some-where outside of herself. *I should have known better.*

She ground her knuckles into the side of the ship; the sharp sting of splinters was the least she deserved. She could only hope Hector had kept his promise. He'd been the only one who seemed to truly care about them, to want what was best for Rose. She had to believe, despite his being part of Veritas and one of Avanna's closest advisors, that he was trustworthy.

And now there was an uncertainty that was part of her, too. The powers she'd felt in Lord Torrant's basement—were they the same as those that Arthur had awoken? A brief spark of desperation causing them to flare up?

Then why had they failed her in the woods when she, Raif, and Rose were attacked? If she had powers, they were unreliable at best.

Or worse—useless, uncontrollable, pointless. She snorted. *Just like me.*

Evelyn was overcome with a burning urgency, and she leaned over the ship to vomit, eyes streaming, mouth filling with bitter bile. When she stood upright and wiped the back of her hand across her mouth, she felt lighter, purged, as though all her rage and doubts and mistrust had left her along with the contents of her stomach.

She was filled instead with a renewed sense of clarity.

Jonah helped me. Not only at Lord Torrant's home, but last night, too —watching over me, expecting nothing in return.

That's not true, though, is it? He brought me here for a reason. Perhaps, if all goes wrong, I will be the one he will blame.

She frowned at herself, wishing she could simply trust someone for once without questioning their motives. After all, he was one man; he couldn't be held responsible for the orders placed upon him by the Commune. Besides, it was clear there was more to his relationship with Lord Torrant, some connection that Evelyn, having never felt it herself, could scarce bring herself to try and understand.

Maybe he was someone she *could* trust. She wrinkled her nose, disgusted at the notion. A soldier of the Commune, and she was helping him.

What will Raif think when I tell him all that has happened? It was unusual to allow herself to consider trusting Jonah, that was certain; he was as foreign to her as the lands she surveyed on the distant horizon. The idea sat uneasy within her now that she gave it her full attention, a burden rather than a comfort, a knot in her stomach she could not ignore. Accepting that Jonah might be able to do what he promised—that he was true to his word—was so much harder than treating him with suspicion and disdain.

She laid a hand to her forehead and rubbed, willing away the thumping headache and inner turmoil that crashed against her skull, making her head swim.

"Morning!"

She groaned as she turned to face the cabin boy. To her horror, he grinned widely back at her.

What did I do to make him think we were friends? She cursed herself for consuming so much wine. Though, at the time, she had wanted only to blot out her pain and anger.

She sighed, taking in the boy. He was younger than her—fourteen years or so. *Same age as Raif,* she realised sadly. The cabin boy had a rugged, sun-reddened complexion, with short brown hair peeking out from beneath a dirty red bandana. Tried though she might, she could not recall his name.

"I was worried 'bout how you was after you took so much wine last night," he said. "I didn't wanna give you so much. But you said you could handle it so, so, um ..." He trailed off, chapped lips pulling downwards.

"I'm fine," Evelyn snapped. "I *can* handle it."

A lie, her mind whispered. She shook her head, frowning at herself, wanting nothing but to be hidden away in her cabin once more.

The boy's shoulders slumped with evident relief and he grinned again, revealing a mouthful of yellow teeth. "Th-thanks for spendin' time with me. I don't get much chance to see people me own age," he said. "Let alone have someone *wanna* spend time wi' me."

Evelyn waved a dismissive hand, aware that she had only spent time with him because of his ability to gain access to his father's stash of wine. Part of her was ashamed for it, and part of her knew it had been her only option. He was a child, and so she could main-tain control of the situation with him; everyone else on this ship was an adult man, and therefore far too dangerous to be vulnerable around.

The cabin boy's brow creased as he leaned in close. "I came to find you for a reason," he said. "There's somethin' you should know or, um, p'rhaps it's best ..." He shuffled on the spot, wringing his hands. He glanced up towards the sun. "We need t' hurry."

Evelyn raised an eyebrow. "What is it?"

"You should c-come to my da's cabin," he said, avoiding her gaze as his cheeks flushed.

"What? No!" Evelyn said. *I should have known ... even in one so young. They're all the same, aren't they?*

That's not true. Raif is different.

And he still believes you a boy, doesn't he? His request is innocent, surely.

Regardless of that quiet, gentle voice in her head, she could not reason herself out of the anxiety that spiked within her. This place, she realised—being trapped aboard a ship with a crew of strange men—was a prison the likes of which she had not planned to find herself in. Fear clamping across her chest, she had to resist the urge to shove the cabin boy away. She clenched her quivering fists at her sides.

Seeing her anger, the boy's face dropped. "Oh no, what's wrong? I just wanna help!" he said, holding his hands towards her.

She flinched backwards. "Don't touch me."

"I thought we was ..." The boy let out a long sigh before peering over his shoulder, as if worried they might be caught by someone. "T-there's something you need t' know," he whispered urgently. "Please."

"I'm sure you can tell me right here," she said, crossing her arms.

"Will you come if I give you more wine?" His sudden offer made Evelyn blanch. It seemed he already knew her real reason for spending time with him. She paused, indignation outbalanced by her own cravings. Wine *would* help her to forget the pain in her head, and to ease the tightness in her chest.

"I've got plenty more," he said. "But you, um, need t' come t' my da's cabin."

She lifted her chin and stared at him until he looked away, willing him to judge her. "Fine, but you will *not* touch me," she said.

He furrowed his brow, small eyes narrowing as he glanced back at her over his shoulder. "'Course not. Quick, follow me. It might be too, um, too late."

Despite herself, Evelyn's interest was piqued. What could he possibly have to share with her? She hurried after him along the main deck and towards the crew's quarters. "How comes your da has so much wine?" she asked. "Are you sure you should be sharing it with me?"

He beamed back at her, all innocent joy, and she knew in that moment he was simply glad to have someone he might call a friend. "There's plenty to go around. Da always brings lots. Hands it out t' the crew as a reward, y'see. Cap'n says it's good for us, keeps us motivated."

As they made their way towards the cabin in question, a tall, bald-headed man called out, stopping the boy in his tracks. "Oi! Ham! Where d'you think you're goin' with a deck to scrub an' lunch to prepare, boy?"

Ham. Of course, Evelyn thought, studying his pink face and upturned nose. The nickname had caused her some merriment the night before, she suddenly recalled, though now it simply seemed cruel.

"Oh! I'm sorry, I was lookin' for ... Um, d'you know where my da is?" Ham asked the man.

The bald man scowled. "He's overseeing the crew at their duties, boy. Why, want me t' tell 'im you're slackin'?"

"Oh! No, no, I'm comin'." The bald man huffed, glanced at Evelyn, shook his head, and retreated. Ham sighed with evident relief. "Go inside. It sounds like Da hasn't visited the cap'n yet. There should still be time ..." He chewed his lip. "You might 'ave to wait, but trust me—there's somethin' you'll wanna hear."

Evelyn opened her mouth to speak, but Ham had already started backing away. "Help yourself t' the wine; it's stashed in the chest beneath the hammock. B-but be careful. Cap'n's cabin is connected to Da's. Be quiet, be alert. Jus' ... *listen*, okay? Listen."

"Oh, uh, okay. Thank you," Evelyn said, watching as he ran towards the kitchens. *Listen for what?* This was an odd game to play, that was certain, but her mouth was already watering, her mind on a single thought. *More wine. Just a little, just to get me through this morning. Just to ease this head pain.*

Inside, she quickly found the chest Ham had directed her to, and within, a treasure trove. She licked her lips in anticipation, eager to escape herself once more. She lifted a wineskin, satisfyingly heavy, and slumped against the wall. Her hands shook as she opened it and poured a generous measure into her mouth, gulping it down, welcoming the slight burn of the alcohol at the back of her throat. She'd had far nicer wine, but this was strong enough to numb her, and that was all she really needed.

She rested her head back on the wall and waited as Ham had instructed. She drank more wine, and as the minutes dragged, found her eyelids growing heavy. Lulled by the gentle rocking of the ship, she slept.

When Evelyn gasped awake, mouth dry and body aching, she did not know how much time had passed. She groaned, head groggy. She rubbed her eyes, making to stand. She'd almost forgotten what Ham had told her and was about to leave the cabin—two wineskins tucked into her belt—when she became aware of the cadence of voices through the wall. *Listen*; that's what Ham had said. Suddenly uneasy, she leaned her head against the wall.

"... makin' the crew uneasy. We have to do something 'bout this *commander*, Cap'n."

Commander. They're talking about Jonah!

Her stomach knotted. *Always a conspiracy. Always danger.*

"I share your concerns, Smith, but we have to be careful." Captain Nem's words drifted through the wood, his usually jovial manner replaced by sombre concern. "Ensure we are *all* well-guarded. We cannot risk him discovering our true purpose. I have watched him closely and now believe that Lord Torrant sent the commander, at the Grand Magister's orders, to watch over us. It can be the only explanation."

"But what of the ruby, Cap'n? I thought that would buy us some time."

"Perhaps it gave us enough time to get away, but that's all. It was a risk to take it in the first place. We must continue to be vigilant for signs of Captain Lence's ship ... I fear I may have placed us all in far more danger."

"I can't see there were another choice."

"No, Smith. I believe you are right." A heavy sigh reached her ears, even through the wall. "It is no matter now. We must do what we can to ensure we reach our destination in one piece. Rest assured, Smith, and spread word around the crew. I will deal with Commander Sulemon before we reach the Noman Islands. We must not lower our guard around that dangerous man."

"Yes, Cap'n." There was a pause, the sound of a throat clearing. "And what of his *companion*?"

"Hmm. The boy may be innocent, though we cannot be sure. It seems strange to me that he would accompany Commander Sulemon if he were not somehow involved in the man's mission. Else he is being held against his will. Perhaps an ally waiting to be saved."

Shit.

"P'rhaps he should be questioned."

Oh, shit!

"Yes, perhaps. Leave it to me, Smith. Now back to work. There can be no suspicion. The ship must run like clockwork. I have no doubt he watches our every move."

A door opened and closed.

Evelyn slumped back against the wall, frozen and fearful, heart hammering.

She had to think.

Jonah was in danger. She might be, too.

She had been in a similar position before, and Avanna had caught her overhearing a plan not meant for her ears. She had to act wisely.

Evelyn made her way back to her cabin to come up with a plan, unwilling to make the same mistakes she had before. She would bide her time rather than panic; she would save Jonah's life, and in doing so, she would take the power in their relationship.

She smiled to herself, deeply comforted by the notion.

And then I will be in control.

CHAPTER 9
RAIF

At the end of the tour of Nook Town, Lebby invited Raif into her home with the offer of refreshment. Exhausted, he agreed, though his mind was beginning to return to thoughts of Rose and Hector. Guilt gnawed at him that he had allowed himself to be distracted for so long. His stomach knotted, for he'd barely spared his sister a thought since that morning. Dog was tied outside at Lebby's polite request. Not wanting to cast a shadow over their day, Raif consented, ignoring Dog's quiet whimpers.

Don't trust anyone, hear me?

Lebby moved about the white-walled kitchen, opening wooden cupboards and humming to herself. As he watched her, he found it hard to reconcile Hector's inherent mistrust. Surely someone like Lebby—someone young and innocent—could not mean them harm? Her father, on the other hand ...

I must be careful of Orion. He nodded to himself, resolved to be more careful going forward. He was alone now, but that did not mean he could simply stay inactive. Rose was still out there somewhere.

"Would you like some tea?" Lebby asked, dragging him away from his thoughts.

At the mention of tea, he remembered Hector's warning at breakfast that morning, what felt like an eternity ago to his racing mind. But Lebby wouldn't do what Avanna had done; it made no sense. Even so, he told himself to remain cautious. Wait until she drank it, be sure it was safe. Satisfied he was taking all the precautions he could, he gave Lebby a nod.

"That would be nice," he said with a smile.

"Good," she said, smiling back at him.

He watched her deft preparations with admiration—pinching various herbs and spices from glass pots lined neatly upon a shelf, sprinkling them into a metal pan above the fire. As she stirred the tea with a long wooden ladle, she gave him a steady gaze. "You seem distracted."

Raif scrunched his face up. "Sorry. It's just ..."

"You're worried about Hector."

Raif looked up, meeting her eyes. They were full of sadness and understanding.

"I am." He tugged at one of his tunic sleeves. "Do you, um, do you know why he was arrested?"

She turned back to her pot, shaking her head, golden hair bouncing. "No," she said, leaning over to check the tea. She retrieved some cups from a cupboard. "He left Nook Town before I was born. Father has mentioned him over the years, but ..." She shrugged before filling the cups. "I am not familiar with his story." She placed a filled mug in front of him and sat in the chair opposite. The dining table was small, with just two seats, and Lebby reached over to pat his arm. "I'm sorry. It must be very difficult to lose your friend."

Raif cupped his hands around his mug, allowing the steam to wash over his face. "I'm not sure what I'll do without his help. Though Orion, I mean, y-your father, said he wasn't in danger, that he wouldn't be harmed ... and I—I hope that means—"

"Hush, Raif, hush," Lebby said, stroking his arm. "All will be well." She sipped at her tea, sighing with satisfaction. Taking that as a sign that it was safe to consume, Raif followed suit. The drink was warming, sweet, and floral. His whole body seemed to relax as he consumed it, and a warmth blossomed outwards from his chest.

"Thank you, Lebby. This is ..."

"Lovely, is it not?" She smiled. "I drink it every day. My mother taught me the recipe before she died."

"Oh, I'm sorry," Raif said. "That—that she died."

Lebby watched him over the rim of her cup as she drank more tea. "It's okay; she died a long time ago." She set her tea down. "Besides, I know she's blessed by Perisma, bathing in His eternal light."

"I see," Raif said, feeling incapable of saying anything useful. He found no such peace when thinking of his own father, only an ever-simmering anger at those who had caused his death. *The Commune.*

"What about you?" She brushed back some hair from her shoulder, her eyes intent upon him. "Where are your family?"

"My family?"

"Yes." Lebby, seeming to sense this was a sensitive subject, reached out to touch his arm again.

"My mother ..." He lifted his mug and gulped down more tea, forcing back a lump in his throat. "I-I don't know where she is. Or whether she's alive. The Commune, um ... they took her. She's gone." As sadness pulled at his heart, Raif wondered when he'd given up hope of finding her again, for he knew, deep down, that was the truth. He'd lost his mother and father when the Commune attacked their home. Rose was the only family he had left. He felt Lebby's hand upon his forearm, soft and reassuring. "My sister, she's who we came to Nook Town searching for." He said the words before he could stop himself, yet when he saw the concern in Lebby's face, he knew he could trust her.

"What's her name?" she asked softly.

"Rose," he said. "It's Rose." His voice quivered as he spoke her name. Lebby eased her chair closer to his and placed an arm around his shoulders.

"I'm sorry, Raif. I see how hard it is for you to be apart from her," she whispered. "What's she like?"

Raif paused. Seeing Rose's bright blue eyes and blonde curls clearly in his mind's eye, he couldn't help but smile. "She's young, just six. No, almost seven now. She doesn't speak much, but she's clever. And strong. Stronger than—well, than you'd expect of a child." He flashed a glance at Lebby, wondering if he'd said too much.

"Well, you only have each other. I expect you've both been strong in your own ways, since your parents."

Raif nodded, flashbacks of the time since they'd fled from Little Haven bursting into his mind: Rose finding Dog, stumbling upon the tavern in which they'd met Evelyn, travelling with her to find help—

And blood. So much blood.

He gasped, body aflame with a sense of fear and panic.

"Raif? Are you unwell?" Lebby furrowed her brow. She gripped him closer. "Slow your breathing, like this." She breathed in and out slowly. Raif mirrored her as best he could, and in a few minutes, his breathing and heart rate had calmed. Lebby stood, taking his mug and refilling it from the pot by the hearth. She put the full mug in front of him and sat back down.

"Sorry, Lebby," he said. "It's just that—"

"Hush. You've been through much. You do not need to explain yourself."

Raif drank more tea, grateful for its soothing warmth. After a time, he said, "It's been really difficult."

Lebby nodded. "When my mother died, I experienced similar … feelings. I tried to deal with my grief on my own. I thought that was what I must do. But sometimes your mind can become over-whelmed, can't it? When you tried to hold it all in." She leaned closer, and he could smell her tea-sweetened breath. "After I strug-gled for a time, I found that the best way to deal with those feelings was to speak them aloud. To stop trying to contain them in and be ... well, strong."

Her frankness astounded him. No one had ever made him feel so understood. Filled with reassurance, he made a decision. "Lebby, can I trust you?"

She regarded him with those hazel eyes and beamed, her whole face alight with kindness. "Of course you can," she said, nudging him in the ribs. "We're friends, aren't we?"

Friends. He needed a friend now more than ever. He returned Lebby's smile, uncertainty tugging at the corners of his mind.

But then he took a deep breath and spoke. "It's just ... well, my sister, she has powers. Really strong powers."

"Oh," Lebby said, her face remaining open and friendly, though a shadow passed across her eyes. But in a blink, it was gone. "How did you discover them?"

"Her powers?" Raif hesitated. *Can I really tell her the truth, including the men who Rose—*

No, no, no.

As if reading his mind, Lebby said, "Did she use them, Raif? Did she hurt someone?"

Raif gulped. "Um, she ... yes. But—but she's not a bad person. She's so young, and those powers, they ... She used them to ..."

"Yes?" Lebby glided closer still, her golden hair brushing against his arm. "You can tell me, Raif."

He nodded, sipping some more tea. "We were running from soldiers. It was after our home was destroyed, and these men, they attacked us. Came from nowhere. Evelyn—that's our friend, but she's gone now—well, she tried to stop them, but they were too strong. And then Rose used her powers.

"I mean, I didn't see it ... but—but Evelyn did. She told me. The men were dead, and Rose, uh, well, she—she did it." *Blood. So much blood. The smell of it, the sight of it.* He shuddered, glancing at Lebby, afraid that she'd somehow reach into his mind and pluck out those awful images. "It's not Rose's fault. It's the Commune. They're to blame. They took our home from us. If we hadn't been running, we wouldn't have been in danger. Rose wouldn't have needed to—to ..." Raif's lip began to tremble. He bit down on it, determined not to cry.

"Oh, Raif." Lebby's arm was back round his shoulder as she comforted him. "I'm so sorry. What a difficult journey you've had."

Raif sniffed, nodding. He found that he was suddenly very tired and wanted nothing more than to return to the tavern, to his room, and to his bed. When he relayed as much to Lebby, she stood and held out her hand.

"Come on. I'll walk you back."

Outside, they untied Dog, who leaped up to lick Raif's hand. At his side, Lebby wrinkled her nose. "You really shouldn't let him do that," she said. Raif found he had no energy to question or argue that point, so he simply nodded.

They walked in silence to Bernard's tavern. By the door, Lebby came to a halt. "Raif, I—" She glanced around. "I just wanted to say thank you. For sharing your story."

Raif gave a lopsided smile, barely able to keep his eyes open. "Thank you for listening."

Lebby studied his face, then gave a firm nod. "I'll come for you tomorrow. Get some rest."

Raif watched her walk away, back towards her home, before opening the tavern door. To his relief, Bernard was bustling about in the kitchen and did not notice him returning. He crept up the stairs to his room. At the top, he spared a glance at the door to Hector's room, a pang of guilt tugging at him. Dog whined

Tomorrow, he told himself. He entered his room, slumped on the bed, and let out a long exhale. He was just aware of Dog burrowing into the woollen blanket at his side as he drifted off.

Tomorrow I'll find out more, he assured himself.

And then he knew no more.

CHAPTER 10

HECTOR

In silence, Hector summoned the barman, holding aloft his empty tankard. He was not as drunk as he desired to be, and the sun had long since set. Raif would wonder where he was, no doubt, would be worried about what his arrest could mean.

Raif.

How I have failed him.

Father ...

He took a deep swig of ale, willing it to numb him.

After all these years, now I must face the consequences of what I did. What Father asked me to do.

"I can't go on like this, Hector. Please ... help me."

Mercy, his father called it.

It hadn't felt like mercy. He rubbed his aching eyes, so like his father's, the guilt burning at his heart even after all this time. Biron would have been open to discussion, would have allowed some merit to the notion of mercy.

Orion ... He was a man whose faith outshone any reason, any discussion, any doubts.

Even when he knew he must return to Nook Town, Hector never

thought he would be in any real danger. He couldn't have predicted the changes that Orion had wrought on his home.

I was a fool. After Avanna, I should have known to expect change here. Biron never would have allowed for ... He glanced around at his surroundings. *This.* To the unknowing eye, it was a rundown tavern on the outskirts of Nook Town. He'd been in worse establishments, yet he would much rather be in any number of those places than here.

The silent barman approached, filling his tankard with frothing, pale ale. He shared the briefest of glances with Hector before flitting back into the shadows of the dark kitchen area behind the bar. There were others here, too, though he'd yet to engage in conversation with them since he'd arrived that morning. He took a generous swig of ale, then glanced over his shoulder at them. They sat in groups and spoke in hushed tones, appearing no different from any patrons he might expect to see in any small tavern. But they *were* different; he knew that all too well.

Their powers. That was what set these people apart. What had caused them to be moved here, little more than prisoners. And it was clear that was what they were seen as, given Hector's own imprisonment in this place.

"Perisma's Blight is the only place for the likes of you," Hector had been told as he was marched to the southwest corner of Nook Town. "Until such time as Perisma's judgement is to be cast." The young men who guarded him were unfamiliar, mere boys to his eyes.

"When will that be?" he'd asked. "Can you pass a message to Raif, to the lad I travelled here with?"

Neither had responded, refusing to meet his pleading gaze.

"At least tell me when I might expect—"

"Keep your mouth shut," one of them hissed.

"Traitor," growled the other.

They reached a locked iron gate that circled what he could only assume to be Perisma's Blight. One of them retrieved a key from his pocket, unlocked the gate, and opened it, letting a screech of unoiled hinges into the chill, bright morning air. Hector was shoved inside, barely able to keep his footing with the suddenness of the movement. He watched as the gate was closed and locked behind him. One of the men spat at his feet, then they both turned and walked away. Hector's gaze remained on their retreating backs, tears prickling at his eyes.

What am I going to do?

A voice not his own responded in his mind. *Stop feeling sorry for yourself, for a start.*

He sniffed, blinking around. *Cara?*

From behind a pile of empty old barrels beside the gate to Perisma's Blight, he saw her white face and piercing yellow eyes. She let out a gentle *miaow*, enough for him to know she was there without drawing any attention to herself from anyone who happened to be nearby.

"It's okay," Hector whispered. "All at the church, anyway."

Still best to be cautious. Cara's gaze darted around from her hiding place.

Hector sighed and scuffed his boot at the rain-sodden ground. *What am I going to do? What about the lad? I've let him down again.*

You weren't to know this would happen.

I should *have known. Should have prepared for the fact that Biron might not be in power anymore. Though I could never've ...* He turned around and looked at the Blight. A miserable place, with rundown wooden homes that appeared to have been built in a hurry and were only barely maintained. *I never expected Orion could be* this *cruel. He was all words when we were children, never had the courage to actually* do *anything. And now ...*

Now we know the truth. Cara was suddenly at his feet, observing the Blight beside him, her fur stark white against the dark mud. Their eyes locked for a moment. *You asked what you're going to do. Wait, watch. I would say listen, but you haven't always been the most observant when it comes to—*

"Enough of that, cat!" he muttered, nudging her with his foot. She affectionately butted his leg with her head.

I'll *do the listening for us. And I'll watch out for Raif, too, best I can.*

Hector knew she said that to reassure him more than anything, for if the lad did get into trouble, her options for helping him were limited. But he appreciated the gesture, nonetheless. It allowed him to maintain the tiniest slither of hope where there had, mere moments ago, been none.

Right, then. Wait and watch. He nodded down at her, and she glanced at him, ran her face along his leg, then scurried away into hiding once more. It would not do for her to be caught now.

And so he had headed for the biggest building in the Blight, the only place that seemed to have any sign of life, and taken a seat at the bar, ordering himself an ale. And he'd waited.

Enough self-pity. Time to watch. Time to listen, too, despite what that bloody cat said.

He put down his ale tankard and turned to properly observe the room.

Eleven people occupied the tavern in all, including the barman. A trio of young men huddled close to the meagre fire, unspeaking and hunched over their cups. A woman around Hector's age was reading a book in a battered armchair nearby. An old couple, man and woman, were dozing within their booth, each clasping a half empty tankard. Finally, around a table sat a group of four children, two boys and two girls, ranging in age, he estimated between six and sixteen. One of them was the young boy who had tended him and Raif and taken Bert when they first arrived.

Too young to be in this forsaken place, Hector reflected. At the sight of the youngest boy and girl, he thought of Rose, of Raif and Evelyn, and his heart ached. He had much to make amends for, and he inwardly vowed that he would do so, no matter the cost.

Somehow, I'll make it all right.

As he watched, he noticed a troubling aspect. Each of these people was dull-eyed or sullen or frail, or a combination thereof. A deep sense of anguish radiated from them all, creating an air of sorrow that seeped into the very walls of the tavern and festered like a slow-growing mould, poisoning the atmosphere. Some spoke in hushed tones, though they seemed almost self-conscious of making any sound, of drawing attention to themselves in this dreadful place. On the wall above the hearth, the symbol of Perisma shone with reflected firelight. Beneath it, the words *Perisma sees all, Perisma judges all* were painted in dark red on the whitewashed wall.

Orion, what have you done to these people?

Before he could think too much about it, he stood and cleared his throat. "Hello," he said. To his dismay, he was spared a couple of throwaway, frowning glances. "Hello, everyone. I'm Hector, and I—"

"Welcome, Hector," the woman in the armchair said, snapping her book shut. She stood, walking towards him. She was of a height with him, with shoulder-length brown hair, and bright blue eyes. He smiled at her, but she did not return it, instead firmly taking his arm and steering him towards the bar. "You're new here, so I'm happy to give you some guidance. But"—she leaned back, looking him up and down—"we don't want to get involved with any of Orion's ... *trouble.*"

"Trouble?" He furrowed his brow. "I—" What could he say that would not require the full truth for his imprisonment here? "I'm from Nook Town. I've been away, and—"

"I know who you are." The woman's tone was blunt, her gaze direct. "And like I said, we don't want any trouble. Hard enough getting along here without Orion sticking his nose into our business." She sniffed. "We keep our heads down, follow the rules, and we're fed and housed. We've children to think of"—she cast a glance over her shoulder—"so I'm sure you understand."

Hector followed her gaze and nodded. "'Course," he said.

"Well, then"—the woman cast him a humourless smile—"the rules. We are all assigned our jobs throughout the week. We are to accept them without question, else all of us are punished, rations taken away or firewood confiscated. Believe me, it's not worth trying.

Fighting back'll get you nowhere, now that you're here. Orion has control over everything."

Hector swallowed. "I see."

"If you don't now, you will very soon."

"Where am I—where will I sleep?" he asked.

"Hut six is empty. You're welcome to it. Do what you can to make it ... yours. May as well get comfortable; it's the only home you'll—"

"Oh, I won't be here for long. I, uh ..." Hector trailed off, suddenly very unsure as to what his future held. Would he ever be permitted to leave this awful place? His gut filled with dread. "I'll leave you. I thank you for your help, uh ...?"

The woman eyed him for a moment. "Beth."

"Beth." He nodded, turned to leave.

"There's one more thing, Hector."

He paused, looking back over his shoulder. "Yes?"

The barman had appeared, holding a cup of some steaming liquid. "That's yours," Beth said, pointing to the cup.

Hector frowned. "What is it?"

"The rules," Beth said. "Veritarra's Gift is to be consumed by all in the Blight, no exceptions."

"What? No!" Hector pushed the cup away from where the barman had placed it. "I will not drink that."

Beth pursed her lips, waving an arm towards the barman, who moved away. "I can't make you drink it," she said, leaning closer to him. "But know that if you don't, Orion will know. And he will punish you somehow. He will hurt someone you hold dear. You arrived with a young boy, didn't you? Under your care, was he?" She watched him for a moment, nodding when his mouth dropped open. "Mm. Think of him. Drink the tea. You do not want to find out what Orion will do if you don't follow the rules." She tapped his cup with a finger before turning and walking away.

Shit. Hector reached for the cup, hand trembling. *Veritarra's Gift.* His father had ensured he drank it when he was a child—one of the conditions that Biron had asked of them to avoid Hector being sent away to the Commune like the other individuals with powers born in Nook Town under his governance. Hector never knew how his father was able to come to that agreement with the church elder; he'd never *wanted* to know. Whatever the arrangement, his powers and his consumption of Veritarra's Gift had been a secret. A shameful thing, known only by Biron, his father, and himself. As he'd gotten older, the effects had weakened, though he'd never admitted that to his father.

But he knew, didn't he? Else he wouldn't have asked me to …

And then he had fled, swearing never again to drink the tea that repressed his very being.

What choice do I have? I cannot allow Raif to be hurt.

As soon as he thought it, a reply entered his mind. *I'll watch over him, Hector.*

Cara. Hector peered around, though she was nowhere in sight. *Cara, I cannot do this. I cannot cut off my connection to you, my love.*

Hush. I will still be here. You must do this. It will be temporary. We will find a way out of this place.

Hector sighed, biting down on his lip.

We will be together again soon, my love. He imagined Cara nuzzling against him and took strength from her belief that this was the only choice he had. He reached for the cup and lifted it to his lips. With a shudder, he drank the dark, astringent liquid within.

It wouldn't be long before it took effect, though he knew all too well what to expect—a vacant, alien otherness. A detachment from himself, from his powers and all they gave him—good and bad.

Part of him welcomed the spreading dullness like an old friend. Part of him wanted to fight his way, kicking and screaming, from this dreadful place, kill Orion and every one of his ignorant, foolish followers, to burn Nook Town to the ground.

I'm sorry, Cara.

It's okay, old man. I'm here. I'm still here.

And then her voice was gone.

CHAPTER 11

RAIF

Raif was awoken early the next morning by a rapid knocking on the door to his room. Outside the small window, the sky was still alight with stars. He sat up, flattening his hair as best he could and wiping drool from his chin, wondering who could be knocking so early and with such urgency.

Knock, knock-knock, knock.

"Coming!" he slurred, stumbling from the bed. Dog, evidently perturbed at being awoken, gave a small, disgruntled growl before settling back down on the bed. Raif did his best to make it to the door without tripping in the darkness.

"Oh, Lebby!"

"Morning, Raif!" Lebby said chirpily. She held an oil lamp, which illuminated her in the shadowy hall. She tilted her head, lips quirking upwards. "Didn't wake you, did I?"

Raif straightened the clothes he'd fallen asleep in, cheeks burning. "O-of course not, I, uh—"

Lebby leaned forward and patted his arm. "I'm teasing," she said. "It's very early; I wouldn't expect you to be up so soon." She smiled at him. "I did wonder whether you'd like to join me for breakfast, though. I've been thinking about you and everything that's happened, and ... I want to help."

"Really?" Raif smiled back at her, relief washing over him. "That would be nice."

"Come on, then. Let's go."

"Dog, we're going for breakfast," Raif called. Lebby frowned though did not say anything as Dog stretched and jumped from the bed, the promise of food evidently far too appealing to ignore.

THEY ONCE AGAIN SAT IN Lebby's home at the kitchen table. Dog had been tied outside, though Raif had ensured he was left a small pot of water and promised he'd bring food out for the whining spaniel.

"I'll make some tea," Lebby said. She glanced at the door as she flitted about the kitchen, gathering herbs as she had done the day before. As Raif watched her, the kitchen door glided open and Orion strode in.

"Good morning, Lebioda," he said. His hard eyes met Raif's. "Raif."

"Good morning, Father," Lebby said.

"Oh, um, g-good morning, O-O—"

"You may call me Church Elder," Orion said, moving to stand next to the kitchen table. Raif risked a glance at him, dressed in his church robes even at this early hour.

"Church Elder, of course." He dropped his eyes to the table in front of him, afraid of this man who seemed to control everything and everyone in Nook Town.

"Perhaps you would join me in my study, boy."

"Oh, uh ..." Raif glanced at Lebby. "We were going to—"

"Lebioda, bring the boy's breakfast to the study. Come." Orion made for the door without looking back. Raif stared after him, wide-eyed and unmoving, until Lebby gave him a gentle nudge.

"Go on," she said. "Don't worry."

He nodded numbly, following after Orion. Had this been the plan all along?

He walked behind the church elder without speaking, out of the kitchen and down the hallway, where they stopped outside a dark-stained door. Orion pulled a heavy key from the pocket of his robes and proceeded to unlock it. He signalled for Raif to pick up an oil lamp from a nearby table before disappearing into the dark room beyond.

Inside, it took a moment for Raif's eyes to adjust, even with the light from the lamp. When they did, he found a room much like the one he and Hector had been kept in at the church, all dark wood and stone, with a great fireplace behind a large desk. The fire was beginning to crackle to life, as though it had not long been lit. To the back of the room was another dark-stained, engraved door. The symbol of Perisma stood out even against the near blackness of the wood.

"Where does that lead?" He asked the question before he knew why. Orion glared at him as he took a seat at his desk.

"That does not concern you, boy. Come. Sit."

Something in his tone drew Raif's undivided attention. Orion sat, hands steepled, watching him. Behind the church elder, flames flickered in the hearth. Raif's heart hammered as he moved to sit in front of the man, mouth suddenly very dry. He placed the oil lamp in front of him, tongue flicking out to moisten his lips.

A silence extended between them, and Raif wondered whether he was expected to talk. Then Orion let out a long, heavy exhale and sat back in his chair. "Lebioda has told me of your sister. Of the reason that you came here."

Raif's stomach dropped. "She—she has?"

I trusted her. I thought she was my friend.

And she told the man who imprisoned Hector.

He wanted to scream and cry simultaneously. Instead, he quashed down his emotions, sat as tall as he could, and waited for Orion to speak.

I have done nothing wrong by searching for my sister.

Orion nodded as though he had been listening to Raif's inner dialogue and approved of his conclusion. "I understand why you did not wish to tell me, Raif, but my daughter told me because she knew I would be able to help."

Raif raised his eyebrows. "You can? How?"

"I have people. Resources. I wonder, though"—Orion leaned forward, his hollow-cheeked face illuminated by the oil lamp—"what led you to come *here* in search of her?"

Don't trust anyone, hear me?

What choice do I have, Hector?

Raif took a deep breath. "We—we were at Veritas. They were helping us with—with Rose's ..."

"Her powers." Orion's voice was low, his eyes burning with hatred.

"Y-yes. Her powers."

"They are strong." It did not seem to be a question, and Raif found himself unable to deny it.

"Yes, she's strong. She needed training. Help to bring them under control because she—"

"Veritas was formed on a lie, boy. Those with powers cannot take control of them. No one can." He waved a hand in the air. "Continue."

"We thought we were safe. Hector was—was ... Um, it doesn't matter. But, well, Rose—that's my sister—was taken."

Orion's black brows shot up. "Taken?" He composed himself quickly. "Yet that does not answer the question I posed. Why here? Why did Hector bring you to Nook Town?"

Raif repressed a shudder at Orion's increasing irritation. "The woman who took her, Avanna. She told Hector that she was coming here with Rose, and—"

"I see. Troubling, that she should tell him such a lie."

"A lie?"

"Of course." Orion steepled his fingers again. "For they never arrived here, this Avanna, nor your sister."

Though he'd known it already, Raif's heart sank.

"But I do not wish for your journey to have been in vain."

Raif looked up. "You—you don't?"

Orion's thin lips twitched into a smile. "You are not alone here, boy. Much as that fool Hector might have made you feel it to be so. The Church of Perisma offers you only—"

At that moment, the door opened, and Lebby entered the study with a tray of food and tea. She kept her gaze down as she walked to the desk, placing the tray in front of Raif. She continued to avoid his eyes as she turned to leave.

"Lebioda, sit," Orion said. She did as she was told, taking the chair next to Raif's. He smiled at her, but she was staring down at her lap.

Raif hated seeing her so ashamed. She'd done nothing wrong, really. Only sought to help. *I need to tell her it's okay, that I'm not upset at her for telling her father about Rose.*

"I was just telling the boy that he is not alone here. That we are his ... friends."

Lebby nodded. "That's true, Father." She glanced briefly towards Raif, then back down again. "We—we want to help, Raif," she said quietly.

"I know," he said. She looked up, her shoulders slumping with evident relief

"All I'll need is a description of your sister, boy. And this Avanna. We will do all we can to bring them back to Nook Town and make the Veritas woman answer for what she has done." Orion leaned across his desk, retrieving quill, ink, and vellum. He poised the quill, raising an eyebrow at Raif. "Well?"

"Oh, yes, um ... She—she has blonde, curly hair down to her shoulders. Blue eyes. And she's small for her age. About half my height, probably." He let out a gentle laugh. "She's strong, though. Stronger than she looks. I call her little bug."

Lebby leaned over and touched his hand. "We'll find her, Raif."

"Very well. And the woman?"

"Brown hair and eyes. Tall, perhaps your height. She … spoke well. Had a way about her. She was … convincing." Raif gulped.

"Mm. I know the sort." Orion continued scratching with his quill for a moment before setting it down. He nodded at Raif. "This should be enough." After allowing the ink to dry, he rolled the vellum, melted a lump of wax, and pressed a seal onto it, then stood from his chair. "I will send people out immediately."

A lump rose in Raif's throat, thickening his voice. "Thank you," he said. "Thank you, Church Elder."

Orion inclined his head. "Now drink your tea and eat your meal. You need your strength." He approached the door. As he opened it, he turned back, lips pursed. "Lebioda, perhaps you could show Raif Perisma's holy text. The first acolyte, hmm?"

Lebby's eyes widened. "Y-yes, Father. I mean, if you're certain that—"

"Do not question me, girl." Orion moved through the door and closed it firmly.

Raif's stomach let out a grumble, and he realised how hungry he was. He ate some of the buttered bread Lebby had brought him, dipping it in egg yolk. He gulped down his tea, too, letting the floral scent calm him. It seemed to hold a certain quality that stilled his mind. He breathed deeply and smiled at Lebby. "Thank you," he said.

"Of course! I invited you here for breakfast after—"

"No." Raif wiped a hand across his mouth. "I mean for telling your father about Rose. I was upset at first, but …" He grinned. "Do you think he can really find her? He seems confident."

Lebby turned to the door and back again. "If there's one thing I know about my father, it's that he *always* does what he sets his mind to." He noticed a glimmer of sadness in her eyes. But then she stood and moved to the opposite side of the desk, running her hands across a large, leather tome. "Now, Raif, this is a very important book."

He stood to get a better look at it. Outwardly, it appeared quite plain. Brown, well worn. Not a book he would have been particularly drawn to. But then Lebby opened the front, and on the first page was the symbol from the front gate. Etched in gold, it shimmered with reflected light from the oil lamp and fire. He reached forward, wanting to run his finger along it.

Lebby tapped his hand away. "Be careful," she said. "This is our holy text. It's best I handle it. Father is very particular about it." She smiled up at him. "Come round here and look."

Raif walked round the desk and shuffled as close to Lebby as he dared. They remained silent for a time as she turned the pages, filled with columns and columns of text he could have no hope of being able to read. He did his best to concentrate despite his growing awareness of the closeness of her shoulder to his and the way her sleek hair hung down in front of her face as she scanned each page before delicately turning to the next.

"Ah! Here it is," she said finally, tapping a finger on a particular passage in the book. "This is one of the first stories I learned." Her voice was full of reverence, her face glowing as she turned to him. "It seems that Father would like you to learn it, too."

Raif swallowed, an unexplained well of emotion stirring in his chest. "I'd like to," he said, voice hoarse. "I—I can't read, though. At least, not very well." His cheeks burned with shame.

Lebby gave him a gentle smile. "Don't worry; I can read it. Follow my finger. Here, sit."

He did so, feeling an instant absence as she moved away from him. He sank into a cushioned seat with a hard wooden back. He realised he was still clutching his mug and gulped the rest of the tea down.

Beside him, Lebby whispered, "Are you ready?"

Raif swallowed. Part of him strangely felt like he shouldn't be here. Like this was a trap and he was only moving further into it by allowing himself to learn this.

But then he chided himself. *What harm can a story do?* To Lebby, he said, "Yes, I'm ready."

"This is the story of Perisma's first acolyte. A woman who lived long ago."

Mistress Esteralla Clinkscale was the sole heir of Lord Jeph Clinkscale, King's Protector of the Scale Isles.

"The Scale Isles." Raif sat forward, intrigued. "Aren't they the Abandoned Isles now, to the west?"

Lebby frowned. "Yes, Raif, they are. But hush, you must listen."

"Sorry." He relaxed back in the chair and allowed her to continue.

As an only child, Esteralla was told she must marry into a wealthy family to secure a comfortable future for herself. After all, as a woman, she could scarce inherit her father's land and title.

From the age of thirteen, Esteralla was paraded in front of a long list of noble families, appraised for suitability. Dressed in her finest emerald-green corseted gown, yellow hair brushed until it shone like spun gold, green eyes outlined with coal from Alpin, she would grit her teeth and do as she was bid and remain silent, the obedient daughter of a powerful lord.

But inside, she had a dormant ability, one that would prove the downfall of her father, her family, and of all who lived in the Scale Isles.

"She had powers!" Raif said, unable to stop his exclamation. Lebby cast him a withering look, and he bowed his head, wincing. "Sorry ..."

Years passed, and still Esteralla refused all suitors. Her father, growing impatient with his daughter's stubbornness, made an oath that the next man would be her husband, whether she was content with the choice or not; after all, he had already given her too much freedom, and he feared his own life grew short. His fellow nobles scoffed that he had, so far, allowed her to make her own decision. But she was his daughter, and he couldn't deny the gnawing guilt in his heart that she must be paraded like a prized mare and ultimately sent away from her beloved home. Besides which, he found that, far too frequently, he could not make her do as he bade. When he reflected upon that, his mind grew fuzzy and vague, as though he were trying to recall memories that were not quite his own.

But now his daughter was nearing her nineteenth winter. She had turned down far too many eligible young men. Lord Clinkscale had to be firm.

"Esteralla, my child," he said, clasping her delicate hand in his. He guided her to join him beside the fire in his study, for his joints protested in his old age and he could not stand for long. "It is time for you to be married. I can no longer afford to allow you the final decision."

Esteralla's bright green eyes flashed. Her father's frailty set her heart to aching, but even so, his words caused a deep-seated anger to awaken within her. She had to be careful; some years before, she'd learned of the power within her—and of how it could swell if she lost control of her emotions.

Raif gasped but held his tongue. *Was this how it was for Rose? Did she know of her potential, how dangerous it could be? She is so young; how could she know?* He chewed on his lip, deep in thought.

Unaware of his inner turmoil, Lebby continued to read.

She'd lost more than a few pets when she'd allowed her temper to get the better of her, such that she no longer allowed domestic animals to be kept within the confines of the castle. Even knowing the dangers of her power, she continued to use her abilities to force her father to agree with her, as she had done since she was thirteen years old.

"Father," she said, her voice even and unemotional. "Must we speak of such things? I see how tired you are, how your hands shake." She summoned a servant to attend them and ordered some tea. "Come, let me guide you to bed." She reached across for his hand and eased her powers into his mind, swift and subtle as could be.

"No, Esteralla, I really must—oh." Lord Jeph Clinkscale was overcome with exhaustion, his mind too slow to piece together his rapidly fading thoughts.

"Hush, Father, hush." She pulled him up from his seat, noticing then how light he was—like a frail bird, so easily crushed. All the more impor- tant to keep her control over him gentle, for the slightest slip might mean he lost himself altogether, like one of those poor cats she'd broken in her early days of experimentation. She put him to bed and gave him some healing tea and sat with him until he slept.

That night, Mistress Esteralla Clinkscale went to her own bed believing she had avoided her father's wishes once more. She was one step closer to remaining within her home, to using her powers to convince her father that she must inherit his land and title—to being free, alone, in control.

She was awoken abruptly in the night, her lady's maid shaking her by the shoulders.

"My lady," the young woman whispered. "It's your father. You must come now."

Fear shot through Esteralla. She hurried to follow the young maid.

In his bed, her father was thrashing viciously, sweat pouring from his brow, face slack. When she went to his side, his eyes were wide with terror, focused upon something she could not see. She reached for his mind with her own, thinking to use her powers to help him. She didn't realise, of course, that it was her powers that had shattered his mind at last, after years of influence, for she was blinded by the selfishness her abilities created within her.

Inside, his thoughts clashed against each other, like a great storm contained within the confines of his weak and dying body. She knew what to do, and she had to act fast. She focused as hard as she could, working to calm Lord Jeph Clinkscale, to bring him back to himself.

There was a moment of silence; he relaxed, his body stilled, and his eyes closed. Esteralla let out a sigh of relief and made to stand.

But then her beloved father let out a cry of agony such as she had never heard before.

"Esteralla," he croaked. "Please."

She knelt and clasped his icy hand in hers. His eyes were lucid, fixed upon her face. "You must marry," he said. "Promise me ... It is for your own ... good. You need protection ... the powers you hide ..."

Lady Esteralla's heart skipped a beat. He knew; had he known she was using them on him all these years?

"Promise me, my daughter. My love."

She closed her eyes and felt her father's delicate hand in hers and made a decision.

"Of course, Father," she said. "I promise."

If only she had told the truth.

But she would not discover the importance of honesty until she had seen the truth and light of—

"But wasn't she using her powers with good intentions?" Raif asked. "Surely, she didn't mean to cause harm?" *Perhaps, like Rose, she simply wanted to use them for the best. To protect herself, as Rose protected us.*

Blood. So much blood.

Lebby raised her eyebrows. "What she intended and what she did are two different things, aren't they? And that's the problem with these *powers*. Those born with them can use them however they wish, without thought for the impact on their victims."

Raif gulped. *She's right.* "I'm sorry, I didn't mean ..."

"It's okay, Raif. You have much to be taught, and there is plenty of time for me to help you learn." She smiled, closing the book firmly. "That's enough for today, I think. How about some more tea?"

Raif looked down at his cup, surprised to find it was empty.

Oh, I drank it already. He frowned. *How did I forget that?*

"That would be nice," he said. "Thank you."

As they walked from the room, Raif's eyes were drawn back to the holy book. Were there answers in there to help Rose? To bring her powers under control, to protect her from them? It seemed so, and he could not ignore the glimmer of hope that ignited within his heart at the thought.

CHAPTER 12
EVELYN

It had been four days since Evelyn revealed what she'd overheard to Jonah.

He'd listened in silence, face an impassive mask. "Do not tell anyone what you know," he said. "Watch for anything unusual. Report back to me."

Evelyn had gawped at him. "W-what if I get caught? What if something happens to you and—"

Stoic as ever, he'd simply said, "I will remain vigilant. Do not worry about me."

Evelyn had not spoken aloud her panic. Jonah appeared unfazed by her revelation—unsurprised, even, as though he had been expecting something of this nature all along. Maybe his years of soldiering meant he was always on his guard, suspicious of all around him. Evelyn knew what it was to be mistrustful, but she hadn't expected this—Captain Nem seemed friendly, eager to assist them.

You idiot, you've put yourself in danger again, haven't you?

But Jonah knows what he's doing ... doesn't he?

Evelyn tried to convince herself it was so as she continued with her days as instructed, blending into the background of the ship's daily workings, making herself an unimportant element that could be disregarded. Inside, she was on edge, her stomach in knots and mind a flurry.

What if he's killed without me knowing?

What if they find out I'm a woman?

What if they—

No. No, no, no.

After four days of endless paranoia and anxiety circling her mind, she was exhausted. "Oh, this is stupid," she muttered. So far, there'd been no sign of anything wrong, of Captain Nem's having a plan to take down Jonah. Determined to find answers and to try to take some semblance of control of the situation, she searched for Ham. He'd been mysteriously absent these past few days, but he *had* chosen to help her. He had led her to his father's cabin, instructed her to listen.

Maybe the fates are finally beginning to favour me, she pondered. But even as the thought occurred to her, she couldn't avoid the veil of negativity that tainted her every waking moment.

Don't be a fucking idiot.

It must have been a trap, an attempt to lure us into a sense of unease. Perhaps they're laughing at us behind our backs, waiting to carry out their attack.

The sun beamed down, but she kept her hood up, avoiding eye contact with everyone she passed. The crew, having quickly acclimatised to her presence, ignored her as they went about their duties. She didn't know anything about sailing a ship. Despite herself, she marvelled at the deft ways they called to each other and worked in unison to keep *Septima's Blessing* on course. More than once, she heard utterance of the word "pirates," and a ripple of fear ran through her. Were they in danger of attack? Just another worry to add to her mind. But beneath her admiration of the crew's work was a constant simmering undercurrent of terror—when would Captain Nem "deal" with Jonah?

And what would a ship full of sailors do when they discovered a girl in their midst?

Nausea rose up from her stomach, burning her throat, making her retch. Waving it off as seasickness to the crew member who raised an eyebrow at her, she continued her pacing. With some days ahead before their arrival at the Noman Islands, Evelyn's mind reeled with possibilities. Though she was concerned about their vulnerable position—certain they were balanced upon a precipice with nowhere to turn—she was unable to voice her feelings to Jonah. Although the smallest level of trust had begun to grow between them, a part of her couldn't help but remember who he had been, how they had met. They were far from friends. If she let him see her true self, she opened herself up to the possibility of betrayal.

When a hand settled upon her arm, her heart jolted and she spun around, fists up and ready to attack.

"Woah! Sorry, it's only me." Ham flinched backwards.

"Oh, Ham," Evelyn said. And then, embarrassment turning to irritation, she flared up. "Where have you been? I've been looking for you."

Ham glanced around nervously. "I-I'm sorry. I've been, um, busy." He looked down at his hands, twisting them together. "My da found out about the wine and ..." He winced.

"Oh." A silence dragged out between them. "Sorry, Ham," she said, stepping closer and giving him an awkward pat on the back. "You just scared me. Hope I didn't get you in trouble with your da."

He sniffed and shrugged. "Nothing I'm not used to, really ..." He glanced over his shoulder, tilting closer. "Y'know, I never did get your name, did I?"

She blanched though quickly gathered herself. A wonder he hadn't asked sooner. A name instantly came to mind. "It's Raif." He nodded, mouthing the name to himself. Then, before he could begin any of his inane chatter, she checked that they were alone and pulled him to a quiet area of the deck, sheltered beneath the stairs leading to the ship's stern and wheel.

"Why did you tell me to go to your cabin, Ham?" she asked, all the while checking around for other crew. "To listen?"

He swallowed, refusing to meet her gaze. "I-I dunno," he said, unconvincing in his lie.

"Ham. Please, you can trust me. We're friends, aren't we?" She smiled, hoping it would come across as genuine, though she was out of practice and almost out of patience.

His lips twitched into a grin, and she felt a slither of guilt for manipulating him. "Well, that's true." He leaned close. "I heard my father, the first mate, talking to, uh ..." He shuffled on the spot, frowning. "Well, my da, y'see, he don't think I can, I can make friends. The other crew, they mock me." His cheeks flushed a darker shade of red than usual. "I proved 'em all wrong, an' I took their wine!" He giggled, beaming with pride.

In that moment, she missed Raif more than ever. This boy might be of an age with him, but he was far from Raif's level of intelligence and maturity. Inhaling sharply and biting her lip, Evelyn grasped Ham's shoulders and squeezed. "Please, I need you to concentrate. Why did you take me to your cabin?"

A glint of confusion and pain appeared in his eyes. "I was upset with Da," he said, as if that explained everything. "After I heard him speaking about your commander, I ..." He furrowed his brow. "You was nice to me. We became friends. And then the next day, when I heard Da, I thought about it an' ..." He shrugged, evidently trying to loosen her grip. "I'd've wanted to know, is all. Please, you're hurting me."

"What?" She narrowed her eyes, attempting to understand his rambling. "Did you know what I would hear?" Her clasp tightened on his arm. She had failed Raif and Rose. She would not do the same for Jonah. She would help him, and they would reach their destination, and they would stop the Commune.

They had to.

As she pressed him into the wall, she suddenly became aware of a faint glimmer of awareness at the edge of her mind, just as she'd felt in Lord Torrant's basement. A flicker of something *other* blending into her own conscious. And, if she chose, she might mould it to her own will, make it obey her.

"Did you know?" she said again, ignoring Ham's increasingly pale demeanour. "What are they going to do to Jonah—the Commander? What did you hear your da say?"

"I-I ..." Ham seemed unable to respond, eyes growing vacant.

His lack of response only served to stoke Evelyn's rage. "You said you heard your da speaking about it! What did you hear?" As she spoke, she began to smother that *otherness* inside her mind, not thinking what it might mean for Ham. It was growing dim, her hands were twisting his tunic, pulling up so he was standing on tiptoes. Just a little more and he would be sure to reveal—

"What's going on here?"

Evelyn let out a shocked cry as she snapped back to awareness. She released Ham, who slumped to the floor, dazed. The fury slipped away, leaving behind an icy chill in her gut.

What have I done?

"Ham," she said, reaching down for him. He shrank away from her touch.

"What've you done to my son?" said the voice from behind. Evelyn had almost forgotten anyone had spoken. She turned to find a fierce-looking crewman, black brow furrowed.

"Da!" stuttered Ham. "I'm sorry, I just wanted to, um, you said, you said ..." Ham's lip quivered. "He knows! 'Bout Cap'n Nem's plan!" He waved his arms towards Evelyn, tears spilling down his cheeks.

Suddenly, Ham's words sunk in. His da was the first mate. *The first mate. Smith, the one who spoke to Nem.*

Shit.

"Does he now?" Smith gave Evelyn an appraising look. With nowhere to run, all she could do was stare blankly back at him. "I think Captain Nem will need to hear of this." He clamped a huge hand on her arm and pulled her away. When Ham made to follow, Smith held up his other hand. "Not you, boy. You've done enough."

Numb, shocked, and ashamed, Evelyn didn't try to fight. Her knees were weak as she followed Smith. She glanced over her shoulder to see a sobbing Ham watching them go.

"Ham, please—tell Jonah," she croaked, hoping he would listen even after what she'd done to him. "Tell the Commander I ..."

Tell him I've failed.

F*ather,*

How pleased the Grand Magister was to hear of the passing of King Arias, a man who, in two short years, tried his hardest to bring a "balance back to our beloved Septima." His implication that the Commune's increasing power was a danger to all citizens caused a great stir, with many noble families beginning to question the wisdom of sending their children to a man they scarce saw within the public realms, let alone understood.

What a shame that King Arias's own ill health meant he was unable to see his plans come to fruition. The Grand Magister assures me that his son, dubbed by some as Cosmo the Coward, will be far more amenable and that there will be no more whisperings amongst the feeble-minded, the power-less, the ignorant.

It is said that King Arias had a fraught relationship with young, frail Cosmo. Before his coronation, the boy was rarely seen in court, an apparent embarrassment to his father's name. It reminded me of our rela-tionship, Father. Of how little pride and honour I brought to the family name and how unwilling you were to love me simply for being of your blood.

My companion, Jonah, tells me that his own father was absent for much of his childhood, was focused only on his own position, power, influ-ence. It left me wondering, is it more damaging to have a father who is emotionally distant, cold, and uncaring, or a father who simply is not there at all?

How distant you were, Father; how steadfast and uncompromising in your cool disdain towards me. Perhaps it would have been better if I had never known you. Perhaps my life might have been easier, my heart and mind less at war.

Even now, as I hate you with my very being, I still crave that which I know I can never have—your love and acceptance.

And that is why I will never send these letters, why I can never—

I find myself drained, Father, and the night draws in. I will write again, though it may not be for some time.

Your son,

Eirik Torrant

Loyal Servant to His Benevolence

Grand Magister Quilliam Nubira Antellopie III

CHAPTER 13

JONAH

Bang bang bang.

Jonah awoke with a start, gasping in the stuffy air of his cabin. His mouth was dry; his eyes ached.

Bang bang bang.

He froze, looking towards the door, body taut and ready to fight.

Bang bang bang.

"Com-commander Sulemon." The voice sounded young and unsure.

Jonah sat forward, remaining wary. "Who is it?"

"Ham, Commander. The cabin boy. I—I have a message from Raif."

He frowned. "Raif?" he whispered to himself.

He bolted upright, realisation hitting him. *Evelyn.* He leaped towards the door and opened it, finding a red-faced boy shuffling nervously.

"Where is she?" Jonah said, glancing up and down the dim corridor, hoping to see her.

"She?" Ham said with a gasp and Jonah realised his error too late.

"Just tell me, boy!"

"Oh, um, he—I mean, she was so angry," Ham said, voice trembling. "I just wanted to be his—" He frowned and shook his head. "I mean *her* friend."

Jonah crouched to meet the boy's teary gaze, knowing that anger would only send him fleeing. He slowed his breathing and spoke as gently as he could. "Where is she, boy?"

"Captain Nem has her."

Jonah didn't miss a beat. He darted forward, nearly knocking Ham to the floor. His boots pounded upon the decking as he ran to the captain's cabin. Outside the door, a huge, bearded man was standing guard.

"I wish to see the captain. Nem! I know you're in there!"

The man crossed his thick, muscled arms. "The cap'n isn't taking visitors," he said, looking Jonah up and down. "Especially not from the likes o' you."

Jonah's fingers curled into his palms, but he kept his fists at his sides. He had to get to Evelyn. Rage would not serve. So he did what he had learned to do in his years working for the Commune—he puffed out his chest and held his head high, speaking with all the authority he could muster. "I will see Captain Nem. That is not a request."

The man moved whip-fast despite his considerable size. He grabbed Jonah's right arm, twisting it behind his back. "I don't take orders from traitors," he hissed. "The cap'n will see to you, mark my—"

"Now, Smith, that's quite enough." Captain Nem stood behind them, wearing a long, purple cloak, ruby brooch gleaming upon the chest of his black tunic. "The commander is here for a reason." He stood aside, allowing Jonah entrance.

Smith grunted, squeezed Jonah's wrist one last time, and flung him towards the open door, where he stumbled across the threshold and to the floor. "Be careful, Cap'n," he growled. "This one has ideas about his position on your ship."

"That will be all, Smith."

"But Cap'n, he might be armed. I can—"

Nem's eyes did not leave Jonah's face as he said, "I'll handle it, Smith."

The captain closed his door with a firm *thud*, turning to study Jonah. The cabin was lit by three large, rectangular windows, which cast beams of daylight upon his face. Jonah did not like what he saw there.

"Well, it would appear that news travels fast upon my ship," he said. "I had no doubt you would come to retrieve your boy."

"Where is she?" Jonah asked, no longer caring to keep up the pretence.

"She?" Captain Nem's lips pursed. "You have been keeping secrets, haven't you, Commander?" He waved his hand. "This way." He led Jonah to the rear of his cabin, where he leaned down and began to pull aside the large, black rug to reveal a wide square hatch in the floor.

"What is this, Nem?" Jonah asked. The captain remained tight-lipped as he retrieved a firestone lamp and handed it to Jonah.

"Come."

Jonah took the lamp and watched Captain Nem open the hatch and then begin his descent down the ladder into the dark hole beneath. He followed, his stomach knotting. *This cannot be good.*

He climbed down the ladder, his mind taking him back to that morning in Eirik's home, to the day he'd learned the horrific truth about his former lover. Fear compounding, his heartbeat roared in his ears. As he made his way down the ladder, his breath quickened and his chest tightened. He could touch the walls on each side, so cramped was the descent.

"Where are you taking me?" he whispered, unable to keep the terror from his voice. Captain Nem said nothing from beneath him, perhaps unable to hear, perhaps not caring to answer. Jonah heard him reach the bottom of the ladder and step aside. As he reached the bottom himself, Jonah held the lamp aloft. They were in a tiny room, a single wooden door before them. The captain reached into his pocket and retrieved a key, unlocking the door.

Unable to contain his anxiety, Jonah said, "Please, Captain, you must tell me. What is—"

Captain Nem glared over his shoulder. "The time for questions is over." Without waiting for a response, he pushed the door open, silent as a breath. Inside, dozens of firestone lamps were scattered about a vast cabin. It took Jonah's eyes a moment to adjust as he squinted against the sudden onslaught of flickering firestones. There should have been cargo here, bound for the Noman Islands.

But why should cargo need to be locked away and lit besides?

Jonah's breath caught in his throat. As he grew accustomed to the light, he saw more and more that he couldn't understand.

"What ..." He stepped forward on shaking legs.

All around, he met the faces of his fellow Nomarrans—men, women, and children. Some were alone, some huddled together, their bunks pushed close. None spoke but all regarded him with wariness. He couldn't comprehend what he was seeing nor what it could mean. They had been given hammocks, appeared to be well-clothed and fed, and yet he was overwhelmed with suspicion. *What is Nem doing with them?*

A groan to his left alerted him to Evelyn's presence. She was semi-conscious, tied to a wooden chair. Her head was slumped forward. Gaining some semblance of himself, Jonah moved towards her. He touched a hand to her shoulder. "Evelyn?" he whispered, but the only reply he received was another moan. "What have you done to her? What is going on here?"

"She is perfectly well, Commander. She has been given Veritarra's Gift and a sleeping tonic. To rest her mind and keep her powers at bay." Captain Nem stood above him, a hand resting upon the knife at his belt.

"Powers?" Jonah gasped. "She is weak, her powers are nothing to—"

"Do you wish to explain that to my cabin boy, upon whom she

used them with no restraint? Lucky enough that Smith found them before the poor boy was killed."

Jonah frowned. "What?" *How can that be?*

"I might have them; did you know that?"

She tried to tell me. Still, he could not believe she had any real strength; he would have noticed, wouldn't he? *Eirik* would have noticed, that awful morning in his—

No.

He narrowed his eyes at the captain. "You have rendered a young woman unconscious because of your own foolish notions. She is no danger."

Nem scowled. "Do you still believe I do not know why you are here? *She* is here with *you* and so is not to be trusted. You have lied about her identity, after all. What else is she hiding?" His nostrils flared as he stared down at Evelyn. "I have no doubt she was trying to gain more information for your mission. Though the true purpose of that remains ... unclear." He began to stride back and forth, his irritation evident in the hunch of his shoulders.

"My mission?" He watched the captain, took in the ruby gleaming upon the man's chest. Jonah felt each Nomarran prisoner's dread and fear like a weight upon his shoulders. "It is all too clear now what my mission must be. I must save these people. *Our* people, Captain. How could you keep them here? You treat them well, I see. Give them hammocks, keep them fed. But that doesn't change what you are doing." Jonah marched towards Nem, hand gripping his sword hilt, fire burning in his heart. He had ignored the plight of his countryfolk for too long. *No longer.* "Where are you taking them? What has the Grand Magister promised you?"

"The Grand Magister?" Captain Nem's dark eyes flashed with confusion. "Is this some trick, Commander? Some way to lure me into trapping myself for your beloved—"

A cry sounded from the top of the hatch, interrupting his words. "Cap'n Nem!"

Jonah and the captain stared at each other, frozen in their

confrontation. Heavy boots hammered down the ladder. The door clattered open.

"Cap'n, we're under attack! Pirates!" Smith was wide-eyed with frenzy.

"Pirates?" Nem swallowed. "How have they approached us without detection? Can it be—"

"Lence, Cap'n. Must be. Only he is strong enough to cloak a ship."

Cloak a ship? Jonah's mind whirred. *How?*

Nem nodded as though unsurprised at the revelation. "Are you sure? Are they flying the flag?" Nem's voice was low, his tone urgent.

"They are, Cap'n," Smith said. "They fly under the red flag. They are the Grand Magister's men." Smith gawped at them both, helpless. "They've found us."

The Grand Magister's men? Why would they attack a ship loyal to the Commune? Unless ...

"Ready the crew," Captain Nem said. "We must fight as best we can." He began to lead Smith away, towards the deck. "Fetch men to guard this room. They must not be allowed to get to the—the—"

"Captain," Jonah said, making a decision. He knew well what the red flag meant, and it was clear now that he did not know the true nature of Captain Nem's mission, nor his relationship with the Commune. All Jonah knew was that he had to help protect his people.

"What is it?"

"I can assist you." In case there was any doubt, he drew his sword.

Nem followed the movement, lips pursed. "I do not trust you, Commander. What is to stop you from aiding these pirates? Perhaps this is part of your scheme ..."

Ignoring the question, Jonah stepped forward. "I am a strong fighter. And I am immune to control, unlike, I imagine, most of your crew. Our quarrel can wait."

"We need all the help we can get, Cap'n," Smith said.

Nem sighed. "It appears I find myself without choice, Commander. But betray us at your peril. Let's go."

On deck, chaos was rapidly taking hold. Crewmen ran back and forth, seemingly without purpose. One man stood unmoving, watching the red-flagged pirate ship that had appeared alongside *Septima's Blessing*. A warning shot fired out from the pirate ship, landing in the water a short distance from their port side.

Briefly, he allowed panic to clamp across his chest. But then he clenched his jaw and grabbed Nem's arm.

"Captain, we need to take control."

"Do not presume to take command on my ship," Captain Nem snapped, snatching his arm free. "I know how to deal with these *bastards*."

Jonah looked around, confused. "But the crew, they are not—"

"I will see to it." Captain Nem marched away, Smith at his back.

The captain's stubbornness could cost them their lives. Why were he and his crew not prepared for this? Jonah had no time to dwell on it. He dashed towards the man who remained rooted, tugged him backwards, and pushed him to stand outside the closed door of Captain Nem's cabin. "Guard this," he said. "Do not leave your post."

Before the man could respond, Jonah dashed back to the deck. Captain Nem and Smith had disappeared towards the helm. He thought to find them, to ask for a plan, but the pirates were moving fast—three grappling ropes were hooked over the ship's port side.

He leaned over the railing and found himself face to face with a black-toothed pirate, grimacing as he heaved himself up towards the deck. The man reached out a gnarled hand, likely trying to use his powers to control Jonah, unaware he wasted his energy. In retaliation, Jonah slashed outwards with his sword, catching the man's shoulder and knocking him loose, the ocean beneath claiming him.

Where Jonah's victim fell, others followed. They scuttled like rats up the hooked ropes, adept and surefooted. He braced himself, preparing for the onslaught.

"Here! I need men here, they're boarding!" he cried, unsure whether he was heard or whether any of the crew were equipped to assist. He had no time to check before another pirate clambered aboard, younger than the last but just as savage eyed. Jonah gave him no time for any futile attempts at using his powers and swung hard with both hands. Steel met flesh, screeched against bone, and the man's eyes widened with shock. His mouth opened but no scream escaped it—only blood passed his lips. The man slipped backwards and away from the blade, dropping to one of the empty skiffs below with a meaty thud.

From the left, a gaunt-faced pirate lunged at Jonah. He grabbed hold with skeletal hands, digging into Jonah's arms with fierce strength, holding his sword in place. "Traitorous scum," the pirate growled.

Nails clawed into the back of Jonah's neck. He twisted and swung round with a roar, pulling the gaunt-faced pirate fully onto the deck, plunging his sword into the one at his back. His arms were still pinned awkwardly by the first wretch. He hauled his sword from the second man's gut and lurched sideways, pressing the pirate who gripped his arms to the side of the ship. The snap of bones was audible even over the surrounding shouts and cries. The man screeched, his grip slackening. Jonah swung his sword up and across, removing his head in one swift blow.

More pirates made their way onto the deck; fights broke out all around. Some of the crew members had succumbed to the pirates' powers and began attacking their own.

Damn it, Nem, why weren't they protected?

He glanced around frantically. *Where* is *the captain?* There was no time to search. Instead, he hurried to intervene.

"Commander!"

He continued running, barging into two fighting crewman and trying to discern which still had his own mind.

"He was gonna kill me! Me own, me own—" said the bloodied man to his left, voice quivering as he stared at his fellow crewman in shock. Jonah ran his sword through the man to his right, whose dulled eyes barely registered his own death.

"Commander!"

He spun round, found Ham gasping at his back.

"What are you doing, boy? Hide yourself below, now!"

"Commander, I *was* below—it's, they're ... come quickly!"

Ham darted away; Jonah ran behind him. They ran past fighting crew towards the bow of the ship, crashing through the door to the crew's quarters and to a hatch much like that in the captain's cabin.

"Down 'ere!" Ham cried, leaping onto the ladder. Jonah followed without question, heart pounding.

The Nomarrans. Shit.

As they moved down the ladder, harsh voices and cruel laughter reached his ears. He gritted his teeth, preparing himself for the worst.

At the bottom, Ham shoved through a door, allowing Jonah to enter behind unimpeded. Fury coursed through his veins when he saw the scene within.

Evelyn had been dragged to this door from the other end of the hold, where the door that led to Nem's cabin was undisturbed. She remained unconscious, laid out on the floor like a piece of cargo ready for transport. The Nomarran prisoners, meanwhile, were being forced into a row, the men facing one end of the hold whilst the women and children were brought forward for inspection. Jonah stood with his sword held up, ready for attack, waiting to be noticed. But the speaker continued, unperturbed by the disturbance. He was pacing in front of the woman and children, hands clasped behind his back.

"This one will do for you, Scab," he said in a low drawl, smirking at the scrawny, greasy-haired man who limped along to his left. "We all know you're not fussy." A ripple of mirthless laughter ran through the other two crewmen walking alongside the speaker.

"No!" One of the Nomarran men turned from his place in line, trying to grab for the young woman in question. The speaker moved with grace and ease; his sabre slashed up in a flash, removing the Nomarran man's hand at the wrist. The Nomarran man screamed and fell to his knees, clutching the bleeding stump.

"Shut him up, Scab," the man said, nonchalantly wiping the blood from his sword.

"Yes, Captain," said Scab, dragging the wailing man away. He placed the man on the ground away from the other prisoners, and without showing the slightest hint of emotion, ran a knife across his throat. A choking sound filled the air, and the man slumped to the floor, blood pouring from his neck. Jonah remained frozen, the scene unfolding too fast for him to stop it. At the sight of the dead man, however, something inside him snapped.

"You should not be here," he roared.

The leader of the pirates turned to regard Jonah. Though his wide-brimmed hat cast his face in shadow, his cruel smile was visible. "What have we here? Come to save your people?" He turned his head to regard the row of Nomarrans, tongue flicking across cracked lips. "But I've promised them to my men, y'see, and they will get angry if they aren't rewarded for their hard work. Besides, after all our dear Captain Nehemiah has put us through ... it's the least we deserve."

In unison, the three pirates at the leader's side, including Scab, faced Jonah, weapons drawn and faces alive with hatred. Behind them, their leader stood, unflinching.

"Ham," Jonah said, aware that the cabin boy was loitering at his back. "Find Captain Nem. Go now."

"Yes, Commander." With a whip of cool air, he was gone.

"Commander, is it?" The captain pushed the brim of his hat back, revealing eyes like bottomless black pits. He was younger than Jonah expected, but his pale face was marred with scars. "Captain Lence Agron, at your service." His thin lips twitched as he gave a mock bow, black curls falling over his angular face.

Captain Agron. The name stirred some distant memory, long buried, from his past. He drew himself up and glared at each of the pirates in turn. "You fly the red flag. Captain Nem of this ship flies it, too," he snapped. "You should know what that means. You are both duty-bound to the Commune. The Grand Magister will hear of what you have done here. You will pay—"

Captain Agron's laugh started low, like a vicious growl. It grew into harsh barks, loud and sharp. He slapped his thigh in mock merriment. His men croaked in mimicry, and Jonah finally understood how powerful he was. *A man with powers enough to control his crew, to cloak his ship. A dangerous man who must be stopped at all costs.*

"The Grand Magister," Captain Agron sighed, sniffing and wiping a hand across his mottled skin. "You fool. Captain *Nem* does not work for the Grand Magister. He's a clever man, I will grant him that. Stealing my ruby was ... inspired."

Stealing ...? Jonah frowned.

"Trust me, the Grand Magister doesn't care what I do, as long as I bring him back the man who has evaded his grasp ... until now, of course."

"You mean—"

"We long suspected he was working to steal Nomarrans from Septima. And here we have it, confirmed at last. It has been a long chase. The man knows how to hide in plain sight, but we have him now."

Shit. Nem was never working for the Grand Magister. We've been on the same side all along.

The pirate captain stepped forward, dark eyes roving across Jonah's face. "But wait. I know you, don't I?" He paused, tapping his lips. Finally, he snapped his fingers. "That's it! Commander Jonah Sulemon. I remember now. Always so serious. Lord Torrant's own man, helping a traitor like Nehemiah Muelaman. Who would have thought it? I think I'll take this prize for myself. Now."

The three pirates moved as one, charging at Jonah, bypassing Captain Agron with a swift sidestep, swords pointing straight ahead. Jonah ducked and rolled to the right, away from where Evelyn lay, away from the Nomarrans who had all moved against the wall by the door to Nem's cabin, as far from the fight as possible.

As he stood upright, one of the crew lunged. Jonah caught the man's sword with his own, steel scraping against steel with an ear-piercing screech. The two remaining men made a pincer move, seeking to corner him and pin him with their swords. He leaped backwards, almost rolling back into a hammock. He lurched awkwardly to prevent himself from falling, landing oddly and twisting his ankle. He winced but did not stop, slashing out at the hammocks on this side of the hold.

"You can overpower him!" he shouted in Nomarran. "He cannot control us!" It was no use; the prisoners remained frozen in place, watching on in horror.

"You cannot appeal to them, Commander," Captain Agron called. "They know what I can do. You think your goddess can protect you here?" And, as if to prove the point, Jonah felt something probing against his mind.

Impossible. He pushed back with great effort, and the feeling was gone, though he was shaken and unsettled. He should not *have* to fight it. His internal defences, present from birth by the grace of Veritarra's Gift, had never allowed any powers to infiltrate his mind before. How was this man so strong?

"There are things you can never understand, Jonah."

All the while, even as he tried to piece everything together, Jonah was pursued by Captain Agron's crew. They followed close at his heels, deftly leaping over the hammocks he'd cut down. Attempting to catch them by surprise, Jonah jumped and turned, thrusting his sword into the gut of one of his pursuers. The man fell backwards without a noise, blocking the path of his fellow pirates, almost tripping them. Jonah whipped round just in time to avoid running into the wall. As he held his arms out to stop himself, one of the crew caught up with him. He jerked to the side, trying to turn and fight, but as he did so, the man's sword sliced into his thigh. He gritted his teeth, raised his sword, and dashed it down, hitting the pirate's collarbone.

Unfazed by the injury, the man kept slashing with his own weapon. Jonah had to pull hard to free his sword as blood gushed from the pirate's wound, bone and gristle causing resistance. When his weapon was suddenly freed, Jonah fell back against the wall. With no time to lose, he kicked out with his uninjured leg, clipping the pirate in the groin. The man crashed to the floor and fell still, a red stain spreading beneath him.

"Commander, stop." Captain Agron's words pierced his concentration. All at once, he was aware of the tang of blood in the air, the heave of his ragged breaths, the sweat pouring down his back. The remaining two pirates, one bleeding profusely from his stomach, had taken captives—a Nomarran woman and child. The pirates were still, faces blank, swords poised at the throats of their hostages.

"No," Jonah croaked. "No, please. Let them go."

"You've given me no choice, Commander. Perhaps I'll let you save one."

Jonah blinked, rubbed the sweat from his eyes, and locked eyes with Captain Agron, realising all too late who he was holding his own weapon against.

"Evelyn!"

Jonah didn't know when she'd woken or how much she understood. Her eyes were fixed upon his, unblinking and glazed, her mind evidently still clouded by the Veritarra's Gift she'd been forced to ingest. Captain Agron's weapon pinched into her neck, dangerously close to piercing the delicate flesh.

"Is she yours?" Captain Agron said. "I'd heard you had other tastes, Commander." He sniffed at Evelyn's hair greedily. "Perhaps I can take her off your hands."

"Stop." Jonah stumbled forward, injured leg throbbing. "Please."

"Ah, ah, Commander Sulemon. Stay where you are, or you'll regret it." To make his point, one of the men under Captain Agron's control—the one clutching the Nomarran woman—sliced his sword sideways. The woman slumped to the floor as blood spurted from her neck, horror filling her eyes and mouth gaping in a silent scream.

"You gave me no warning!" Jonah shouted. He held his free hand up. "Please, no more."

"Consider yourself warned, Commander. Weapon down."

Jonah dropped his sword. Captain Agron smiled that hollow, unfeeling smile and nodded his approval. "You put up a good fight," he said. "Killed Scab there. I'm impressed. He's been with me for some time. You wouldn't know this, of course, being ... as you are, but it takes a remarkable amount of energy and willpower to create so perfect a link." He gave a dramatic shake of his head. "Awfully inconvenient to have lost him."

"You think I care? You're a monster!" Jonah spat.

"Ah, but you will care, Commander. When I make this girl here my new connection, you'll care. I'll let you watch when I *take* her. You'll enjoy it, I'm sure, despite your particular *perversions*." He chuckled, drawing Evelyn closer. Finally gaining some semblance of understanding, Evelyn whimpered.

"Jonah?" she said, her eyes wide, brimming with tears. "What's—what's happening?"

"Don't worry. I'll save you, Evelyn. I'll save you; I promise."

Captain Agron laughed coldly. "You know, I'd always heard stories about you, *Commander*. Your pride, your arrogance, the way you flaunted your connection with Lord Torrant. Strutting around like some prized peacock." He scoffed. "I didn't believe them at first. How could one of your birth be so above his station? But then I met you, d'you remember? In Taskan. A meeting with the Grand Magister following a new intake. No doubt your dear Lord Torrant was inspecting them, checking that they were *up to par*. And there you were, refusing to meet anyone's gaze. Eyes only for Lord Torrant. I knew straightaway the stories were true. And do you know what I thought, Commander?"

Jonah's lip curled into a sneer. "What?"

"I knew it would be up to me to bring you down a peg or two. A

Nomarran commander! What a notion. Look how the fates have aligned, my dear Commander Sulemon. By His benevolent powers, indeed!" Captain Agron shrieked with laughter, eyes closing as he showed his first seemingly real emotion—insane happiness. Jonah tried to make eye contact with Evelyn, to reassure her she would not be controlled by this abhorrent man. He would get them out of this ... He would save her as he'd promised. He just had to work out how.

He quickly glanced about the room—at Agron's man still holding his sword against a young Nomarran boy's throat, at Scab's bleeding corpse, at the last crewman who, seemingly having succumbed to his gut wound, slumped by the door to Nem's cabin. During the course of the fight, they had all moved to that end of the hold and away from the crew's entrance. Flitting his glance towards the opposite end of the hold, Jonah saw a movement in the doorway's shadows.

"By His benevolent powers, Captain," Jonah said, keeping the pirate's dark-eyed gaze upon him. "Yes, perhaps you are right. My eyes have been led astray, my loyalty taken into question. May the Grand Magister's justice be done."

Captain Agron narrowed his eyes. "Indeed, Commander. I am glad you agree. For once, you are speaking— Oh." Confusion slackened his features as blood bubbled from his mouth and down his chin, appearing as black as his eyes in the dim light of the cabin. The end of a sword appeared through his front, just below his ribs. He gasped, dropping to his knees.

"Commander Sulemon, I am sorry for the delay," Captain Nem said, stepping from behind the pirate captain. "I had some business to attend to on deck." He glanced at the choking pirate. "Here our game ends, Captain Agron," he said, spitting on the ground. "May Ezzarah watch you burn."

Captain Agron grasped at the sword in his stomach. His mouth flapped open as though he meant to speak, but the only sound he made was a gargling wheeze. As he died, his eyes locked with Jonah's. There remained, even in defeat, a glimmer of satisfaction that Jonah believed would haunt him for a long time to come.

With the demise of his leader, the last of the pirates fell to the floor, motionless in death. As relief flooded him, Jonah's legs gave way. His mind was exhausted, for it was only when Captain Agron fell that he noticed how hard he'd been fighting to stop the man's powers from reaching him. Evelyn stumbled to his side, grasped his hand, and laid him on the floor.

"Jonah," she whispered, frowning. "What happened? Who are all these people down here?"

He blinked towards the row of Nomarran prisoners. "Help them. Nem, he is—he is not who we thought."

"What? What d—"

But Evelyn was pulled back by Captain Nem, who looked down at Jonah with a frown. "Get him upstairs," he said to someone at his back. "In my cabin."

It seemed that Nem still did not trust him. The danger was not over yet.

CHAPTER 14

HECTOR

Loitering in the shadowy doorway of an empty shop, Hector spied on Orion's house. That morning, he'd received his first job as an inhabitant of the Blight—tending to the gardens of some of Nook Town's wealthier residents. He was to return without delay to the Blight after he was finished. To disobey was to be punished. And yet he'd known he must take this opportunity to seek out Raif, to check the lad was well. To try and make some plan for escape, perhaps.

There had been no sign of Raif in or around Bernard's tavern. Hector had wandered the streets for a time, keeping his head down, trying to avoid attention. And then something deep inside—likely a tiny tendril of communication from Cara, pushing through the blockage created by the Veritarra's Gift he had been consuming—said, *Go to Orion's house.*

And so it was that he stood in vigil in the cold morning air, watching Orion's house, waiting for his moment. Any who saw him observing the property might have believed he was speaking to himself, but he was, in fact, holding an imaginary conversation with Cara.

"I've already waited too long," he said. "I know that. Should've tried to get out of that damned place sooner." He imagined his beloved companion's response.

Now's the time to stop moping, old man, and to bloody well do something.

In the few days he'd been in the Blight, he had kept to himself. After his first attempt at speaking to the other residents there, it was clear they were not willing to offer him any friendship. He had walked the perimeter of the small section of walled-off town, taking in the muddied streets, the dreary homes, the sheer misery of the place. Now that he was being forced to consume Veritarra's Gift again, his mind was as dull as his powers. He found it difficult to think outside of the grim reality he found himself in, though he desperately wished to find some solution to save Raif, to return to searching for Rose.

You pathetic bastard. You've swept yourself up in self-pity and forgotten about what's important.

"If only it were that simple," he muttered. "Damn, but I hope the lad is well. It doesn't bode well that he's ..." He stared at Orion's home, moustache twitching. "Right, then; no use delaying any longer. More time I spend here, more likely it is I'm caught and punished."

As he was about to step out from his hiding place, a brown-cloaked townsman walked by. He drew himself back, tugging the hood of his cloak to cover his face. As soon as the man had passed, Hector pushed up from the wall and moved his hood back to observe the street once more. It was quiet, the odd merchant passing by on business, a handful of children playing, three old women gossiping amongst themselves close to Orion's house. None of them appeared to notice him, though it would not remain so when he walked into the street.

Suddenly, two Nomarran men appeared, rounding a corner and approaching Orion's home. Their long, burgundy robes flapped behind them as they hurried for the door. One of them rapped his fist on it whilst the other glanced around. Hector drew himself back, sure the man's gaze had met his own. When he looked back, however, the man was facing the house again.

A young woman with blonde hair opened the door and allowed the two men in without question. She checked the street before silently shutting the door.

"What do you suppose that's about?" Hector whispered.

Could one of them be the man I saw at Bernard's, the man who Avanna was in contact with? They'd both been bald like the man at Bernard's tavern, though Hector was too far away to have been able to make out their features and to be certain of it. Even so, his gut told him it was likely so.

With a sigh, he straightened his tunic and brushed down his greasy hair, wishing he'd had the opportunity to freshen himself up. He told himself it was because he hadn't wanted to take the limited daily supply of fresh water away from the other residents—especially the children—though part of him acknowledged that he had been complacent in his personal care since being imprisoned in the Blight. A sudden surge of anger fired through his veins, and he found himself grateful that his powers were repressed, for he wasn't sure what he might have done to Orion in that moment if he had the ability to wield them.

He has taken too much from too many, especially the children.

He gritted his teeth. *Now is not the time for such thoughts. I must get answers, powers or no.*

Puffing himself up, he marched towards Orion's home. The three gossiping women paused in their conversation as he drew near, eyeing him with ill-concealed suspicion.

"Good day, ladies," he said with an elaborate bow. He continued, feeling their eyes upon his back. Perhaps he should have hidden his identity, for he had no doubt they knew exactly who he was, but he was weary of playing games. This place was full of secrets and scorn; he could hardly bear it any longer and had no desire to add to it. He turned and gave the women his brightest smile, and though their expressions remained wary, they soon went back to their hushed gossiping, undoubtedly at his expense.

Leave them to it.

He inhaled deeply and confidently rapped on Orion's door. His tenacity faltered somewhat when there was no response. He peered over his shoulder, suddenly uneasy, before knocking once more.

Nothing.

"Orion," he called. "It's Hector. I've come to speak to you." He banged the door this time, frustration rising. "Orion!" He raised his hand again just as the door was flung open to reveal a furious-looking young woman—the same who had let the Nomarrans in minutes before.

"Oh," he said, hand hanging in midair. "Hello." At the sight of her innocent young face, his anger deflated.

"Master Haralambous," she said, glancing behind her. Before Hector could follow her gaze, she pushed the door closed so only a crack remained. "What are you doing here?"

"I ..." Hector stood upright and cleared his throat. "I've come to speak to Orion. I need to know that Raif, the lad I came here with, is safe. He's my charge, and I made a promise to a friend to protect him. It's important that—"

"My father is not here," she said.

Father? She is so unlike him.

"Where is he?"

"He's not able to speak with you, Master Haralambous. He's undergoing church business."

Church business. With the Nomarrans, no doubt. Hector shook his head with frustration. "Perhaps you might know about Raif, then. I have not seen him since I was ... taken. And I need to make sure he is well."

The young woman stood tall. "He *is* well."

"You know him? You've seen him?"

"Father has placed him under my charge. Raif was alone here, was he not?" A flash of defiance alit in her eyes. She looked very like Orion in that moment.

"Yes. I suppose he was, and I thank you for taking him in. But ... there are matters that we must—"

"You mean his sister?" The young woman smirked. "Father has taken care of that, too. He is doing all that you could not."

What have you done, lad? Hector frowned, trying to focus. "Please, let me just speak to the lad. Let me see him with my own eyes."

"That's not a good idea," she said. "He is ... studying."

"Studying?" Hector repeated. *Shit, they have him in their grasp.*

"Yes, and I think it's best you go." The young woman made to close the door, but Hector put his foot in the way. Though his mind was clouded, he knew that this might be his only chance to see Raif.

"Please," he whispered. "Just for a few moments. Your father doesn't need to know, does he? Have mercy."

Her face softened. "Very well." She stepped aside. "You may have a few moments." Hector moved into the hallway, and she closed the door firmly behind them.

"What's your name?" Hector asked.

"It's Lebioda. Lebby." She sniffed. "Come, this way. Quickly." With a brisk pace, she led him down a dark hall, up a flight of stairs, and along a short corridor. She gently tapped on a door, and without awaiting a response, pushed it open.

"Raif," she whispered. "Someone is here to see you."

Inside a rectangular bedroom, the lad sat in front of a desk, head bent over a vast leather tome. When he turned around, Hector gasped. In just a few days, his face had grown thinner, his expression more serious. In that moment, he looked much older than his fourteen years. There was a feverish brightness to his grey eyes, their colour seeming to shift like dark storm clouds swirling in a vortex.

Oh, fuck. He's been given it, too. They've got him. It was all Hector could to keep walking into the room, even as his legs threatened to collapse beneath him. *I'm too late.*

"Hector," Raif said, beaming. "Can you stay? I've learned so much. Lebby's teaching me to read, and somehow, it's ... it's working! It never has before!" He let out a delighted laugh.

Hector gave a subdued smile. "That's good." He glanced around. "Where's Dog, lad? You know Rose would want you to keep him safe."

Raif's expression clouded. "Dog?"

Lebby stepped forward. "He's downstairs, shut in the kitchen. He is looked after. But a bedroom is no place for a pet, is it?" She gave a sickly-sweet smile.

Raif sat forward. "Oh, I'm glad you came. I've got so much to tell you. And Orion says the search for Rose is ongoing. He's going to find her, Hector; I'm sure of it."

Hector swallowed, giving Lebby an uneasy glare. "Slow down, lad," he said, approaching Raif. As a reflex, he placed a hand on the boy's arm as if to calm him with his powers. "Come away from the book for a moment. Let's talk. Tell me about what Orion has said about Rose."

"Oh," Raif said, glancing down at Hector's hand, then towards Lebby. "I think I should—"

"Raif, it's fine," Lebby said, though a flash of irritation passed across her face.

Perhaps she's not as innocent as she appears.

"I'll make some tea. Sit, catch up with your friend. And then we'll return to your studies." She left the room, closing the door behind her. Hector heard the turn of a key in the lock. He focused his attention on Raif; the boy was manic, sweat glistening on his brow, cheeks flushed.

Tea, fucking tea. They've got to him already. Shit, shit, shit.

"Come on, lad," he said, leading Raif to the bed. "Let's sit for a moment." Hector nudged the boy down and sat beside him.

"I'm sorry I didn't come to see you. Lebby said it's best to avoid the Blight, you know ... She told me it's not a place for me. She's been very kind." Raif gave a boyish grin. "She's so nice to me. She told me the story about Esteralla Clinkscale. Well, she started to ... I'll need to hear the end." Raif's face grew vacant, as though he was trying to remember something. "And Rose—Rose is going to be found. I told Orion all about her, and he sent men to search for her. And Avanna."

"You told him everything about her?" Hector's heart skipped a beat. "About her powers?"

Raif blinked too slowly, his brow creased. "No," he said. He chewed his lip for a moment. "I told Lebby, though; she's been a good friend. She said it didn't matter what Rose has done. We can help her. By Per—"

"By Perisma's light," Hector said. He patted Raif's shoulder, trying to ignore the wave of despair that washed over him. "I see."

"It's okay, Hector." Raif smiled. "Orion has been very kind."

"I'm sure, lad. I'm sure." Hector glanced at the door. "Now, listen to me. You must not drink any more of the tea, you hear me? It's got—"

"Oh, Hector! Don't be silly," Raif said. "I know you're worried because of, of Avanna's tea, but Lebby would never do anything to harm me. She's my friend. Orion, too."

Hector saw in Raif's face the sincere belief that those words were true. Yet how could they be? What did Orion hope to gain from this? The more he thought on it, the more clouded his mind felt.

When he was a child, Hector's father made him a wooden puzzle. The pieces were intricately carved to slot together, as long as he could find the right sequence. He'd spent hours with it, determined to complete it. As he focused in that moment, he thought of the puzzle for the first time in years. As he had then, Hector tried to piece together all the parts of the puzzle— Raif, Rose, Orion, the Nomarran men, Avanna; they were all linked somehow. Eventually, they would slot together, and all would make sense. He chewed his lip. Without his powers, he would have to think on his feet.

"Raif, I don't wish to scare you, but—"

The door opened and Lebby stepped in, a tray of tea in hand. He had to act now or lose his chance altogether. He stood. "What's in that? Veritarra's Gift, is it? Raif, lad, you have to be careful, you might—"

"I think it's best you left," Lebby snapped. "My father would be angry if he found you here. You've seen Raif; you know he's well."

"*Well?*" Hector cried. "He is far from it. He's not the same lad I brought here. I don't know what you've done to him in such a short time, but mark my words—"

The sound of barking filled the house.

"Is that Dog?" Raif asked. "He's got out, Lebby!"

Hector hurried from the room, followed closely by Raif and Lebby. Downstairs, Dog was scratching at a dark door beneath the stairs.

"That's Father's study. Away, beast!" Lebby made to push Dog.

"No, Lebby!" Raif shouted, the most emotion Hector had seen from him that morning.

He's still in there. His mind is not gone yet.

"Hector, will you take him?" Raif asked. "Please, he … he can't be here."

"Yes, that seems best." Lebby turned to Hector, face flushed with anger. "You have to take your creature and leave. Now." She smiled at Raif. "Go back upstairs, Raif. Father said we weren't to leave your room or see anyone. Your studies are very important."

Raif looked to Hector, then back to Lebby, his mouth down-turned. Perhaps the emotion of the situation had broken through some of the fog in his mind.

"Now, Raif," Lebby snapped, indicating the stairs.

The lad nodded. Before leaving, however, he turned to Hector. "Be careful with Dog," he whispered. "Rose would be so upset if anything happened to him." With that, he headed back upstairs.

Hector approached Dog, who remained standing outside the door, though his barking had ceased. He was aware of Lebby's eyes on his back, but still he knelt down and said, "What is it, boy? What's in there?"

"That is none of your concern, Master Haralambous," Lebby said. "Your welcome is well and truly overstayed."

She's worried. Why?

Another piece of the puzzle, Hector was certain.

"Come on, boy," he said, retreating from the door. As he walked away, he rubbed his temples. A headache was taking hold, as much from stress as from the Veritarra's Gift in his veins. Lebby marched him to the front door and opened it.

"Rest assured, Father will set your trial date. Until then, you will remain in the Blight. I will ensure you are not given any more tasks that might tempt you to return here." The words seemed like they had come straight from Orion's mouth. Her father's daughter, after all. Hector nodded as the door was slammed in his face.

Outside, Dog whined. Hector dropped to his knees and held his hand out, receiving a lick in return. "I can't do anything now, Dog. But whatever's in there, I'll find out. You have to come with me. We'll get to the bottom of this."

He felt foolish speaking so frankly, though when he looked into Dog's eyes, he thought he saw a level of understanding. Perhaps he wasn't without intelligence, even for a dog.

"Let's go." There was much to think about, and he did not want Orion to catch him here. He knew with icy clarity he couldn't continue to dose himself up if there was any chance of helping Raif and discovering the truth. Punishment be damned; he needed his mind clear. He had to risk the wrath of setting his powers free to save the lad, to stop Orion, to get away from this place. It was their only hope of getting out of Nook Town alive.

CHAPTER 15
RAIF

"Do you recall what I told you about Lady Esteralla?" Lebby asked, sitting beside him as he studied Perisma's sacred text. Momentarily distracted by her closeness, Raif swallowed, thinking back to the morning in Orion's study. Lebby tapped his arm. "I knew I shouldn't have allowed him in," she muttered.

"Who? Hector? He's a good friend," Raif said. "He looked after us when Evelyn left ... She didn't even say goodbye." He frowned and looked towards the door. *Why did he come to visit?* He glanced around the room, at the holy book before him, at Lebby's irritated expression.

How long have I been here?

And then another voice, barely more than a whisper in his mind —*Help.*

"Raif, concentrate," Lebby said. "Drink your tea; you seem tired."

He nodded numbly, picking up his mug and gulping it down. It was almost an impulse now, so sweet and calming did he find the tea that Lebby made him. Hector was silly to be concerned about it.

Lebby's my friend. She wouldn't hurt me. She's helping *me.*

Besides, with her close by and keeping him focused on his studies, it was easy to forget his concerns. Her soft blonde hair draped over her shoulders so he might even touch it if he dared. Her hazel eyes, however, were filled with impatience. She smacked her hand down on the desk and Raif jumped.

"I told you to concentrate. Esteralla Clinkscale," she said, clapping her palms together. "The lesson is an important one. You should know this by now. The beginning of our teachings. You must understand the reason for the story. Father wants to ensure you are ready for …"

"What?" Raif asked, sitting up. "Ready for what?"

Her face softened as she looked at him. "Don't worry for now, Raif." She tapped the book in front of him. "Come on, find the page. Read it to me again. It's important you remember it so you can recite it to Father."

"Esteralla Clinkscale," he said. "Yes, she had powers. She used them to … she …" *Powers. She used her powers to kill them, she protected us, she didn't know what she was doing.*

Powers to protect.

"Raif?"

He froze; his head was heavy, his thoughts thick and difficult to separate. Orion and Lebby had been nothing but kind. Why should there be anything to be concerned about? He reached with a shaking hand for his mug and drank more tea. It seemed the more he consumed, the more he wanted. Lebby really did have a gift for creating the perfect, relaxing concoction.

"She used her powers for her own gains." Lebby stabbed a finger at the page of the book with every word she said. "She killed her father. She chose the abilities given to her by a false god—a *cruel* god —over the honour of her family."

"Her powers are bad," Raif replied, voice quiet. *She killed two men. Injured another.*

"Yes, Raif. *All* powers are, as we learn from Lady Esteralla's story.

They cannot be allowed. When we step into Perisma's light, we see the truth. You want that, don't you?"

"Yes, Lebby," Raif said. "Do you ... do you think there'll be any news about Rose soon? From your father?"

Lebby nodded. "I think we must have faith that Perisma will guide our men to find her." She squeezed his shoulder. "All will be well, Raif. Now I'll fetch us some food. It's been a long morning."

Raif watched her leave the room before turning back to the tome, studying the page. Though he was still learning, some of the words were becoming clearer through Lebby's teaching. *Esteralla Clinkscale* ... A woman who used her powers against her father. She harmed others, just like—

No, powers help. To help.

Help.

Raif frowned. *No, that's not true.* In his mind, he drew up a defensive wall against that tiny, deceptive voice, silencing it abruptly. To distract himself, he flicked through the text. The more he learned about the faith here in Nook Town, the more he felt certain it was where he and Rose would be safest. These people would know how to control her powers, to stop her from using them to hurt others. She should never have been put in a position to do it, and that was his fault, not hers. She was far too young to understand the implications of her actions. He wasn't, though, and he knew now that he had to protect her fully—from herself as much as from outside dangers. Yes, with Perisma's guidance, Rose would be found, and they would be safe.

Head down, he smiled as he focused on his studies.

Yes, all would be well.

CHAPTER 16

EVELYN

Evelyn's head pounded. She sat forward and rested her face on her palms, fighting her rising nausea. *What happened?* The last she remembered was speaking to Ham ... but then something inside her had flared up. After that, her memory was fractured, as though her mind was protecting her from the truth.

But when she searched deep down, she knew what had happened. It was as it had been with Arthur, with the poor, broken man in Lord Torrant's basement.

Powers. She scrunched her face up, ashamed of the memories flooding back. *My powers are out of control, just like my emotions.* She'd used them on Ham. She could have seriously hurt him if she hadn't been caught.

This isn't right. I'm dangerous.

Why had her powers failed her when she *willed* them in the woods with Raif and Rose all those weeks ago? Her emotions had been heightened then, too, but consciously pushing to use them seemed to bring the opposite effect. It was as though they were locked away the morning she'd used them on Arthur, returning only in Lord Torrant's basement. But that answer did not satisfy

146

her, for she had let Raif and Rose down when they'd needed her most.

Pathetic, useless, as always.

"Bring him some *i'ra* for the pain," Captain Nem said, his words piercing through her thoughts.

Reluctantly, Evelyn raised her head and watched as one of the crewmen handed the captain a bottle of deep-brown liquid. "What is that?" she asked, narrowing her eyes.

The captain frowned at her. "It is alcohol from our homeland to ease the Commander's pain."

Evelyn's throat constricted with an acute craving for alcohol. Her mouth salivated in anticipation of the burn she imagined it would provide, the sense of numbness that would spread through her limbs that she so needed. She gritted her teeth and bowed her head, tearing her eyes away from the bottle of amber liquid. As she did so, the unpleasant smell of blood and sweat hit her nostrils. She swallowed back the bile in her throat and rubbed her tired eyes.

It had been some hours since the attack. After the pirate captain was killed by Nem, his remaining crew had fled back to their ship, apparently aware instantaneously of their leader's demise. Nem's men had let them go, relieved to find themselves no longer in danger. Afterwards, the bodies of the dead—both those from Nem's crew and the dead pirates—had been removed in a remarkably swift manner; returned to the sea, Nem said, as was expected for sailors killed on duty. Even so, the scent of death seemed to hang in the air around them. Captain Nem hadn't told her how many had died, but the strained expression on his face told Evelyn all she needed to know—the attack had left its mark.

Jonah was lying on Captain Nem's bed, still unconscious. He must have put a lot of himself into the fight, or he had been left far weaker than he'd let on after what happened at Lord Torrant's home. A man approached and cautiously checked his bandaged thigh. Evelyn made to stand.

"Where are you going?" Nem asked sharply.

"I want to check my friend," she snapped back.

"You will sit back down, girl. Your *friend* has questions to answer, and so do you. Do not take my crew's care for compliance in whatever mission you two are carrying out. I will not allow any more secrets on my ship. It is time the truth was spoken."

"What of *your* secrets?" She narrowed her eyes. *Nem is not who we thought.* "Why did I overhear you saying you would kill Jonah?"

"*Kill* Jonah?" Captain Nem raised his eyebrows. "You are extremely forthright for someone who has been caught out."

Evelyn's head swam. She stumbled backwards and slumped into the seat. *Caught out?*

There was much unsaid here, and her muddled mind struggled to keep up. What *had* they given her? She massaged her forehead. And who *were* those Nomarrans belowdecks? "You—you owe us answers, too," she said weakly. "You did something to me, you—"

Jonah let out a groan and began to rouse, trying to sit up. Nem was at his side in a flash. Though it was apparent the captain remained suspicious of Jonah, he also showed great tenderness towards him. He placed a gentle hand on Jonah's shoulder, easing him back onto a folded blanket, preventing him from moving too much and agitating his freshly stitched leg.

"Leave us," Nem said to his two crewmen. "Wait outside the door in case of trouble." He took the bottle of *i'ra* in hand and waited for them to comply.

"Yes, Captain," they said in unison.

The cabin door closed, the atmosphere becoming thick with unspoken tension.

"Commander Sulemon," Captain Nem said.

Jonah groaned in response, still only half-conscious.

Evelyn moved to stand beside the bed. "Jonah."

His eyes fluttered open. "Eirik," he cried, gaze unfocused. Evelyn tried to get closer, but Captain Nem shot her a dark look from where he perched on the bed.

"Commander Sulemon," he said. "Do not try to move." He laid a hand on Jonah's.

"Captain Nem?" Jonah inhaled sharply and tugged his hand free, eyes widening. He took in his surroundings before touching the fresh bandage on his thigh with a wince. "Where is Evelyn?"

"I'm here," Evelyn said, leaping forward. "Jonah, are you—"

"Stand aside, girl," Nem said. He looked down at Jonah, expression guarded. "Commander Sulemon, I would like to thank you for your help in defeating those Commune pirates."

Jonah flinched. "Pirates," he muttered. His eyes were glazed, sweat glistened on his brow. He suddenly sat forward, staring at Nem. "You were expecting him, weren't you? Captain Agron."

Captain Nem let out a long exhale. "I was. And now he is dead. We no longer need to worry about him. Yet it is curious that you were so eager to fight off a man whose loyalties aligned with your own." He looked between Jonah and Evelyn.

"What?" Jonah's voice was low, his nostrils flared. He made to get up, grimacing as he tried to swing his uninjured leg to the floor. "Speak plainly, Nem."

"Commander Sulemon, stay down. Your leg has not long been stitched." Nem placed a firm hand on Jonah's shoulder. "Perhaps I have been too lenient until now, but it is time for answers. I have lost too many men to allow any further risk." Captain Nem poured some *i'ra* into a mug and held it out to Jonah, who turned his head aside and waved it away. Evelyn caught a whiff of its strong, fruity odour, and her mouth watered.

Captain Nem drew the mug back. "I hope you see, Commander, that the care I have provided is in gratitude for what you have done. I dread to think what could have happened had you not been here to assist ..." He shook his head. "But that does not discount the fact that you are aboard my ship and you may yet be an *enemy* to me and my people. *Our* people. We may be plain about that now that you have seen the truth. I should not have accepted your passage, but what else was I to do? Risk the Grand Magister's wrath just as we had almost made our escape from Taskan?"

Jonah lurched up once more, pain flitting across his face. "An enemy?" he croaked. "*I* am an enemy?" He sneered. "Captain, those prisoners you are keeping below—those are *our* people, yes. They might have died at the hands of those pirates if not for me. And you call *me* an enemy?"

"Prisoners?" Captain Nem raised an eyebrow at Evelyn. "Why would they be prisoners, Commander? I am escorting them safely away from Septima. From a land where Nomarrans are taken advantage of, promised freedom but treated with disdain. The Grand Magister's decree has only fixed that treatment in law, made it all the more likely to occur." He turned away, staring out the port side cabin window. "They are not prisoners. I thought you knew that. Else why did the Grand Magister send you to spy on my ship? To catch me out in my treachery?" He paused, running a hand over his chin as he turned back to Jonah. "What trap do you yet seek to set for me, Commander Sulemon?"

"Trap? Captain, I ... I—" Jonah's head slumped backwards, his face shining with sweat. His eyes fluttered.

"Hush, Jonah. Rest," Evelyn said, frowning at Captain Nem. "He's exhausted. You said he helped you, so let him sleep." She reached for a nearby damp cloth and mopped Jonah's brow.

Captain Nem stood close by, still holding the mug of *i'ra* he'd offered Jonah. As Evelyn watched, he gulped it down. She swallowed, biting back the urge to ask him for some.

He met Evelyn's gaze. "Why did you come to my ship? Who sent you?"

"We weren't sent," Evelyn said, moving to join him in front of the window. "I'm Evelyn. Friends of mine are in serious danger from the Commune, and ... well, Jonah offered me the chance to save them. So we need to travel to the Noman Islands."

"Evelyn, is it?" Captain Nem bowed his head. "Nice to meet you at last, hmm?" His eyes glinted, though he spoke on before she could reply. "But why my ship? That is what troubles me. The timing ... It could only have been because the Grand Magister—"

"We're trying to find a way to stop the Grand Magister!" Evelyn shouted, immediately regretting her impulsive outcry.

Captain Nem's hand drifted to the glimmering ruby still pinned to his robes. "You—you were not sent by him?"

"Of course not," Evelyn said quietly. She lifted her chin. "I would *never* do his bidding after all he's done. I've lost my friends, the woman who took me in, who loved me like a daughter." She sucked in one cheek, doing her best to hold back the tears pricking at her eyes; she refused to cry in front of Captain Nem. Finally, she looked him squarely in the face. "We do not work *for* the Grand Magister. We mean to *stop* him."

"But how do you ... Oh." His dark eyes gleamed in the dim cabin. "The Noman Islands, of course. Could it be so simple?" He moved to a vast wooden desk and began removing objects from one of the drawers. Lifting a drawstring leather pouch with such care that it might have been made of glass, his lips curled upwards into the ghost of a smile. "This is what I used to stop your powers. This is what you need, is it not?"

"Is that ..." She stepped forward, holding out a hand, afraid to touch the pouch. She knew now what it could do. Her mind had been clouded, her powers dampened. *This might work.*

"Veritarra's Gift," Captain Nem said.

Evelyn nodded. "Jonah told me of a flower. He said it could render them powerless, all of them—the Grand Magister, Lord Torrant, anyone using their powers to hurt others."

"Lord Torrant?" The captain flashed a glance towards Jonah. "Curious."

"He said it could be used with a weapon—on the tip of an arrow, along the edge of a sword. He said it could disarm them."

"A weapon?" Captain Nem frowned. "A violent option, and an unusual one. It hasn't been done in some time, not since the Seven Year War over a hundred years ago."

Evelyn frowned. "But Jonah … he said that would be how to bring down the Grand Magister."

Nem nodded, giving a gentle smile. "He has lived a soldier's life, and that shows. The flower is sacred, and we Nomarrans seek to avoid violence whenever we can." He moved towards the bed and looked down at Jonah. "Perhaps there is another way," he muttered. He was quiet for a long moment, the creaking of the ship and cawing of nearby seagulls all that could be heard. "It has been a long time since he left."

"Captain Nem?" Evelyn studied his face, trying to grasp his meaning.

He turned to her, sighing. "I owe you both an apology," he said. "I've been a fool." He traced a finger across the ruby on his chest and let out a bitter laugh. "I don't know why I'm still wearing this." He removed it, clamping his fingers around it. "If your friend hadn't been aboard my ship, we might all have been doomed. I swore to help my people and only endangered them further by stealing this damned ruby. I owe Commander Sulemon—Jonah—a great debt. I will talk to him when he is awake."

Evelyn raised an eyebrow. "Anything you have to say to Jonah, you can say to me as well. We are here on a mission together."

Nem eyed her, dark eyes roaming her face before he gave a curt nod. "Yes, I am sorry." He stood tall, placing a hand on his chest. "You have my word as a captain and as a Nomarran that I will do all I can to help both of you achieve your mission. My crew and I are at your disposal. Now get some sleep. It has been a long and trying day for all of us. We shall speak in the morning."

Evelyn nodded, heart filled with renewed hope as she headed for the cabin door. With Nem's help, they might actually have a chance of succeeding.

Raif, Rose, Hector … please hold on.

CHAPTER 17

HECTOR

In Perisma's Blight, Hector would find the help he needed; he was sure of it. He had to be, for there was no hope to be found anywhere else. It was time to get to know the people who had been imprisoned here—to help them see that they had other options, and that they did not need to allow Orion to dictate their lives.

The tavern door's hinges creaked as Hector entered, Dog at his side. He wiped the rainfall from his eyes and scanned the room. In the silence, the water dripping from his soaked clothes was all too audible. Hector cleared his throat, but no one looked up. They remained in their groups, huddled around tables, nursing their drinks. These people had lost themselves and accepted Orion's conditions upon them; perhaps Hector could give them renewed purpose.

He moved to the bar and tapped it. When the ever-silent barman approached, Hector pointed towards a barrel of ale and watched as it was poured. He gave the man a nod of thanks, paid him a handful of coppers—noting how empty his purse was becoming—and turned to survey the room once more, grateful for the crackling fire. Still, no one met his eye. They even ignored Dog, who was eagerly snuffling at the rushes on the floor with immense interest, leaving trails of water wherever he went. Three young men were playing a card game, their words few and smiles strained. Beth, the woman who had told him the rules of the Blight and where he could stay, was once more reading a book in a ragged armchair by the fire. The old couple were sharing a meal, unspeaking. The group of children, two boys and two girls, were the most animated. The youngest, a girl who must have been around Rose's age, seemed to be regaling the others with a tale about a frog she'd tried to befriend. Hector pursed his lips, wondering what her powers were. How strong were they? He doubted any could contend with Rose, but they would never know if they were forced to repress that part of themselves by consuming Veritarra's Gift.

He let out a sigh. He needed to find a way to appeal to them. The younger might be easiest to convince if they still held some slither of hope of their lives improving. The elders, however, were likely to have given up on ever having anything differently.

The scourge of the town.

A pestilence upon the purity of Perisma.

Hector had heard those with powers called such things and worse in his youth, and that was before Orion had instilled even deeper hatred in the town. Yet how could a god who encouraged such judgement be true, just, or good? He'd never understood, even when his father tried to explain. And now Raif was being brainwashed by Orion and his daughter, and it was his fault for bringing the lad into this place without proper planning.

Self-absorbed, useless bastard. Lost in the past when your mind should have been focused on what's important now.

Irritated, he swigged down his ale and slammed the cup on the bar. The sudden bang drew the immediate attention of those around him. He stepped forward, swallowing down his anger. He had to make it mean something, all that had happened. It was now or never.

"Some of you might know who I am," he said, voice breaking through the constant tension in that dank tavern. Some of his audience looked at each other, clearly alarmed or confused; some simply stared at him. The old couple openly frowned at him. Dog stopped where he was and looked up, ears pricked forward. Dog came to sit beside him, as though understanding the importance of this moment.

"I'm like you," Hector continued. "I was told that my existence did not comply with the laws of Perisma's sacred church. That I was somehow *other*, a foreigner in my own home. I know what—"

"We know who you are, Hector," Beth said. She'd placed her book down on a nearby table and watched him with her clear, blue eyes. "Though you left this place behind long enough ago."

Hector bowed his head. "You're right," he said. "It's been some years since I left Nook Town, and I did all I could to forget it. I'm sorry. If I had known what had become of it, what Orion was forcing upon you all ... I would have come back to help."

"To help?" Beth shook her head sadly. "There is nothing you could have done." She glanced around. "Some of us didn't even know we had powers until Orion introduced the compulsory consumption of that beloved Nomarran concoction."

"What?" Hector frowned. "He forced—"

"Everyone in the town to drink it, yes. Spouted some nonsense about Perisma telling him to *root out the traitors*." She spread her arms. "And here we are, the ones who chose to stay rather than be sent to the Commune."

Hector cast his eyes around the room. "I'm sorry."

"Mm. That's as well, Hector, but I *know* you. I remember you, though you kept to yourself, always at your father's side."

Hector bit down on his cheek to stop himself from reacting at the mention of his father. Beth paused, studying his face, seeming to understand the impact of her words. She gave a small smile, turning back to the others. "You say you are like us, but ... you haven't been here. You weren't here when Orion took power. When he hunted us down, tore our families apart, forced us—or our families—to choose."

Hector had never considered how it must have been for them, so young, so alone. "I-I didn't realise," he said weakly.

Beth shrugged as if she knew that already. "This is all we have. The only place we can call home. Anything that jeopardises that will not be taken lightly."

I must tread carefully. They are afraid.

As Beth spoke, the other patrons listened closely, some giving fervent nods. Hector couldn't disagree with the woman's statements. He'd lived a privileged life in comparison to those before him. His father was a kind, loving, and generous man who'd shielded him from being sent to the Commune, and he'd left Nook Town before Orion's changes had been implemented. His childhood was as normal as one as he might ask for in Nook Town. All he'd needed to do was drink a cupful of bitter liquid each morning.

As he dwelled upon his past, he became aware that all eyes were on him; some seemed envious, some afraid, some closely guarded. Each individual appeared to be waiting for him to respond. His mind was clearing of the Veritarra's-Gift-induced fog, his clarity returning by the moment, perhaps sped on by the decisiveness with which he now acted.

He had to make a change. He had to save Raif, to find Rose, to put right all the failures he had allowed to happen. But he needed help.

And, suddenly, he knew what he could offer these people: freedom. Freedom from this place, from the judgement of the citizens of Nook Town, from the church of Perisma. He met each gaze in turn.

"I can't deny your words," he said to Beth. "And I wouldn't try to, either. You deserve better than that, all of you." He turned to face the room. "Better than the lies you've been fed by Orion, by everyone who follows Perisma. None of you deserve the life that's been forced upon you."

Beth sighed. "We chose to stay here because we thought it would be better than being sent to the Commune. Now ..." She pursed her lips. "I'm not so sure that's true."

Hector almost reached out to touch her arm, so intense was her sadness, but he held back. "Believe me when I say it's not much better out there in Septima. I've worked to fight the Commune, seen what they've done to those like us. How they've sought to control us. But perhaps there's another way." His eyes lingered upon the group of four children, his sense of injustice flaring. "Truth is, I need your help."

"Our help?" It was one of the young boys who spoke. "What can we possibly do t' help you?" Dark eyes shining and cheeks flushed, he stared with an air of defiance. Hector thought he must be the eldest of the four, for the others seemed to defer to him, not daring to look up at Hector as he did.

"I can understand your suspicion," Hector said. "Why should you trust me?"

"How do we know you have powers at all?" said one of the three young men, green eyes narrowed. He pushed his mousy hair back and uncovered a deep scar across his forehead. "This is what my grandfather did t' me the first time he witnessed me using my powers on a wild rabbit. Struck me, lashed me to the back of his horse, and rode me back t' town. Left me outside the door o' this very place. I was eight. I wasn't allowed near my family again. My brother was brought not long afterward. Our mother was too ashamed t' visit, and our father, he ..." The young man shook his head, fists clenched atop the table. One of his companions—his brother, Hector guessed, from the similarity in their appearance—grasped his shoulder.

Hector knew then there was only one thing he could do. He moved towards the young man and clutched his arm.

I hope this works.

At his side, Dog let out a quiet whine.

It had only been a couple of hours since he'd last consumed Veritarra's Gift, and it would remain within him for some time yet, working to counteract his powers and prevent their use. They weren't likely to return to full capacity for a few days. But for this simple task, he should be able to push just enough through the fog to calm the young man. He concentrated as hard as he could, felt the sweat spring up on his forehead.

To his relief, it didn't take long for his powers to take effect.

The young man's face flickered from angry to serene in a matter of seconds. His brother drew his hand back as though he'd been jolted, gasping.

A chair scraped behind Hector as utterances of shock and wonder filled the room. This was a place where powers had long been scorned. Any who used them within the walls of Nook Town faced a heavy penalty, with severe punishment if they were used on another person. But Hector had a point to make and this was the only way to do it. Somehow, he knew no one here would betray him to Orion; in his display of powers, he had shown himself to be one of them—an outsider, undeserving of Perisma's blessing.

His joy was short-lived. As he released the man's arm, he became lightheaded. He stumbled backwards, groped to find something to lean on, almost fell. It had taken more effort than he'd realised. He blinked, trying to rid his eyes of the flickering lights dotting his vision.

"Here, Hector, sit down," Beth said. He felt hands guiding him, settling him onto a chair.

"I'm sorry," Hector said. "I-I don't know why ..."

"It's the dosage."

"Elussius has made it stronger."

"Perhaps he shouldn't have ..."

Muttering voices surrounded him, and Hector's head spun. He kept his eyes closed, so he could not be sure who spoke. Dog's wet nose touched his hand, and Hector stroked his soft fur, seeking comfort, wishing Cara were close.

"Don't crowd him," Beth said. She reached for Hector's shoulder. "Take deep breaths. Here, drink some of this."

"No, no, I can't—"

"It's just water."

Hector gulped down a mouthful. The liquid's coolness brought him back to himself, steadying him so he felt able to open his eyes once more.

The young man he'd used his powers on was the first to speak. "Your powers must be strong," he said. "You've been in this bar for the past four days, drinking your daily requirement. I've seen you having Max prepare your drinks, same as all of us. T' still be able to use them ..." He glanced over his shoulder as if seeking agreement from the others.

"Hush, Ben," said Beth, signalling everyone to move back. "Give the man a minute to recover. And then I think it's time we all introduced ourselves. We'll be ready when you are." She looked at Hector with a hint of warmth in her blue eyes that hadn't been there before. He nodded gratefully as everyone sat around him. They were closer to each other than before, placing themselves in a loose circle. He sensed a shift in the atmosphere, away from the anguish and melancholy that usually permeated the very walls of this place. A tiny flicker of hope had been lit, so faint as to be almost indiscernible. He had to choose his next words carefully, for the flame might be set alight or extinguished with a mere whisper.

He took a deep breath and pushed himself up. His legs were slow to respond, the scar left by the Commander aching abominably in his moment of weakness. He limped towards the circle of waiting people.

"I'm sorry if I caused alarm," he said, voice hoarse.

"I'm sorry I doubted your abilities," said Ben.

Hector shook his head. "Think nothing of it," he said. "As I said, I understand your suspicion. No doubt I'd be the same in your position." He seated himself amongst them, the air of hostility he'd sensed earlier all but melted away.

"So we'll introduce ourselves, and then you can tell us what you need from us," Beth said.

The old couple were Lenny and Elaina. Both had moved to Nook Town late in life—unfortunately, just as Orion's reign began. Next to them sat the three young men: Ben; his younger brother, Tamwen; and Barnaby, friend of the brothers. The unspeaking barman was introduced as Max. Of the four children, Charlie, the one who had spoken earlier, was the eldest at sixteen; Flo was next in age at fourteen; the youngest, Mayla and Theodore—known as Toad—were twins, just seven years old.

"So," Beth said, focusing on Hector. "You need our help."

"I came back here with a boy, Raif. He's young, only fourteen"—his eyes passed over the group of children—"but he's been through a lot."

"Does he have powers, too?" asked Toad, face glowing with excitement.

"He doesn't," Hector said. "But his sister Rose does. Her powers are …" He blew air from his lips. "Well, the strongest I've ever seen. And it's her we came to Nook Town to find. You see, I was part of a camp, north of Septima, in the Crystal Mountains. I thought we were working for the greater good, to bring down the Commune, to help those like us who needed shelter." He pulled at his moustache, trying to push away images of Avanna's face. If he could go back, would he have been able to sense her betrayal?

Or was I too blinded by loyalty, by years of friendship?
By her lies?

"Veritas," Beth said, tone strangely reverent.

"We've seen the posters," said Ben. "There were soldiers, Commune … they brought them into town, stuck 'em t' buildings, began asking around. There was a picture o' your face, along with another man and a woman. Orion had the men removed and the posters torn down, but we all wondered what it could mean."

"Hm," Hector grunted. "Yes, Orion mentioned the town had been visited. Well, I'm not ashamed of it. I worked with Veritas, and we did what we could to rescue those who would have been taken by the Commune. But I placed my trust in someone I shouldn't have …

Believed that after years together, I knew who she was." He shook his head, anger bubbling up. "She took the child—Rose, that is. We were told she was coming here, seeking out Veritarra's Gift from the Nomarrans in town. She meant to harm the girl, of that I'm sure. To do what we've long suspected the Grand Magister has been doing ..." He rubbed his temples. At his feet, Dog whimpered as though he knew what Hector said. "Well, not that his awful actions matter to us, not right now. The point is, it would seem that Rose was never brought here."

"Though we keep to ourselves, we try to keep watch on the comings and goings in town when we are about our work. We haven't seen such a girl arrive in the company of a woman, for the little assurance that might provide you," Beth said.

"That dog," said Mayla, eyes bright with curiosity. "Is he your com ... com ..."

"Companion," Flo said, smiling gently.

There was a pause, as though everyone was holding their breath, waiting for Hector's response. He wondered how many of them might have had their own companions, whether any had been lost when Orion took control of their lives. "He's not," he said, giving Dog a pat. "But he is Rose's. He was left behind when the girl was taken."

Mayla gasped and jumped from her seat, rushing to give Dog a cuddle. "Poor thing." Dog, for his part, seemed happy to receive the attention, tail wagging as he licked the girl's face, much to Mayla's delight. Hector's heart twinged at the sight; she wasn't much older than Rose, and her life and freedom had been stolen from her.

"Why don't you and your brother take him outside to play?" Hector asked. He didn't want the children to have any part in what was to come, having no doubt that Orion would exact punishment on any involved, regardless of age. Once Mayla and Toad had eagerly run outside with Dog, he sat forward in his chair. "The boy I came here with, Raif. I need your help saving him."

"Where is he?" asked Beth.

"Orion has him."

Gasps of shock rippled round the room.

"What can we do?" Ben asked.

"He would punish us," Barnaby muttered.

"A ceremony? What kind of ceremony?" Lenny asked.

Hector continued, knowing he had to push past the overwhelming anxiety caused by years of Orion's lies and deceit. He held his hand up, and everyone fell silent. "I mean to free the boy. And there's something else. A room in the back of Orion's house—I need to get inside it. He's keeping a secret in there, I'm sure of it. Dog knew it, sensed it somehow. I mean to find out what it is." He lifted his chin. "It might explain everything. About why he hates the powers. Why he keeps you hidden here, why he—"

"Or it might explain nothing," said Lenny. Despite his old age, his voice was sharp and clear. "You haven't been here, Hector. You haven't known what we've known these past sixteen years." There were mutters and nods of agreement around the room. "It might not be much to you, but for us, it's the only home we have. Don't you think we've thought of escape over the years?" He shook his head. "No. Orion keeps us under an ever-watchful eye. If we help you, if we do what you ask, we risk everything."

"Isn't it worth the risk?" asked Beth, an unmistakeable fire in her tone. "To take our revenge against Orion? To show we are *more* than he's made us?"

Lenny gave her a patient nod. "Might be it is," he said. "But we have to be aware our decision will mean more than a simple yes or no. It could cost us our homes, our security ... our lives."

"I know what I ask of you is no easy thing," Hector said. "It's your choice, all of you, whether you want to be involved. For what it's worth, I will do what I can to minimise the risk. To protect you all. To help you flee Nook Town."

A prolonged silence hung in the air, weighted with unspoken fears, anxieties, concerns.

"How do you mean to do it?" said Charlie. "How do you mean to break your friend free?"

Hector scratched his chin. "Ah, well ... I'd hoped someone might have an idea on that," he said, smiling weakly. "My mind has been slowed since I've come back here." He sighed. "No matter. Your help would be much appreciated." *And the sooner the better, for who knows when Orion will set my trial.* Hector swallowed, guilt at not revealing the full truth gnawing at him.

Another lull in conversation, each person appearing deep in thought.

"Perisma's Light," Beth said, voice ringing out. "The day of worship."

Hector's heart skipped a beat. *Of course.* How could he have forgotten? It had been many years since he'd attended the day of ceremonies with his father, but it all flooded back in that moment.

"It could work," Charlie said, eyes ablaze. "Orion will be—"

"Distracted," Flo interrupted, sitting up, sharing a look with Charlie. "We'll be released from the Blight. His house will be unguarded."

"We'll have t' be careful," said Ben, "but it might just work." His brother Tamwen, however, had a guarded expression. Beside him, Barnaby scowled.

"I understand I'm asking a lot," Hector said. "I know you will be putting yourselves in danger. But if there's any chance of this working, I ask—I *beg* of you, please help me."

Beth stood. "Those who would rather not get involved, there will be no ill feeling. But I am certainly willing to do all I can. I would see Orion pay for all he's done to us."

Hector tilted his head towards her, grateful for her support.

"I'll help," Ben said, standing to join Beth. Tamwen held his arm out as if to stop him, but Ben shook it off. Barnaby remained seated as well.

"So will we," said Charlie, taking Flo's hand as they stood alongside Ben and Beth.

"And me," said Lenny. "You'll excuse me if I don't stand, though; my old legs aren't what they used to be." He gave his wife's knee a gentle squeeze. "Elaina will stay and help with Mayla and Toad. Tamwen and Barnaby, I expect you to do so as well. And Max, hmm?"

The two young men grunted, and Max nodded.

"It's agreed, then," Beth said, smiling.

"Thank you, everyone," Hector said, gratitude swelling in his chest.

"Don't thank us yet." Beth's blue eyes danced in the firelight. "We have a plan to make. The ceremony is yet ten days away. Max, I think we'll need some more ale. There's much to discuss."

Those who had agreed to aid him sat around a table. The flicker of hope had grown; still an ember, it would need coaxing and tending to reach its full potential, but he could see it growing stronger by the minute.

Yes, there was much to discuss, plans to make.

Tankard of ale in hand, Hector listened to his new friends' ideas, heart brimming with optimism.

CHAPTER 18

JONAH

After three days abed in Captain Nem's cabin, Jonah's endless tossing and turning and restlessness had become too much, and he could bear his confinement no longer. His leg wound was well stitched and bandaged, Nem's first mate Smith having tended to it with an expert hand, though it remained tender and swollen. He winced as he swung his feet to the ground and tested his weight on it. He gritted his teeth as he stood, whole body trembling. *You have allowed yourself to become weak.* He flushed with shame at his vulnerability, though part of him knew that he was not at fault for what had happened and acknowledged the value of resting after such an injury.

Using the wall as a support, he made his way to the cabin door and pushed it open, all the while ignoring the throbbing in his leg. Outside, the sun was beaming down from a cloudless blue sky. He squinted, holding up an arm to cover his eyes. He'd been inside too long; fresh air was what he needed. *Fresh air and movement to regain my strength.*

He took a deep breath, head beginning to clear. Ignoring the glances and frowns from the crew, Jonah limped down the stairs that would take him to the ship's aft rail, sucking on his tongue to stop himself from outwardly reacting to his aching leg wound. As soon as he reached the rail, he leaned against it with a sigh of relief. He didn't like to admit how much effort it had taken him to get there and made a great show of casually observing the rippling waves of the Great Sea. The air was thick and humid, a sure sign that they were drawing nearer to the Noman Islands. He huffed and wiped his forearm across his sweaty brow, as much a result of the increasing heat as from the effort of hauling himself around on his injured leg.

Pitiful. Oh, how Eirik would have mocked me. He breathed slowly in an attempt to calm his racing heart. It was that *bastard* Agron's fault he was in such a state.

Captain Agron. His stomach knotted. *"Your pride, your arrogance, the way you flaunted your connection with Lord Torrant."* Jonah shuddered at recalling the man's words.

Was I so awful? So blind to all around me, except ... him?

He rested his head upon his forearms and closed his eyes. Was that how he'd been seen in Septima? As Commander Sulemon, he'd wanted to be a man revered, respected, looked up to ... but his men could never quite conceal a glimmer of mistrust, scorn, or scepticism. After all, how had a Nomarran been chosen to command above someone born and raised in their beloved Septima?

Jonah had believed the true nature of his relationship with Lord Torrant was a well-kept secret. In that, he now realised, he'd chosen to remain ignorant as well. *Damned idiot, did you think that no one knew?* No wonder his men never respected him. A deeper flush of shame ran through him, warming his cheeks, sending a pulse of burning rage through his body.

Were the past seven years a lie? Eirik gave me that cloak alongside a promise that we would return to what we were. What I actually got was a position in which he had me carry out whatever he wished without question. The more Jonah thought on it, the angrier he grew with himself. It was as though he'd interpreted everything wrong, as though even his own mind had concealed the truth from him. He thought back to the day seven years ago when everything had changed.

"You can't stay here any longer, Jonah. You need to leave the estate." Eirik clutched a scroll to his chest, its contents obscured from Jonah's view.

Jonah was instantly on edge, his whole world threatening to crumble around him. "Eirik, what—what's happened?"

"I've been given a choice." A steely gaze, cold as ice, sent shards into Jonah's heart. "I must do this. My brother ... The Grand Magister, he ..." Eirik shook his head, his black hair falling about his pale face, lips twisting strangely. "You wouldn't understand."

"Eirik, my love—"

"Don't call me that." A sharp inhale, a withdrawing of mind and body and soul. "It cannot be that way ever again. You cannot stay. Please. I'm sorry, Jonah, but ... there are things you can never understand. It is for the best."

For too many years, he'd pushed away what happened. He'd clung onto the hope that they would one day return to what they had been.

Until finally when that fateful morning in Eirik's basement provided him with the long-sought truth. How he wished it wasn't so. He understood now what Eirik had chosen over their love—the callous murder of his once beloved brother so he might be granted his family name and estate. *That* was the path Eirik's loyalty to the Commune had taken him down. He wasn't the man Jonah had believed him to be for thirteen years.

So why does leaving him hurt so much? Even as it sickens me to my stomach that I have loved a man who is so ...

"Cruel," he whispered. "A man so very cruel."

In the periphery of his mind, Jonah was aware of the gentle movements of the ship beneath his feet, of the ache in his thigh. But he was too embroiled in the pain within, memories spilling forth that he'd kept locked inside for too long. He covered his mouth with his forearm, wanting to scream.

Some months after being forced away, he had been summoned by Eirik once again. Alongside the scroll, he received a red soldier's cloak. He read the scroll with trembling hands, already knowing he would return to Eirik without hesitation. He could no more stop himself from doing so than he could stop his own heart from beating.

Six sweet years together; seven years of hopeless, endless longing. Of a promise that would never come to fruition because Eirik was already too far gone.

"Jonah ..." A hungry kiss, a sigh of pleasure as their bodies entangled together, connected as one.

The day they met, their whole futures ahead of them.

"You could call me Jonah for short."

"Yes. I think that will suit."

The day they parted, so many questions unanswered.

"There are things you can never understand, Jonah."

"Jonah."

He jerked his head up, Evelyn's voice shocking him back to the present.

"Jonah," Evelyn said again, moving to stand beside him. "Are you well?"

He peered at her, then quickly looked away. "Of course," he said, staring steadfastly at the distant horizon. He felt Evelyn's eyes lingering on him, disbelief radiating from her.

"Here," she said, handing him a water skin. "I thought you'd still be resting."

He took the skin and gulped down its contents, pushing back the lump in his throat. "Thank you," he croaked. "I am done resting."

"But your leg—"

"Will recover. I need air, sunlight on my skin. I thought I might lose my mind if I had to look at the cabin walls any longer."

Evelyn studied him before giving a hesitant nod. He found her concern surprising. *Not so long ago, we were enemies.* Perhaps this was his chance to redeem himself for the wrongs he had done while so blindly following the Commune and Lord Torrant. She had powers, but ... perhaps he could trust her. She did not seem to wield them as Eirik had.

"The captain says we'll arrive in a day or so," Evelyn said. "The winds have been kind, apparently, and the damage to the ship from the attack has not slowed us. We've been lucky, all things considered." She looked up at him again, the subtlest of smiles playing on her lips. "What's your home like?"

His stomach lurched. *Home.* He had been asked the question once before, some years ago as he lay beside the man he'd loved so dearly. He closed his eyes, almost able to smell the beard oil and sweat, hear the crackling of the fire in the hearth at his back, feel the soft fur rug beneath his bare skin.

"Jonah?"

He blinked his eyes open, inhaled the salt breeze that blew across his face. "Home."

"Do you have any family there?" Evelyn asked.

He blanched. Family. *Mother.* Would she even recognise him? Thirteen years was a long time. Some part of him knew he should have gone back to her, written her a letter, anything to let her know he was still alive. But his love for Eirik had been all-consuming, his mind unable to dwell on the home he'd left behind. Now, confronted with his inaction, the guilt nestled in his gut like an insidious rot. He must do what he could to make amends, else be consumed by it altogether.

"My mother is there, I believe." He sighed. "Though it has been some time, so I am not sure ..."

"Oh, I see." Evelyn scuffed her boot against the deck. "Sorry."

"It, uh ... Do not worry," he said. Evelyn gave a curt nod. A long silence followed. They stood side by side, and Jonah tried to ignore the heaviness pressing down on his chest.

To divert himself, he reflected on what he had learned about Captain Nem and the Nomarran prisoners since the pirate attack.

Not *prisoners after all. They are returning home, free and safe.* The discovery had been a shock. Visiting him often over the three days since the attack, Nem had refused to discuss anything in depth while Jonah recovered.

With his head clearer than it had been in days, it was time to start planning in earnest—and to speak to Captain Nem. Veritarra's Gift was a precious resource, sacred to the Noman Islands. He thought of his own pouch of the dried flower, taken by Avanna, and of the test he'd been required to undertake to obtain it. He hadn't yet thought about how he and Evelyn might obtain a large volume of it, though Captain Nem might be able to offer insight on that.

Hoping to lighten the mood, he gave Evelyn a conspiratorial smile. "So, we have an ally in Captain Nem. It is a *relief* that he will not kill me."

Evelyn snorted.

"We should speak to him further. I would like to know more about his plans and how he might help us."

Evelyn looked up at him, expression becoming serious. "Good idea. I saw him near the crew's quarters."

"Well then, lead the way."

SINCE THE ATTACK, Captain Nem had lost some of his jovial nature. He was stricter with his crew, checking in with everyone regularly, apparently blaming himself for what had happened. A valuable lesson had been learned but at the cost of half a dozen crewmen's lives. *Losses that should have been heavier. We were lucky that Agron was cut down relatively quickly.* Despite this, the Nomarrans who had been secured belowdecks were now allowed freedom to roam the ship, and they passed many young men, women, and children as they sought out Nem's whereabouts. Jonah wanted to speak to them, to ask them where they were from, but he held himself back, afraid of what they'd think of a man who had served the very people who had driven them from their homes in Septima.

As Jonah and Evelyn approached Nem, who was speaking to two Nomarrans outside the crew's quarters, Jonah noted how weary he looked. When he had finished speaking to his crew, he turned to them. "Ah, good morning to you both. It is good to see you out of bed, Commander," Nem said, lips twitching into a smile.

"Captain." He bowed his head. "And it is Jonah, please. I am a commander no longer."

Captain Nem's hand floated to where the ruby brooch had been pinned. "Of course, Jonah. Of course." He sighed, running a hand over his close-cropped curls. "I was ignorant and blind. I am, after all, a simple merchant." He gave a weak smile and shrugged, slapping his hands lightly against his sides.

"We all were, Cap'n," said Smith, approaching from behind Jonah. "Should've known he'd find us. An unnatural man." He glanced towards Jonah, then down at Evelyn. "Evil."

Jonah pinched his lips, watching Evelyn from the corner of his eye. She remained still, face impassive, though her hands twitched into fists. To change the subject, he asked, "How are the repairs going?"

"We were fortunate to sustain such little damage," Captain Nem said. "Some minor repairs, that's all." He stared into the distance, eyes glazed. "It's likely Agron planned to take the ship back to Taskan, to add her to the Grand Magister's fleet."

Jonah nodded. "All that matters now is that he did not achieve it."

Nem's shoulders slumped as he rubbed a hand across his chin. "You are right there, I think." He flicked his head, directing them to follow. "Come," he said. "Let's share a drink now that I have my cabin back." He winked at Jonah. "No doubt you have questions. And there are things I would say to you both before we arrive at the islands."

Inside the cabin, Captain Nem sat behind his great wooden desk and directed them to the chairs in front of it. He retrieved some *i'ra* from a drawer and poured himself and Jonah a generous measure.

Evelyn waved away the offered glass, though there was a pained expression in her eye as she did so. "Are you sure? From my personal stores. Straight from Samalah's Isle," Nem said, lifting his tumbler. "It's the least I can do for you both."

Evelyn's lips pinched tight. "No, thank you, Captain. I ... I'd best not."

Jonah wanted to pat her on the back, sensing the struggle she was experiencing. Instead, he smiled at Nem. "Your home island, Captain?"

"It is. Though I have been away for longer than I care to admit, even if it was for a good cause."

Jonah sipped his *i'ra*. The taste on his tongue instantly transported him to his last evening at home when he'd shared a meal with his mother before his ship departed. Her face had grown blurred with the passing of time, but her voice remained as clear as it had been that day. *"You do not have to prove anything, Jonasaiah; you are not your father."*

Ah, but I am more like him than you believed, Mother. A self-righteous imbecile who has caused great pain to others because of his ignorant beliefs.

"You know, I knew your father before the uprising," Nem said. "I was a young man, learning my trade from my own father. We were travelling a trade route when ..."

Jonah shifted in his seat, unable to meet Nem's gaze. Evelyn gave him a curious glance though remained silent.

"What happened was simply awful." Nem bowed his head. "One's name should be a badge of honour, should it not? It is a point of pride for us as men to bear the names of our fathers, as the women take their mother's names. Yet, after all your father did, I do not blame you for taking your mother's family name."

Jonah did not respond for a moment. The decision to change his name had been part of his new life in Septima with Eirik. Shed the ghost of his father's family name; be who his father was not. Someone *good. I became Jonah Sulemon. Look where that got me.* He sat forward, clasping the glass of *i'ra* between his hands. "My father was not a moral man. He chose to act for his own benefit. To lead those with powers in a cruel uprising." It was all the explanation he could give. The rest was buried too deeply in a place he dared not unlock. "I could not in all good conscience bear his name."

"I understand," Nem said. He placed his empty glass down. "Now. What did you wish to ask me? We have spoken briefly, and I am sure Evelyn has filled you in on some matters. Nevertheless, I am sure there are still some answers you would like from me."

Jonah gulped down the last of his *i'ra*, grateful to move away from the discussion of his father. "The Nomarrans you have aboard this ship. Where are they from?"

"All over Septima." Nem sighed. "I'm sure you know how Nomarran refugees are being treated of late. Not all can be so lucky as to be appointed a commander of the Commune."

Jonah nodded, guilt gnawing at him.

Nem's expression grew clouded and distant, as if he was unaware of the discomfort his comment had caused. "Most travel from the islands with hopes of a better life. It was so, for a time. Nomarrans were welcomed in Septima in years past. We allowed ourselves to become comfortable there. A place many called home. But now ..."

"The Grand Magister's decree," Jonah growled.

"Mm. Even after all we did during the war."

"Decree?" Evelyn asked, brow furrowed. "What did he do?"

"His decree dictated that Nomarrans had to report to their nearest town or city. It was made to seem as though this was simply a consensus, a means of ensuring all Nomarrans were being treated fairly in Septima." Nem's face darkened. "The reality was that the Grand Magister wanted our people rounded up and removed from the kingdom."

Jonah bowed his head, ashamed. *Eirik hid this from me.* "I knew of the destruction of our homes in Castleton." His knuckles tightened around his empty glass. "I did not question it. I should have done more," he said, voice raising with his building anger. He breathed deeply to calm himself. "Despite that, I thought our people were safe. There were areas of refuge, too—where our people could be together, live in peace, away from the cities, if they wished. North of Castleton. A place where—"

"Gone. Not two weeks past," said Nem, face grim. "Discovered by the Commune. Any who tried to defend themselves were killed, and the rest taken for the Grand Magister. I could not do anything to help them. I was in Taskan making my plans, too far away to stage a rescue."

"No. No, that cannot be." Jonah studied Nem's face, a hard lump rising in his throat. "It was not so long ago that I sent a woman there myself. Imarra. I saved her from her brute of a master. And *Samalah* ..." He closed his eyes. "One who was looking over the community. She took Imarra away, and I thought ..." He clenched his hands into fists, fury building once more. "I should have known, should have been told. I was a *commander*."

Eirik, you bastard. You knew, you knew all along.

Captain Nem refilled their glasses. "Why would they tell you?" he said gently. "You are a Nomarran, my friend. Despite all you might have done for the Commune, they would never truly trust you."

Jonah knew it before the words were spoken. Had known it all along, deep down. His men followed his orders, true, but always with an air of disdain. He wondered what man had led the charge against the Nomarran camp, whether he would ever have the chance to exact revenge against him.

"The people I am returning home have been carefully gathered from Taskan, Cragside, Haven's End, Ambleside. One of my men attempted to infiltrate the Torrant Estate, too, though to no avail. Lord Torrant ..." Nem's dark eyes flashed with anger. "He is a man I would not wish to cross. His estate is, as I'm sure you know, kept under constant guard."

Jonah moistened his suddenly dry lips. "You are best to stay away from that place."

Nem paused with his glass held to his mouth. "Perhaps, one day, I will breach its walls."

Jonah lifted his own glass, staring at the amber liquid within. "Perhaps." He took a sip, appreciating the alcohol's snaking warmth.

"How did you come to be in Taskan, Captain?" Evelyn asked. "It seems that, despite the misunderstandings we've experienced, our meeting there was fortunate."

Nem sipped his own drink. "Mm, it seems so, does it not? I was a merchant, a trader between the Noman Islands and Septima. When I discovered the Grand Magister's actions against the Nomarrans in Septima, I did all I could to appear loyal to the Commune, worked with that bastard Agron, all the while gaining what knowledge I could to save our people and return them home. I was in Taskan, finalising the plan to smuggle those now aboard."

"Of course," said Jonah.

"Your pride, your arrogance, the way you flaunted your connection with Lord Torrant."

Rage coursed through Jonah's limbs as he recalled those words. He stood, wishing nothing more than to tear apart the entire cabin. Instead, he moved to observe the view from one of the rear windows, taking in the clear blue waters churning beneath the ship's stern.

"I should have been doing the same. Had I been less focused on my own position and status and loyalty to ..." He gritted his teeth, repressing the urge to smash his glass against the floor.

"Jonah," Nem said gently, standing from his desk and joining Jonah by the window. "You are here now. From what I understand, you intend to make amends. To change the fates of all in Septima. Both of you."

"You saved me, Jonah," Evelyn said. "I don't know what Lord Torrant might have done, but I was certain I would die in that place. But you helped me to escape."

"No doubt Lord Torrant wanted you for your powers," Nem said.

Jonah turned to see her response, and she glanced towards him before responding. "Yes. He wanted to test me. But I didn't know if ..." She gulped, holding back whatever words she'd meant to say. "Well, anyway, if Jonah hadn't been there, I don't know where I would be now."

Jonah bit his lip and looked towards the Great Ocean again, unable to speak of what had happened in Lord Torrant's home. *"Now you know the truth ... We can go back ... Please, Jonah."* He returned to his seat as the echoes of Eirik's words whispered in his mind.

Captain Nem moved back to his desk, drank the last of his *i'ra*, and placed his glass down. "In the hands of the Commune, no doubt. Anyway, I need to speak to you about Ham."

"Oh." Evelyn's cheeks reddened. She fidgeted, tugging at her tunic, not meeting their eyes. "That was ... I didn't mean to hurt him. It was a mistake. I won't do it again. I promise."

Nem raised an eyebrow. "Tell me the truth, Evelyn. Can you control your powers?"

Evelyn glanced between them both. "I-I'm not sure," she whispered. "It seems like when I want to use them, they disappear. I didn't *intend* to do anything to Ham." She shrugged, staring at the floor. "I don't know. I'm sorry."

"It is as I thought," Nem said. "And it is for this reason that I must ask you to keep your powers concealed when we arrive at the Noman Islands."

"Concealed?" Jonah sat forward. "Is it so fraught with tension, even after all these years?" Though he despised the powers, he believed Evelyn had no intention of using them against anyone. *At least, not again.* He frowned, glancing at her. *But perhaps her intentions are not enough.*

"Things have changed since you left. It's part of the reason why I was charged with returning as many of our people to the islands as I could. For years now, ever since Ezzarah's uprising—"

"Please, Captain. As you know, I am *intimately* aware of the uprising; we need not speak of it now. Tell me plainly—why must Evelyn hide her powers?"

"Since the rebellion, there has been growing suspicion of *any* with powers. Understandable, is it not? After what happened, our homeland was left in disarray."

"It was complete chaos." Jonah grunted; the words were barely able to scratch the surface of the horrors he had witnessed. "It is so."

Nem spread his arms wide. "With the spread of the Commune's control, there has been a certain reluctance to allow those with powers to venture onto the main islands. Ezzarah's Isle, perhaps, where the rebels who surrendered were allowed to form a new community ... but the other islands, no."

"I see," Jonah said, unable to meet Nem's eyes. His father had been amongst the rebels, hung for his lack of repentance.

"In recent years, *Samalah* has decreed that those with powers are, well—"

"Unwelcome." Jonah looked to Evelyn, his lips pursed.

"Yes. It would seem she was right, given the Grand Magister's recent actions."

Evelyn gave a weak smile. "It's fine. I understand. I don't want to cause any trouble. It's clear that, promise as I might, I *could* unintentionally hurt someone. Like poor Ham." She sniffed. "I'll do as the captain says and keep my powers concealed."

Jonah nodded, thankful for her agreement. *Still, will it be so simple? If she is unable to control them ...*

"If I may make a suggestion," Nem said, as if reading Jonah's mind. "A drink containing a pinch of Veritarra's Gift every day will ensure they are kept under control."

"Veritarra's Gift?" Jonah frowned. *It could work.* "Evelyn, what do you think? You have felt it, experienced its dulling effects."

"Though you would need *far* less than what I gave you," Nem said, giving an apologetic smile. "I can assure you of that. You would not be knocked out. Your powers would be dulled; that's all."

Evelyn chewed her lip. "After what I did to Ham, I think it's the only way."

Jonah let out a resigned exhale, his relief intermingled with concern. "Well then, no one will know of Evelyn's powers."

"Very well," Captain Nem said. "I will ensure you have a small supply. You only need a small pinch in your water every day. Do not let anyone see you take it, for they will know what it means." He placed his hands on the desk as though to finalise the subject before turning to Jonah. "I understand it cannot be easy for you. Despite years of loyalty—and whatever else Lord Torrant might have been to you—you have chosen to be here. To act against him."

Jonah heard no judgement, only kindness and acceptance. Despite this, he could not stop his own self-derision and judgement. *I have been fighting all these years on the wrong side.* The realisation was like a knife in his gut.

"Thank you," he said. "Now I just need to find a way to get enough Veritarra's Gift for our purpose. I have none of my own, after it was taken by … Well, it does not matter now."

"Mm. A challenge, indeed." Captain Nem cleared his throat, a satisfied glint in his eye. "But there is something more I have kept hidden from you. Now that I know your true intentions, I can tell you what's happened since you left the islands."

Jonah's stomach lurched, and he expected the worst despite Nem's demeanour. "Tell me."

"It took time for us to recover after the rebellion, as you know. About ten years ago, the place was near unrecognisable. People were afraid, you see."

"That it might happen again," Jonah muttered. *That is why I left. I could not have faced such violence, not again.*

"Yes," Nem said. "They were afraid of being defenceless. It was then the *Samalah* from each island joined together, knowing they must take action. They visited the Temple of Veritarra and spoke to the Goddess Herself. After seven days of prayer, they were given the answer. It was there all along, of course—Veritarra's Gift. But the Goddess revealed how it might be made more potent."

Jonah's eyes widened. "You mean …?"

Captain Nem nodded. "We have found a way to strengthen our defences, Jonah—*without* the need for violence. The new batches are stronger. Their ability to repress powers far greater. In some cases, remove them altogether."

Remove them altogether. Jonah hardly dared believe it. In some distant part of his mind, he couldn't help but wonder what this could mean for Eirik. What kind of man would he be without his powers? The man he once was, perhaps. *One for whom love was enough.*

"This is just what we need, Captain," Evelyn said.

Jonah ran a hand along his jaw. "That is so, but we still need to find a way of obtaining enough for our cause. I have been away from my home for too long. I have been working for the enemy. Why should anyone there help us?"

"Mm. It is closely guarded, as well you know." Nem pulled a desk drawer open. "For a start, I insist on giving you my own supply."

Jonah gasped. "Captain, I cannot ask you to—"

"You have not asked. Besides, it is the least I can do. I cannot speak for anyone else, but for myself, it is an honour to aid you."

"Captain Nem, I—" Jonah thought of his own pouch, and his heart burned with regret. He had so easily given it away and told that wretched woman what she'd wanted to know so he could return to Eirik's side. Was he expecting too much, to obtain enough to actually carry out their plan? "I cannot accept."

Captain Nem chuckled. "I think you will find that the choice is out of your hands." He held up a black leather pouch. "Please allow me to be the first to assist in your cause." He placed it into Jonah's open palm, closing both their fingers around it.

"Nem, I ..." Jonah swallowed back the pressure in his throat. "Thank you."

"There is no need for thanks. Just be sure to use as much as you can against that bastard the Grand Magister." He retrieved the bottle of *i'ra* from behind his desk before sitting once more. "I think we need more drink. To celebrate our alliance."

"To our alliance, Captain." He looked to Evelyn. This time, she agreed to take a glass of *i'ra* and raised it high alongside them both.

"To new friends."

"I will drink to that." Jonah gulped the fiery liquid down. "And to the Goddess Veritarra, whose gifts will see us take down the Commune once and for all."

And, for the first time, Jonah truly, fully believed their plan could work.

Father,

How can it be so?

I heard the news, yet I could scarce believe it. A messenger brought me a scroll; I saw the family seal. My heart filled with joy and fear. Though I have written all these letters, each have been tossed into the blaze in my hearth, my own cowardice stopping me from sending them. And yet ... I thought, just for a moment, that you had written to me. That you had sought me out. Despite all that has passed between us, despite the passing of so many years, you had reached out at last—perhaps wishing to see me once again, to acknowledge the son you abandoned as a child ...

But it wasn't from you, was it?

Ythan wrote to tell me. He said that there was no pain. You passed peacefully in your sleep. I should attend the estate without delay should I wish to see you buried.

You must forgive my shaky hand, but I cannot stop my laughter. It began when I read those words and has not stopped since. I feel half deranged; Jonah is most concerned for my wellbeing, but how can I explain to him what I am feeling when I do not understand it myself? Such a deep-seated, long-held emotion that has surged to the surface, leaving me unable to think straight.

"No pain. Passed peacefully." How can that be fair?

I wanted to do it myself, you see. To see the life drain from your eyes, to know my powers had grown in strength, enabling such an act. A fitting end for you, I thought—the man who abandoned me all those years ago for possessing those very powers. I was certain it would have finally dulled the endless, burning hatred in my heart.

But now it can never be so.

Of course, it's exactly like you, Father. To take away my one hope of vengeance.

My only consolation is that you have left behind a far better man than you could ever hope to be: Ythan. I wonder if he remembers me as I do him —a brother I once loved dearly. Maybe it is time I reached out to him once more, sought to rekindle the relationship we once had.

Goodbye, Father. I hope you have found eternal suffering for all the wrongs you committed.

Your son,
Eirik Torrant
Loyal Servant to His Benevolence
Grand Magister Quilliam Nubira Antellopie III

CHAPTER 19
EVELYN

Evelyn's heart thrummed with excitement and trepidation as *Septima's Blessing* approached the docks of a beautiful island. The beach of pure-white sand stretched away into the distance, lined by tall trees with long, slim trunks and pointed leaves that swayed in the gentle breeze. Her breath caught in her throat; it was like nothing she'd seen before, so far removed from the grey, dreary shores of Septima and all the horrors she had faced there that some part of her wanted to sob with relief.

"The Isle of Veritarra." Jonah's eyes roved over the shoreline towards the small wooden docks that jutted from the beach, finally settling on the people who stood waiting to greet them. Evelyn followed his gaze, sensing the doubt that seemed to simmer within. "This is where I was born," Jonah said.

Evelyn nodded, smiling. "It's beautiful. Will your mother be here to greet us?" she asked, glancing towards the crowd once again. "Are there usually so many people around the docks?" *Will they like me? Or will they see that I'm hiding something?*

"It is usual," Jonah said. He coughed and turned his face aside. "I cannot say whether my mother will be present, though. It has been …

some time since I was here. As I told you before, I do not know if she still lives."

Evelyn looked up at him but found his face an impassive mask. Whatever emotions he might be feeling in that moment he was not willing to share with her.

Captain Nem waved to them as he approached, smiling broadly. "Come. We are home." Behind him stood the Nomarrans he had smuggled to the Noman Islands. Many of them looked towards the shore with tears in their eyes. They waved to the people there, faces alight with happiness and relief. Evelyn couldn't help but smile, too, at seeing their joy. As she scanned the crew's faces, she locked eyes with Ham. She waved to him, and he waved back, grinning. Relief washed over her that he had accepted the apology she had extended to him last night—that he had promised to keep her secret, despite what she'd done, told her that he was far more mature than she had given him credit for.

Not everyone is as bad as you think they are. Not everyone wants to hurt you.

At her side, Jonah let out a brief grunt, drawing her attention back to him. "Let's get this done," he said, apparently more to himself than Evelyn. As they walked towards the gangplank, he pulled her to one side. He allowed the Nomarrans to go past them before he said, "Have you had your drink?"

"Of course," she said, touching a hand to the small pouch of Veritarra's Gift Nem had supplied her with, safely concealed within a coin purse. Jonah gave a curt nod, lips pulled tight, and walked on.

As they made their way to the beach, a strange sensation prickled across Evelyn's body. She realised how exposed and vulnerable she was—a foreigner to this land, her white skin and auburn hair and masculine dress marking her as an outsider, not to mention her almost complete lack of knowledge or understanding about the Nomarrans, their culture or beliefs. *I am an ignorant child.* She had to keep her eyes open, her listening active, be prepared to learn all she could.

Evelyn set her feet down on the wooden pier beside the ship, doing her best to adjust to being on solid land after almost two weeks at sea. She had barely gained her bearings when she looked up to find herself face to face with around thirty women and children alongside a scattering of men, all waiting to greet the new arrivals. Each individual was dressed in robes of all colours, ranging from red and orange to yellow and gold to purple and green. There were smiles and open arms and hands holding out fragrant, colourful flowers. She'd never seen anything so vibrant and full of life. Her own drab, brown tunic and trousers had never seemed so dull.

Would they be as welcoming if they knew the truth about me? About who—and what—*I am?*

They spoke in Nomarran so she understood nothing, though it was clear from the delighted expressions on their faces that they were pleased to meet her. Even so, she looked over her shoulder, waiting for Jonah to catch up. With him by her side, she was far more comfortable, less out of place, better able to walk with some semblance of confidence. She wondered when she had to come to rely on him and bristled slightly at the realisation.

Captain Nem was ahead of them on the docks, being welcomed by an old woman no taller than Evelyn. Despite her small stature, there was a respectful gap between her and the crowd around her, an air of undeniable authority in the way she held herself. She spoke in a soft yet clear voice to the uncharacteristically bashful Nem, who replied quietly whilst waving a hand towards Evelyn and Jonah. He turned and walked towards them. "Come. *Samalah* would look upon you."

Evelyn gulped, suddenly afraid to meet the old woman's scrutinising gaze. Yet even as she tried to look away, her eyes were drawn to *Samalah*'s. The old woman's face was wrinkled, her expression kindly, her short, white curls decorated with small, white flowers. Her robes were also white, a stark contrast to the richly coloured robes of those around her and to her own dark skin.

Samalah smiled at Evelyn, holding her hands out in greeting.

Evelyn took them, cheeks warming under the woman's scrutiny. "My child," she said, switching to the King's tongue of Septima. "You are welcome here." Her clutch was warm, her gaze friendly, and Evelyn was soon calmed. She realised that was all she needed to hear—a simple statement of acceptance, an acknowledgement that she would not be sent away. A weight lifted from her shoulders as a lump rose in her throat.

"Thank you."

The old woman bowed her head, smiling. "You will join us in our festivities. Some of our lost children have returned today, and—oh." Evelyn turned in time to see Jonah fall to his knees, head down, arms spread wide.

"*Samalah*," he croaked. "Please, forgive me. I saw your kin in Septima. I took a woman to her, seeking refuge ... I did not know the Commune would find them. I did not know what would become of them. Please, forgive me." Jonah's voice quivered.

The old woman moved forward, white robes billowing behind her as a sudden breeze gusted along the docks. *Samalah* reached down, cupping Jonah's chin and lifting his face up. She spoke in Nomarran, her voice barely discernible. Though Evelyn didn't understand the words, she saw the impact they had on Jonah. He let out a long sigh, tears spilling down his cheeks that were wiped away by *Samalah's* soft touch. When *Samalah* held out her hand to him, he stood and bowed his head to her.

"Thank you," he whispered.

She gave a nod, eyes shining, before turning to the crowd behind her. "My people," she said in the King's tongue—for her benefit alone, Evelyn knew. "Nehemiah has told me of the struggles he encountered to return our countryfolk to us. There are some who did not reach our shores; may Veritarra protect them until Nehemiah is able to return to Septima with his crew, until they are home once more."

A murmur of agreement rippled through the people, with many clasping the hand of their neighbour.

"But"—*Samalah* held her arms out wide—"some *have* returned to us this day, thanks to brave Nehemiah and his crew—and by the grace of our beloved Veritarra."

A great cheer emitted from the people as flowers were thrown into the air. Jonah received claps on the back, hugs of welcome, gentle touches of greeting. His eyes met Evelyn's and he smiled, though there remained a glimmer of some unspoken sadness in his gaze. She wanted to go to him, to ask what troubled him, surprised at her own concern. *When did he turn from enemy to friend?*

And then, amongst the noise and celebration, a woman's voice rang out.

"Jonasaiah?"

At first, Evelyn appeared to be the only one who heard. Then there was a ripple through the gathering. A tall, lean woman with long, black curls and the same dark, serious eyes as Jonah emerged.

"Jonasaiah?" she said again.

Jonah turned, meeting the woman's gaze. They stared at each other for a moment, faces mirroring each other's surprise and joy. Finally, the woman moved to stand in front of him. "*A'laha.*"

"Mother." Jonah blinked, eyes glistening with tears.

"My son," she replied, mirroring his use of the King's tongue. She held a shaking hand to his chest. "You have come home."

As Evelyn watched them embrace, a well of warm happiness and spiking jealousy filled her heart, and her legs trembled beneath her. She exhaled shakily, suddenly struggling to breathe.

Bessie.

She could never again find someone to whom she could bring such joy, no matter how far she travelled—of that she felt completely certain. The only woman who had been anything like a mother to her was gone. Killed in cold blood.

The Commune. She bit her lip hard, quivering with anger. *Calm yourself. You can't get emotional; not here.* Despite the Veritarra's Gift flowing through her veins, she feared the powers that remained so out of her control.

She focused on slowing her breathing, tearing her gaze away from Jonah and his mother, pushing back the wave of grief their reunion had awoken within her.

"Evelyn." Captain Nem was at her shoulder. She didn't know how long he'd been there, and she sniffed, surreptitiously wiping away a stray tear before turning to face him. He smiled at her. "We are moving to the village. There is to be a feast. My crew and I cannot stay long, but ... It will be a welcome respite."

"That sounds nice." Evelyn's stomach grumbled in agreement; she couldn't recall when she'd last eaten anything other than biscuits, hard sausage, oatmeal, and eggs.

"This way," Nem said. He merged into the moving crowd, walking away from the beach into a dense grove of trees. As she followed, Evelyn peered up at the crown-like leaves that formed a canopy above them. Turning her gaze downwards, she saw bright yellow spheres, about the size of her hand, scattered around their bases. As they passed, each person bent to retrieve one and continued on their way, clutching them to their chests like sacred relics.

"What are they?" she asked Nem, watching as he picked up his own.

"Ah," he said, eyes gleaming. He held the object up for her to view. "Here, take it." She did so, finding it to be heavier than expected. Its skin was smooth yet very hard. She sniffed its sweet, earthy aroma.

"It is *Sha-mulon Fyra*. Fruit of the family," Nem said, leaning down to pick up another one for himself. "We are fortunate to have returned when they are at their ripest. We will open them to drink the juice. You must try it." He held up the fruit as if to admire its perfect form. "With its consumption, we will begin our celebration."

Evelyn clutched the fruit, enjoying the way it sat perfectly between her palms. She glanced around at the procession. Captain Nem's crew appeared to still be with the ship, so she was the only foreigner in their midst. She filled with gratitude at being given the opportunity to join in with this Nomarran tradition. At the same time, she was self-conscious at being granted such a privilege.

Especially as I'm hiding who I truly am.

She searched out Jonah, seeking some comfort from knowing he was nearby. He knew her secret; he trusted her to keep it, though she barely knew whether she trusted herself or not. Some way ahead, he walked arm in arm with his mother. He seemed to walk taller, his shoulders less weighed down with the worries he had appeared to carry throughout their journey here.

Perhaps things will work out. I will keep consuming Veritarra's Gift. I will keep my mind calm. We will succeed in our mission. She clenched her jaw and nodded to herself, determined to keep her own word.

Jonah turned as though sensing her thoughts. He gave her a solemn nod, lips turning upwards into a brief smile. She smiled back and watched him walk on with his mother.

I have to do this. For the plan. For Raif and Rose and Hector. For Jonah. She touched a hand to the small purse containing the Veritarra's Gift at her waist and followed Captain Nem onwards. Around her, people chattered excitedly, each clutching their fragrant fruits, their bright robes flowing behind them as they walked. The ground beneath her boots was hard-packed sand, a path that had been trodden many times before. She enjoyed the cool breeze that flowed between the trees' tall, slim trunks, allowing it to dry the sweat on her brow as she lifted her face. Through the tree line ahead, a scattering of white houses began to emerge. The air was heavy with the aromatic scent of cooking meat and sweet spices.

It was time to join in the Nomarran celebrations.

CHAPTER 20

JONAH

Jonah's mother smiled at him, patting his hand with her own. She had aged in the past thirteen years, grey now streaking the hair at her temples, wrinkles around her eyes and mouth deepening when she spoke, but as soon as he'd seen her, he'd wondered how he could ever have forgotten her face. Besides, he had changed too, had he not?

And not just outwardly.

As they walked towards the village, he did his best to ignore the throbbing ache in his injured thigh. To distract himself, he glimpsed back over his shoulder. In the crowd of beaming Nomarrans, it wasn't hard to spot Evelyn's auburn hair and pale face. She was smiling and appeared content. The mood here *was* infectious when he allowed himself to be swept up by it. He laughed with those who passed him and his mother, even as his heart pulsed a steady beat of guilt through his body.

I am home after thirteen years. So why do I feel like a stranger here, like my home was never here at all ... but with Eirik?

Jonah bit down on his cheek. He had to try harder. There was no turning back; he was as far from Septima as he might ever be, far from the person he'd been with Eirik. He focused on placing one foot in front of the other, one arm through his mother's and one clutching the dense *Sha-mulon Fyra.*

"Jonasaiah," his mother said.

"Jonasaiah. That's quite a mouthful." Jonah flinched at hearing that name, for it had been thirteen years since he had shared it with Eirik, thirteen years since he had become Jonah. His mother must have detected his unease. She stopped walking and looked at him, brow creased with concern. "My son."

"Su'mula," he said. *Mother.* His native language was heavy on his tongue, and he felt unduly clumsy saying the word that had once been so natural. He bowed his head, ashamed.

His mother touched his cheek with a soft hand, her skin as sweetly fragrant as it had been when he was a child. "Are you not happy to be home?" she whispered, lips downturned.

Around them, the crowd trailed on towards the Isle of Veritarra's central village, where he was born and raised. No one disturbed Jonah and his mother, everyone seeming to understand how sacred this moment was—a reunion after too many years apart.

What must they think of me, for abandoning the woman who gave me life? He looked into her eyes and gave a weak smile. "Of course, Mother," he said. He placed a delicate kiss on her forehead, aware of how coarse his stubbled chin must feel against her skin. A flash of memory jolted him, of a black beard against his own face, the softness of a tender kiss.

"You seem distracted." She cupped his chin and moved his head from side to side, mouth twitching upwards. "But I think you are still the same boy who left here all that time ago, so eager to find a better life." She touched a hand to his chest. "To prove yourself."

Jonah let out a trembling exhale. "Mother, I am so sorry. I did not—"

"Hush, *a'laha,*" she said. "We can speak later. The celebration first."

Grateful for the reprieve, he nodded and looked up to see the last of the crowd disappearing between the trees ahead. "Everyone is gone."

"We can catch up."

And they did, just in time to join the start of the ceremony. They cut open their fruits with small, wooden-handled daggers passed between them, and drank the rich, pulpy juice. The bright orange flesh was as sweet and succulent as it always had been, though Jonah barely tasted it. He recalled the foolish notion he'd once held that he would bring Eirik here—that he'd share the sacred fruit with the man he loved. Around him, people cheered and shouted as *Samalah* declared their celebrations had begun, but all he could think of was that he owed his mother an explanation as to why he had not returned home sooner, even as the thought made him sick to his stomach. What would she think of him for once loving such a cruel and callous man?

For loving him still?

At the front of the crowd, *Samalah* spoke of their beloved Veritarra, of a fruitful harvest season, of successful trades with the other Noman Islands—and beyond. Jonah was quietly greeted by old friends with gentle smiles, touches, and nods. They kept their distance, though, seeming to understand his simmering anxiety at being home again after so many years. As *Samalah's* voice carried across the crowd, Evelyn found him.

"Jonah!" she whispered, merriment evident in the gleam of her eyes and flush of her cheeks. She had sticky streaks of juice down the front of her tunic, though she didn't seem to mind—or perhaps she hadn't noticed. Jonah had always been fastidious at making sure he did not spill any of his juice, but others around them were equally marked by their enjoyment of the fruit.

"Evelyn," he whispered, despite *Samalah's* speech having finished and others around them beginning to speak or to spread out around the village towards the food and drink supplies being readied around them. Jonah turned a hand to his mother, who stood quietly at his side. "I would like you to meet—"

"Oh, uh—tell me later!" Evelyn giggled as she was dragged away by a group of women. Music started then, with drumming, fluting, and soft singing washing over Jonah. He so wished he could let it drown out the thrum of his heartache.

"Who is that, Jonasaiah?" his mother asked, brow furrowed as she watched Evelyn, women tying ribbons into her short, auburn hair.

"She is ... a friend," he said. The word felt strange to say, but it was the right word. Their friendship was delicate but in his heart, he knew it would grow. She had shown her kind nature, the one she hid so carefully beneath a prickly façade. She had not spurned him when he had revealed his truth.

Before long, Evelyn was lost from view as she joined in the dancing. Drums and pipes and bells provided a joyous beat. Jonah was uplifted to see such happiness, though he refused the invitations to join them.

The feast included various dishes Jonah had long-since forgotten the taste of—sweetly-sauced fish, spiced chicken and pork, and salted berries and root vegetables of all colours and flavours. Their *i'ra* was dark and sweet and honeyed, such that his head was soon swimming. Some part of him wondered if Evelyn was drinking it, too, though the thought drifted away from him before he could find her and check. A concern for later, perhaps. His mother stayed close to him all night, as though afraid he was a mere figment of her mind who might disappear if she left his side.

"No more, Su'mula," he said with a laugh as she tried to hand him another helping of food.

"Nonsense." She placed a bowlful of fruit and chicken in his hand, cupping her own fingers around his. "You have been gone for thirteen years; think of all the meals we have not shared." She stroked his arm. "Besides, look how tall and thin you have become. You need to keep your strength up, my boy."

Jonah had lost weight since his flight from Lord Torrant's home. His heartache had left him numb to the food he'd once delighted in, every mouthful turning to ash on his tongue, such that even the meagre portions aboard Nem's ship had been a struggle to consume. His mother was right, though; he would need to keep himself strong. He took the food with a snort and a shake of the head, shovelling mouthfuls in without appreciating the aromatic flavours in the slightest. As he did so, he watched his mother from the corner of his eye. Though she glanced around with a smile on her lips, her true feelings simmered just below the surface of her expression; there was a deep well of sadness that she could not conceal from her dark eyes. He sensed a fear within her that he would soon be gone again.

How can I tell her she is right?

"Jonah," Evelyn said, stumbling to his side. She was bright-eyed, yellow and pink ribbons fluttering in her short, auburn hair, a robe of deep burgundy tied over her plain, beige and brown tunic and trousers.

His mother raised an eyebrow. "Jonasaiah?"

"Mother, I have used Jonah for ease during my time in Septima. It is a name ... I have become accustomed to." *It is the man I have become.*

"I see," said his mother, expression guarded.

"I'm sorry; I didn't know," said Evelyn, not meeting his mother's eyes, her pale cheeks flushing a deep shade of red to match her gifted robe.

"No, do not be sorry, child," said his mother. "If you are a friend of my son, it is my honour to meet you." She bowed her head. "I am Tiah'sulemon. Call me Tiah."

Evelyn turned her face towards him, trepidation darkening her amber eyes. "A friend? Oh, well, I suppose ..."

"Yes," Jonah said. "As I told you, she is a friend. Mother, this is Evelyn."

Without hesitation, his mother pulled the girl into a tight hug. "Thank you for bringing my son home," she said, voice thick with emotion. "You are from Septima?"

Evelyn stiffened for a moment before stepping away from the embrace. "Uh, yes. Septima."

His mother said no more on the subject, for which Jonah was grateful. Instead, she beamed at Evelyn. "It is a pleasure to meet you. I would be happy to join you in the morning to take you to *Samalah* for a proper introduction. To help you learn of our customs."

"That's very kind of you," Evelyn said, glancing down at her feet as she fiddled with her robe.

"For now, Evelyn, I am sure you will understand that I need some time with my son. We have much to speak of."

"Oh, yes. Of course."

"I will see you tomorrow," Jonah said, touching her shoulder. "You will receive many offers for somewhere to sleep tonight. You are safe here."

"Thank you," Evelyn said. He watched her join the crowd of dancers, knowing she would not be short of company.

"So," his mother said, grasping his hand. "Shall we go home?"

Home. A lump rose in his throat, and all Jonah could manage was a hoarse "Yes" in response.

As they turned to leave, he heard his name called from amongst the crowd. Captain Nem waved and marched towards him. "Jonah, my friend," he said. "I am sorry to disturb you. I need a moment."

Jonah nodded, taking Nem to one side. "What do you need, Captain?"

"I will be leaving early in the morning."

"Leaving? But—"

"Do not worry. I will return. Before I can take you back to Septima, however, I will be making a small journey around the other islands, trading news and goods. Most importantly, returning the Nomarrans I have transported here to their homes. Some are eager to see their families, as I am sure you understand." Captain Nem glanced over his shoulder before leaning closer. "I will return in three weeks. And then, my friend, we shall leave."

"Three weeks," Jonah said. "I will speak to *Samalah*, explain the plan, hope she understands that—"

"I think she will, Jonah. I think she will."

Jonah nodded in gratitude at Nem's confidence. "Until then, Captain." They clasped hands, and Nem moved back into the crowd.

"Are you ready, *a'laha*?" His mother took his arm in hers once more.

"Yes, Mother," he said. She led him to his childhood home, though he would never forget the hardpacked sand path decorated on each side with colourful flowers. Other dwellings, similar to his mother's, had white-washed walls and painted doors. Some had dedicated shrines to Veritarra in their gardens, white marble or painted wooden statues with offerings of food, flowers, and *i'ra* beneath them.

When they arrived at his mother's home, he recognised it immediately. The white walls, curtained windows, small garden—his mother's pride and joy—were all much the same. The sickly-sweet fragrance of her favourite pink-petalled flowers hit him as they approached. Her shrine was freshly tended, the white statue polished to a sheen, firestones casting an orange glow on the smooth face of her beloved Goddess.

"I wanted to stay here," his mother said, turning to him as they neared the red front door. "For your return, you see. I did not want you to think I had forgotten you. You will always have a home here."

She pushed open the door and walked inside. The sun was still blazing upon the western horizon, painting the sky to match the multi-coloured robes of his people, but his mother's home—*my home*, he reminded himself—was dark. She retrieved a lamp, muttering under her breath as she tried to light some firestones.

"Let me," he said, taking the stones from her and deftly striking them together until they burned bright in his hands. He placed them into a white bowl, and their light grew stronger and spread up the room's white walls.

"I see you have not lost your skill. You know I could never get the hang of it," she said. "Come, I will light some candles. Your chair is still by the mantel."

He moved into the dim house, and for a horrifying moment, saw it as it had been during the uprising—the chairs thrown aside, jars of tea and herbs smashed, ash from the fire spread around to stain the walls and floor, the carcasses of his mother's chickens carelessly tossed about, their necks broken. The words 'Power to Ezzarah' had been daubed on the walls in a deep red, the colour of—

No. He shook his head and blinked. The damage and destruction had long since been repaired. The kitchen was as it had been for most of his childhood—small but well-stocked, a stove for cooking and brewing tea, shelves lined with jars of herbs and dried food aplenty, two wooden chairs sitting in front of the stove. He sat down, and his chair creaked beneath him. He sucked in a breath as his healing leg wound stretched.

"Are you well?" his mother asked, concern creasing her brow.

Jonah waved his hand in the air, dismissing her worry. "A minor wound; that's all." He patted the arms of his chair. "This has shrunk."

His mother laughed, a light, tinkling sound that sent a thrill through his body. "Or perhaps you have grown," she said, taking the seat opposite his, eyes gleaming. "Has it really been thirteen years, Jonasaiah?"

"It has." He exhaled, long and slow. "How the time has flown."

"Would that I could turn the time back, my son. I ..." She frowned, shook her head, seemed to grasp for words. "I wanted to stop you from leaving. Despite all that happened with your father, Ezzarah's uprising, the aftermath ..." She watched him, lips clenched tight as though she was trying to stop them from trembling. He had no doubt she recalled the atrocities of that awful time over twenty years before. "I felt there could still be good here in our home. And I was right—look how far we have come."

He couldn't deny it; the passing years had been kind. The leaders of those who had risen up against Veritarra were dead—*executed, they were executed; I saw it with my own eyes*—his father included. Those who had sought Veritarra's forgiveness were granted exile to Ezzarah's Isle, allowed to start again, though they were outsiders to the rest of the islands. There were scars left behind, some physical, some unseen, but the community had moved on as best it could. Still, Jonah dared not lie and tell her he wished he had stayed. Despite recent revelations, he could not pretend that he would have chosen differently. His father's actions had been terrible, leading to devastation and destruction in his home, and yet ... they had also meant he left the Noman Islands, that he had boarded a ship for Septima and never looked back.

That I found Eirik and had six short, sweet years of love with him, even if the next seven were filled with despair and longing.

No, he knew deep down that, if given the choice, he would still choose the path that led to his time with Eirik.

His mother gave a brief nod, as though his silence told her all she needed to know. "Would you like a drink?" She stood and moved towards the wooden shelves.

"Please. Your tea was always a treat," Jonah said, smiling.

For a time, they remained in contented silence as his mother prepared the tea. She placed a pan of water over the hearth and waited for it to heat. When she handed him a mug of steaming liquid, he cupped it in both hands, allowing the warmth to wash over his face much as he had done when he was a child.

"I am glad you did not stop me," he said finally. "I could not have been happy here. Not after the rebellion. I needed to find a way to remove the knowledge of what Father caused—of where I came from."

"I see," she said, pursing her lips. Speaking of the past was difficult for both of them. What good would bringing his father up do? *None at all. Nothing can be changed after all these years. But she deserves the truth, and it is time to tell it.*

"Mother, there is a reason why I did not return to you. Perhaps you will understand. Perhaps you will see what a fool I have been."

His mouth twitched into the echo of a smile as he tried to overcome his fraying nerves.

"What is it?" She frowned. "Tell me, *a'laha*."

Jonah paused, wondering whether it was the last time he would see such an expression upon his mother's face. "I met someone in Septima. I know it is no excuse for my lack of contact with you, but Mother, I could not ..." His lips trembled and his heart raced.

His mother reached for him, but he brushed her away, knowing he had to either speak now or lose the courage to say the words altogether.

"I could not come home because my heart and spirit, my life, belonged to someone else. To someone who—whose powers twisted and corrupted them, just like Father and his damned rebellion. All this time, the powers were all ..." Jonah choked, trying desperately to hold back tears. "Even now, I am afraid my heart is still ..." *His.*

"Jonasaiah, oh, *a'laha*." His mother grasped for his arm. "My son. What was her name? You could have told me, written to me, brought her home to me. Anyone who you love would be loved by me as well; you should know that. We could have used Veritarra's love, shown her the way back."

Jonah blinked back the tears that threatened to fall. *Her?* He could have laughed. Here was the crux of the matter. In Septima, he and Eirik had kept their relationship hidden, though somehow it had still been known—and judged—by those who did not understand. No one had spoken the words to him or Eirik directly, but the scornful whispers had reached his ears on more than one occasion. But the truth was he was not worried about his mother's response to him loving a man; it was not frowned upon in the Noman Islands to share such love. The real truth that he feared her knowing was ...

He swallowed, staring into his tea. *She must know. It is the least I owe her after thirteen years of silence.*

"It was not a woman. His name was Eirik, and he—he had powers. Like Father." The words, though spoken as quietly as a breath, seemed to echo around the room. He stared into his tea, feeling his mother's gaze upon him. She stood, shuffled away, sighed.

It is done. She knows who I am, and she can no longer look at me.

He could not bring himself to feel angry at her reaction; if anything, he understood. All that sat within him was a well of desperate misery. He put his mug down and stood. "I am sorry," he muttered. "I will go, Mother."

"*A'laha.*" Her voice was soft, though he could not tell what might be behind it. Perhaps she was fighting hard to hold back the anger she must be feeling.

He froze, facing away from her, afraid to see the shame in her eyes.

But she was suddenly behind him, her hand stroking his back with gentle tenderness, warmth spreading from her touch. "Oh, sweet Jonasaiah. Why did you not tell me sooner?" she whispered. And when he turned, her face was streaked with tears.

Jonah let out a long, quivering breath. "I thought …"

"You are my son. Nothing will change that. You found someone you loved deeply, and that is all there is to it. You could not have removed those wretched powers from him, just as I could not with your father." She looked into his eyes. "You cannot help who you love, *a'laha.*"

He shuddered with relief, collapsing to his knees and pressing his head into his mother's stomach. "I am sorry." Tears rolled down his cheeks as he spoke, the pain in his chest growing with each moment. "I could not leave him. If I left, my heart would have shattered into a million pieces. And I believed that if you knew, you would …" He looked up, imploring her to understand. "I could not leave him, I could not leave him, I swear it. But then— But then he …" Jonah could say no more as the sobs overcame him. As his mother held him, Jonah cried and cried until he had nothing left inside him.

CHAPTER 21
RAIF

Raif followed Lebby into her father's study. His mind repeated the stories he had learned from Perisma's holy book such that he was barely aware of his own body as he moved behind her.

Orion looked up from his desk, the oil lamp at his side casting half his face in shadow. Raif shuddered inwardly, though Orion had been nothing but kind to him since Hector's imprisonment.

Why would I be afraid of him? He was vaguely aware of his face twitching into a frown, even as the thought drifted away, preventing him from exploring it any further.

"Is he ready?" Orion's deep voice reverberated across the quiet room.

Lebby stepped forward, face cast downwards. "I believe he is getting there, Father. I think he has started to … He is getting used to what we are giving him." She glanced over her shoulder at Raif, lips pursed.

She really is quite beautiful. Raif smiled at her, and she gave him a nod before turning back to her father.

"He understands the truth of Perisma's light. He is willing to study."

"Very good. Then he should be ready for the ceremony. He's had his dosage for today?"

"Yes, Father."

"Is there any change in his demeanour? Has he become adjusted yet?"

Lebby hesitated, looking at Raif again. "Not as quickly as we might expect. It is as though something ... as though, er ... something—"

"Spit your words out, girl. I know it can take some time. Believe me, we went through enough trials to ... Well, no matter. But if there is an issue, I can speak to Elussius about it. Ensure the boy has what he needs to be brought into Perisma's fold."

"Something inside him is fighting it. His mind remains slow, as it was when he first drank the tea."

Orion stood, steely gaze fixed on Raif. "I see," he said, clenching his jaw. He moved to stand in front of his desk. "Boy, step forward."

Raif did as he was told, hands clasped in front of him, eyes down. Their words meant little to him. All that was important was studying, proving his knowledge of Perisma, learning all he could to—

What was it again? Why *had* he come here?

Fight it, Raif.

He pushed the thought away, snuffing out the pervasive whisper that tried to invade his mind. He focused on the floor at Orion's feet as best he could, though his vision swam. He sensed it was time to have more tea. That would help. If only he could stop the random, niggling voice at the back of his mind, like an itch he couldn't reach no matter how hard he tried.

Too late, he realised Orion was addressing him. He focused just in time to hear the final few words.

"... have you found it?"

Raif looked to Lebby for help. She shrugged, face pinched with frustration. When he met Orion's eyes, the anger he saw there made him flinch.

"Are you listening, boy?" he said, crossing his arms.

Raif's mind, pleasantly clouded as it had become of late, was slow to respond, though he retained enough self-awareness to berate himself. "Yes, Church Elder. I mean ... I ... sorry, Church Elder Orion, could you repeat your question?" *Idiot. What will Lebby think?*

Lebby? Not Lebby. Remember me, remember why you came here, remember—

NO. I must remain focused.

"I asked how you have found your studies of our most sacred of texts," Orion said, walking back behind his desk and placing his hand delicately on the leather tome that rested there. "Perisma's gospel and truth. You have been reading it for some time now. The day of Perisma's Light approaches. If you are to join in our most celebrated of days—to be brought into Perisma's congregation fully—we must be sure you have learned all you need to. That you understand the work we do."

A shudder ran down Raif's spine at the feverish glow emanating from Orion's eyes. For a brief moment, something inside him relaxed, and he recalled there was something he was looking for. Something he should ask Orion about. Something—or someone— was missing ... If only he could remember their face or name.

Rose. Help Rose.

Orion slammed the sacred book of Perisma shut, and the thought was blown away like a cloud of smoke. Raif concentrated on Orion's words, on what he must do.

"I understand, Church Elder," he said. "We must condemn those born with powers. We must learn from the story of Esteralla Clinkscale, Perisma's first acolyte. Turn away from the abilities of false gods and all will be well. Embrace the powers and we are all doomed to death and destruction, as the lady herself experienced before her conversion to the light."

Orion nodded, a smile pulling at his thin lips. "Very good, boy.

Lebby, you have done well. I will speak to Elussius about the dosage, but for now, keep it the same."

Raif beamed at the praise and bowed his head. "Thank you, Church Elder."

"Come, Raif." Lebby touched his hand. A warm thrill ran through his body at feeling her soft fingers on his. "I'll make you more tea."

"Tea." Raif nodded, mouth salivating at the thought. "Yes, please."

Help, Raif. Help.

He batted away the thought like he might a buzzing fly as he followed Lebby to the kitchen. After his tea, he would return to his room. There was still more studying to be done, and the day of Perisma's Light would be here before he knew it.

CHAPTER 22
HECTOR

Hector sat at the bar in the Blight's tavern, Dog at his feet. After days of discussion, their plans were finally made. The group would need to split up to accomplish everything needed on the day of Perisma's Light. They'd gone over what to do again and again, ensuring everyone knew their part and place. Additionally, they'd all agreed to stop drinking their Veritarra's-Gift-dosed tea two days before the ceremony. Hector had wanted to stop sooner, though it was made clear that the consumption was checked regularly by Orion's lackeys. If suspicion was raised too early, their plan would be forfeit before they'd had any chance to put it into action.

Even with these precautions, it may not work.

He retrieved his tankard from the bar and took a swig of his ale. Dog looked up at him and huffed as though joining Hector in his worry. He wondered if he could reach out to the animal and read his mind, though the idea sent a stab of guilt through him. Cara was his companion; to try and connect with another animal felt deeply wrong. Hector rubbed his temples, glad that his head had cleared. He had stopped drinking the tea the day the group had agreed to help him, fearful that continuing to cloud his mind would cause him to make a grave mistake. The others were covering for him, and he knew how to pretend he was dosed up, though it was certainly a risk. He was counting down the six remaining days until the ceremony, until they could flee from this awful place.

He wished there were another way, one that didn't involve endangering the lives of these people, but the strength of Orion's sway over the rest of the town left him little choice. He had seen with his own eyes that Orion was using Veritarra's Gift as more than a means to repress those with powers. Somehow, he had created a drink that made the town complicit in his utter madness, in his notion that Perisma spoke directly through him, which meant Hector would be overpowered if he tried to carry out the plan alone.

Hector turned to study those around him. The faces of Beth, Lenny, Ben, Charlie, and Flo each showed a renewed sense of purpose. In those staying behind, an array of emotions was on display. Some, like Lenny's wife Elaina, were happy to look after the youngest children, Mayla and Toad. Max remained silent and vigilant as ever, keeping them watered and fed whilst they made their plans. Tamwen and Barnaby, however, watched them with tight-lipped suspicion. Seeing them, Hector's stomach clenched.

Ben was nearby, drinking some ale and chatting to Charlie and Flo. Hector tapped him on the shoulder and signalled for him to follow, away from the others.

"Is everything okay, Hector?"

Hector ran a hand over his moustache. "Now, I don't mean any offence. This is a question I wouldn't ask if I didn't think it necessary. Do you trust your brother, lad?"

Ben peered at Tamwen over his shoulder, then met Hector's gaze. "With my life. We've been through too much together."

"And what of his friend?"

"Barnaby?" Ben frowned. "He is ... *bitter*, it's true. He's been through a lot. But I don't believe he would do us any harm. We don't know much about him, though he's been here since he was a child, just like me an' Tamwen." He paused before shaking his head firmly. "I don't think he'd betray us, though. Why would he choose to do so when he was abandoned to the Blight just like the rest of us?"

Hector nodded. "Thank you, lad." As Ben moved away and Hector returned to his seat, his niggling uncertainty remained. After everything he'd been through, he was loathe to ignore it. He should speak to Tamwen and Barnaby, seek to understand their feelings. Until he could be sure of them, he would keep Cara concealed from everyone. He couldn't risk her being caught if anything should go wrong.

Again, he longed for another way. Some other solution that would save Raif, discover what Orion was hiding, and find Rose. *If only it were that simple.* He rubbed his temples, cursing his inner turmoil. His mind kept taunting him with the repeated thought. He couldn't ignore the feeling he was missing something that he might see clearly if only he tried hard enough, if only he had searched for a means to escape his imprisonment, to force Orion to give him answers. As it was, he had a feeling that Orion was keeping him here without answers as a means of punishment.

There is no other choice, old man. Nothing else you can do. Focus on the plan.

Cara. She must be close. *Or perhaps my mind is playing tricks on me, simply wishing it were so.* He sipped his drink, casually looking around the tavern in the hope of catching a glimpse of his beloved's snow-white fur; nothing, as ever. Even so, he reached out for her and repeated the message he had imparted upon her for the past four days: *Watch Orion's house. Keep an eye on the boy. You must make sure—*

"Hector," said Beth, pulling out the stool beside him. "We are ready to run through the plans once more."

"Must we do it again tonight?" he said. He felt Beth's hand upon his forearm. It was the first time she'd touched him, and the thrill he experienced from it surprised him.

No time for such foolish notions.

Beth's eyes widened and then narrowed, her lips curling up into a smile, but if she somehow sensed his thought, she said nothing of it. "We have days to go over it, I know." She turned to face the group of volunteers. He followed her gaze. "But I want everyone to know the plan as well as possible. Like the back of their hand ... or a beloved companion."

His heart jolted; what did she know? Had he given something about Cara away? Beth was still watching the group, expression unreadable. "Come, Hector," she said, squeezing his arm. "Some more talk will keep our minds alert."

He finished his ale and stood, trying to push aside his weariness. "Another round, Max, if you will."

When he approached the group, newly-filled tankard in hand and Dog alongside him, a fervent discussion was underway about what it would be like when everyone finally stopped taking the wretched tea that Orion forced upon them.

"It's been so long," Ben said to Lenny. "How can you be sure? You might be stronger than you recall!"

Lenny chuckled, dark eyes hidden within the wrinkles of his weathered face. "Believe me, boy," he said. "It might've been sixteen years, but I remember that day like it were yesterday. I know my strength, and I shan't tell myself lies nor try to taunt myself with ideas that it might be otherwise."

Ben looked around for help, and seeing Hector draw near, beckoned him over. "You might know," he said, face animated with excitement. "I've heard rumours we can strengthen our abilities if we train. Really put our minds to it."

Hector took his seat amongst the others and regarded the young man, and pulled at the corner of his moustache. "Where might you have heard a rumour like that, I wonder?"

Ben's cheeks flushed. "I—er ... It was—"

"It was our father," said Tamwen. It was the first time Hector heard him address the group, and his voice was full of bitterness.

"Your father?" Hector asked, glancing between the brothers. "Did he have powers himself, then?"

"Yes," Ben said, looking at his lap.

Hector frowned. "So why isn't he here with you?"

Tamwen scoffed. "Because he left Nook Town before he knew we had powers. He chose the Commune. He never came back for us." Though Tamwen was only nineteen years old, his eyes told of a lifetime of pain. "You should know the temptation of forgetting all about this place. You say we're all the same, but it's not true. You haven't been here for my whole lifetime, Hector. You don't know how we've had to live. You're selfish, simple as that. And now you come here and expect us to risk everything for you." His voice grew louder, eyes aflame with anger. Beside him, Barnaby nodded fervently.

No wonder he's so mistrustful.

"I had no choice but to leave, lad," Hector said softly, trying to calm him.

"Come on, Hector, do you expect us to believe that?" Barnaby said, glaring round at the group. "There's always a choice. You could have stayed here, tried to help those like yourself. But you didn't want to because you believe yourself *better* than all of us, don't you?"

Hector inhaled deeply. He could see that the only way to win Tamwen and Barnaby around was with the truth, and it was a truth he hadn't spoken aloud in eighteen years.

"The truth is ..." He held his breath, heart hammering a vicious beat. *It's time.* "I killed my father."

A gasp of shock rippled round the room. Hector was unable to meet anyone's gaze.

Beth shifted in the seat beside him. "What happened?" she asked gently.

Hector allowed the memories he'd kept barred away for so long to flood back.

"My father was unwell for some time. In the weeks leading up to his death, he grew weaker and weaker until he was bed-bound. He wasn't himself anymore. Not the man who raised me, kept me safe against the influence of the church, came to an arrangement with Biron to shelter me from being sent to the Commune."

He glanced up to see that everyone was watching him. He stroked his moustache and let out a deep sigh.

"When he summoned me on that final morning, I think I already knew what would be asked of me. I went to him, on his final morning, believing I could do what he requested of me without hesitation."

Yet when he'd entered his father's bedroom and smelled the sweetly rotten scent of imminent death, he faltered in his decisiveness. His father's face had been cast in grey, mouth pinched into a hard line. "I can't go on like this, son. Please ... help me."

"Father, don't ask me to. I-I could never hurt you. I can't." He grasped his father's hand in his own, trying not to tremble.

His father's eyes closed. He took a sharp, hissing breath and gritted his teeth. "Will it hurt more'n this?"

The question took Hector by surprise. He'd never taken the life of any living creature with his powers, though his father often encouraged him to test them on animals in the nearby woods so he might learn to control them. Every time, the minds of the birds and mice and squirrels had given over willingly with no hint of pain or panic. As long as he was slow and gentle, his powers took over with ease ... until, if he chose, he could smother them entirely, extinguish their life in a flash. But he would never, could never, do such a thing. The thought terrified and excited him in equal measure; to be so powerful—it was a truly dangerous thing.

"Hector?" his father croaked.

"No, Father. It wouldn't hurt more." He swallowed, willing the tears away. His father gave an almost imperceptible squeeze with his hand. "I can't; please don't ask it of me."

"I have protected you, Hector. This is all I ask in return. Don't let me ..." His father paused, took a long, whistling breath, stared into his son's eyes. What had once been bright green, much like Hector's own, were now dulled, glazed with pain. "Don't let me linger on like this."

"Father ..."

"Don't make me beg. It's a mercy; can't you see that, lad? You must understand." For a second, there was a glimmer of the man he had once been—proud, intelligent, kind.

He kept me safe and close where others turned their children aside.

This is the least I can do for him.

Before he knew it, the decision was made.

He nodded, saw the shadow of a smile pass over his father's face. "Thank you." The relief was palpable in those two words, whispered into the air of that foul-smelling room.

"Do you want anything before I ...? A drink, perhaps. Or something to eat?" Desperate to stretch out their last minutes together, Hector cast about the room. It was no good, though; the time was now. His father's suffering had to end. He had to see it through before he changed his mind.

"Hector," his father said. "Don't ... don't let them control you. You are more than they say you are. You always have been."

"I won't, Father, I won't," Hector whispered, lip trembling. "Thank you. For everything."

Their eyes locked, and they shared a knowing look. Hector clasped his father's hand in both of his, tears blurring his vision. With a deep breath, he focused his powers to a pinpoint. He could almost see them threading into his father's hand, slow and creeping, reaching and smothering his aged mind, stopping his withered heart.

It had been easier than expected, barely taking a conscious effort on Hector's part. Like snuffing out a candle. Perhaps that was what had scared him the most.

"Goodbye, Father," Hector said. There was no response. The silence was a dagger in his chest. Overcome with grief and exhaustion, he slumped forward, resting his head upon his father's chest and letting the tears flow.

He didn't know how long he had remained that way when the sound of an opening door brought him back to the room.

"Hello? Master Haralambous?"

It was the doctor, come to check on his father. He stood, frozen with indecision, numbed by grief.

The bedroom door was opening wider. Hector remained by his father's side, unable to move.

"Oh, Hector. Good morning. I thought you'd be serving in your father's shop."

"Good morning, Doctor Samson," Hector said, not turning around. "I'm afraid you're not ... I—My father, I mean ... He needed me to—He ... He's ..."

Doctor Samson glanced between Hector and his father. "I see." He stepped forward and placed a gentle hand on Hector's shoulder. "I'm sorry, Hector. It was his time. Did he go in his sleep?"

Hector's face crumpled, his mouth contorting into a silent cry. He shook his head. "I'm sorry. He—he—"

"Hector?" The doctor withdrew his comforting touch, frowning. "What have you done?"

"I-I—" Hector turned to find the doctor's face darkened with contempt, but there was nothing he could say, no words to prevent the man's growing suspicion. Hector's heart was broken, and it was his own fault.

No, you helped him; it was what he wanted.

But I killed him. I'm a monster.

Doctor Samson frowned, ignorant to the tumult of Hector's thoughts. "Now that I think on it, he seemed well when last I saw him. He was talking about his plans for the shop, how he hoped to be back on his feet before the harvest festival." He was edging back towards the door, glaring. "How long have you been here, Hector? You said your father needed you?"

Hector held his arm out imploringly. "Please, doctor, my father was not well. He would never have left this bed again. He asked it of me; you have to believe me."

"So, you admit it? What did you do, man? Was it ..." The disgust across the doctor's features told Hector all he needed to know—there would be no respite, no understanding. "Did you use those god-forbidden powers?" The last word was spat, the venom within it unconcealed.

"Please, Doctor Samson," Hector said, stumbling forward. The man

flinched backwards so that he was pressed against the door, the sudden fear in his eyes unmistakeable.

What does he think I am?

Fury coursed through Hector's veins. He'd just lost his father, and all this man could do was regard him as an accursed creature, unworthy of sympathy.

I'll show him what I can do.

He reached out with his mind, the flare of power like a bolt of lightning through the air. The doctor's face grew slack; his arms dropped to his sides, and his mouth drooped open.

"He was my father," Hector said, grimacing with rage and heartache. "He asked to be free of his pain."

Somewhere in a distant corner of his thoughts, he could sense the doctor trying to fight back. In the man's blue eyes, he could see a hint of the distress his conscious mind was experiencing.

"P-p-p—" Drool ran down Doctor Samson's quivering chin. "Please." Saying the word must have taken an immense amount of effort, for he slumped to the floor as soon as it was spoken.

Hector realised only then what he was doing. In horror, he withdrew his powers from Doctor Samson. The man was unconscious, though his chest fluttered with shallow breaths; he would recover. With a final glance towards his father, Hector heaved the doctor away from the door and fled. He had to get away. The circumstances of his father's death would be spread around the town, and Church Elder Biron, accommodating as he had been, would surely see him face retribution for this crime against their blessed Perisma.

He had to leave this forsaken place. Had to somehow be the man his father had believed he could be, even as his own monstrous actions played in his head over and over again.

"And so, I left my home and didn't look back," Hector said, staring into his tankard. The tavern remained tensely silent. "This is the first time I've been back in eighteen years. As soon as I returned, Orion imprisoned me here. That's why I'm in the Blight. I didn't even come here by choice, and I'm sure I'd have avoided it if I had been given such a choice." Hector swallowed. "Tamwen and Barnaby are right; I'm selfish, and what I'm asking of you is ... Well, it's too much. I understand if you wish to leave me to carry out the plan alone. I never meant for any of this."

Within the space of a heartbeat, Beth had taken Hector's hand in her own. "Don't be a fool, Hector. I don't believe you to be selfish or cruel or anything else you might think of yourself." She flashed a glare towards Tamwen and Barnaby. "And I don't think anyone else does, either." There were murmurs of agreement around the room.

"I appreciate that," Hector said. "But it doesn't change the truth of it. Of what I'm asking from you all." His eyes lingered on the two young men who had questioned him, both of whom stared at the floor.

"We know what we're doing, don't we, Flo?" Charlie said.

"Yes, we do." Flo nodded and smiled at Hector.

"As do I," Ben said.

"Then we're all agreed," Beth said. "There'll be no more nonsense. Seems to me, Hector, that what you did for your father was a mercy. And Doctor Samson died years ago. You have no need to fear judgement from any of us, does he? Barnaby? Tamwen?"

The two young men glanced at each other and then towards Beth and Hector.

"I'm sorry for what I said," Tamwen said quietly. "I won't stop my brother from helping you, but I'm afraid I'd still rather not get involved. I-I can't. I'll stay with Elaina, help with the children."

"And I'm sure she'll be grateful for the help, boy," Lenny said.

Barnaby sighed, staring at Beth for a drawn-out moment. "You do what you need to," he muttered. He pushed himself up to stand. "You'll hear no protest from me. Just don't expect me to get involved." Without a backwards glance, he stalked out of the tavern. Instinctively, Hector reached for his mind as he walked away. It did not take much to push past the wall provided by Veritarra's Gift to reach a dizzying swirl of anger, sadness, guilt, bitterness.

"Don't worry about him," Beth said, brushing his arm. "He has his own demons to contend with."

"I see," Hector said, staring towards the closed door. "What happened to his parents?"

A glimmer of some unspoken pain passed across Beth's eyes, gone before he could grasp its meaning. He thought to reach out to her mind, too, but held himself back, not wanting to probe into a sadness she did not wish to share with him. She shook her head. "It doesn't matter now. Leave him be. It's for the best." She turned her attention back towards the group. "Come. We have plans to go over."

Before long, however, Hector was focusing on more important matters than the young man with the suspicious eyes and bitter heart.

"So, the celebrations will begin early; we all know that. The whole town will descend upon the church. Every year, Orion extends an invitation to those in the Blight as some kind of ... act of *benevolence*."

"To help us understand 'the importance of Perisma's light and truth,'" Beth said, rolling her eyes.

Hector sneered, unable to conceal his disdain. "Whatever the reason, this time, it helps us. The invitation will be extended as always; we will accept. Or, at least, some of us will."

Beth stood beside him, blue eyes blazing. "Ben, Flo, and I will attend the church to try and determine the boy's whereabouts. Orion has, by all reports, kept him closely concealed, and that can only mean one thing."

"He intends to take the boy into the church's arms," Lenny said.

Not long after Hector's arrival in the Blight, Lenny had shared his past in Nook Town. "I've seen that ceremony more times'n I can count, over the years." Fear had filled his rheumy eyes. "If it goes ahead, your boy'll be lost forever to Orion and his church." Knowing that, Hector had wanted to move their plans forward, not wanting to risk the boy any more than he had to, but it couldn't be done. Orion was too powerful, the community around the church too close-knit, now more than ever, it seemed. It was a painful countdown to the day of Perisma's Light, but there was no other option. This would be their one and only chance, when the entire town's attentions would be drawn together in a single place, when Raif would be brought out of the concealment of Orion's home.

Beth gave a curt nod. "The three of us will keep watch on the boy. If the ceremony begins, we'll know we must act to retrieve him at any cost. Though if we can wait for you, Hector, to join us after you've completed your task, we will."

Ben and Flo assented, and Hector's heart ached at the thought of the danger he was placing them in. They were still young and innocent, their whole lives ahead of them, if only they could be free of this place. He made a promise to himself that he would see them away from Nook Town when everything was done. They would be free of Orion's control.

"Hector?" Beth was looking at him expectantly.

"Oh, sorry." He forced a smile.

Beth laughed softly. "Do you want to go over *your* part of the plan?"

He bowed his head. "Please."

He reached down to pat Dog's head for comfort, causing the animal to stir from his sleep. "So that leaves Lenny, Charlie, and me." Dog licked his hand. "And Dog, of course. We must break into Orion's home and find out what he's hiding. Mayhap if we learn the truth, we'll be able to confront him with it and use it as a way to save Raif. I don't know. All I know is Dog was fiercely upset by whatever Orion was keeping in that room." He stroked his moustache.

Beth laid a hand on his shoulder. "We understand."

"Thank you." Overwhelmed with a sudden, deep exhaustion, he pushed himself to his feet. Dog stood, too. "Please, you'll have to excuse me. I need to rest."

He moved towards the door with Dog, aware of everyone's eyes upon his back. Outside, he opened his mind and searched for Cara. He didn't know Beth had followed him until she spoke.

"How long have you been connected?" she asked.

His heart skipped a beat. "What? I don't know what you mean, I—"

"Hector." She tilted her head, smiling. "It's written all over your face." She reached up to touch his cheek, though quickly pulled her hand away, as if afraid of prolonged physical contact between them.

She felt it, too, the spark between us.

"I had a companion once myself. I know that look because I've been there." Beth followed his gaze out into the black streets and dark shadows—anywhere his beloved companion could be hiding. "So, are they close?"

Hector stretched his mind to its farthest reaches. "Yes, though I can't see her. She's good at hiding." He sighed, his breath clouding the air. "I never wanted to return here, to put her in danger. And the lad, though I never even thought that would—"

"I know," Beth said softly. "I know, Hector. It's best she keeps herself safe. If Orion found out about her—about your connection." She shrugged, lips pulling down. "It's just not worth the risk."

"I know. Doesn't make it any easier, though." Hector gave the dark night one last hopeful glimpse before turning back to Beth.

"I've been meaning to ask you something ..." Beth hesitated, eyes down.

"You can ask me anything," Hector said. "You've helped me more than I could have hoped for."

Beth looked up at him. "When you first came to us, you mentioned the Commune."

Hector's stomach lurched. "I did."

"You said you were fighting them. That they are no better than Orion and the church, though *they* state they are helping those with powers."

"It's true," Hector said. "The Grand Magister is a man working for his own ends, no one else's. He takes in children with powers, but it *isn't* to help them."

Beth's eyes shone. "I've heard those under the Commune's care

are free to use their abilities how they wish. Encouraged to nurture them, to control them, to ... well, to be themselves."

Hector nearly choked with disbelief. "Where did you hear that?" He glimpsed back towards the tavern; hadn't Ben said something similar to him? Before Beth could answer, he took her hand in his and stepped closer. He could feel her warmth against him and tried not to let it distract him. "Beth, that's not how it is. The Commune, they're not to be trusted. The Grand Magister isn't benevolent; he isn't good or wise. Just, *please*, believe me on that."

Beth gave a wistful smile and squeezed his hand before releasing it. "Very well, Hector. I'll believe you." She peered up at the moon. "I always admired you, you know. I would see you around the town with your father, always so impeccably dressed."

Hector chuckled. "Yes, my father insisted on it. 'They'll criticise us for everything else, lad, but it will not be how we dress.' He was a proud man. Proud and kind." Hector sighed, missing his father more than ever.

"It must be hard for you, coming back here after all these years. Seeing all the places you used to go with him. If you don't want to be alone, perhaps you'd like to ..." Beth trailed off, toeing the ground with her shoe.

"Are you well, Beth?" he asked. He tried to reach for her mind but found a barrier around it. *Of course. She is still consuming the tea.*

Beth let out a low laugh, and butterflies stirred in Hector's stomach. "I know what it is to be lonely," she said. "Since I lost my companion, I've been afraid to let anyone else in." She stepped closer, meeting his eyes; hers were like pools of deep blue light, drawing him in. "Would you like to join me for a drink?"

"In the tavern? No, I—"

"No, Hector. In my home. It's just down the road ... In the Blight, of course." Her voice was soft, welcoming, warm.

Despite his earlier misgivings and belief that he didn't have time for such ideas, there was a sudden awakening of a long-dormant part of his heart, an area he'd closed away years ago that not even his connection with Cara could touch. As he looked into Beth's face, he allowed himself to smile.

"I would like that very much," he said, body afire with anticipation. *You're acting like a young lad, you fool.*

Joy alighting her face, Beth looped her arm through his own, no hesitation or doubt in her movements this time. "Come on; this way."

As she spoke, Hector glimpsed, from the corner of his eye, two glowing specks in the darkness. *Cara.* He hesitated, the pull towards his companion magnetic in strength.

Go. I will see you tomorrow.

Gratitude and love bloomed in his heart. In the blink of an eye, his beloved Cara slunk back into the darkness.

"Hector?" Beth said.

"Lead the way."

Together, they walked into the night.

CHAPTER 23

EVELYN

The sun beamed in through the glassless window. Evelyn shielded her eyes with her forearm and turned onto her side, groaning as her temples pulsed with pain. When she forced her eyes open and saw the white stone wall, she sat up with a start. *Where am I? How did I get here?*

The last she remembered was … dancing. Lots of dancing. *What came over me?* She ran a hand through her hair and found it still laden with ribbons. *The celebration.*

I'ra. There had been *i'ra* as soon as the music had started, it seemed, and the Nomarran drink was a delightfully sweet delicacy that was far too easy to consume. She had been surrounded by women who all wanted her to join in, to taste their food, to drink their honeyed *i'ra*. She'd felt so welcome here; she'd let her guard down, gone back on the promise she'd made to herself on Nem's ship that she would not drink again.

So much i'ra.

Idiot.

The men, she recalled, had kept what appeared to be a respectful distance, watching and smiling from the edge of the crowd. The realisation had put her at ease, made her more comfortable than she had been in a long time. No harm would come to her here; she'd felt so sure of that last night.

This morning, though …

Where am I? As her panic rose, her chest tightened. Jonah wasn't here; he'd gone with his mother. She could be anywhere, with anyone.

You put yourself in danger again, stupid bloody idiot. Have you learned nothing?

Suddenly, the sound of movement from an adjacent room reached her ears—footsteps, shuffling, a gentle cough. Evelyn froze, afraid to look round. She was still staring at the wall when she heard someone enter.

"Good morning," said a cheerful woman's voice.

Evelyn turned stiffly, her expression guarded. "Good morning," she said. The woman had a kindly expression, and her thick black curls, piled high on her head, were still decorated with colourful flowers from the night before.

"Are you well, child? You look pale." The woman approached, brow creased with concern. She reached forward, and Evelyn flinched back. The woman's dark eyes widened, her hand hovering in the air between them. "I mean you no harm, young lady."

"I—I'm sorry," Evelyn muttered, hugging herself. *Why am I like this?* This woman had clearly welcomed her into her home. She might have slept under the trees otherwise. "I just couldn't … I don't remember what …"

"Ah," said the woman, pulling up a chair. "You can call me Ayah. Might be that we were over generous with the *i'ra.*" Her eyes twinkled with amusement.

"No, don't worry. I'm used to alcohol. Wine, usually," Evelyn said.

"I see," Ayah said, studying her closely.

Eager to leave the woman's scrutiny, Evelyn sat forward on the bed and made to stand, though her legs appeared to have other ideas. "I agreed to see Jonah's—sorry, Jonasaiah's mother today. Perhaps I'd better go."

"Nonsense, girl." Ayah stood. "We will get you washed and dressed, and then it is time for our morning meal and blessing. We eat together. Come, I will fetch you some water. Your journey was long, and your clothes are ..." She wrinkled her nose as she held them up. As she did so, the coin purse containing her Veritarra's Gift fell to the floor. Before Ayah could lean down to pick it up, Evelyn darted an arm out and retrieved it.

"What is that?" Ayah asked, watching as Evelyn tucked it under her pillow.

"Oh, nothing," Evelyn said. "Just ... my coin purse. Empty." She forced a smile, though her stomach churned uneasily as she remembered Captain Nem's words: *Do not let anyone see you take it, for they will know what it means.*

Ayah raised an eyebrow but said no more on the matter. "Hmm. Well, I'll find you something fresh."

She bustled from the room, red robes billowing behind her. Her bare feet pattered against the floor, and Evelyn recalled that many people had gone without shoes the night before. She eyed her seen-better-days leather boots, battered and in dire need of resoling, before lifting them from where they'd been placed at the foot of the mattress. Perhaps she should embrace this local custom. She stretched her feet, enjoying the feel of the cool earthen floor. When she stood, she attempted to stretch when a wave of cramps took hold of her abdomen.

"Shit," she muttered. As always, her monthly bloods were unpredictable. She would need to find a way to deal with it.

"Oh, what is wrong?" Ayah asked, hurrying back into the room.

"Uh," Evelyn said. She held a hand to her lower stomach. There was no use in being shy about it, she decided. "My, uh ... My bloods have started."

"Oh!" Ayah nodded, handing Evelyn a deep orange robe. "Take this. I will find you some cloths. Do not worry."

Evelyn was grateful for this woman's kindness. Her earlier mistrust melted away as she examined the robe. It would be strange not wearing trousers, but there was little choice. She nudged the stinking pile of clothes at her feet, wrinkling her nose. She held the robe up, taking in the long skirt hanging from the fitted bodice. Bessie would be proud. *"Wearing a skirt at last,"* Evelyn imagined her saying. It brought a smile to her face, though the grief simmering beneath the surface soon washed it away.

Ayah popped her head back into the room. "Come, you can wash in here." She waved Evelyn forward. "Then we will get you dressed." She smiled warmly. "And then some food. Your monthlies, especially, are a time to keep your strength up, hmm? I will take care of you. Veritarra would expect no less."

The early morning sun beamed down on the bright sands and white houses of the Isle of Veritarra. Evelyn squinted against the light. Her head was beginning to pleasantly fog, a sign that the Veritarra's Gift she had quietly consumed whilst she washed was taking effect.

"This way," Ayah said, smiling and leading her down the path away from her home. Evelyn followed. The robe Ayah had given her hung loose around her chest and hips but was tied tightly around the waist with her own battered leather belt—coin purse included—which just about stopped it from dragging on the floor. She tugged at the clothing self-consciously as she walked behind Ayah, trying to get used to the excess material hanging about her legs.

"We will soon see you well fed," Ayah said cheerily. "Until then, my daughter's old robes will suffice."

"Your daughter?" Evelyn asked, glancing down at her outfit before looking back up. "Where is she?" Pain flashed across Ayah's face, and Evelyn realised she'd spoken too boldly. "I'm sorry, I shouldn't have pried."

Ayah shook her head and held up a hand. "No, we speak plainly about such things here." She sighed. "This place was not always as you see it. There was war, fighting, death. My daughter, Talliamon—

Talli." Ayah smiled. "She is with Veritarra now." She made a hand movement that Evelyn didn't recognise, kissing her right thumb, placing it on her forehead, and then opening her palm towards the sky.

Evelyn gulped. "Was it ... was it those with powers who ...?" *Killed her.* She couldn't bring herself to say those words, sure as she was of the answer.

Ayah smiled sadly. "Yes," she said. "Ezzarah's Cursed."

Evelyn nodded weakly, wishing with every part of herself that she did not possess those same powers. "I'm sorry you lost her," she whispered.

"I have not lost her," Ayah said, eyes sparkling. "She was blessed by our beloved Goddess. I will see her again."

Evelyn nodded, unsure what to say. She admired the woman's staunch faith but could scarce bring herself to believe it. After all she'd been through, all the atrocities she'd witnessed, how could she?

Ayah has been through worse and retains such faith. How?

As though sensing her thoughts, Ayah gave her a sharp look. "You will see." She paused in her walking, touching Evelyn's shoulder. "When you speak to *Samalah*, you will see. She knows the truth of all. She is one of Veritarra's guides in this world."

Evelyn met the woman's eyes. *I hope she doesn't see* everything, she thought. Ayah only gave a brief, satisfied nod before marching onwards.

Evelyn kept her head down as she followed Ayah towards the long, white-walled building at the heart of the village. Like all the buildings in the village, it was a single-storey stone building, painted white and adorned with flowers. Through the glassless windows, she saw long tables laden with food. The smell of fresh-baked bread and rich spices reached her nose, and her stomach flipped. *Shouldn't have drunk so much i'ra.*

Inside was a large, airy room, the tables occupied by villagers. The walls were adorned with paintings that appeared to depict the

Goddess Veritarra granting various blessings. There were flowers along the tables, too, decorating the long, wooden serving platters that were still being laid out by some of the men, who then moved to sit at separate, smaller tables at the outer edges of the room, keeping their eyes down and voices quiet. In contrast, the women were voracious in both their eating and gossip, creating a cacophony.

"Come, child," Ayah said, gently guiding her. They sat at a long table alongside several other women. Evelyn looked around, noting the difference in dress between those seated at each table. At the table Ayah had chosen, all the women were dressed in bright robes, with long hair piled high or pulled away from their faces, interwoven with ribbons or flowers. Evelyn touched her own short curls, which held remnants of the ribbons that had been delicately woven in at the celebrations yesterday. At another table, the women had short hair like her, with ribbons tied around their necks and wrists, their robes more muted in tone.

"Here, you must try this." Ayah passed her a dark, round fruit about the size of her thumb. Evelyn realised she would have to eat; it was clearly an expectation. She lifted the fruit to her lips, immediately smelling its strong, citrussy scent. She bit into it, and it seemed to melt in her mouth, releasing cool, refreshing juice.

"It will settle your stomach," Ayah whispered, winking at her. She handed over some fresh bread laden with thick, creamy cheese. Evelyn smiled and took it, already feeling better.

"Eat what you can, girl," Ayah said. "We will get your strength up." All around them, the women gave vehement nods. Evelyn felt her face flush; she was unused to—and unfond of—being the centre of attention.

When the room fell silent, all eyes turned to the door, and the old woman entered—*Samalah*. The hush was reverent, respectful, full of awe. As last night, she was dressed all in white, her short grey hair decorated with small white flowers. At her side was Jonah's mother, Tiah, along with three other women, each with dark curls hanging down their backs, their hair intricately tied with braids, ribbons, and flowers.

Samalah held up her hands, cast her gaze about the room, and spoke, her lyrical voice ringing through the room. Evelyn recognised the word "Veritarra" but nothing else. When *Samalah* was done, she was led to a circular table at the head of the room, where a plate of food was placed before her.

"What did she say?" Evelyn asked, watching the old woman as she took delicate nibbles of some nut bread.

"She blessed us all in the name of our Goddess, Veritarra, and bade us all to follow Her ever-present example," Ayah said. "It is a tradition on this, our day of rest."

"Thank you," Evelyn said. She was relieved the Nomarrans were so adept in the King's tongue and so willing to accept her ignorance.

As long as I hide my true nature.

Even with the warm welcome, Evelyn imagined she could feel all eyes upon her as she sat once more. Around her, the women spoke to each other in the King's tongue, even though she was the only Septiman present. She slumped her head down, pulling apart the bread on her plate. *I am not worthy of their kindness and attentiveness.*

"Evelyn."

Evelyn jolted upright. "Tiah," she said, glancing round to find Jonah's mother at her back. "Uh, good morning," She peered behind the woman. "Is Jonah here?"

"My son is resting," Tiah said. "He is … tired. After your journey."

"Of course," Evelyn said, sensing something unspoken beneath her statement.

"*Samalah* has requested your attendance this afternoon."

"Oh." Evelyn looked between the old woman and Tiah, blood rushing in her ears.

"That is a great honour," said Ayah, squeezing her shoulder.

"Once you have finished eating, I would speak with you," Tiah said. "I would like to tell you a little of our customs."

Evelyn looked at the crumbs on her plate, surprised at how much she'd eaten. Her stomach was full, her head much clearer. "I'm ready now."

"Very well," Tiah said. "Come."

"Go well, child," Ayah called after her. Evelyn gave Ayah a brief wave, trying to push away her growing unease.

"This way," Tiah said, beckoning for her to follow. "I will show you our place of worship."

Evelyn nodded and sped up, following Tiah through a line of those tall, slim trees along a path of white sand. Beside the path were low, green shrubs, tall plants with sharp spines and bright flowers, and the occasional marble statue and shrine to Veritarra. Each shrine was full to bursting with written devotions and prayers, offerings, and blessings. These people loved their goddess dearly. She wondered what it must be like to have such a keen sense of faith in something they had never seen with their own eyes.

They walked for a short time, the sounds of the village falling away. The ocean washed against the shore somewhere close by as a swirling flight of large, white birds circled above their heads. A warm, pleasant breeze blew by. Tiah remained silent as she marched on. Eventually, they emerged at a clearing in the trees. At its centre sat a tall white building, a great spire reaching towards the cloudless blue sky. Evelyn gawped upwards. She had never seen a place so beautiful.

"The temple of Veritarra," Tiah said, breaking her reverie.

"It's ... so peaceful." Looking at it, Evelyn felt a sense of calm wash over her. She felt she could happily stay in this place forever.

Tiah made the same hand gesture Ayah had earlier—kissing her thumb, placing it to her forehead, then opening her palm to the sky. "Come," she said. "I would be honoured to share our home with you."

She moved towards the temple's open door, an archway of flowers greeting them with their sweet, heady fragrance. Evelyn inhaled deeply, wanting to take in every detail around her. Inside, white marble benches were scattered all around, their legs and edges carved with tiny flowers and vines. Tapestries of Nomarran people, adorned in their colourful robes, hung upon the white walls. Some appeared to be worshipping statues of Veritarra, much like those around the village. Others showed a giant, broad-chested, bearded statue, with robed men bowing down at its feet. Evelyn frowned, uneasy at this new, unknown entity, though unable to comprehend why. She moved away, taking in the white marble statues around the edges of the room, each carved into the likeness of a different woman. The air was rich with the deep, sweet scent of flowers, so strong as to be almost overpowering.

Tiah must have noticed Evelyn's fascination, for she stopped in her tracks and followed her gaze towards the closest statue. "Veritarra's chosen," she said. "Former *Samalah*. Those who gave their lives to protecting and spreading the message of our beloved goddess."

Evelyn marvelled at the fine carvings. Their faces were almost lifelike, their eyes seeming to watch her every move.

"This is where *Samalah* gives her monthly blessing," Tiah said, placing her hand upon a high-backed seat of white marble. It was carved with tiny flowers and vines, much like the benches, and rose from the ground on a small dais. Evelyn moved closer to it, almost able to imagine *Samalah* sitting on it, speaking to her people, sharing her wisdom. A deep pang of sadness shot through her that she had never known such a sense of belonging, faith, and community during her own life.

"Why have you come here?" Tiah asked abruptly, snatching Evelyn's attention away from the seat.

Evelyn was taken aback at Tiah's bluntness. "I ... I came with Jonah."

"Jonasaiah. My son." Tiah sighed. "Do not mistake me, girl; I am pleased he is home. But I cannot ignore the turmoil within him." Her expression was tinged with sadness, and Evelyn realised the woman wasn't angry with her—she was worried about her son, seeking reassurance. But for what ... that he wouldn't leave her again?

I cannot give her what she wants. Unable to find any words of comfort, Evelyn pointed towards the tapestries and said, "Can you tell me about these?"

"Ah," Tiah said, walking towards the closest one, which depicted a huge, muscular figure, the same as was depicted in the statue that Evelyn had noted earlier.

"Who is that?" Evelyn asked, trying to pull her gaze away from the statue's rage-filled face. "Who are those men worshipping?"

"Ezzarah," Tiah said. "The creator of—"

"Powers." Evelyn's stomach lurched. *Ezzarah.* Wasn't that who Captain Nem had mentioned? Something about an uprising, the reason why she had to keep her abilities hidden. "There was ... an uprising?" she asked, examining the images closer.

"What do you know of it?" Tiah said, raising her eyebrows.

"Oh, not much," Evelyn said, not wanting to admit what she had heard Jonah and Nem speaking of back on the ship, remembering that Jonah's father had been involved somehow. She waved a hand in the air. "I've heard it mentioned, that's all."

Tiah narrowed her eyes as though assessing whether Evelyn was worthy to hear the story. Eventually, she gave a curt nod and said, "Ezzarah and Veritarra were there at the beginning of all things, hundreds and hundreds of years ago. They granted us life and light. But where Veritarra encouraged love, kindness, and compassion, Ezzarah believed fear, admiration, and daily struggle were needed to prove loyalty. He was a ruthless god, always seeking to test the faith of his worshipers.

"To encourage them to fight for his attentions, the great and arrogant Ezzarah granted a chosen few the power to control animals, and even other people. A blessing, they believed. Those who followed Veritarra, in their wisdom, saw the truth. It was a curse—Ezzarah's Curse—that he might further control those who proclaimed his might."

Evelyn's heart hammered so loudly she was sure it would give her away. *Was this where it all began?* "What happened?"

"Those who were *blessed* by Ezzarah turned on those who were not, the followers of Veritarra most of all. They began to exert control over them, using their accursed abilities for their own gains, following in the steps of their beloved and terrible god. The more they used their abilities for ill, the stronger they appeared to get. They believed themselves superior. Ezzarah's chosen, they called themselves. They sought to raise themselves as rulers of our beloved islands." As she spoke, Tiah led Evelyn round the room towards the tapestries, each depicting a different stage of the battles that had taken place hundreds of years ago.

"How were they stopped?" Evelyn asked, hand hovering over the pouch of Veritarra's Gift at her waist.

"In Her infinite wisdom, the blessed Goddess Veritarra gave us Her Gift so that we might defend ourselves against the Curse of Ezzarah. So that his chosen might see the truth of their actions, unfettered by the blindness of their love for a twisted god." Tiah bowed her head, placing her hand upon the pouch at her own waist with a wistful smile upon her lips. "In time, it was discovered that most mothers who ingested the dried petals of Veritarra's Gift whilst pregnant were able to imbue their unborn child with the natural ability to defend themselves against the powers."

"So that another uprising couldn't occur," Evelyn said.

Tiah's smile faded, her expression becoming anguished. "It should have been so," she said. "Hundreds and hundreds of years have passed since then. Ezzarah's chosen were cast away from the islands. They spread far and wide, across the world itself, and so, too, did Ezzarah's influence—and curse. To your kingdom, too, is it not so?" She paused and watched Evelyn for a moment, tightening her lips.

"Yes," Evelyn whispered, guilt pulsing through her veins. "It is."

Tiah looked back to the tapestries. "Those cursed by Ezzarah were no longer a trouble to our home because the cruel god himself had turned his attention elsewhere. We became complacent, relied too much upon Veritarra's blessing, believed ourselves safe from

Ezzarah and his followers. They were not in our homes anymore, and so ... Well, for centuries, we were at peace.

"But twenty-two years ago, Jonasaiah's father, my husband, was cursed by Ezzarah. Or, at least, that is when his power rose to the surface. It must have laid dormant within him for some years until ..." She turned her face away from Evelyn for a moment, shoulders slumping as she sighed. "He led a misguided group against the rest of his people. They aimed to take control of the islands for themselves. We were not expecting it, and ..." Tiah ran a trembling hand across her face. "These powers ... this *curse*, it has shaped the world around us. It has caused much pain and suffering."

Evelyn held back any questions, knowing now was not the time to press for information. Nevertheless, her mind reeled at the revelation. *I knew of something of his father's involvement; I should have guessed sooner. This is why Jonah hates the powers so much. This is why he was drawn to the Commune. A means of controlling those with these powers, this curse.* She would need to speak to him, surprised as she was at her new understanding for all he had done. *I wonder why he has been so lenient with me, knowing that I have them, too.* She chewed on her lip.

When Tiah spoke once more, Evelyn put her thoughts aside, determining to speak to Jonah later. "Suffice it to say, we will not make that mistake again. Thanks to the love and guidance of our Goddess, we have a stronger concoction of Veritarra's Gift. She showed us the way to strengthen it so that we might better protect ourselves. Those Nomarrans still born accursed have two choices: Submit to the wisdom of Veritarra, consume the Gift She has given, and live as one of us, unimpeded by the curse. Or live on Ezzarah's Isle amongst others like them. Keep to themselves, along with the remaining few who were granted a new life after the uprising."

"What about those from across the world with—with this curse? From Septima? Don't you receive any outside visitors to the islands?"

Tiah's eyes darkened; her brow furrowed. "Uninvited Septimans are no longer permitted here." She gave Evelyn a fleeting smile. "Do not worry. You came with Jonasaiah and Nehemiah. We know, then, that you may be trusted."

Evelyn nodded and smiled as best she could, guilt knifing at her gut.

"We must protect our community," Tiah continued. "The balance is a delicate one; we see that now. Veritarra has permitted us Her Gift, but we must remain vigilant. It cannot happen again. The curse has spread; we are not strong enough to fight the whole world. We can only shield ourselves against the terrible repercussions of Ezzarah's vanity and cruelty."

Evelyn nodded, finally appreciating the importance of Captain Nem's words. She could never reveal her powers here—they were feared and despised in equal measure. She was ashamed to be hiding from these people who were so kind, so open to her presence, but what other option was there? She and Jonah had a plan—possibly their only chance to defeat the Commune.

Evelyn explored the tranquil temple while Tiah sat in apparent prayer. She inhaled the scent of the flowers and felt some sense of peace fill her heart. At the back of her mind, a quiet voice acknowledged that this was the calmest she had felt in a long time. Possibly her whole life.

I could stay here forever. But then Raif and Rose's faces swam to the forefront of her mind. *They* need *me.*

When a distant bell rang from the direction of the village, Tiah placed a hand on her shoulder. "Come," she said. "It is time for you to meet *Samalah*."

THEY MADE their way back to the village. *Samalah's* living quarters, a small white house close to the larger building where they had eaten breakfast that morning, weren't far from its centre. It was much like the other homes in the village, fronted by a small garden with an array of different flowers, including the small white buds that

Samalah wore in her hair. It struck Evelyn then how much Jonah's home village was like Little Haven. The way the entire community seemed built around the central building, where they could share their feasts and speak of village news. *Hopefully not too similar.* She recalled the harsh judgements and cold indifference of the Little Haven elders towards her, a parentless orphan left in their midst, especially after the incident with Arthur.

"Here," Tiah said, pushing open the white-painted door. "Please." She proffered her hand to indicate that Evelyn should enter.

"What about you?" Evelyn asked, eyeing the dark interior with caution.

Tiah smiled. "I cannot enter with you," she said. "*Samalah* must see you alone. To know *your* heart." Her hand hovered over Evelyn's chest for a moment. "When you are done, you may visit my home and see Jonah."

Evelyn swallowed, guilt and shame snaking through her body. What if Samalah could detect the curse within her? She had no choice but to enter with Tiah watching her expectantly. She had to trust that Nem's plan was enough, that the Veritarra's Gift she consumed would sufficiently conceal her abilities.

Evelyn squared her shoulders, held her head high, and entered the building. The door closed behind her. The room was lit by a single window, the thin white sheet that hung across it muting the sunlight. Despite the warm weather, a crackling fire blazed before her. Evelyn blinked and rubbed her eyes, realising there was a fine, mist-like quality to the air. A light, floral fragrance filled her nose, and she felt calm, as she had in the temple. She moved as though in a dream, taking a seat on a white rocking chair that eased her into a rhythmic sway. Her gaze was drawn to the fireplace. She stared at it, realising it wasn't burning logs at all but rather a small pile of pulsating, glowing stones, much like there had been on Nem's ship.

"Let us sit in silence," *Samalah* said. She was seated opposite Evelyn—*Has she been there the whole time?*—smiling warmly. She was dressed in the same white robe she had worn to greet everyone at the docks when they arrived on Nem's ship. "There is pain in you, my child. I feel it." She rocked slowly on her own chair, watching Evelyn with dark eyes that danced in the glow of the firestones. "If you wish to be free of your pain, you must learn to embrace your own heart." She began humming, low and gentle, a sound that vibrated into Evelyn's very core.

Evelyn couldn't speak. A strange meditative state had taken hold, enveloping her in serenity. She couldn't have drawn herself back from it even if she'd wanted to. She leaned her head against the chair, allowing it to continue rocking her. She drifted away, the subtle incense and soft humming blanketing her as she sank into a deep unconsciousness.

But inside the depths of her mind, the calm did not—could not —last. A frantic, heart-clenching, panic overcame her.

She thrashed and turned and fought, but the darkness engulfed her.

Blond hair, blue eyes, an arrogant smile.

You'll never amount to anything.

A deep stab of pain.

He hurt me.

An inescapable sense of guilt, of wrongness.

This is my fault.

"My son wishes to marry you, and it shall be so."

"No. Your son, he ... There was no ... He forced himself on me ..."

I let it happen.

"Enough! I will not hear such lies. You are to be married. That's the end of it."

I am useless, weak, stupid.

I let it happen.

No, no, no ...

There was a flicker of fire in her heart, a power that might be unleashed...

Yet it was blocked, smothered before it could take hold. A white shield held it back, deceptively strong despite its delicate appearance.

The fire was gone. Smouldering embers, nothing more.

A distant voice spoke, drawing her back.

A dream, just a dream.

"Come back to me, my child," *Samalah* whispered. "You can come back now. I feel your pain. I see what you have suffered. I see you."

Evelyn blinked her eyes open, glad to be away from those awful memories and the feelings—*powers, it's your powers*—they unlocked within her. When she saw *Samalah* kneeling beside her, a reassuring smile upon her wrinkled face, her breathing slowed.

"You are safe here," the old woman said. "I am with you, my child. I am with you. Together, we will move through this." She patted Evelyn's hand with her own.

She must not be able to sense my powers. Veritarra's Gift has worked. She swallowed against the bubble of emotion that welled up her throat, though could already tell she would not be able to hold it back.

Their goddess accepts me. Samalah *accepts me. I am ... welcome here.*

Unable to speak, relief flooded through Evelyn as tears she'd held in for two long years began to flow down her cheeks.

CHAPTER 24

JONAH

"Here, *a'laha*. You must eat."

Jonah stretched on his bed, exhaustion flooding his body. "Thank you, Mother," he said, dragging himself to sit up and taking the bowl from her hands. She nodded and retreated to the corner of the room, sitting on a wooden chair. He eyed the sweet rice, nut bread, salted eggs, and fruit. This was the food of his childhood; it should be a comfort to him. Instead, he felt nothing. Numbness gnawed at his heart, filling his gut with a heaviness that left him with no appetite.

He ate what he could and drank down some fruit juice to keep his mother satisfied. Once he had eaten enough to do just that, he turned his attention towards her. She sat watching him, mouth downturned and hands fumbling with her robe.

He sighed. Even though she seemed to accept what he'd told her last night, he feared the light of day had cast doubt on her heart. "I will not stay here for long. If you need me to stay with the other men, I can—"

"Oh, no no." His mother rushed forward, laying her hand atop his own. "That is not my concern. You may stay here as long as you

wish—you must. Any who question it can answer to me. It's just ..."
She turned away from his gaze.

"Please," he said. "Speak openly to me. I cannot bear the idea of
unspoken thoughts between us." He gave her a weak smile. "I have
had enough of secrets." *Except for those I must keep from you, Mother.
For your own sake.* He swallowed, knowing he lied to himself, yet
powerless to stop it.

"Of course," she said, lips flicking upwards. "I want you to be
content, Jonasaiah. Happy. You are not who you were when you left
here, so full of hope for the future. I see it in your face, in your heart,
in the way you hold yourself—that *place* has hardened you. Taken
something from you that I am afraid I cannot bring back. It is as
though you have forgotten your people, forgotten our ways and
traditions and what is important in the eyes of Veritarra." She stiffened, sitting upright and pushing her shoulders back. "I wish I could
have protected you, *a'laha,* though you always had to find your own
way."

"Nothing that happened is your fault. I was a fool. I fell in love
with a man who lied and deceived me and sought only his own
power." Jonah closed his eyes, seeing Eirik's face with crystal clarity
in his mind. His heart ached with every beat. *Why must the love
remain, even amidst so much hate?*

"I see what he has done to you, Jonasaiah. The pain within you.
You must speak to *Samalah.* Allow her to see all that has happened.
To help you deal with your sadness ... To process it. It is the only way
I might get you back. Only then can you begin to rebuild your life
here with me and your people. Where you belong." Her joy was so
evident that Jonah could not bring himself to contradict her—not
yet. Let her believe he intended to stay, no matter the guilt and regret
it solidified within him.

*Let her believe she has her son back, though I fear that can never
be so.*

"I will speak to *Samalah,*" he said, squeezing her hand and standing. "Is she at home?"

"Oh, yes, but ... Well, you may need to wait." She cast her gaze downwards.

He frowned. "Why, Su'mula? It is a day of rest."

His mother hesitated a moment before speaking. "She wanted to see the girl," she said, holding her hands out and helplessly shrugging. "It is not for me to question her wishes."

Evelyn. "Why did you not wake me?" he said. "She is not used to our ways, our traditions. She is not—" *Who you think.* "I should have been told. She is my responsibility."

"No, *a'laha*, you cannot interrupt—" She grabbed his arm, attempting to pull him back, but he snatched himself free, fury blooming in his chest.

"Perhaps I have been gone too long, as you say. Perhaps I have forgotten our ways." Jonah knew the rage was not truly for his mother, but that didn't stop the furious words from pouring forth. His mother's face dropped as her eyes filled with tears. He left without a backward glance, too concerned for his friend—for the secrets they both kept—to dwell upon his mother's hurt.

By the time he reached *Samalah's* lodgings, the anger had melted away. Jonah stood in the garden in front of *Samalah's* door, burning with shame.

What have you become?

If people hadn't been watching him, he would have screamed, held his hands up to the sky, sought Veritarra's forgiveness for all the pain he had wrought on his mother, on Evelyn, on his own people from ignoring their plight because he was blinded by foolishness and love. But he held it in, pushed it down, for he could do nothing else. He cast about, meeting the eyes of any curious individuals who had stopped in their rest-day activities to watch him.

He gave a broad grin. "Good morning," he said, receiving smiles and nods and waves in return. Even so, he sensed their wariness of him. He'd been away a long time, forgotten their ways. If his mother believed it, everyone else did, too. In many ways, Evelyn appeared to have been embraced and brought into their fold with far greater ease than he had.

Mother was right. I have changed.

He drew himself up, focusing on the white door. As he did so, a memory returned. He was young, perhaps five or six, and the door was smeared with blood. Inside, the smell had been awful—blood, shit, piss.

Death.

Animals had been sacrificed in the name of Ezzarah, women raped, the home of Veritarra's chosen desecrated; a way for the rebels to show their contempt for *Samalah* and her kindness.

Women's weakness, they'd said. *See the might of Ezzarah, granted to his chosen men.*

Such atrocities were burned upon his young mind, though he rarely allowed himself to think on them.

As he stood outside *Samalah's* home, he remembered his mother's screams, his own confusion and fear.

It had been the start of the uprising that would ravage his homeland for almost a decade. By the time it was done, his father—along with many other men and women—was dead, and he had known he must leave this place.

Now was not the time to dwell on what had passed before. Jonah rose a shaking hand to the door, long since re-painted, the stains of war so easily removed. He wondered if he should knock or enter unannounced. What might be occurring within? *Could Evelyn be in danger?* It was a strange thought, for he knew *Samalah* would never cause harm, and yet the idea invaded his mind so sharply that he had no choice but to obey the impulse that followed. He pushed the door open, holding his breath as his eyes adjusted to the dim interior.

"Ah, Jonasaiah. Or Jonah, is it now?" *Samalah* greeted him from a seat in front of a hearth of firestones. "Come, join us."

Jonah blinked and saw Evelyn sitting opposite her. She sipped from a mug of steaming tea.

"Jonah," Evelyn said, smiling. "Good morning. I was going to come and see you."

Something had changed about her manner, her way of holding herself. She sat a bit taller, gave off a sense of confidence he had never before seen in her. He smelled the burning incense and glanced at the mug in her hands.

"*Samalah*," he said, falling to his knees in front of her. "I came to ensure that my friend was well and that you ... I-I was—"

"Afraid." *Samalah* nodded, studying his face. "Yes, you are full of fear and hatred; I feel it. But there is also love within you, *a'laha*, though you wish to forget it. Love intermingled with confusion, anger, lies." Her dark eyes danced; Jonah could not pull his gaze away. *I see you,* her expression said. *I know what you believe.*

You still think you can save the man you love.

But the words were not spoken aloud. Jonah could not be certain whether it was *Samalah's* voice in his head or simply his own mind finally admitting the truth to itself.

"Come, sit," *Samalah* said. "I will prepare you some tea and we will talk, all of us. I sense there is much that the two of you must share with me."

Jonah blanched at those words. *What does she know?* But he had to be patient and wait for his answer, so he did as he was told, retrieving a seat from the edge of the room and placing it next to the others. "Are you well, Evelyn?"

The pulsating light played upon her pale face, brightening her eyes. "I ... It's hard to describe," she whispered. "There is more work to do. The memories and experiences remain, but for the first time since it happened ..." She waved her hand as though to trying to catch a passing thought. "I believe I might be able to feel ... *better.*"

Jonah nodded. Though they'd never spoken outright about Evelyn's experiences, he knew well the pain she carried, had seen it in the way she used alcohol to numb herself, in the mistrust she wore like armour, and in the unspoken truth she had revealed to him in her cabin aboard Nem's ship. "I am glad."

"I understand you have both come here on a mission," *Samalah* said, handing Jonah a mug of sweet tea.

"Did Captain Nehemiah speak to you before he left?" Jonah asked.

"He did, briefly," *Samalah* said, brows creasing. "But well you know, Jonasaiah, that I see your heart's truest wishes and desires, even if you try to hide them from me."

He bowed his head. "Of course, *Samalah.* I did not mean to—"

"Hush, my child. You do not need to explain yourself here." There was an amused tone in her voice as she drank her own tea, eyes ever watchful over the rim of her mug.

Jonah had to speak, to explain his plan. With *Samalah's* support, perhaps they could obtain enough Veritarra's Gift to stop whoever they needed to—the Grand Magister, Lord Torrant, whoever else threatened innocent lives.

Eirik ... I might bring his powers under control. Bring him back to me.

He shook the thought away and inhaled sharply. "It is as you say," he said. "I have returned home for a reason, and Evelyn ... She is to help me."

"You do not mean to stay," *Samalah* responded. "How could you, with so much unfinished business to return to Septima for?"

"I left my friends behind," Evelyn said, leaning forward. "They are in danger as long as the Commune controls the kingdom. A lot of people are. We mean to stop the Grand Magister and those who carry out his orders. Lord Torrant, too. He is dangerous. Evil."

Samalah glanced at Jonah at mention of Lord Torrant's name. He dropped his gaze, unable to meet her knowing eyes.

"And how do you believe you can stop such great powers?" *Samalah* asked.

"We require Veritarra's Gift. As much as we are permitted to take. We do not know how much will be needed. Whether it will even work." Jonah sighed, suddenly aware of the great mountain of doubt and danger that stood before them. "But we must try. Nem told us of the changes that have taken place since I left. Of the ways in which it has been strengthened."

Samalah closed her eyes, letting out a low hum. Jonah glanced at Evelyn, saw his own uncertainty mirrored back at him. Had they asked too much?

"I see your true wish, Jonah." Her eyes opened, pinning him to the spot. She placed down her teacup, clasping her hands over her lap. "Our people cannot go to war. Our sacred gift from Veritarra cannot be used as a weapon."

We have come for nothing. Jonah's heart grew heavy. "I understand."

Samalah reached forward and touched his hand. "It does not need to be so, *a'laha*." She patted him before leaning back in her seat. "One man, that is all he is."

Jonah glanced up. "*Samalah?*"

The old woman stood, eyes cast towards the ceiling. She was small, what some might describe as frail, with delicate arms resting against her white robes. She remained as she was for a time, unspeaking, unmoving. Jonah looked at Evelyn. She gave him a tight smile.

Finally, *Samalah* gave a brief nod, as though answering some unheard voice. "It will be so," she whispered. She turned to Jonah and Evelyn, pulling a leather pouch from the pocket of her robe. "This is for him." She placed the pouch in Jonah's hands. "The stronger concoction of which Nehemiah spoke. It is more potent than before. Enough to paralyse any powers possessed, even *his*. This is for the sake of our people. That man must be stopped. His corruption grows by the day."

Jonah felt the weight of the pouch in his hands as though it were filled with firestones, though, in truth, it was as light as the flower from which it took its namesake.

"The Grand Magister," Evelyn said. "The head of the Commune. It could work. Take away his powers, take away the Commune's influence."

Not Eirik. Though perhaps a pinch would be all it would take to—

"The Grand Magister." *Samalah's* words broke through his thoughts. "No one else. Use it all on him. His powers are strong, drawn from others over many years; it will be necessary."

"How?" Evelyn asked. "On a weapon, perhaps?"

Samalah shook her head firmly. "No," she said. "Violence is not our path. We do not use the ways of Ezzarah to get what we want. It must be consumed."

"Consumed?" Jonah looked down at the pouch. "That is the only way?"

"It has to be eaten or drunk." *Samalah* lifted her chin towards Jonah, dark eyes studying him. "Your anger may have led you to believe you must use violence against all in the Commune, but it is not so. It is the Grand Magister who must be stopped. It is he who holds far more control than one man should. Veritarra's Gift will be enough to stop his powers. The rest will be up to you." She paused, glancing towards Evelyn, then back to Jonah. "You must promise that violence will not be used, *a'laha*. No matter what that man has done, our Goddess shows us the way. That way does not involve the spilling of blood."

Jonah looked to Evelyn, making a decision he knew she would agree with—no matter how hard it made their mission. "Then it will be so," he said. "You have my word." *Though I do not know how we will succeed.*

"And mine," Evelyn said.

Samalah bowed her head approvingly.

"Thank you, *Samalah*," Jonah said, mind whirling. *Perhaps there is still a way to save Eirik. Even without Veritarra's Gift.*

"Of course," *Samalah* said. "Evelyn, I would see you carry out our sacred rite of passage. There is some part of you—" she narrowed her eyes, grasped at the empty air before her—"that is hidden to me. The ceremony will help to clear your mind. To prove your worth. You may then receive your own pouch of Veritarra's Gift. It will bless you on your journey."

Evelyn nodded, eyes gleaming, cheeks flushed.

Her own pouch. Perhaps that will be the answer, Jonah thought. *This might be just what we need if I am to try and save Eirik.*

But will Evelyn understand?

He lifted his chin. *She will have to.*

"Thank you, *Samalah,* thank you," he said, kneeling before the woman once more, taking her weathered hands in his own. He kissed them, their warmth pressing against his palms.

Samalah gently pulled them free, and he tilted his head up to face hers. "Know this, *a'laha,*" she said. "I have granted you this pouch, but it must mean one thing: you cannot do what your heart yearns for. You must act for the good of Septima. You will fight the Commune, and you may defeat them if you are true to your cause. You cannot do this if your mind is clouded by your own desires. Your mission is against the Grand Magister; no one else."

A lump rose in Jonah's throat as he realised the true meaning of the words. *This cannot be used on the man you love.* "With Evelyn's help, we will do what must be done," he croaked. He wondered if *Samalah* knew it was a lie. Yet, if she did, she said nothing—only touched a hand to his cheek and looked down at him with those deep, brown eyes.

He stood, legs trembling, and cleared his throat. "We will do as you say."

Samalah gave a sad smile and lowered her head. "Then you choose the path of Veritarra," she said. She turned to Evelyn. "And now we will prepare for your rites. You will need to shed your past life. To show your true self. Step outside of your pain, overcome that which has caused your heart to be so heavy with doubt, hatred, and grief."

"To show my true self?" Evelyn asked, glancing at Jonah.

Jonah stepped towards her, placing a hand on her shoulder and gently squeezing. "It is okay," he said. "*Samalah* will explain. She will need some days to prepare. And I will help you."

Evelyn chewed her lip. "Okay," she said.

He smiled. "I hope you are able to find the peace you deserve." *The peace that so eludes me, especially after* Samalah's *words.*

Suddenly, he wished to be alone with his thoughts, to think about everything that had been said. "Please excuse me. I need some fresh air." He bowed his head and turned to leave. Outside, he took a deep breath, the sun warm on his skin. His legs were shaking, his wound throbbing, but he set a rapid pace, heading as far from the village as he could, away from prying eyes and concerned voices.

Before long, sweat ran down his back. He picked up some ripe *mu'ira* fruit from the ground, eating the dark flesh, the sweet juice relieving his parched throat.

When he reached the beach, he made his way towards the pier and dangled his bare feet into the ocean's cool, lapping waves. The sound of the waves settled him as he stared towards the Great Sea. Try as he might, he couldn't stop his mind from drifting where it always did—to Eirik. Where was he now, what was he doing?

Has he thought of me at all since I left?

He looked up at the sky, lips trembling. "How am I ever going to forget him?"

"Jonah?"

He wiped his face before turning to Evelyn. She tugged on the burgundy robe that swamped her slim frame and watched him from along the docks.

"I'm sorry to disturb you," she said. "It's just, I thought you might need some company. After ... Well, you seemed upset."

"I ..." Jonah shifted. "Thank you, but you did not need to check on me."

Evelyn sat beside him, splashing her feet into the sea. "Your mother took me to the temple."

"Ah. She wishes you to know of the importance of Veritarra. My mother has always been passionate about sharing our Goddess's wisdom. How did you find it?"

She was still for a moment, looking down at her lap. "She told me what happened. The uprising ... You must have been very young."

Jonah's heart jolted; blood roared in his ears. His mouth opened and closed but no words came.

"I can see why you have such hate for those with powers. Why everyone here does. The Curse of Ezzarah. I see why the Commune must have seemed the best place for you when you arrived in Septima."

"Evelyn, I—"

"It's okay. I understand, I think. After what happened here, with your father, you must have despised the powers. What they did to your home."

Jonah exhaled. "I am sorry," he said. He peered out to the distant horizon. "It would appear that I ran away only to find myself on the other side of the battle. Things are not so cleanly divided, are they?"

"No," Evelyn said. "They're not."

The soothing ocean waves washed over their feet, and a curiously comfortable silence settled over them. It was a clear day; they could see for miles out to sea.

"What *Samalah* said ... about focusing on the Grand Magister. You wanted to help him, didn't you? Lord Torrant." Evelyn didn't meet Jonah's eye as she asked the question, her gaze fixed on the distant horizon.

Jonah briefly thought about lying. But no, he had to be a different man now, a better man than he had been these past thirteen years. "Yes," he said simply. "I had hoped I could, even after ..." Jonah sighed deeply, heart aching. "Would you believe me if I told you he was a good man once?"

"No," Evelyn said firmly. "But I believe you want to believe that."

Perhaps she is right. "He was ... corrupted. Twisted by the Grand Magister."

Evelyn scoffed. "He still had a choice. *Has* a choice," she said. "As you did."

"Hmm." Jonah stared out at the waves for a moment, their gentle undulating a far cry from his endless crashing thoughts—thoughts of his early days with Eirik, of the stories they'd shared about their childhoods, their fathers. "He had a difficult upbringing. I do not think we can fully comprehend what it must have meant for him— how it must have felt—to be abandoned to the Commune at a young age."

"I was abandoned, too," Evelyn whispered. She looked up at him, eyes hardened with anger. "Not to the Commune, but my parents left me without a hope of my ever knowing who they were. Why they didn't want me." She exhaled, nostrils flaring. "It is no excuse for what he has done. For the man he has become."

Jonah bowed his head. "Perhaps." He gave Evelyn a weak smile. "Perhaps nothing is that simple."

"You said something like that to me before," Evelyn said. "Not so long ago. You told me I had a child's understanding of life."

Jonah glanced down at her, expecting to see anger in her expression but finding only resignation.

"I know I'm lacking in experience. I know my past has ..." She frowned, eyes becoming glassy. "I'm not a child, Jonah. But you were right. People do not get what they deserve. And it's shit, but it's life. If they did, Lord Torrant wouldn't have the power he does. He wouldn't have the love of a man like you." She looked away, as though embarrassed by her own words, then shook her head. "I can't say I understand it. Love does strange things to a person, doesn't it?"

Jonah snorted. "It does."

It really does.

"So," she said abruptly, casting her eyes back towards the clear blue waters of Veritarra's Bay. "You changed your name. Jonasaiah."

Jonah nodded, grateful for the subject change. It sounded strange to hear that name spoken aloud by Evelyn; it didn't belong to him anymore, hadn't since he had abandoned it for a man whose love he had been desperate to attain since the moment they met. Like the sand snake shedding its skin, it was a name long left behind.

Evelyn shifted beside him. "You don't have to explain anything to me. I just wanted to tell you—I understand. You wanted to leave behind who you were. It was the same for me when I left Little

Haven. I ... I wanted to be someone else. Forget what happened before."

He rubbed a hand along his jaw. "As did I," he said. It was all he could say, his emotions too raw, his memories too fraught.

"Well, if there's anything you need to talk about, anything you want to ..." Evelyn moved again, seeming uncomfortable. "I mean, if you need someone, that is. Since you've helped me more than once." She looked at him, eyes like precious amber reflecting the sunlight. "Sorry. I've never been much good at this kind of, well ... Anything, really."

Jonah glanced away. It was still too soon. His mind was too muddled, a confusing mix of hatred, heartbreak, love. He could hardly comprehend it, nor the plan that was weaving together in his mind even as he tried to deny it ... How could he possibly try to explain it to Evelyn? "It is enough to know you are here," he said, smiling weakly. "A friend."

"A friend," Evelyn repeated, glancing at him from the corner of her eye. She nudged him with her shoulder. "Isn't that strange?" she said, chuckling.

Despite himself, Jonah laughed. "Yes, I suppose it is."

"Not something I ever saw coming." Evelyn grinned.

"Nor I," Jonah admitted.

When their laughter had stopped, Evelyn frowned, picking at the wood of the pier. "This will work, won't it?"

He hesitated.

"Jonah?" Her voice was quiet and unsure. "It will be difficult, I know, to get close to the Grand Magister, but ..." She left the words hanging between them, the hope that he could somehow bridge the gap between reality and their destination evident.

He forced himself to smile. "Of course," he said, afraid to say more in case he should somehow betray his own determination to still try and save Eirik. "But first we must focus on your rites."

A flash of fear crossed Evelyn's eyes. "Yes," she said, staring out at the ocean. "What am I going to do?"

"You'll get through it," Jonah said. "And I'll help you."

He heard her sigh of relief, saw her shoulders relax, and felt a sense of joy at having been able to calm her. It was a feeling he had not expected, and he found a genuine smile on his lips.

"What?" Evelyn asked, narrowing her eyes up at him.

"Nothing," he said. "But ... if I am to help, I will need to know everything. You must tell me of your past, and what Veritarra will see. Perhaps, in doing so, we can understand why your powers are out of your control. And then we can seek to bring them *under* your control."

Evelyn ran her palms over her lap. "I suppose it's worth a try."

He touched a hand to her arm. "Take your time," he said. "I am here to listen when you are ready." And he was surprised at the blossoming of warmth in his chest when she smiled up at him.

"Thank you," she said.

He bowed his head and swallowed back the tightness in his throat.

23rd Day of Flourishing
5th year of King Cosmo Septimus
25th year of Grand Magister Quilliam Nubira Antellopie III

ather,

    In the months since your death, I have become increasingly distracted. I have retreated into myself, my thoughts tumbling together, my body growing weak. Jonah has been at my side, his presence a constant reassurance, and yet ... I cannot allow his love to comfort me, such is the depth of my despair.

And so it was that the Grand Magister, in his benevolence and wisdom, offered me the one opportunity that provided me a small glimmer of hope in the blackness of my misery. Until he offered it, I hadn't known I could be redeemed. I believed myself beyond saving, that the rest of my life was to be lived with this darkness engulfing my heart and soul.

Even thinking of it sets my heart to racing. I can hardly bring myself to write it down ...

Revenge.

Not against you, Father, for that chance has slipped through my grasp. After all you did to me, your lack of love, your lack of pride and honour in your own son. After forsaking me when I was just a child, leaving me to wonder what I had done to be left in that place, little more than a prisoner. My position rose, it's true, when the Grand Magister understood my powers, my worth. But there was a time when I was afraid. Afraid and alone. Unable to make a friend for fear they would be taken away. Not knowing why you did not send for me.

And still, the revenge is not against you. But there is another who may be held accountable. For what was worse than all that you did to me? It was Ythan, my beloved brother, who allowed it to happen.

Perhaps, I began to realise, it was Ythan who my deepest rage was aimed at. I always hated you. I knew you never loved me. The way you looked at me with such disdain told me all I needed to know. But Ythan ... he professed to love me. We used to play together; he taught me to fight and ride and write. We knew each other's greatest desires and fears.

Even so, Ythan allowed you to send me away. He was fifteen at the time; he could have done something, anything, to stop you. And he never came for me. For all I knew, he never spared me a thought. The letter declaring your death was the first I heard from him in fourteen years. It was curt, cold, distant—just like you always were, Father.

I am beginning to believe death might be too swift for him. My mind reels at the possibilities. One thing is certain—Ythan must pay for what he did. And when he does, I will inherit my rightful title. The Grand Magister has promised it shall be so. How I will smile to know I have taken the family estate against all of your wishes.

I know I cannot reveal my plans to Jonah; he would never approve. And so, I must choose—exact the revenge that will ease the rot in my heart, or remain as I am, the man I love by my side.

I fear the decision is already made.

Your son,

Eirik Torrant

Loyal Servant to His Benevolence

Grand Magister Quilliam Nubira Antellopie III

CHAPTER 25

HECTOR

Hector brushed his fingers across his moustache and gave a fleeting smile to those sitting around him. "Perisma's Light is finally upon us. Tomorrow, we'll enact our plan. Is everyone ready?" The eyes of his newfound friends reflected the fierce determination that burned within him, unaware as they must be of the nerves fluttering in his stomach.

"Everyone knows what's to be done," Beth said, standing beside him. After their night together, Hector had been surprised at the ease with which they'd returned to their normal routine, as though there was an unspoken agreement between them, a recognition of what they could never be.

Does it have to be so? Could we be more?

As Beth spoke, he was all too conscious of the way her shoulder brushed against his.

Grow up, old man.

That thought, he knew, was Cara's. He did his best to remain focused and not seek her out as was his reflex.

A man in his fifth decade distracted by a shoulder.

He coughed to cover the laugh that almost escaped his lips.

Beth raised her eyebrows at him. "Anything to add, Hector?"

"Hmm? Er, no. I don't think there's anything else to do but wait. Make sure you get some rest. We'll be up early tomorrow." With muttered agreements and scraping chairs, everyone moved away into their own separate groups.

"Are you okay?" Beth asked, eyes roaming his face. "You seem, I don't know, different, somehow. I'm sorry if our time together these past few days has been—"

"No," he said abruptly. "Beth, it's been wonderful spending time with you, really. I don't regret a thing." He touched her arm before turning to observe the room. "It's just … this time tomorrow, it'll be over. And I can't say with any certainty whether we'll succeed."

"I know." Beth squeezed his hand, letting go before anyone had a chance to notice. "All we can do is try. You've given us something to work towards for the first time in … well, years. A lifetime, in some cases. Don't take that onto your own shoulders as though we didn't have a choice. Everyone who's coming is old enough to know what they're getting into."

"I suppose so," Hector said, letting out a long sigh.

"I'll get us some more drinks," Beth said, moving towards the bar. Alone, Hector was left to ponder Beth's words. The fact was, if he'd been more careful in the first place, kept his eye on the boy, not been so absorbed in his own self-pity, things would have been very different. *This damned town was always going to cause us a problem.*

Of course, this all went back to his misplaced trust in Avanna. His stomach leaped at the thought; he wondered where she could be … And Rose, poor child; did she understand what had happened, why her brother and Dog weren't by her side? With a stab of regret, he realised he had been all too focused on rescuing Raif and discovering Orion's secret these past days. He'd allowed himself to forget why they'd come here, reasoning to himself that retrieving Raif would have to take priority, else he would be torn in too many directions … He didn't dare admit that he'd lost hope of finding Rose when it became clear Avanna had never arrived in Nook Town.

Rose could be long dead. We wouldn't even know. Dog, as though reading his mind, let out a low growl at his feet.

"I'm sorry, boy," he said, leaning down to pet him. "I'm trying not to lose hope. Mayhap … Mayhap everything will all work out." He allowed a brief smile, not believing his own words as much as he would like, though they seemed to settle Dog.

If all went to plan tomorrow and he was able to save Raif, they would leave Nook Town without delay. But where should they begin looking for Rose? If Avanna lied to Mak about coming to Nook Town, she could have gone anywhere in the kingdom. Heading back to the Veritas camp seemed the only option. Though it had been his home for many years, a distinct sense of dread filled him at the thought.

Cara's voice entered his mind without hesitation. *Don't distract yourself now. Not tonight. Focus.*

Her words cleared his doubts in an instant. She was right; now was not the time to think of Rose. The lad first, then uncover Orion's secret. Then flee from this place and never look back, continue hunting for answers as to where Avanna might have taken poor Rose.

"Here," Beth said, placing a fresh cup of ale before him.

"Thank you," he said, taking a grateful sip. And then, like a ray of sunshine through a dark cloud, a thought occurred to him. He began stuttering the words before he could convince himself not to. "Beth," he said. "Can I—I mean … Could you possibly, d'you think, er—"

Beth laughed, her eyes the colour of a clear summer sky. "What's wrong? You've turned the colour of a beetroot."

Hector felt himself blush even deeper, cursing himself for being a stupid old fool. *Just say it.* He drank some more ale, wiped his moustache with the back of his hand, and looked at her. "Will you leave with me? With us, I mean. Me and the lad. And Dog and Cara. She's my companion, the one … well, you know. Anyway, when we leave Nook Town, I just wondered if you'd like to join us. We'll go as soon as we can after the plan is complete."

For a moment, Beth was silent. Her eyes dropped. "Oh, Hector. I don't know."

It was his turn to smile, though it was an unsure smile that questioned itself even as it formed. He swallowed. "I'm sorry; perhaps I stepped out of line. It's just, well, I thought maybe I had nothing to lose for asking. And after the other night, you see ..."

Stop talking, you idiot. He ran a hand through his hair and picked up his tankard, ready to drown his embarrassment with a steady stream of alcohol.

"Hector," Beth said, slowly lowering her own cup to the table. Clearly flustered, she almost tipped the entire contents on the floor. "This is my home. I can't imagine leaving. Besides, there are ... others to think of." She wouldn't meet his eye as she spoke.

The others; of course. He should have known she would put her friends first. She was a mother-figure to the younger ones; it had been selfish of him to ask.

"I'm sorry. I didn't think," he said. "How could I ask you to leave and not bring everyone else?"

"Everyone else?" Beth glanced about the room. "Oh, yes, the others ... We would have to take them with us."

Hector's heart soared. *Take them with us?* He hadn't dared imagine it. Could it be possible? But doubt coursed through him. *I've shown my inability to take care of others who are left under my charge ...* Yet as he thought on it, another part of his mind—perhaps it was Cara—wondered if this was his chance at redemption.

We could save them all, take them away from this wretched place.

He sat up, looked around at everyone in the tavern, and made a decision.

"Yes," he said, briefly touching her hand. "You're right. We'll take them with us. Barnaby, too, though I haven't seen the boy in a while. I hope he'll be happy to join us."

Beth's lips quirked into the shadow of a smile. "Okay, Hector," she said. "We'll leave together."

Beth is coming with me! Hector could scarcely contain the joy in his heart. They would start anew, somewhere far from here. They could seek out Rose together. His whole body thrummed with excitement, and it took all his self-control not to lift her up and whirl her around. Instead, he cleared his throat and nodded curtly.

"Well, that's good news, indeed," he said. "Yes, excellent news." He drained his tankard and met Beth's gaze, feeling giddy enough to fly.

RAIF

"Tomorrow, the whole town will be celebrating our beloved Perisma. My daughter assures me you have studied hard every day in preparation for your admittance into our congregation. You've remained obedient, haven't asked questions." Orion's stare was hard as steel, but Raif believed he could see through the man's hard façade; he'd welcomed Raif in, hadn't he? When he had no one else to help, nowhere else to go. He was where he was supposed to be, and he filled with a growing sense of belonging. It was the first time he'd felt so content since …

Since what? What am I forgetting? He pushed the thought away, though a sharp pain prodded at his temples as he did so. He rubbed at them absentmindedly, casting Lebby a smile. With her by his side, he could be happy in Nook Town.

Help.

He shook his head, ignoring the tiny voice inside his mind, even as the pain in his temples flared. It had tried to invade his thoughts for some days now; a test of his devotion to Perisma, he had come to believe. He turned his attention to Orion, bowing his head. "Yes, Church Elder," he said.

Orion gave an approving nod. "Well, let's see. Tell me what you've learned. Let us start with Esteralla Clinkscale. What does her story tell us about those who are *accursed* with powers?"

"Powers ..." *Rose. Two dead men.* "Yes, they are a curse. Lady Esteralla used them for her own gains ... because of her selfishness. Perisma punished her with her father's death."

"No," Orion said, frowning. "Perisma did not cause her father's death. Lady Esteralla did that herself, snuffing out his mind like it was nothing." He pinched his fingers over a candle flame to illustrate his point. "Should any one person have such power?" Raif stared at the thin curl of smoke that snaked towards the ceiling.

Help me.

"Boy, pay attention." Orion slammed a fist on his desk. Raif flinched, blinking hard, his temples throbbing.

"Yes. I mean ... no, Church Elder. No one should have such power."

Rose does, your sister does, remember Rose, remember why—

Raif flitted a hand in the air, batting away the incessant thoughts. He clenched his jaw, frustrated that his mind was testing him so. "Lady Esteralla *should* have taken the death of her father as a sign. But she didn't. She chose to continue using her powers."

"She did. And well we know what happened." Orion gave a satisfied nod, his angular face cast in shadow. "Please, I would hear the story again before the morning. Lebby, sit beside me. Raif is going to regale us with Lady Esteralla's tale."

"Yes, Father," Lebby said. She smiled reassuringly at Raif.

Raif swallowed, feeling the scrutiny of their gazes upon him. "Where would you like me to begin?"

"After Lord Jeph Clinkscale's death, I think," Orion said, waving his hand with impatience. "Begin, boy."

Raif, wake up. They're lying

Please.

This time, the pain in Raif's temples flared through his whole head, down his face, and into his body. He cried out, laying a hand to his forehead, grateful that the pain ebbed away as quickly as it had started.

"Raif!" Lebby leapt to his side.

"Get back," Orion roared. Lebby did so, shuffling back to her seat. "Raif, do as I have bid. Now."

"Y-yes, of course," Raif said, rubbing at his temples. The pain dimmed enough to allow him to concentrate, though he feared it could return at any point. He swallowed. "After her father's death ..."

"Speak up," Orion snapped.

Raif waited a moment to see whether the voice or agonising pain would return. Nothing. He cleared his throat. "After her father's death, Esteralla Clinkscale was married to Lord Yeward Weystone, son of her family's closest ally, from a family of ancient bloodlines. In her state of grief, she was unable to use her powers to fight the marriage. But it didn't stay that way for long."

Lord Yeward was clear on what he expected from his new wife: a still tongue, an obedient mind, a willing lover. In their first weeks together, he'd shown himself to be even-tempered, kind, and chivalrous.

"When we have children," Yeward told his wife, "you shall be in charge of their care and education." He studied his new bride with his deep-set brown eyes. He was not a handsome man—his nose crooked, lips thin, hair receding—but he had a certain charisma about him that commanded a room. "Will that not be a position to be proud of?"

"Yes, husband," Esteralla said.

"Of course, if we're to have children, we shall have to try harder. I appreciate that you've been grieving for your father, but I did not appreciate you turning me away from your bed last night. You must learn, Esteralla, that ..."

His words faded away as she focused on pushing her untouched breakfast around her plate. Since her father's death two months prior, Esteralla had little appetite. Her once lustrous blonde hair had grown dull, her hazel eyes ringed with dark lines, her clothing loose about her delicate frame.

"Will you not look at me when I speak to you?" Lord Yeward said,

reaching forward. Lady Esteralla didn't move, allowing her husband's hand to press over her own. "My dear, did you hear me?"

At his touch, Esteralla felt a spark in her mind, like a flint being struck. Her powers had returned to her, as quickly as they had retreated two months ago. She was shocked at what they revealed about the man she had married.

His words were gentle, but the thoughts that cascaded within him were not—they were angry, full of lust and entitlement, pride and arrogance.

"Esteralla, my love," he said, lifting her chin so she had to meet his gaze, then reaching for her hand once more.

"Look at me, ungrateful bitch," said his thoughts.

Disgusted, she snatched her hand away, almost falling from her seat in her eagerness to stand. "No," she whispered. She edged away from the table, seeking to escape.

"What's wrong, my dear?" Yeward batted his eyelids, the picture of innocence. He approached her with upraised palms. "I'm not going to hurt you."

"I'll teach you a lesson, you filthy whore. How dare you turn me away? I'll show you," his mind screamed.

Her powers were coming back in earnest, and with them, the reality of the man before her; like floodwaters bursting through a dam, his vitriol washed over her, threatening to drown her beneath its sheer weight. She fell to her knees, squeezed her eyes shut. Lord Yeward's hands clamped on her shoulders as he heaved her upwards.

"Can you not hear me?" he said. "You are my wife; why will you not look at me? Why do you turn me away?"

And now the anger was pouring from his mouth as well, his thin lips curling into a sneer. His fingers pinched into her skin. She let out a cry. "You're looking at me now," he whispered.

"Husband," she said. "I am ... I am feeling unwell. May I be permitted to—"

"No," he snapped, shoving her backwards. A portrait of her father shuddered as she collided with the wall. "You have mourned for long enough. I will not stand for it, woman. I am the man of this house."

"Please," she croaked.

But he wasn't listening. His hands were clenching into fists, his rage building. She had to do something; that much was clear. A scream escaped from Lady Esteralla's lips, so loud and piercing it vibrated the glassware that sat—

"Stop." Orion sat forwards, eyes dark with rage. "What was that? Do you mock us, boy?" He turned to Lebby. "Has he been reading the sacred text?"

"Yes, Father. I made sure of it. He knows the true story."

Raif stared at her, confused. *What did I just say aloud if not the true story?*

"Explain yourself, boy."

"What do you mean?" Raif asked.

Lies, said that strange whisper in his head. This time, his temples did not hurt so much as tingle. *Whatever I said to Orion and Lebby was not the story they know, but it was the truth ... Their faith is founded on a lie.* He blinked towards Orion, squaring his jaw, sudden defiance coursing through him. "I told the story, didn't I? The true story."

"The *true* story?" Orion spat, standing up and striding towards him, his fury almost palpable in the air. He grabbed Raif by the arm and heaved him towards his desk, surprisingly strong for a man so lean. "Show me where you have read such a story." He retrieved his copy of Perisma's holy book, slammed it down, waited.

Raif stared at the tome, mouth agape. The defiance that had set him on this course was melting away all too fast. "I-I read it in here. How Lady Esteralla used her powers to overcome her husband and to find her own—"

"*No!*" Orion cried. "That is not the story of our blessed Perisma. Lord Yeward Weystone showed his lady wife the *light*, little though she deserved his mercy. He helped her to overcome her accursed powers. Though she almost killed him due to her own blind selfishness, he remained by her side." He flicked through the book and stabbed a shaking finger towards the text. "Here, boy. See the truth."

Not truth, Raif. Lies.

Raif blinked at the page. He suddenly did not feel certain about anything. Something had changed, for he no longer felt the reverent awe that had encompassed him. His mind had cleared; the strange pain seemed to have cleansed it of whatever was fogging his thoughts, and with it came a sense of overwhelming panic.

What am I doing here?

Where's Hector?

Help me, brother.

With intense clarity, he understood whose voice it was he heard. He scowled at Orion. "Where's my sister, Orion?"

Lebby stood from her seat. Orion snatched at him, trying to stop him from backing away. But Raif was too fast. He ducked away from the church elder, rolling beneath his desk. "Come back here, you ungrateful—"

"What have you done with her?" Raif shouted, filled with furious certainty. *Rose is here. Orion is keeping her from me.*

"Raif, what are you talking about?" Lebby stepped towards him, eyes wide. "Father, what's wrong with him?"

For a brief moment, Orion looked unsure, the hardness leaving his eyes. He regained himself quickly and joined his daughter's side. "He needs more tea, my dear. He's confused. Go, go quickly. Make it as strong as you can." Lebby nodded and briskly followed her father's instructions, closing the study door firmly behind her.

"No, no more tea," Raif cried. He stood on the opposite side of the desk, the church elder blocking access to the door. Raif's eyes darted about the room, his mind cycling over the same questions.

How long have I been here? Where's Hector? Where's Rose?

He narrowed his eyes at Orion, anger pulsing through his veins. "There's something in the tea, isn't there?" He clenched his hands into fists, furious at himself for being caught by the same trick Avanna had used to take Rose. "I won't drink it."

Orion stepped around the desk towards him. "Oh, you'll drink it, boy," he whispered menacingly.

Raif felt rooted to the spot by the man's iron gaze. Trying to remain defiant, he squared himself up; he was almost of a height with the church elder, and broader besides. "You can't make me."

"But what about your sister, boy?"

Raif's heart skipped a beat. "Rose? What have you done with her? You have to—"

Orion let out a low, bitter laugh. "If you wish to see her again, you'll do as I say. You'll drink your tea without question. If you don't, you will never—"

Orion froze mid-sentence as Lebby returned to the room, turning away from Raif.

She doesn't know about Rose. Some part of him was comforted by that. *Lebby hasn't deceived me.*

"Place it over here, Lebioda." The church elder now stood beside Raif. He clicked his fingers towards the desk.

Lebby placed the tray down on her father's desk and gave Raif a gentle nod. "It's your favourite. Sweetened how you like it."

Raif bristled. She may not have deceived him, but she was still complicit in whatever her father had done to him. But perhaps, if she knew the truth, she would help him. He could tell her what Orion was doing. They could save Rose together. "Lebby, your father, he's taken my—"

"Silence!" Orion roared. "Raif knows what's best for him. He knows no harm will come to *anyone* if he does what he's told." He turned to Raif, eyebrows raised. "Don't you, boy?"

He had no doubt that Orion would hurt Rose to make him comply, though he wasn't certain yet what Orion needed *him* for. "So, you admit it?" he asked. "You have my sister?"

Orion's eyes flashed darkly. He glanced at Lebby before giving the briefest of nods. Raif knew then that he could not leave this place until he had freed Rose. Until they could both flee, together.

I'll come for you, Rose.

He approached the desk and lifted the cup of steaming liquid. Bile rose in his throat at its sickly-sweet aroma. *For Rose.* He drained the cup in one.

"What do you say to my daughter, boy?"

"Thank you." Far too quickly, his legs weakened, and he grew dizzy.

"Fetch him a chair," Orion said. Lebby did as she was told.

By the time he was seated once more, the clouds were again enveloping his mind. Raif leaned his head back and sighed, the fear and anger replaced with numb indifference.

"We'll start again," Orion said, sitting behind his desk and steepling his hands. "Tell us of Lady Esteralla's story and how she was saved by the blessing of Perisma."

"Of course," Raif said. "Lord Yeward's guidance and Perisma's light was all she needed to learn the true evil of the powers bestowed upon her at birth."

And he recalled the tale word for word as it was written in Perisma's holy book, his conscious mind once again forgetting Orion's lies.

CHAPTER 27
JONAH

The firestones flickered, casting their orange glow on the blank parchment before him. Jonah rubbed his temples and let out an exasperated breath. He'd barely slept these past days, his mind torn and fraught.

He picked up the bone quill, provided without question by his mother along with two blank pages, and let the tip hover until a black drop of ink dripped onto the page. He left it there, a sign of his hesitation that he hoped Eirik would notice. Before he could over-think his words or convince himself not to write them at all, he put pen to paper and poured out his pain.

Eirik—my love,

Can I even call you that anymore? All I know is to say it is to be true to myself and to the endless aching of my broken heart, damned fool that I am.

I scarcely know what to write or how to explain the thoughts cascading through my mind. They have been there since I left you that awful morning, which feels a lifetime ago, though it is mere weeks and days.

Sometimes I wish I could turn back, return to that moment, see you again—but would I make a different decision? In honesty, my dear Eirik, I do not know. I do not wish to ever see what you did to that poor young man again. The horror of your actions was too far from the man I love, the man I thought I knew after so many years together.

Even so, my abrupt departure, whether the right thing to do or not, has left a gaping hole within me. What happened that day gave me the answer I had been seeking for seven long years, and yet ... it also left me with further questions, still unanswered.

In the days and weeks since, I find myself thinking of your last words and your face, never fading from my memory, a mask of anguish. You begged me to stay. You told me we could go back to what we were before. But after you admitted, that awful morning not so long ago, what you chose over our love, how you came to inherit your title and family land ... How could you believe we could ever be the same again after I had seen the truth of it? Perhaps you knew what would happen when I found out; and so, you kept it hidden for as long as you could.

Were you always so filled with vengeance? Should I have known what you were capable of when, in our early days together, you spoke to me of your hatred for your father? When you spoke with bitterness about your beloved brother?

Having seen what you kept locked away in that damp, miserable base-ment, I know the door has been closed on what we were. We can <u>never</u> go back.

And yet ... there is a part of me that dares to hope. Perhaps we cannot go back, but can we go forward?

So I write to you with that singular thought in mind, one that I am not sure you will even—

There was a sharp rap upon the door.

"Jonasaiah?" his mother called. She'd awoken early to help prepare for Evelyn's rite of passage. "A'laha, are you ready? It is time."

Is it morning already? He scanned the page before him, the words he'd written barely scratching the surface of what he wanted to say.

The door creaked as it was pushed open. He folded the page swiftly, tucking it within his robes for safekeeping. He must keep it concealed, sure as he was that no one would understand why he had to write it.

He would finish it as soon as he could. When he and Evelyn returned to Septima, he would find a messenger to dispatch it as discreetly as possible. Until then, he would hold it close to his chest and bide his time.

CHAPTER 28
EVELYN

"Are you ready, my child?"

No.

"Yes," Evelyn said. *Samalah* gave her a measuring look, deep brown eyes shrouded by wrinkled black skin. *She knows my doubts.*

"If you submit yourself to Veritarra, you will be free," *Samalah* said. "But you must surrender completely or the ceremony will not work. Our Goddess bestows Her kindness and love on those who are willing to accept themselves. To reveal their soul"—*Samalah's* hand hovered over her chest—"and their heart."

"Okay," Evelyn whispered, trying to ignore the strange way her stomach fluttered at the words. *My powers. This could be dangerous.*

Samalah began chanting under her breath, affixing small white flowers to Evelyn's hair. Though unable to understand the words, Evelyn found it soothing to have the old woman close, deft hands working to prepare her for the upcoming rite of passage. She drank the tea, prepared by *Samalah*, without question, its sweet and flowery flavour helping to assuage her nerves.

"Thank you," she said. "For allowing me to do this."

"You wish to do the work of Veritarra, but there will be a choice to make. It is not an easy path. You will need to look into yourself, to discover who you truly are." *Samalah* briefly cupped Evelyn's chin. "You will need to *choose* who you will be."

Evelyn drank more tea to avoid responding, her trepidation growing. There was a knock on the door. For a moment, *Samalah* whispered under her breath, eyes closed. When she was done, she stepped back and regarded Evelyn. Giving a satisfied nod, she turned to the door.

"Enter," she said.

Jonah entered wearing dark brown robes, his face fresh-shaven and black curls cropped short. Despite this, exhaustion glazed his eyes. His hand rested upon his chest as though trying to soothe a deep ache.

"I will give you a moment," *Samalah* said. "And then we must begin."

"Thank you," Evelyn said. The old woman moved towards Jonah, placed a hand upon his shoulder without a word, and then left the room. "Are you well?" she asked.

Jonah laughed and moved to sit opposite her. "You do not need to be so formal," he said.

"Sorry," she said, grinning. "Nerves, I suppose." She shifted in her seat, careful not to loosen the flowers in her short hair. She pulled at the white robe she'd been given, self-conscious about the significance of its colour. "I haven't seen you properly in days. I came to see you at your mother's house, but she said you'd been leaving early, before sunrise. I couldn't find you anywhere." She studied his face, though it remained unreadable. "Are you ... okay?"

"I ..." He let out a shaky breath, gave an unconvincing smile. "Please do not worry about me. I thought it was best to give you space while you prepared." He reached forward and patted her leg. "How are *you* feeling?"

Evelyn looked down at his hand, now back at his side, wondering when she'd started taking comfort from physical contact rather than shrinking away from it. "Scared," she said. "This is an important ceremony, isn't it? What if my, my—"

"I am not worried," Jonah said firmly. He sat back in his chair. "There have been those before who have had powers and have submitted to Veritarra. Being true to *yourself* allows the ceremony to be a success. This is a tradition, and it is one many have been through over the years." He nodded, dark eyes locking with hers. "No, I am not worried. Veritarra bestows Her gifts on those of us who are worthy, shows us who we are."

"Worthy?" Evelyn's stomach lurched. "What if—"

"You are not worthy?" Jonah laughed, not unkindly. "Evelyn, that is the fear that each of us has before it begins. But you must hold the belief in your heart—you *are* worthy. We all are, if we are true to ourselves. Submit yourself to Veritarra, allow Her to see who you are. You are stronger than you know."

You'll never amount to anything. She swallowed. "Has anyone ever ... failed?"

A darkness flashed across Jonah's face. He hesitated before saying, "Yes."

"Who was it? What happened to—"

A knock at the door stopped Evelyn from saying any more. Tiah peeked into the room. "It is time," she said. "Come, Jonah. Evelyn must be alone." She glanced at Evelyn. "Wait here, child."

"I will see you soon," Jonah said. He touched her arm, the warmth of his hand giving her a small modicum of strength. But when he departed and she was alone, she couldn't help but wonder, *Will I be one of the unworthy? What of my powers? I should have done more to prepare.*

Perhaps I should have been honest with Samalah *about who I am. Revealed the truth. Faced the consequences.*

But it was too late; all she could do was wait. With each passing moment, Evelyn's apprehension grew. She finished her tea and placed the cup down. She fidgeted her legs, fiddled with her robes.

Her gaze kept flitting towards the door; she was impatient to begin yet afraid of what was to come.

What's taking so long? She shifted in the seat and straightened her robes. Finally, she could stand it no longer. Heart pounding, she stood. With forced determination, she marched towards the door and reached out to open it.

"Evelyn."

That voice was like a punch to the gut, driving the wind from her lungs. It took all her effort not to collapse to the floor. She leaned a hand against the wall, her breathing fast and shallow.

"Evelyn, what are you doing?"

"I ... I ..." She closed her eyes, inhaled sharply, and turned around. Her heart drummed a thunderous beat; the blood roared in her ears. "Arthur," she whispered. She rubbed her eyes, hoping he would disappear. But when she opened them again, there he stood, smiling in the same easy, self-satisfied manner he always had.

"What are you doing here?"

No. How is this possible?

He walked towards her, his movements full of self-assurance and arrogance. "It's good to see you."

Evelyn choked with indignation. "I asked you a question," she said through gritted teeth. "How are you here? Little Haven ... the Commune took everyone. No, this isn't possible."

Arthur's laugh was a harsh bark of indifference. "And yet here I stand. I always thought you were ... *slow*." Without warning, he darted towards her just as he had two years ago. He grasped her wrists, pushing her back against the wall. "And I was right, wasn't I?"

Pinpricks rose along her arms and down her back, and she did her best to twist away from him. "Get off me," she spat. To her surprise, he did.

"Please accept my apologies," he said, straightening his tunic. He walked towards *Samalah's* herb cabinet and leaned down to examine the jars, hands clasped behind his back. "I know it's been some time since we last saw each other. It must be a shock for you."

Evelyn edged towards the door, wondering whether she could make her escape. Jonah must still be close by; perhaps she could call for him. He would help her since they were friends now.

"If truth be told, I was sorely disappointed when you ran away. The thought of marrying you ... Well, I must have wanted it more than I thought."

Her hand was resting on the door handle. All she had to do was turn and pull.

"Evidently, you didn't feel the same." Arthur turned with the suddenness of a striking snake, a strange smile playing on his lips. It was almost wistful. "Going somewhere?"

Evelyn shook her head, ashamed of the fear that spiked through her. It was then she realised the truth—he'd taken everything from her. Even with all that had happened since that day, this boy, what he'd done, lay at her core. Dictating what she did, who she trusted, the choices she made. She despised what she had become because of him—a shell of her former self, the very thing he predicted would be her future.

You'll never amount to anything.

In that moment, she made a decision and formed a plan.

"Good. Here, sit. I'll make us some tea."

Evelyn shuffled towards the seat *Samalah* had prepared for her not so long ago. *Where is she?* As she glanced around the room, she took note of a sword leaning against the fireplace. Not just any sword but the very sword, battered and tarnished as it was, that she'd taken from Little Haven. She hadn't seen it since ...

Lord Torrant's home.

Her heart soared, though she kept her expression as blank as possible. Strange that it was here, but then, so was Arthur. If it gave her an advantage over him, allowed her to see through her plan, all the better; she wouldn't question its presence. She sat down in the seat closest to it, ensuring it was within reach.

Arthur completed the tea preparation and brought her a steaming mug, grinning proudly. Inside was a bitter-smelling liquid. "It's a special concoction of mine," he said, sitting opposite. Despite the steam curling from it, he took a generous gulp and let out a satisfied exhale. "Won't you try some?"

She looked down into her cup. The tea appeared to be swirling of its own accord. It was dark and dense, with the consistency of thick blood gravy. "No," she said, bile rising. "I don't think so."

Arthur's face dropped. He wiped the back of his hand across his mouth and stood, dropping his mug so it shattered, its remaining contents splashing across the floor. He didn't even flinch at the sound, instead moving to stand over her. He placed his arms on either side of her, leering.

"You always were ungrateful. I gave you my time and energy, teaching you to hunt when you didn't even *belong* in Little Haven. You were abandoned, a baby who no one wanted." He tilted his head. "Now drink before I lose my patience." He jerked the mug towards her mouth, splashing some of the foul liquid down her front. The stain spread like blood, far too red against the crisp white of the robes.

Don't drink it, don't drink it.

Despite her inward resistance, Evelyn's trembling hand, as though it was completely out of her control, moved the tea the final distance to her lips. The smell and taste hit her at once, and she fought not to gag on the rancid concoction. When she was finally able to swallow, she looked up and saw the satisfaction in Arthur's eyes. The liquid burned all the way down to her stomach. Though the liquid was scorchingly hot, a cold chill coursed through her body.

"There, that wasn't so hard now, was it?" He turned from her and began walking about the room again, hands once more clasped at his back. "Do you know how upset my mother was when she discovered the wedding wouldn't go ahead? She knew how *privileged* you were to be chosen by me. It simply made no sense. Are you listening?" He paused, frowning at her.

Evelyn had leaned to the side while his back was to her, trying to get as close to the sword as she could. With Arthur's attention back on her, she relaxed into the chair and nodded briskly. "Of course," she said. "Your mother was upset."

"She was," Arthur said, sighing. "She had already begun to make preparations, you know. Such an embarrassment for a village elder."

He was facing away; this might be her only chance. She leaned towards the sword again, stretching her arm as far as she could. Her fingers brushed the hilt. She had to be careful; just a nudge might knock it over. But her arm was shaking, her mind was slower than it should be, her confusion at the strange situation marred her thoughts, and—

Clang.

The metallic sound of the sword hitting the floor reverberated around the room, and Arthur smirked. "I'm sorry, do you need some help with that?"

"No, I, uh ..." Evelyn shrank back into the chair. Arthur knelt down and picked it up, removing it from its sheath and examining the blade.

"It's rather well used but could do the job, no doubt." His blue eyes glinted. "Perhaps we should find out how sharp it is."

"No!" Evelyn couldn't stand it any longer. As he approached, she flung her foot out, and it connected with his groin. He cried out and crumpled over. With no time to hesitate, Evelyn leaped from her chair and made for the door. Her hands fumbled with the handle as she heard him stand.

"You'll pay for that," he wheezed.

No, no.

She pulled the door open, blinded for a moment by the beaming daylight.

"Jonah!" she cried. "*Samalah!*" A few paces outside and she realised there was something very wrong. She glanced about in disbelief.

This can't be.

She was ... home.

Little Haven.

"Welcome back," Arthur said, watching her like a hawk from the doorway. "You never could escape this place, you know."

"What is going on?" she said, temporarily forgetting the sword now sheathed at Arthur's waist. The village was intact. No fire had destroyed the central hut, as Raif had described had happened. Little Haven was as it had been the morning she'd left. She could even hear birds singing in Haven Forest. "Where is everyone?"

"They're out on a hunt," Arthur said, examining his fingernails. "It's as I said—you really are abominably slow."

"A hunt? What are they hunting?"

"Oh, Evelyn." Arthur sighed, hand hovering over the sword hilt. "You, of course." He drew the sword and lunged towards her. Evelyn willed her leaden legs into action, darting towards the tree line behind them.

Though she almost tripped on the undergrowth more than once, she somehow kept her balance. Her robes snagged and ripped and tore with every step, but still she kept going. Pulse rushing in her ears, she could hear no other sound but was sure Arthur remained close.

Don't stop. Don't let him catch you.

Mouth dry, legs heavy, lungs burning, she wove her way through the trees of Haven Forest.

Go, go, go. Remember what Bessie said. Don't look back.

She ran faster than she thought was possible. Her arms were covered in cuts and scrapes; the scent of the forest's sweet decay filled her nostrils.

Run, or he will kill you. Don't stop, no matter what—

Suddenly, she passed from the dense tree line into a clearing. She leaned over to catch her breath, wishing she had a skin of water—or, better yet, wine—to ease her parched throat.

Leaves rustled behind her. "You can't escape me, you know," Arthur said. He wasn't even out of breath. *No.* Frozen to the spot,

Evelyn watched him walk across the clearing behind her. *The clearing.*

She knew this place.

The Old Woods. Raif and Rose, Dog and Bert. Two men, so much blood.

We were running.

I was supposed to protect them. I failed.

I was never good enough. I could never have helped them.

She ran a hand over her forehead, dripping with sweat, and tried to fathom how they could be here, even as part of her knew it was all part of the trial she faced. Still, she could not quell the terror rising within her.

"What shall we do about this?" Arthur said, drawing her attention to where he stood. He was leaning over something long, wrapped in a green cloth, toeing it with his fine black boots.

Unable to walk another step, Evelyn fell to her knees and crawled forward. *My robes will be ruined.* She almost laughed at the absurdity of the thought.

Arthur was kneeling down, regarding the object with interest.

Object ... no, it was no object.

She almost screamed.

Not green cloth; a green cloak. *Her* green cloak. Long auburn hair fanned out on the rotting brown leaves. Lying on her side, face mottled with bruises and dried blood.

"She's still alive," Arthur said. He stroked a hand across the face —*my face*—with surprising gentleness. Without warning, he moved the unconscious body—*it's me, how can it be me?*—onto its back and loosened the cloak. "And now to make use of the sword." He retrieved it in one swift movement, poking the point of the blade to the top of her—*my*—tunic.

"No!" Evelyn cried, leaping towards him, trying to pry the sword out of his hands.

"How dare you touch me!" he shouted, flinging her backwards. She landed with a thud. Winded, she lifted her head, unable to do anything but watch as he hacked the sword downwards, apparently caring little for any injury he might inflict. The sound of cloth ripping was almost too much to bear.

"Hmm, sharp enough despite its dull appearance," Arthur said in a carefree tone.

As he cut clothing away, the other her began to stir. A quiet groan passed her lips—*my lips, they're my lips. Please don't do this*—though her eyes remained closed.

"Please," she whispered, though it was useless; she already knew how this would play out. "Please, please, please." She'd been here before. As she had then, she remained unmoving, frozen, petrified. All she could do was watch.

Arthur's excitement was clear. Beneath the tunic, the other Evelyn's pale white skin was marked with dark purple bruises. He glanced over his shoulder, lips peeled into a grin. He dropped the sword at his feet and began to undo his trousers.

"Won't be long," he said. "I just need to see to this."

It was the casual tone in which he spoke, or perhaps the easy grin he gave her, that sent a surge of anger through Evelyn. This time, she would not let him see his plan through. She ran forward, shrieking at the top of her lungs. "No!" she cried. "No, no, no!" She ran into him, knocking him to the ground with a satisfying thud. She pummelled him with her fists, teeth bared, wanting him to feel the pain she had carried for over two years.

Yet still, he laughed.

He fought back, slapping her fists away with ease. He clamped a hand around her throat. He was so much bigger than her, so much stronger. He threw her off him to the ground again, so hard she couldn't even gain a breath to sob.

Where are my powers?

From somewhere distant, a voice whispered, *You do not need powers to overcome this, child. You are strong enough without them.* Evelyn was barely able to comprehend the words before Arthur was leaning over her.

"Now lie there and *watch*," he hissed. He moved over to the half-conscious, other Evelyn, and began fumbling with her trousers. He sneered back at her, a smug glint in his eye that she recalled all too well from that awful day.

And then it began. He was atop the other Evelyn, thrusting and grunting. Beneath him, the other Evelyn's eyes fluttered open, and her mouth flew open in a silent screech of terror. The moment came when her powers should have come—*had come*, two years ago—but they didn't.

I cannot rely on them; they are never there when I want them. It's up to me to end this. She grimaced as she eased herself up from the ground. Arthur was too distracted now, too focused on his own pleasure.

"No," she whispered. She looked down, meeting the gaze of herself, though the other Evelyn's eyes had become glazed and distant, as though she was no longer present in the moment. Arthur's terrible groans continued. A quiet rage bubbled within her, though she sensed it was not linked to her powers, but rather, to the injustice she had faced at the hands of this young man who had taken everything from her. No longer would she shut it away; no longer would she blame herself.

"No more," she muttered. Evelyn peered around for the sword. There, on the ground behind Arthur. "No more, you bastard." She stumbled forward, legs shaking. She lunged for the sword, clasping her hand around it as Arthur let out one last, loud groan. He turned to her, about to say something—and saw what she held. His eyes widened. Evelyn lifted the sword. There was to be no hesitation.

Now.

A scream burst forth, a cry of anguish that had been held back for two long years, walled inside and buried deep.

Her pain and trauma, expressed at last.

She took hold of it and set it free from herself, from the deepest parts of her mind where it had been locked away, where it had rotted her from within like black mould. As she did so, she became aware that her powers were also surging to the surface, but this time, they were in her control.

Despite what that voice had said—that she did not *need* her powers—she revelled in the strength they gave her as she swung the sword. It met Arthur's chest. He choked, surprise, irritation, and then pain passing over his blue eyes. He fell to his knees as blood bubbled from his lips.

"Please," he wheezed. He looked his age in that moment, a boy of sixteen, unsure and afraid. "Please don't do this."

Evelyn smirked down at him with grim satisfaction. "No. You don't get to beg." She hacked the sword downwards, jolted as it connected with his perfect, hideous face. The blade bit into his flesh and bone, jarring Evelyn's arms. The sound he made was inhuman in its agony.

She did not care.

She pulled the sword free, lifted it, slashing down again and again.

And again, again, again ...

Until there was nothing left but blood, bone, and pulp, the overwhelming stench of iron, the sound of her racing heart. Only then did she know she'd done enough.

She slumped onto the forest floor, hands slick and red, robes soaked with crimson, and glanced over to where the other her had lain ... yet she was gone, nothing remaining but the emerald green cloak she'd been wrapped in as a child, the one she'd had for so many years until Lord Torrant had taken it from her.

Evelyn stared up at the sky, letting out a breath she'd been holding for far too long. "He can't hurt you any longer."

He can't hurt you.

CHAPTER 29
HECTOR

This is it. This is our chance. The thought floated to the forefront of Hector's mind as he roused himself from sleep. It was the morning of the town's sacred ceremony. The morning when their plans would be played out, and one way or another, be seen through to the end.

To his left, Beth was curled beneath a white woollen blanket, letting out deep, peaceful breaths. He smiled. *When did she come to mean so much to me?* The growing feeling was quite alarming in its voracity, and he scolded himself for allowing it to take hold. He reached towards her, wanting to run his hand through her long, dark hair.

Hector.

He drew his hand back and turned to find Cara's bright yellow eyes peering up at him.

"What have I told you about coming here?" he whispered, irritated he hadn't sensed her approach.

I wouldn't have come, old man, but there's someone at the gate. Wants to see you.

Hector frowned. *How do you know?*

He told me. Cara blinked nonchalantly.

What? He spoke to you?

He did. Cara stared up at him, infuriatingly unhelpful. Hector rolled his eyes and hurried to retrieve his shirt from the floor where it had been abandoned the night before, doing his best to move quietly so as not to waken Beth. He hissed as he stood back up, rubbing a hand across the scar on his thigh. *Come on, I need to find out who this is.*

Cara turned and stalked from the bedroom towards the front door of the rundown home. On his way past, Hector leaned down to Dog, who had taken to sleeping on a pile of musty old blankets in the sorry excuse for a kitchen. "Stay here, boy. Won't be long." Dog blinked up at him, then nestled back down into his makeshift bed.

Hector picked up his cloak from the rickety kitchen table and followed Cara into the chill morning air. It had rained overnight, so the ground was slick with mud and puddles. His companion darted away, bright white in the early morning darkness. He hurried behind, careful not to slip, eager to see who was waiting for him. When he turned the corner around the last of the houses and gained sight of the gate, he let out a gasp.

"It can't be," he muttered, his guard immediately up.

Come on. Cara stopped and waited for him. *He seemed scared when he spoke to me. I don't think he means you any harm.*

Hector grunted. *Bit bloody late if he does, isn't it?*

He approached the gate and frowned at the Nomarran waiting for him. "Elussius, I presume."

The bald man regarded him, lips pursed and eyes unreadable. "Yes. Hector, you will forgive me for using your animal to reach you. I did not think it wise to simply approach your home and expect you to listen."

Hector frowned down at Cara. "How did you know she was mine?"

"She appeared in Nook Town when you did." The Nomarran gave Cara a nod. "She is good at hiding, but I spotted her a few times."

"And you didn't tell Orion?"

Elussius shook his head and glanced over his shoulder. "No. There is no time to explain, but my relationship with that man has changed of late. I have seen ... well, I have seen enough to know that my people and I must leave Nook Town. I can no longer do what he asks of me."

Hector's heart skipped a beat. "And what *has* he asked of you?"

Elussius reached into his pocket and retrieved a jangling ring of keys, which he passed through the gate to Hector. "You will see."

Hector took the keys, mouth dry. "See what? How do I know I can—"

"This key opens your gate here. Go to Orion's home. He will not be there, for he has spent the night in the church, preparing for the ceremony. This key will open the front door, and this the door in his study. He has trusted me because I have done as he's ordered me for ten years. My people were happy here, and so I did not question it. Even as his madness worsened, I did not withdraw my aid and support. I granted him the use of our sacred gift"—he touched a hand to the pouch at his belt, expression pained—"but no more. He has asked too much of me."

Hector took the keys, cold in his palm. "You mean to leave."

Elussius nodded. As if on cue, a Nomarran man in a dark brown robe approached. "It is time, Elussius."

"I must go." Elussius made to leave, then glanced over his shoulder. "I only ask that you forgive me for what I have done. I will pray to Veritarra for Her forgiveness, though I cannot say I deserve it." With that, he and the other Nomarran moved down the street towards the Nook Town gate.

Hector looked down at Cara. "Well," he muttered, "what do you make of that?"

Cara flitted round his legs. *I think it's time to visit Orion's, don't you?*

"I don't see that we have any choice." Hector lifted the key to the Blight gate and slotted it into the lock, half expecting it not to work.

When it clicked open, he raised an eyebrow. "That's one down, anyway." He looked over his shoulder, checking that no one else had noticed. He'd make sure he was back before they were due to gather in the tavern. And perhaps he could fill them in on some of the mysteries they had been seeking to uncover that day. He imagined Beth's face when he was able to tell her of Elussius's help, of the secrets Orion kept.

With a firm nod to himself, Hector and his Cara stalked out of the unlocked gate into the eerily quiet streets, making their way towards Orion's home. "Keep to the shadows, girl," he whispered to his companion.

She looked up at him with those bright yellow eyes. *I think the time for caution has passed, old man. It's now or never.*

He harrumphed, though he did not disagree. He would need to be quick and return to the tavern in time to meet everyone else.

Outside the Blight, the streets were empty, though lamplight flickered in the windows of most homes. Hector kept his head down, hood pulled up, and stalked through the pre-dawn morning like a shadow.

Before he knew it, he was in front of the church, peering up at its steepled outline, dark against the deep pinks and purples of the early morning sky. The symbol of Perisma, gold hands raised up towards the sun, glowed even in the pre-dawn light. Beside the church was Orion's home, windows shuttered, black door sealed tight. Hector took it as an ominous warning to any who might think of trespassing: *This is a place where sinister secrets are kept; do not dare enter.*

Hector shuddered. *Despite his preaching of Perisma's light, Orion is a man of darkness and deceit.* Cara purred her agreement. Hector looked up, studying the windows. From the outside, all appeared eerily quiet. Suddenly, his gut filled with doubt. He swallowed. "This seems too easy, doesn't it?" He glanced down at Cara. "Elussius coming to us, giving us the key. Could be a trap. Perhaps we should tell the others. Let the plan go ahead as expected."

Cara gave him a scathing look. *This might be our only chance to get in there.* She ran for the door, a white blur across the street.

"Cursed, headstrong creature," Hector muttered, running after her. He retrieved the ring of keys and opened the door, his palms moist with sweat. Inside, the house was still and dark. Cara disappeared behind the door, and Hector hurried behind, not wanting her to be in that accursed place alone. He blinked as his eyes adjusted to the dimly lit hallway beyond the door. *Where has she gone?* He stepped towards the stairway, wondering whether Raif was still in his room. "Cara," he hissed, irritation rising. He cast his gaze all about, creeping further inside. "Where are you? Stubborn bloody—"

He froze mid-sentence, mouth agape. His companion was sitting by the door beyond the staircase, the locked door behind which Orion's blackest secrets lay. His fingers curled around the ring of keys as he crept closer to Cara.

"This is it."

Elussius wanted us to see whatever was behind here.

Hector nodded, his heart pounding. "He did. Come, come here." His companion obeyed, likely sharing in his apprehension. "Stay out here. Keep watch."

Always.

With a final nod towards Cara, he moved forward with a confidence he did not feel. Inside the room, an oil lamp burned atop a small wooden table beside the door. Hector retrieved it and held it high, surveying the room. There was a great wooden desk, bookcases piled high with ancient tomes, and an empty fireplace, the air musty and cold.

What needed locking away in here?

The silence in the room was suffocating. Hector's breath caught in his throat as he looked around, willing himself to find something, *anything*, that might explain Dog's reaction to this room. Why Orion kept it locked.

And then he felt it—a near-imperceptible breeze in the air. He followed it towards a bookcase at the rear of the room.

It was crooked, a gap visible behind it. He put the lamp on a nearby cabinet and pushed the bookcase with a grunt. It moved with ease, as though used to being slid back and forth in this very motion. Retrieving the lamp, he held it into the open archway he'd revealed.

"A concealed stairway." He pursed his lips. "Suitably suspicious." He glanced back to the hallway where Cara awaited him and considered fleeing. Something was very wrong here—he sensed that in his core—and yet, he had to know. "I've come this far."

Be careful.

He steeled himself, trying to ignore the fluttering drumbeat of his heart, and began his descent into the gloom-ridden stairwell. As he made his way down, his discomfort and unease grew into a tangible feeling. His head pounded, shoulders tightened, stomach clenched into a hard knot.

Only one explanation ...

At the bottom was a door. His legs moved as though through water, slow and clumsy. He reached for the handle with a quivering hand, turned and pushed his weight into it. As soon as he stepped inside, he collapsed to his knees. Leaning forward, he placed his head on the floor as an agonising pain stabbed into his skull. He released his hold on the lamp and pressed his fingers against his temples, sucking on his lips to keep back the scream threatening to burst forth.

This was much worse than he could ever have imagined.

Orion, what have you done?

He inhaled slowly and deeply, lungs burning.

Pull yourself together.

He gritted his teeth and opened his aching eyes, pushing through the abominable agony that near paralysed his whole body.

You have to fight through it.

Though he knew Cara's thoughts could not reach him in such a place, he imagined her encouraging him on.

We've come too far to let them win now.

After several jerking movements, he grasped for the lamp and heaved himself to his feet using a nearby table for support. Once upright, he took a moment to regain his focus, to ground himself, feel his feet on the floor, his hands upon the smooth wooden surface against which they rested.

I have to hurry.

Blinking through his blurred vision, he examined the room. On the floor, he could just make out the scattered powder of Veritarra's Gift. *Orion, you bastard. What is this?* Elussius had told him, though, hadn't he? That he had provided secret knowledge of the Nomarran flower. Provided some way of rendering Veritarra's Gift even more effective against those with powers. It took all of Hector's willpower to remain upright. His mind was a flurry of desperate thoughts as he fought to stop from blacking out.

This room must have been used to contain someone extremely powerful.

Or dangerous.

To his left was a wooden chair; beside it, a table covered in jars, a burner lamp, various metal instruments. He stumbled towards them, needing to learn all he could. The chair had leather straps on its arms and legs—and it was *small*. Hector would barely have been able to fit in it, despite his slight stature.

This held a child.

His heart thudded as the pieces clicked together.

Hector edged from the chair to the table of instruments. His vision grew more and more unfocused; he was running out of time. He had to get away from this room or risk falling unconscious and being discovered here by Orion. He fumbled with the items on the table, the likes of which he'd never seen before. He knocked one of the jars aside, watched it fall and smash, saw the powder inside spill to the floor.

It was then that he saw it, sitting inside a small bowl, glinting in the flickering light of the lamp.

He pinched it between his fingers, half expecting it not to be there, hoping his mind was playing tricks on him. Somewhere deep in the recesses of his mind, he chanted an old prayer that his father had taught him as a boy.

Perisma protect me,

Grant me your light,

Perisma guide me,

To see the truth in all things.

Shit.

Please, please, don't be what I think you are...

But there was no denying it as the light played upon its surface.

A ringlet of blonde hair.

"No!" He crashed to his knees once more. "Forgive me, Rose." He clasped the curl to his chest. Whatever had transpired here, Raif could have had no part in it. The lad had been kept as much in the dark as he had.

What has Orion done with her?

All thoughts of the plan fled from his mind; he had to help Rose, and now. There could be no delay; waiting might cost the young girl her life. Whatever Orion was doing, this room proved that Rose was in grave danger. This was something undertaken over the course of weeks, perhaps months. This room hadn't been set up quickly ... Had Orion been waiting for someone to test it on?

Once they heard about Rose from Avanna, learned of her powers, they surely couldn't resist.

"No, no, no, what have I done?" he croaked.

He turned on his heel and lurched back towards the door, his body and mind weakening by the minute. By the time he reached the bottom of the stairs, he was crawling. The determination not to fail Rose again spurred him onwards. "Come on, get up," he said through gritted teeth. "Fuck. This is your fault. Get up, old man. Save her." His own words urged him up, each stair like a vast mountain for his unresponsive legs.

As he dragged himself further from the room, its effects on him waned. He reached out for Cara, wanting to tell her what he'd found.

Cara, my love, we must go to the church.

No response.

Cara, where are you?

Something was wrong.

He was at the top of the stairs. He pulled himself up at the door, lurched into the dim hallway, searched for his beloved ...

"Cara! We must—"

Someone stepped out of the darkness. Hector glimpsed a face, a townsperson whose name evaded him, as a blunt instrument was raised over his head. His hands were half-raised in a useless protective gesture when the object connected with his temple.

As he fell to the ground, consciousness fading, he had one final thought.

I've failed again.

39th Day of Reaping

5th year of King Cosmo Septimus

25th year of Grand Magister Quilliam Nubira Antellopie III

J onah,

I know it has been some time since last we saw each other and that the manner of our parting was difficult. Too much has happened to explain in writing. Perhaps there are some things that must remain unsaid between us.

Nevertheless, I am writing now to ask for your forgiveness—despite my lack of explanation—and to invite you to join my household once more.

It is my hope that the enclosed red cloak will convince you of my sincerity in requesting your return. Be assured, your position as commander will be a great honour. Together, we can do the work of the Commune and ensure the safety of all in Septima.

Should you choose to accept this offer, I will await you at the Torrant Estate. I will be here until the end of autumn harvest.

I trust you know ~~how much I have missed you~~ *this is the best course of action for both of us.*

Sincerest regards,

Lord Eirik Torrant

Loyal Servant to His Benevolence

Grand Magister Quilliam Nubira Antellopie III

CHAPTER 30

JONAH

Jonah started, awaking from a restless nap, squinting at the sunlight glaring through the uncovered window above him. The dream had been so real, as they always were—his mind taunting him, remembering things as they could never be again. He looked down at his hands, half expecting to still be holding the letter he'd received from Eirik all those years ago.

I am writing now to ask for your forgiveness.

After they had spent some months apart, he recalled the tears that had spilled as he read the words and clutched the red cloak in his arms, joy overcoming any hurt or anger he might have felt. He hadn't hesitated for a moment. He'd packed his humble belongings and paid his meagre pile of coin to a local farmer for an old nag of a horse. The poor creature had been ridden close to death in Jonah's eagerness to return to his love.

He'd arrived at the Torrant Estate within three days. Their eyes locked across the courtyard, the spark between them untouched by the passing of time. As soon as they were alone, their hands and lips and bodies were drawn together in desperate longing. For that night, they were as they had once been, together as one—heart, body, and soul. Yet when the sun rose the next morning and the night's passion had burned away, Eirik spoke with a strange formality. He'd told Jonah of his new duties as a commander of the Commune, ignored his questions and confusion.

"You will see in time," he said, hand hovering over Jonah's shoulder, not quite touching. "This is the best for both of us."

And so it had been for the years since. Their love remained an unspoken tether between them, ever present but scarce acknowledged.

And what now? What will happen when I send the letter?

What of *Samalah's* comments? She told him in no uncertain terms that he must focus only on the Grand Magister and no one else. His hand drifted to his chest where the unfinished note remained tucked beneath his robe. He pulled it out and held it up to the light of day, reading over his own words.

Is there a way that I might get back the man I met all those years ago in the harbour?

That was what it came down to, wasn't it? He tried to convince himself it wasn't so—that he'd be satisfied with one more night together, one last touch, kiss, taste, smell of each other. If he had that, he would be strong enough to move on. He had to be.

Jonah didn't acknowledge the tiny part of himself that knew it could never be enough. He wanted back the man he had loved for so long, the man for whom he would have done anything.

Evelyn cannot know. No one can. This was a selfish endeavour, yet one he could not stop himself from undertaking. He sighed, folded the letter, and put it back beneath his robe. For now, it could wait. He had to find out how Evelyn had fared in her rite of passage.

As he stood from his seat, the front door opened and his mother stepped in, eyes downcast.

"What's wrong?" Jonah said, seeing the concern etched on her face.

"*A'laha,*" she said. "We need your help."

Jonah's stomach lurched. "Is Evelyn well?"

His mother didn't respond, simply turned and retreated. Jonah followed, blood roaring in his ears.

Outside *Samalah's* home, a small group of grave-faced women was gathered. *Samalah* herself was nowhere to be seen. His mother stopped outside the white front door, surrounded by the rich scent of flowers.

"What happened?" he asked impatiently.

"The ceremony began as normal. *Samalah* had already given Evelyn her tea when we left. The girl was alone. We waited, expecting nothing out of the ordinary, until ..." His mother's brow creased, her fingers hovering over her lips as her eyes glazed over.

"Mother," he said, taking her hand to draw her attention back to him. "Please."

"There was shouting from inside," she said, shaking her head with evident upset. "Screaming. We tried to go in to help the girl. To see what could be done. But the door was locked."

"Locked? How could that be?"

"We do not know. The girl must have done it herself." His mother shrugged.

"Why did you not come and get me sooner? She is my responsibility. My friend." Jonah could not stop his rising irritation.

"By the time I thought to, the shouting had stopped. And then, without warning, the door opened. *Samalah* rushed inside and has not come out since. But it is tradition not to ... Well, we cannot enter until *Samalah* gives permission." She looked around at the other women, each nodding in silent agreement. "I came to you because you can ..." She trailed off and looked away.

The realisation hit him like a punch to the gut; they did not see him as one of them anymore, not truly. He had returned to them, and they had welcomed him home, but all had changed. He had been away for too long. They believed he would break their traditions without a second thought.

Who am I to question them, then? Too furious to respond, he marched towards the door and pushed it open with more force than necessary. The door swung inwards with a resounding crash, and *Samalah* looked up. Evelyn lay unconscious on the floor.

"Jonasaiah," *Samalah* said, signalling him forward. "Please, help me take her to the bedroom."

Jonah bent down and picked up the unmoving Evelyn with ease. She weighed so little, looked so delicate and innocent—like a child.

She is a child. Too young to shoulder the pressure he'd put on her. He should not have let this go ahead. He knew what it entailed, the price it asked of a person. He knew what she had been through. What she concealed.

He could only imagine what memories Veritarra had brought forth to test the girl with. Their goddess was generous with Her gifts, but She also required a measure of sacrifice, of self-reflection, to obtain such rewards ...

He placed Evelyn on the bed, and she let out an anguished groan. He knelt beside her and waited for her to regain consciousness, aware of *Samalah* standing at his back. *You should have prepared her better,* he scorned himself. He thought of the note in his robe, shame burning in his chest.

"What happened?" he asked, noticing dried blood beneath Evelyn's fingernails.

Samalah placed a warm hand on his shoulder. He felt calmer, though his rage still simmered within. "We could not have known the strength of the girl's demons," the old woman said. "Nor how fiercely Veritarra would test her." She gave a weary sigh.

"Surely you knew?" he snapped, even though he knew the powers Evelyn concealed were likely the root cause. He was angry at everything—at himself, those wretched powers, at *Samalah*, his mother, the traditions he'd left behind, the sacrifices he'd made, the home he had lost.

And most of all, at Eirik.

"*Samalah,* you know when you meet a person what they have been through." Still unwilling to tell the truth about Evelyn, he stood and looked down upon the holy woman. For the first time in his life, he saw her for what she was—frail, afraid, and unsure, just like the rest of them.

"I could not see it all," she said. "The girl protected herself from me ... Yet I sensed her strength." She let out a weary sigh. "I failed her, Jonasaiah. I failed her."

Jonah glanced between *Samalah* and Evelyn. "As did I," he said. *I should have been here to protect her.*

The old woman stood beside him. "The women are afraid after what they heard. I sensed an immense power from inside my home. Such pain and despair, Jonah. I have not felt anything like it since ..."

"The uprising," Jonah whispered.

Samalah looked up at him, eyes brimming with sadness. "Yes," she said.

Jonah nodded, running a hand over his hair. "And Veritarra? What of her decision?"

"I await Her word, *a'laha*," *Samalah* said. In her eyes, he saw the truth—Evelyn's powers were all but confirmed.

"*Samalah*, I—"

She held a finger up, silencing him in an instant. "Ezzarah's Curse." She touched a hand to Evelyn's forehead. "It seems the girl was *blessed* by another of our gods." She glanced up, apprehensive. "Had I known, *a'laha*, I could have taken precautions. She can still be worthy of Veritarra, but ... we were all put in grave danger with this secret." She pursed her lips, and he was certain—she was aware of their betrayal, of what he had concealed from his own people. He remained silent, afraid to speak and unwilling to admit the old woman was right.

After a time, he said, "What will happen now?"

"Perhaps the ceremony was what she needed to release the anger within her. The anger that would have turned Ezzarah's Curse into such rage as we have seen before," *Samalah* said. "But these powers —this curse—may yet overwhelm her if they remain a part of her."

"Will she be granted Veritarra's Gift?" Jonah asked. "Perhaps it is what she needs to keep her safe. To prevent the powers from consuming her. Is that not why they were granted to us in the first place?"

Samalah did not speak at first. Instead, she placed a warm hand on his arm. "No matter Veritarra's decision, I believe it is the only way. I will not speak of them to the others. I will keep her secret, but … you cannot stay here, either of you. The powers she has, they have caused too much anguish here before. As well you know, *a'laha*. Yet the girl's path remains … important, somehow." She watched Evelyn for a moment, apparently grappling with some inner turmoil. She kissed her thumb, placed it to her forehead, and held it in the air. For a few moments, her eyes remained closed, and she gently hummed to herself.

Conversing with Veritarra. Jonah watched her with fascination. Witnessing *Samalah* at work had always filled him with peace.

Finally, *Samalah* turned back to him and said, "The Curse of Ezzarah cannot be discovered here again. The girl will be granted Veritarra's Gift. And then you must go."

At that moment, Evelyn began to stir. She opened her eyes and blinked a few times as she glanced around the room, appearing unfocused and confused.

"Evelyn," Jonah said, kneeling beside her once more.

She locked her gaze on him. "Jonah," she said, clasping his arm. "Where were you? I was alone. And he came, he came for me. I didn't know what else to do so I, I killed him." She dropped her head back, staring at the ceiling with wide eyes. "I killed him."

Jonah understood; Veritarra could present visions of such intensity it was impossible to separate them from reality. With the accursed powers seeking to break free, who knew what the Goddess had done. He reached for Evelyn's hand, squeezing it gently. "Who did you kill?" he whispered.

"Arthur. He was a boy in Little Haven, and he … What he *did* followed me for so long." Her lips trembled. "He's gone now."

Jonah nodded. In her eyes, a new light glimmered. Whatever the girl had seen, Veritarra had granted her some much-needed release; that was clear. "It's okay," he said. "You're safe now."

There was a momentary silence before *Samalah* stepped forward. Jonah moved aside to give the woman space. She ran her hands up and down the length of Evelyn's arms, legs, and torso, muttering words under her breath. It was all part of the ceremony, but Jonah found his patience growing short. They had been here for too long. He knew now he would never be able to settle here again. He had changed in some fundamental way; his mother had understood that since the moment he had returned.

I changed the moment I laid eyes upon Eirik, Veritarra forgive me.

"*Samalah*," Evelyn whispered.

"Yes, my child?"

"Am I worthy?"

Without hesitation, Samalah bowed her head. "You will have Veritarra's Gift."

With that, Evelyn's smile widened. She let out a shaky exhale. "I'm worthy, Jonah," she said. "I'm worthy."

"Of course you are," he said, returning to her side. "I never doubted it." He glanced over his shoulder towards *Samalah*.

"Veritarra will show you the way," she said softly. "Remember what I said, *a'laha*." And with that, she left them alone.

"What will happen now?" Evelyn asked.

"Once you are rested enough, we will prepare to leave. Captain Nem should be back from his trip in two days," Jonah said. "It is time for us to return to Septima."

CHAPTER 31
HECTOR

"... We look upon Perisma's blessed light and know He has brought this before us as a trial. A test of our faith and knowledge of His truth on this, our most holy of days."

Orion's voice penetrated Hector's unconscious mind, dragging him towards wakefulness. Even in the depths of sleep, his aching body told him everything was wrong. He'd been given Veritarra's Gift, that was certain ... Yet there was something else, too, such that the concoction rendered him far more powerless than usual, his mind sluggish and body drained. He shifted, feeling the hard floor beneath him. His hands were tied behind his back, his cloak removed, his tunic torn. A chill ran through his body.

His head throbbed abominably, a pain that started in his right temple and spread across his scalp. He grimaced as he forced himself up, determined to see where he was and what was happening. As he did so, his eyes focused and he saw Orion's dark figure standing in front of him. His back was to Hector as he addressed the gathered townsfolk inside the church, and he spoke in impassioned tones about their blessed Perisma. Hector felt as though he was observing the entire scene outside of himself.

What is happening?

Apparently aware of his stirring, Orion turned to look down upon him with a sneer. "Our fallen son awakens," he declared. "See him, know Perisma's truth. This is what happens when you turn from His light. When you are called to face His judgement."

All eyes were upon Hector, and he jutted his jaw out in defiance even as the room swayed around him. Orion knew what had been done to him, how weak he had been left. The church elder wouldn't want the inconvenience of Hector's powers being unleashed in this room full of people; there was a plan playing out here, and Orion was in full control.

"Damn you, you bastard," Hector spat, words slurring slightly. At least he had been caught alone. He could only hope Beth and the others remained free to enact their plan without him. How much time had passed since he'd crept into Orion's home? Were they, even now, devising a way to rescue him? Did they even know where he was?

No, he had to concentrate on what was unfolding before him. *Cara. Rose, Raif.* With his dulled powers, he couldn't sense any of them nearby, but they must be. "What have you done with them? Where are the children?" he croaked.

Orion smirked. "What children, traitor?"

Rage surged through Hector, clearing his mind and strengthening his limbs. He heaved himself up. With his head lifted, he could see the whole interior, lit by burning lamps. He fought back a choke at the thick incense hanging in the air. He quickly scanned the crowd, but there was no sign of Elussius or Rose, Raif, or Lebby. He focused on the man in front of him through tear-blurred vision. "You know damn well who I mean."

"Even now, he remains insolent." His fury-filled eyes locked onto Hector. "It is truly astounding you should dare to question me in this place—you, a murderer. A *monster*. This man killed his own father using those selfish, accursed powers!" Orion stalked closer to Hector and squatted down beside him. "I will give you one last chance, Hector Haralambous, to regain the respect your family name once held. Will you choose to relinquish your old life, to cast aside the accursed powers with which you were born, which you used to take an innocent life, and step into the blessed light of Perisma?"

Hector let out a harsh laugh. "*What?* You truly are insane, aren't you? I killed my father because he was *dying.* He was in terrible pain, and he—he—" He glanced around, hoping to see just one person who understood what he was saying, understood why he had done what he'd done. But it was no use; everyone here was under Orion's thrall, and all stared back at Hector with open disdain or fear. "I hated myself for it, I hated what he asked of me, but ... would I change what I did? No." He turned to Orion, scowling. "And I will *never* sacrifice who I am for your *beloved* god."

The church elder bowed his head as though pained by Hector's words, as if he really would have released Hector if he'd submitted to Perisma's truth. "Very well. Your choice is made." Orion stood and turned back to his audience. "And now I must reveal to you all the true nature of this man, born and raised in our sacred town.

"Hector has been keeping a dark secret from you all. Though he grew up under Perisma's light, he has confirmed today he is not and never will be one of us." Orion clicked his fingers at a nearby man, who moved to retrieve something from the rear of the dais. Unable to move, Hector could only wait. "Yes, he has the powers which we all know to be a plague against Perisma ... But there is more, my friends. Bring *it* forward."

Orion's man came back into view carrying a sealed wooden crate. Hector's stomach lurched. *Cara.* He tried to reach for her, roved his mind into that box, pushed as hard as he could.

Nothing.

Whatever had been given to him, it was strong. Perhaps Cara had been drugged as well. He gritted his teeth to hold back a scream of rage. "Orion, I swear, if you've done anything to harm her, I will—"

"What? Kill me? In front of all these people, in the church of our beloved Perisma?" The church elder's laughter was mocking, his dark eyes gleaming with a mix of malice and pleasure. Hector was powerless, helpless, alone, and Orion clearly delighted in that fact. "Your abilities make you arrogant. What will you do without them? *I see you for what you truly are. All here who are bathed in Perisma's light see it.*" He held his arms out to the church, and a murmur of agreement echoed through the building. "All here are protected in the arms of Perisma."

"By Perisma's light," came a cry from the crowd.

"Praise Perisma," came another.

The calls continued until Orion held his hands up to hush the townsfolk. "But what abomination, you might ask, has he brought among us?" The crate containing Cara was at Orion's feet. The church elder knelt and removed a knife from his belt, using it to loosen the lid.

"I mean it, Orion. I will fucking kill you."

The man ignored him, reaching inside the crate. With a theatrical flourish, he pulled out the unconscious Cara by the scruff of her neck. She hung limp in his hand, so small and fragile. Hector reached for his companion's mind once more. There was the slightest flicker of a response, a tiny light in his mind, then nothing.

Orion displayed the white cat before his congregation as a ripple of shock ran across it. "I can only imagine your suspicions, my friends—and you are correct," he said. "Hector and this *creature* are connected by this man's abhorrent, ungodly powers. She is his *minion*. A foul agent of evil." Orion placed Cara on an altar behind him as gasps, cries of dismay, boos, and hisses filled the room. Hatred emanated from the crowd, filling the room with vitriolic tension. They had always been mistrustful of animals in Nook Town, afraid that each and every one was an abomination, linked to someone with powers.

I should never have come back here.

"Your shock is understandable, my friends, for this man has

brought others like him into our beloved town and endangered us all." Orion waited for the muttering crowd to quiet before speaking on. "Bring the girl forward."

Rose.

Hector stopped probing for Cara's mind and turned to see a man emerging from the room behind the dais, Rose draped over his shoulder. The girl was uncovered, her young face pale and sunken, blonde hair lank.

"What have you done to her?" Hector cried, the strength of his anger providing a burst of energy. "She is a child!"

"A child, yes, but do you dare deny what she is capable of?"

"No, Orion, no, you cannot hold her responsible for—"

"Found with a woman," Orion cried.

Avanna.

"Or should I say, the *body* of a woman. Killed by this child's own hand, by the accursed powers she wields, we have no doubt." The townsfolk obliged with shouts and gasps, making prayer gestures against this new evil brought before them.

"You have no proof, Orion!" Hector shouted. "You can't know she did it."

Orion smiled, seeming satisfied that he was three steps ahead of Hector. "If only it were so ... But the girl's brother was more than candid with my daughter. We know the truth of her nature. Raif has been brought into Perisma's light. He understands the importance of honesty when seeking enlightenment," the church elder said. "Bring the boy out."

Marched out by Lebby, Raif was adorned in the burgundy robes of the acolytes of Perisma. Hector tried to catch the lad's gaze, but his grey eyes were clouded, his expression faraway. *He scarcely knows what's happening.*

"Come forward," Orion said. Raif did as he was told, and Orion placed a hand upon his shoulder, gently encouraging. "Tell the crowd what you told Lebioda."

Hector couldn't see Raif's face, though he heard the lad stutter, saw him turn to look at Orion with a frown. "No. You—you made me ... My sister, she ..." Raif's words hung in the air, his brow furrowed.

Something was wrong. Orion's jaw clenched. He nudged Raif. "Go on, there's nothing to be afraid of. You're doing the right thing, under Perisma's light."

"Raif, no!" Hector called. "Don't do what he—" A sharp kick to the ribs from Orion's lackey knocked the wind from Hector's lungs. He spluttered and curled in on himself, waiting for the next blow. Instead, Orion stalked towards him and crouched down, his hot, stale breath washing over Hector's face.

"Another word from you and I assure you, *murderer*, you will regret it."

Unable to speak, he could only watch as Orion joined Raif once more.

"There was blood," Raif was saying. "Two men, they attacked us ..." He looked around, face contorted with confusion. His glazed eyes met Hector's, and his mouth dropped open. "Hector ...?"

"The boy struggles with the truth," Orion announced. "This girl is his sister, after all. He seeks to protect her. We all understand how hard it can be to relinquish family attachments even when the possession of abominable powers becomes apparent." Murmurs and nods of concurrence passed around the room. "But I assure you that what I tell you came directly from him." Orion squeezed Raif's arm. "This girl *has* killed. She may appear young and innocent, but she has already used her powers to murder."

The words hung in the air like knives poised to strike, and they had the impact Hector knew Orion wanted. The townsfolk, too stunned to utter a single sound, simply stared aghast as the townsman brought Rose, still unconscious, to the front of the dais and laid her down. Even in their revulsion, those in the front benches leaned forward, morbid fascination overcoming disgust and fear.

Rose, can you hear me? Hector concentrated with all his might, trying to force through the drug-induced wall around his powers. Though it was near impenetrable, it had worked with Cara, briefly.

He had to keep trying, had to break it down. *Rose. Cara. Raif.* He reached for all of them in turn, desperate to connect with one of them, even for a moment.

Meanwhile, Orion had moved behind his altar. Upon it sat a copy of the holy text alongside an orb-shaped object covered by a black cloth. "I tell you now, my friends, on this, our most sacred of days, Perisma has sent this child to test us. I declare that she is Esteralla reborn."

The townsfolk burst into a flurry of gossip.

"She has blonde hair."

"The power to kill."

"Esteralla, the first acolyte."

"Sent to test our faith."

Shit. Orion has won.

"Esteralla," Raif muttered. His eyes drifted to his sister. "Like the stories."

"Yes, Raif, the stories," Lebby said gently. "Come." She pulled him aside, away from Rose and Hector. Orion's daughter was just as blinded as the rest of them.

This whole town is cursed.

"Esteralla Clinkscale—and beside her, a man who has gone astray from Perisma's arms. This is what we have been waiting for, my children," Orion announced. "All these years of faithful worship have come to this, here and now. These two faithless wretches have been brought to us so that we might burn the wickedness from their souls and show the world Perisma's way is the *only* way!

"It is not the Commune, that power-hungry liar the Grand Magister, who can lead us forward. It is Perisma who grants us the blessing of His light. It is He who allows us to live under the peace and protection of His righteous glory!" Orion held his arms up until the townsfolk's cheering dulled. "Bring the traitor forward!"

At Orion's words, two men dragged Hector to the front of the dais and threw him down beside Rose. With his hands still tied behind his back, Hector was unable to stop himself from landing on his face, teeth clamping together with a *crack* that resonated around the entire church like a clap of thunder. He let out a moan as the pain in his head renewed, and he tasted blood. No time for self-pity; he had to focus on Rose. Now that he was next to her, he could see her face clearly. More importantly, he could see her eyes fluttering beneath their lids, her mouth twitching. She was waking, yet Orion was oblivious.

This was their chance.

They haven't been able to fully contain her powers.

And then, with ice-clear clarity: *This will not end well.*

"And now we will see what Perisma decrees must be done."

Rose, please hear me. Wake up.

"The light of our beloved God will show the truth to all. By His light, we shall be cleansed. Ignite the thuribles." Orion's voice rose; his palms lifted towards the ceiling. "Do not shield your eyes, faithful followers. See the true beauty of His might."

There was the sound of a cloth being whipped aside before the church was filled with a blinding whiteness that emanated from a large, glowing orb. Even facing away from it, Hector squinted against the light, feeling an immediate wave of heat against his back. And, worse, a blinding pain flashed through his head, his temples aching, his mind momentarily blanking. It passed, though a dull throb remained, timed with the beat of his heart.

"Orion," he cried. "What have you done? What is that thing?" He squinted against the light, just able to make out the church elder's silhouette behind it. Either Orion did not hear or he did not care to answer.

"Perisma blesses us all!" he shrieked.

He is a madman.

Hector turned his focus back to Rose. The orb was not important now; she was.

Rose, wake up.

He had to keep trying—keep pushing and reaching. The scent of incense grew stronger as robed churchgoers walked up and down the aisles, swinging the thuribles, a light fog filling the air. Hector coughed and spluttered, inhaling more of the cloying smoke.

Beside him, Rose's eyes flickered open and closed, a quiet groan passing her lips.

"Behold His magnificence!"

Hector edged forward so he could whisper in her ear. "If you can hear me, girl, then forget all I taught you in training. Unleash everything you have. Free your brother. Free my Cara. Please."

"By the light of Perisma, we judge the unworthy!"

Hector glanced over his shoulder to see Orion holding the sun-bright orb above his head, his expression steeped in reverence. Hector averted his eyes from its still painfully-bright light, afraid that the pain in his head would worsen again.

Whatever that object is, whatever other explanation there might be here, he has truly lost his mind.

Atop the altar, Cara remained unconscious. *I have to reach her.*

Lebby and Raif stood close by, their mouths agape, eyes wide with wonder, apparently, like most of the townsfolk, hypnotised by the orb, its light ebbing from blinding to dim and back again.

They're distracted. Now's my chance.

He tore his gaze away from the orb, thankful that the pain in his head remained dull, and focused on loosening the ties at his back. They'd been knotted tightly, the cord biting into his wrists as he tried to wriggle free.

No good. Rose needs to wake.

He moved his body to shield the young girl from the mysterious orb.

"Rose, do it now," he whispered. "Please."

Please save my beloved. Save your brother. Save yourself.

He scrunched his eyes closed and concentrated with all his might.

Orion continued to cry out praises and blessings to Perisma, the townsfolk mirroring his chants. And then, gentle at first but growing stronger and stronger, Rose began to tremble.

"You can do it," he said to her. "Fight through it."

"See how they cower from Perisma's light," Orion cried from behind them. "Let's see what Perisma does to this *cursed creature!*" He moved the orb down towards Cara, teeth bared, the whites of his eyes reflecting the glaring light.

"No, Orion!" Hector screamed. "No!" He lurched backwards towards the altar, flipping awkwardly and landing on his stomach, biting his tongue.

"This monstrous demon will be punished!"

The orb was almost touching Cara now; the smell of scorching fur filled the room. The congregation stood with their hands up, chanting a prayer to Perisma even as the horrifying act was carried out.

"Orion, no! Leave her, please, leave her. Cara, my love, I'm coming." Hector snaked forward on his stomach as sobs of despair escaped him.

He had to save her. Had to stop Orion.

I'm coming, my love.

A searing pain was blooming in Hector's side as though the orb was being held against his own body and not his companion's. It was burning, burning, burning ...

Without warning, the door to the church slammed open. A stream of air rushed in, breaking through the fog of incense, a chill wind that washed away the suffocating scent.

"What is the meaning of this disturbance?" Orion looked up, pulling the orb away from Cara's side.

Hector wasted no time in completing his journey towards the altar. He pushed himself to his knees, and by sheer willpower, to his feet. His hands still tied, he couldn't pick her up, though he noted that her eyes were open, glazed with pain. He focused on Orion, meaning to confront the man, to use whatever means he could to inflict as much pain as possible ... But the church elder was staring wide-eyed at the door.

"What are you doing here?" Orion said, looking past Hector.

Hector turned, a feeling of uneasiness settling over him. But it was Beth and Dog, Lenny, Charlie and Flo, Ben, even Barnaby. The whole group; they'd come for him. His heart soared.

"Here, up here," he called, nearly collapsing to his knees as relief flooded through him. "We need help."

But something was amiss. There were others with them ... Hector shook his head and blinked; his eyes must be playing tricks on him.

Barnaby moved forward, a scowl creasing his young face.

What has he done?

"It's time for you to pay for what you've done, *Father*," he spat. "These men are here to bring you to justice."

Father?

Barnaby stepped back to join Beth and the others; in their place came soldiers.

Soldiers in red cloaks.

The Commune.

"Orion Weystone. By order of the Grand Magister, you are under arrest for treason."

"No, boy, what have you done?" Hector whispered.

"How dare you! Leave this place at once, you treacherous—" But Orion's words were halted by the sound of a young girl's scream, filled with hatred and fury and unleashed power.

Rose.

And then all was chaos.

CHAPTER 32
RAIF

The orb's light was near blinding, yet warm and comforting, its pulsating drawing him in. There were voices all around —chants, shouts, cries—but they washed over him without meaning.

And then a scream pierced through him, shattering his fixation. In front of him, Orion's face slackened. The orb fell from his hands, crashing to the floor with an almighty *crack*. The light faded to a dull ebb, no longer holding its hypnotising allure. Like the parting of storm clouds, Raif's mind cleared. He peered around, trying to make sense of what he saw.

"Raif?"

Lebby gazed up at him. Their hands were still clasped; in her eyes, he saw his own confusion mirrored back. In the background, he heard shouts and cries and ... barking?

Dog?

"In the name of the Grand Magister, surrender yourselves now or you will be arrested."

"We'll never give in to you!" shouted a woman.

"You desecrate the sacred church of Perisma!" Orion cried.

Raif blinked, finally noticing the men in ...

"Red cloaks," he muttered. *Shit. The Commune.*

The soldiers were trying to fight their way through the lines of townspeople who blocked their path to the front of the church, to Orion. Through it all darted a small, black spaniel. Dog was a blur of movement, weaving his way up the aisle and towards the dais.

"What was that scream?" Lebby asked, voice quivering. It was the first time he'd seen her look so scared, so unsure, so afraid. "It was—It sounded so ..."

The scream. "I don't know," he said, equally shaken. "I don't know what it was." But as he pulled his eyes away from Lebby, he watched Dog, saw to whom he was running.

To a young girl sitting at the front of the platform.

Though she faced away from him, he would recognise that blonde hair anywhere. His heart skipped a beat. "Little bug." He released Lebby's hand and rushed forward. "Rose!"

Rose, you're here.

Everything seemed to happen in slow motion.

She turned towards him, and he almost sobbed at the sight of her; her face was thin, *too* thin, her normally bright blue eyes dull and underlined by bruise-like circles. Dog licked her hand, whining and nuzzling at her.

What happened here? I confronted Orion about Rose, and then ... I don't remember. He scrunched his face, frustrated at his own lack of answers. He stumbled forward awkwardly, wanting only to be by his sister's side.

"Stop there, boy," Orion's voice rang out, jerking his strained mind away from Rose.

"You can't make me do anything anymore. Whatever you did to me, it's over."

"If you move another step, I will kill this creature." Orion was holding a knife against the neck of a white cat upon the altar. *Cara.*

"Please, lad," Hector said, voice full of pain. "Please listen to him." His green eyes were wide, imploring him with a desperation

Raif had never seen from Hector before. He glanced between Hector, Orion and Cara, then towards Rose—*so close*. And yet he thought of Rose and Dog's connection; what would she do if anything happened to her beloved companion? Could he allow such a thing to happen to Hector?

"Hector," he said, voice hoarse. "The soldiers. We have to save Rose. We have to run."

"I can't leave without Cara."

Raif knew he had a choice to make. Behind him, Rose was curled around Dog. It wasn't clear whether she understood the level of danger she was in.

What has Orion done to her?

He had to get her away from this place.

And yet it was apparent from Orion's face that the man wouldn't hesitate to hurt Cara in his desperation to re-take control of the situation. On top of that, the soldiers were getting closer, heedless of Orion's earlier shout, cutting their way through the congregation without a second thought. Some of their own screamed in agony, but still the townsfolk tried to hold the soldiers back, steadfast in their self-righteous beliefs that Perisma would protect them, that protecting Orion was their top priority.

They would give their lives for him. Orion has turned this whole town to his own will. As he did with me.

"Listen to my father, Raif. Please," Lebby said, standing beside him once more.

Raif's anger flared. He looked at Lebby as she spoke, recalling how excited he'd been when they first met, how his stomach fluttered to see her smile. *How could I have been so stupid?* She regarded him now with tear-filled eyes, and all he felt was disgust rising like bile in his throat.

"I will not listen to you anymore," he spat. Lebby flinched, but he didn't care. *She hid Rose from me. She must have known what her father was doing.* He swallowed against the bitterness flooding his mouth.

"You can't keep me from Rose any longer." He leapt forward. "Rose, I'm here. I'm here." He took her hand, so delicate and frail, in his.

"Raif," she whispered. "Dog."

His momentary joy was shattered by Hector's agonised shout.

"Cara, no!"

Orion was smiling at Hector, his expression full of malice. The church elder's knife was poised, his hand tensed. Raif waited for the final blow, for the scream to erupt from Hector's lips ... But it didn't come. For some reason, Orion was unable to finish the act. His flint-grey eyes became blank, his jaw slack. Though Cara remained in his grasp, his arm drooped so she rested on the altar, untouched by the knife.

"Father!" Lebby cried, darting to his side.

The acrid smell of urine filled Raif's nostrils as Orion's knife clattered to the floor. He became aware of a wave of *something* in the air, some unspoken power that terrified him. He glanced at his sister, his understanding finally dawning. Her eyes were focused intently upon Orion, her face contorted with so much rage that she no longer looked like his sister, nor even a child.

"Rose?" He touched her shoulder. As soon as he did so, he let out a gasp of shock. His mind became one with hers. He felt the flood of her powers towards Orion—*smothering, pushing, crushing*. Raif gritted his teeth and pulled away from her. "Rose, stop," he whispered, struggling to comprehend what he had felt. Perhaps there had been some modicum of truth to the teachings Orion and Lebby had impressed upon him. These powers were ...

Evil.

Despite all that Orion had done, did he deserve to suffer in such a way? Regardless of his hatred for the man, Raif couldn't bring himself to believe that he did. And then he identified the feeling at the centre of his core: *I cannot allow my sister to take another life with her powers.*

"Please, Rose, listen to me." Though he pleaded with her, she showed no acknowledgement of his words. Her face was flushed, eyes shining, lips peeled back in a snarl. She didn't even blink.

"Orion Weystone, you are under arrest." The voice was close behind Raif and Rose, nearing the dais. Bodies of men and women alike were strewn in the church aisles. The smell of blood filled the air, overpowering even the lingering scent of incense. Soldiers were clearing the way towards the platform, moving ever nearer.

"Rose, please stop or they'll catch you. Please." He touched her face. To his immense relief, she blinked and let out an exhale. She looked at him with wide eyes, becoming the sister he knew once more. "Rose." He smiled weakly, pulling her to his chest. "I've got you, little bug."

The soldier who had spoken climbed onto the dais as Orion collapsed, first slumping to the altar and then falling to the floor. His skull hit the floor with a hard *thud*, just as his sacred orb had done.

"Powers above," muttered the dark-haired soldier, brow creased. "What's going on here?" Before anyone could respond, he called to one of his fellow soldiers. "Auras, come up here."

"Yes, Commander Brodell." A blond-haired soldier beat a fist against his chest before joining his commander.

"Did you feel that?" Commander Brodell asked.

"Someone here has very strong powers, indeed," Auras responded, lips pursing. The two men glanced around the room before turning away, speaking in hushed voices. As they did, Raif fixated on their red cloaks, so bright against the dingy, incense-dimmed grey of the church interior. His mind flashed back to the attack on Little Haven, so many weeks ago now. His heart raced, fear and fury flooding through him. Instinctively, he moved to shield Rose from the two men. *They killed Father. They took Mother. They will not have my sister.*

The soldiers finished speaking and turned towards Orion and Lebby. They knelt to examine the unconscious church elder, escorting Lebby with a brusquely spoken order, ignoring Hector and Cara altogether.

"Still breathing," Commander Brodell muttered. "What do you make of it?"

Soldier Auras's eyes flitted about the dais and came to rest on the gently flickering orb. He retrieved it and took it back to Brodell, both men studying it with intense interest.

"I've heard of this place. They were allowed to continue worshiping some ... god of light," Auras said, nodding towards the symbol of Perisma that decorated the wall behind the dais. "Shunned the Commune."

Commander Brodell let out a mocking laugh. "Foolish west coasters. Worshiping a being that none can see. Who would choose that over the might and wisdom of His Benevolence?"

While the two men were distracted, Raif pulled Rose upright and led her and Dog to stand beside Hector. "What are we going to do?" he whispered, gesturing for Hector to turn around so his hands could be untied.

"Thank you, lad," Hector said, cautiously glancing over his shoulder towards the soldiers. "But I fear we've run out of options." As soon as his hands were free, he cradled Cara to his chest. Her yellow eyes regarded Raif, their usual cool indifference replaced by a glaze of pain.

Raif squeezed Rose's hand in his own, panic rising. "We can't just stay here. We might be able to slip away now if we move quickly." *They won't take my sister.* He tried to grab Hector's arm, pulled with all his might, but the man was a deadweight.

"It's too late, lad," he said, eyes shining.

"What do you mean? You can't just—"

"You there, what are you doing?" It was the one called Auras.

Raif didn't like the way the man's eyes lingered upon them. He shifted to push Rose behind him, lifting his chin and glaring back at the man. "Stay behind me, Rose," he said. "I'll protect you." *Please don't kill anyone else.* She placed a palm on his back, an affirmation that she would do as he asked. At his feet, Dog growled at the two soldiers.

Brodell smiled as he stepped forward, holding his hand out towards them. "You're safe now. We will protect you." His expression appeared genuine—friendly, even. Raif didn't trust it one bit.

"You can't take her," he said bluntly.

"Don't be a fool, boy," Auras said, standing beside his colleague. "You are too young to—" Suddenly, Auras paled, eyes narrowing. "Powers above. Blonde hair ... So young. Now I think on it, I'm sure I have hunted one such as her before. With Commander Sulemon, some time ago." He gulped. "If she is the same child we pursued then, it's imperative we take her in without delay. It would explain the surge of powers we felt."

"No!" shouted Raif.

"You speak out of turn. It is treason to keep such a child away from the Commune. It's a mercy we don't hang you along with so many others in this town," Commander Brodell said matter-of-factly. He clicked his fingers. Suddenly, the dais was swarming with soldiers. "Take them. Be careful with the girl."

"Stop." Hector stepped in front of Raif, Rose, and Dog. Still holding Cara against him, he looked with the other three as one towards the soldiers surrounding them. "Take me in their stead. I'm a member of Veritas. A rebel, sought by the Grand Magister for some years." He exhaled, shoulders slumping with defeat. "Let them go and I'll answer for my crimes. I'll show you where our camp is located."

"What are you doing?" Raif asked, horrified. "You can't do this. I won't let you."

The sound of laughter pulled his attention back to Brodell and Auras. "Hector Haralambous. Yes, I see it now." Commander Brodell looked him up and down. "You've seen better days, I'd wager. The Veritas camp, you say?" The soldier's eyes gleamed. "Haven't you heard?"

Hector gawped back at him. "Heard? What do you mean?"

"The Veritas camp has already been located. Your rebellious group is no longer a threat. Lord Torrant led his own men to it."

Brodell smirked. "By the Powers, we are granted the wisdom and strength to hunt down such traitors."

Hector's mouth dropped open. "No," he croaked. "No, no, no." Trembling, he buried his head into Cara's neck.

Raif placed a hand on his shoulder, offering what scant comfort he could. "What happened to them?" Raif asked. Despite what Avanna and Mak had done, none of the other members deserved to die. *Arturo, Griff, all the others ... Gone.*

The soldier sniffed, evidently unmoved by Hector's distress. "The adults were executed. Hung as traitors," Brodell said. "The children have been taken by the Commune to be trained by His Benevolence. To serve the kingdom of Septima however the Grand Magister deems fit."

Executed? No.

"Benevolent?" Hector sneered. "You don't know the meaning of the word."

Commander Brodell glowered down at Hector. "I see your traitorous ways remain unbroken. That will change before this is over. You will be shown the way before you are hung."

"Leave him alone!" Raif cried. "He isn't a traitor! He doesn't hurt people, hunt them down, kill for no reason."

"Speak in such a way again, boy, and you will be hung for treason alongside your friend here." Commander Brodell's easy manner was fast melting away, impatience taking its place. "As I see it, none of you have a choice but to hand yourselves over to us. There are no bargains to be made. You'll answer to the Grand Magister for what you've done, Hector Haralambous, make no mistake." He summoned forward one of his soldiers. "Take the cat. I'll not have him doing anything foolish. This will be our insurance."

"No, please, you can't—" A hard slap to the cheek knocked Hector to the ground, where he slumped down with an agonised groan.

"The creature will be returned to you in Taskan so you may say goodbye," Brodell said. "It is the one mercy I will grant you." Apparently satisfied with his decision, he nodded and turned to the front of the dais, hands clasped at his back.

Raif bristled and made to step forward, determined to vent the rage building up inside him. *They killed Father. They destroyed our village. They took Mother. This is all their fault.* But then, from behind, he felt a tiny hand tugging at his arm. "No, Raif. No," Rose said, voice almost inaudible. "No."

Raif exhaled, anger melting away. He knew then they were defeated. He took his sister in his arms. "It's okay," he said. "I'm sorry. I'm here."

"Powers above. Enough of this," Commander Brodell said. "It's time to leave this forsaken place." He snapped his fingers again, and the soldiers responded without delay. When they tried to remove Rose from his arms, Raif pulled her close.

"I'll bring her," he said, resigned. "Let me hold her. I'll follow you." Commander Brodell gave a curt nod.

The soldiers led them from the dais with Hector and Cara. Lebby, silent and deathly pale, walked beside her father as he was carried away by soldiers. They walked down the blood-soaked aisle of the church in silence. Raif looked at the faces of the slaughtered, townsfolk whose names he had never even known. *What a waste,* he thought. *Where was their beloved god when they needed him most?*

As they reached the door, he glanced back at the symbol of Perisma. It looked duller, dark and unappealing, no longer the gleaming symbol of hope he'd once believed it to be.

"So much for Perisma's light," he muttered, shaking his head. He felt ten years older than when they'd come to Nook Town. Just fourteen years old, yet exhaustion dragged at his entire being. Still, he kept putting one foot in front of the other. He had to be strong for Rose. He would remain by her side, no matter what.

Outside, the morning sky was darkened by iron-grey clouds. The air was filled with the smell of recent rainfall, the ground glistening with puddles. A storm rumbled somewhere in the distance, though Raif couldn't tell whether it was approaching or passing.

"In the wagons," Brodell said. "We'll make directly for—"

"Hector!" A woman's voice pierced the air. Before any of the soldiers could stop her, she shoved through the crowds. Though Raif didn't recognise her, Hector's face lit up at the sight of her.

"Beth," he said. "Where have you been? Are you okay? Where are—"

"There's no time to explain," she said, glancing around. "You, soldier." She waved Brodell over, drew herself tall, and stared into his face with an unflinching gaze. "My son, Barnaby, he's the one who fetched you to this town. We made an arrangement, you see."

"What?" Hector's face dropped. "Your *son*? Beth, what have you done?"

"Hush now," Beth said, placing a hand on his cheek. "There'll be time to explain later. Soldier, you must listen. There's been a misunderstanding here." She directed her gaze towards Raif, took in Rose —still clutched to his chest—and Dog at their feet. "My son had an agreement. We were to ensure the traitor Orion was handed over to you. The townsfolk who colluded in his treachery were to be executed. My friends and I"—she waved her hand at them as if to underline her point—"were to remain here. To rebuild Nook Town under the guidance of the Grand Magister, a place where those of us with powers could flourish with the Commune's support. To create a new oath, a new alliance between us."

The Commander nodded as though considering her words, rubbing a hand over his chin. "I see," he said.

"So it's settled then?" Beth asked, eyes glimmering. "They will remain here, with us." She placed a hand on Hector's arm, appearing not to notice when he visibly stiffened beneath her touch.

"Settled?" Brodell stared at her, eyebrows raised. "Oh no, I don't think so."

"What do you—"

"You see, I believe your son failed to mention two things. Firstly, that you were harbouring a wanted rebel and traitor to the Commune, Hector Haralambous."

"But he—"

"And secondly," Commander Brodell said curtly, "we weren't told about this child." He nodded towards Rose, and Raif instinctively hugged her tighter. "The oath in place protected Nook Town, but it didn't allow you to hide those with such *dangerous* powers amongst your ranks. It is clear that this place has been concealing much from the Commune these past years. How can any trust be placed in you to work with the Grand Magister now? His Benevolence has surely been tested, and you have shown yourselves unworthy."

"I've never seen that child before," Beth said, frowning. "I don't—"

"Beth, you fool," Hector spat, regaining himself after the evident shock of this woman's revelations. He glared at her, a venomous look in his eyes. "This is Rose, the girl I've been searching for. Orion had her. We could have saved her. And now you—or rather, your *son*— have brought the very people we've been fleeing from into our midst. They've taken Cara, they're taking Rose, we can't ..." He shrugged, appearing at a loss for words.

"Hector, please believe me. I didn't—"

"I told you the Commune weren't to be trusted. What did you think would happen?" But there was no fury in Hector's voice, only a deep, weary resignation.

"I'm sorry," Beth said, reaching for Hector's arm. He shook her away. "Barnaby. Orion was his father. I didn't think you would understand." She looked around as though seeking support for what she was saying. "Orion had to pay for what he did, Hector. You have to believe me. This was the only way."

Commander Brodell gave his men a nod, cutting off any more explanations or arguments. Hector was dragged away, his beloved companion caged, Raif, Rose, and Dog prisoners alongside them both.

"Please!" Beth cried. "Please, we had an agreement."

The commander turned his back on her. "Gather those left alive," he ordered. "Those without powers will be executed. Those with powers must be tested." He glanced at Beth. "The Grand Magister will decide what will become of this place."

The woman fell to her knees as the Commune's soldiers carried out their work around her. As the five of them were closed inside a wagon, she let out a last cry. "Hector, I'm sorry."

"Who was she?" Raif asked.

Hector, mouth downturned, flitted his gaze towards the church before returning it to his empty lap. "She—she was no one, lad. She was no one."

Before long, the wagon began to rumble along the road. Raif watched the gates of Nook Town recede behind him, wishing with all his might they'd never set eyes upon the place.

CHAPTER 33
EVELYN

Jonah came to get Evelyn the next morning, so early that it was still dark outside. She was already awake, prepared for the journey back to Septima. Despite the three days of bedrest since her ceremony, she remained bone-weary. She'd discovered a new part of herself, confirmed the powers long locked away. Though a weight had been lifted from her, she also needed to come to terms with who she was now.

Samalah had visited her on a few occasions, checking she was recovering well, feeling her pulse, muttering Nomarran prayers. Yet something was different about the way the old woman regarded her; the usual kindness was still there, but there was also a wariness in her eyes and the way she held herself around Evelyn. *It may be my imagination.*

Or she knows.

"*Samalah*," she said on the woman's last visit. "Will I be able to return here one day?" She swallowed, fidgeting with her hands. "It's just, everyone has been so kind. I've felt welcome here. I thought, maybe, well, when Jonah and I have finished what we need to do ... I might come back. With your blessing, of course."

The silence dragged on for too long, the self-doubt taunting Evelyn from deep within the recesses of her mind, quieter than before but still present. *I'll never be fully rid of that, will I?* She was lightheaded as she sat forward on the bed. "*Samalah?*"

The old woman stared out the glassless window. "When it is done," she said, smiling over her shoulder. "When it is done, my child."

Then she produced from her robes the item Evelyn had been waiting for—her very own pouch of Veritarra's Gift. The pouch was made from a fine-grained leather, stained the colour of rich red wine. Evelyn took it and clasped it in her hands. "Thank you," she said, tears filling her eyes. "Thank you."

The old woman left not long after, and Evelyn hadn't seen her since.

Maybe I'll never see her again, she thought, though she shook her head to bat away the notion. *No. No more of that. No more doubting. I am worthy, after all.*

I am worthy. She grinned to herself as she sat up in bed, seeing Jonah gathering her few possessions.

"Has Captain Nem returned?" she asked, standing and stretching with a jaw-cracking yawn.

Jonah gave her a brief nod, lips pursed. "We set sail before sunrise," he said. "Come. Dress yourself and we will go."

Evelyn rubbed her eyes, choosing to ignore his brusque tone. *He must be sad to be leaving his home again.* She moved to her washbasin and splashed her face with cold water before retrieving her tunic and trousers. It would be strange to wear them after so long in Nomarran robes. As a recognition of her time on Veritarra's Isle, she kept some ribbons in her growing hair. Finally, she retrieved her sacred pouch and knotted it to her belt.

"Ready?" Jonah asked.

Evelyn took one last look around the room. "Yes," she said. "I think so."

Without a backward glance, Jonah led her out of the room, out of

Samalah's home, away from the village. Evelyn didn't have time to dwell on why there was no one to send them off as she kept pace with Jonah's quick strides.

"Jonah," she called. "Why are you rushing?"

He slowed down and turned to her, his eyes narrowed. "Oh." He gave an unconvincing smile. "Nem wants to be underway as soon as we can."

"Oh, okay," Evelyn said, hoping to catch her breath for a moment. Jonah, however, was already marching away again. She hurried to catch up, and they walked in silence until they reached the beach.

They'd alighted here many days ago. She and Jonah had sat here, feet dangling into the ocean, confirming their newfound friendship.

How much had happened in such a short time. How different she felt. *Finally starting to know myself,* she thought. *To know my friends.*

Though the pain of what Arthur had done was still part of her, something inside her had changed. A barrier within her had been broken down. She could be whatever she wanted without allowing memories of Arthur to drag her backwards.

I will amount to something, she thought. *Jonah and I will succeed.* She patted the pouch at her belt as Captain Nem's silhouette appeared on the deck of *Septima's Blessing.* The sky was beginning to lighten on the horizon, dappled in streaks of pink, purple, and orange, but he held up a lantern nonetheless, likely to ensure their safe passage along the narrow gangplank.

"Good morning, friends," Nem called. "It is good to see you again."

"And you, Captain," Evelyn said. Jonah grunted.

"Is no one seeing you away?" the captain asked, looking behind them as though expecting a crowd of well-wishers.

"No," Jonah said.

Evelyn reached out to touch him; as her hand drew close to him, she was hit by an immediate wave of sadness, guilt, and anger. She gasped and pulled back, shocked by the intensity of the emotions and her ability to detect them. She shouldn't be able to; the Veritarra's Gift she'd continued to consume was supposed to keep any powers contained. Jonah raised an eyebrow, and she quickly recovered, not wanting to cause any undue concern.

"Is your mother not coming to say goodbye?" she asked, hoping to cheer him and distract herself.

He turned away again, shoulders tensed. "No," he said. "She is not." At that, he began to walk away. "I will see to our cabins."

When Evelyn made to follow, Captain Nem held a hand out to stop her. "Leave him," he said. "He needs some space. Trust me. He has likely already made his farewells. A difficult task, to be leaving again so soon."

Evelyn watched Jonah's retreating back for a moment, hand still tingling. "Yes, I think you're right."

"Well, now," the captain said, eyeing the pouch at her belt. "You must tell me how you came to own that. Come, my cabin will be warmed. I have some delicacies from my tour of the islands I would share with you."

Evelyn followed him. The captain paused so he could pass his orders on to Smith. The broad-shouldered first mate gave Evelyn a nod of greeting before going about his work, any sign of the acrimony he might have felt towards her on their outward journey gone.

"We'll be setting sail before long," Nem said as he led the way to his cabin. Inside, he pointed her towards a chair. The room was lit by the same glowing orange stones as before.

"What are those? I've seen them in a lot of places here yet never thought to ask." Evelyn moved closer to look at them. "There was too much else to think about."

Captain Nem smiled. "Ah," he said, handing her a cup of hot, sweet-smelling liquid. "A unique phenomenon found only on *A'la-ha'a*—the islands of the Sons. Firestones." He sat and took a generous sip from his own cup, giving a satisfied exhale.

"I see. They're beautiful." She took her seat and looked down at the drink he'd given her. "What is this? I do not want any alcohol."

As she said the words, she swore to herself that this time she would not falter in that decision. Drinking had been a defence, a way to prevent herself from feeling all the roiling emotions she'd held within. She would not shut off from those parts of herself again, not willingly.

"Ah, do not worry. There is no alcohol, I assure you. It is spiced juice from the fruit of Ezzarah," he said. "Ezzarah may be reviled, but the fruit is quite delicious." As if to emphasise his point, he took a gulp. "So, tell me what happened." He raised an eyebrow. "You are not the same girl I left here some weeks ago. I sense a change in you." He sat forward. "You seem ... surer of yourself."

Evelyn sat up, flushing under his scrutiny. "Everyone was very welcoming," she said. "I kept my powers hidden, as you advised."

Captain Nem nodded. "Very good. And did you speak to *Samalah* of your plan?"

"Yes. Well, Jonah did," she said. "She agreed to help. But she could only provide one pouch. For the Grand Magister, she said. No one else."

The captain bowed his head. "*Samalah* saw the wisdom in your intentions, I am sure. And will have been guided by Veritarra in this. It is what must be done, I am sure. Avoiding violence has always been our Goddess's way." He sipped his drink, pausing for a moment before lifting his chin towards her. "And you, child?"

Evelyn cupped the pouch of Veritarra's Gift given to her and recalled all that had happened to obtain it. "*Samalah* granted me the rite of passage," she said. "She said I would be tested."

"Mm," Captain Nem said, eyes gleaming. "I remember my own ceremony well. It can be challenging, but I see you were able to gain Veritarra's approval nonetheless."

"Challenging, yes," Evelyn said, unwilling to discuss the truth of the matter, nor of what she had felt with her powers that very morning. *Could they be stronger from the ceremony?* They certainly now seemed within her control, though the thought gave her little comfort. She smiled at Nem, his dark eyes on her. "But I got through it. With Jonah's help."

"Well, I had no doubt it would be so. No doubt at all." He stood and retrieved some of the delicacies he'd mentioned, handing Evelyn a small cloth pouch. She glanced inside to see an assortment of brightly coloured strips.

"Thank you," she said.

"Now I must attend to my crew." He stood and moved towards the door. "Please, make yourself comfortable. We will be underway once the final checks are complete."

Evelyn absentmindedly watched him go. It was time to return to Septima. To put their plan into action. She placed a sweet, red strip in her mouth and chewed, setting her head back against the chair.

Raif, Rose. I'm coming back.

I'm coming for you.

CHAPTER 34
HECTOR

er son. Barnaby was Beth's son, Orion his father.

Try as he might, Hector couldn't fathom this new discovery. As the wagon rumbled ever closer to Taskan, he thought back on everything Beth told him over their weeks together in Nook Town. Had she put the evidence in front of him, waited for him to pick up on the truth? Or had she simply lied the whole time?

She was so eager to help.

To help herself, not me. To get revenge on Orion.

Shit. I was so stupid.

He curled his fingers inwards, nails biting into his palms. He stopped short of punching the wall of their wheeled prison, not wanting to wake up the sleeping Raif, Rose, and Dog. It had taken long enough for them to calm from their ordeal, to accept that he would watch over them and keep them safe. A promise he would do his damnedest to see through now they were back under his eye.

He almost scoffed at himself. Under his eye, but for how much longer?

Oh, Cara. What are we going to do?

A quiet whisper replied, *Everything we can.*

Hector gave a sad smile. Cara always did her best to bolster him, even when she was injured and locked away from him. He wished he could hold her. He had failed her, failed them all at every turn. He let out a long sigh, watching the children and Dog. Soon they would awaken. He would have to try and explain how they'd ended up here, heading for the Commune with no way out.

How he had failed to protect them from Avanna.

From Beth and her foolish plan.

You should never have allowed her in. He berated himself over and over again, remembering the way his stomach fluttered at the sight of her. He thought back on their time together. Some part of him couldn't completely believe it had been false, that she'd used him as part of her own vengeful plot. And yet, she could have told him the truth at any moment ... couldn't she? *Would I have understood?*

He recalled her asking about the Commune, mentioning her belief that any taken in could use their powers however they chose— have them nurtured, even. He should have told her then what he'd seen over his years with Veritas, made her realise how abominable the Grand Magister was. What happened to those who didn't meet his expectations, powers or not. Instead, he'd allowed that seed to grow unimpeded.

Stupid bastard. This is your fault, as always.

Stop. You are too hard on yourself, old man. Your anger is directed the wrong way.

Hector sat up at that, running a hand across his overgrown moustache. Cara was right. There was no point in his burning fury towards himself or Beth or anyone else. Before the week was out, they would be in front of the Grand Magister. He would be made to pay for his role within Veritas. Both he and his beloved Cara would be executed; that was a certainty. It would be a long and painful process, of that he had no doubt.

But what of the children? Hector couldn't think about it, not wanting to consider what the Grand Magister would do with Rose's powers once he discovered them.

What Avanna had tried to do.

Avanna. Dead, Orion said. Now was not the time to ask the girl what happened. Might be it no longer mattered. Avanna had made her choice; she had betrayed Veritas ... She deserved what she got, didn't she?

And now Rose was as good as the Grand Magister's pawn already. She was young enough to be moulded into whatever he chose.

I've failed in every way possible.

There was no escape.

He felt an unspoken attempt at comfort from Cara, a prickling of warmth at the back of his mind.

He leaned his head back and closed his eyes, trying to push the image of Beth's face from his mind. Eventually, the rocking of the wagon lulled him into an uneasy sleep. For a while, he was back with his Cara. They were safe, they were together.

All would be well.

He was awoken by a quiet voice and gentle hands gripping his shoulders.

"Hector."

He inhaled sharply, forcing his heavy, aching eyelids open. "Raif, lad. What is it?" He pulled himself upwards with a groan. On the opposite bench, Rose and Dog were sleeping soundly. Raif was hunched beside him, eyes hidden in shadow.

"I wanted to ask you something." Raif glanced over his shoulder. "About Orion."

Hector lifted himself onto one elbow, trying to ignore the wave of nausea that washed over him. "Nothing good can come of talking about that man, lad."

Raif's expression was pinched. Sadness radiated from him. "What did Orion do to me?" He rubbed a hand across his forehead, brow creasing. "It's slowly coming back to me the further we get from Nook Town. Orion made me promises about Rose. He swore he'd find her. And he made Lebby teach me about Perisma until that became all that mattered. How can what he did to me be *good*? How can those people in Nook Town have followed him so blindly?" His words tumbled out, a barrage of confusion and anger.

Hector sat up, temples throbbing dully. "Perhaps not blindly, given that there was something more at play than Orion's dictatorship over the people … That orb, I suspect, holds some answers, though the true extent of Perisma's power and influence over that town will remain a mystery to us, I fear." He touched a hand to Raif's shoulder, unable to calm him with his powers and wishing he could. He let out a long sigh, Cara purring beside him.

"It's a madman's hope, lad, that keeps such fervent faith in place without question. Orion held all the convictions of a man who believes he has the answers, but there was more to it, wasn't there? He did *something* to those people to ensure they followed him, to place himself in a position of unquestioned leadership." He puffed air through his lips. "My childhood in Nook Town was full of lectures and sermons about Perisma's light and blessing, but I don't remember that orb. I don't remember the townsfolk being so cruel, even against those with powers. The people, my father included, had faith in a god they believed would protect and guide them." Hector's voice lowered, his free hand clenching into a fist, yet he couldn't say more to explain his rage. It was too deeply rooted, too painful to release in its fullness lest it destroy anyone or anything close at hand. "Orion took that faith and corrupted it."

"I think you're right," Raif said after an extended silence, lifting his head, Hector able to see the clear grey of his eyes. "I think he is mad. I think he extends that madness to all who follow him using Lebby's tea and that strange orb of his." He shuddered. "I've never felt so—so—"

"Mm. I know, lad. I felt it too."

Raif gave a nod. "I feel like these last weeks have been a dream. I'm getting flashes of memory. Orion kept me locked away, drugged up, sought to control me ... All for what? So he could control Rose. So he could use her to make some point about his god's law, or as a pawn for his own gains. Just like Avanna before him. He spoke so much of Perisma and truth and light, but he lied to and deceived me, and everyone else in Nook Town. I don't know what was in that tea, Hector, but it really ..." His throat bobbed. "It really made me ignore everything but what he told me."

"It's my fault, lad. You were left alone there because of me, because of what I did. I should have known what would happen as soon as I returned there." Hector bowed his head. "Forgive me."

Raif reached over and touched his hand. "Hector, there's nothing to forgive. I should have listened to you. You told me not to trust anyone, but I ignored you because ..." He turned his face away, cheeks flushing. "Because I liked Lebby. I thought she was a friend at a time when I had no one else. And then Orion told me he'd help with Rose, and before I knew it, I—I was—"

Suddenly, the carriage lurched to a halt. Outside, agitated voices and shouts of alarm permeated the night air. Raif leaped up to gaze out the rear of the wagon, hands clasped around the iron grates that served as the window.

"What's going on?" Hector asked.

"I don't know," Raif said. "It's getting dark, hard to see. I think there are more soldiers, a man in black clothes ..."

"Let me look."

Raif moved aside, and Hector took his place. He saw the dark-clothed man speaking to Commander Brodell. Though he held a lantern, he was turned away from the wagon, face concealed.

"Who is it?" Raif asked, face pinched with worry as he moved to sit beside Rose, who was stirring with the sudden lack of momentum.

"I can't see yet, he's—oh. Oh no."

"What?"

The man's piercing blue eyes, dancing with reflected lantern light, locked with Hector's.

"Yes, Lord Torrant," said Commander Brodell. "We'll see to it right away."

"Get back," Hector whispered, the knot in his stomach tightening. Lord Torrant's appearance here could not be a coincidence. The commander must have sent word of his discovery. Lord Torrant was one of the Grand Magister's closest agents, often testing new prisoners to check the strength of their powers. Hector glanced back at Rose, gulping down his rising panic.

When Brodell came to unlock their wagon, Hector whispered, "What have you done, man? These are the Grand Magister's prisoners. Why are we here?"

Commander Brodell frowned. "I do not answer to you, traitor. Stand back."

"Please," Hector said. "Whatever you have planned, don't take the children. I need to stay with them, I can't—"

"Be quiet or I will *make* you do so," Brodell said calmly, clasping the hilt of his sword. "Get out, all of you."

Mind and body still weakened from all that had transpired at the ceremony, Hector was unable to fight back. "What are you doing?" He turned to the waiting Lord Torrant, heart hammering. "Why are you here?"

"Bring it here," Brodell said to one of his men. A soldier moved beside the commander, clasping Cara's cage in his arms. Hector gasped. "Unless you want us to kill your *pet*, Haralambous, I suggest you do as I say. Bring the children out. Now."

Hector understood. If he tried to fight, he would be killed, and the children would be taken. He had to wait for his powers to return to him. Until then, he had no choice but to obey or risk his companion and lose the children anyway.

Internally, he screamed. *Damn you, Orion.*

"Raif, Rose," he said, voice as calm as he could make it. "Come on."

"What's happening, Hector?" Raif asked, clutching his sister's hand as they jumped down to the ground.

"I'm sorry, lad, I—"

"Silence," Commander Brodell hissed. "Take them before Lord Torrant."

Hector placed a hand on Raif's and Rose's shoulders, gently moving them forward. "Don't be afraid," he said. "I won't let anything happen to you." He sorely wanted to believe his own words, but the situation was far beyond his control; always had been, now he thought on it.

"What have we here?" Lord Torrant said, lantern held up to study each of them in turn. He paused on Hector's face before giving a satisfied nod. "Good work ... Brodell, was it?"

"Yes, my lord," the soldier said, beating his left hand against his chest. "Commander Brodell, sir. Recently promoted to replace a soldier I believe was in your service, Commander Sul—"

"Yes, thank you, Brodell." Lord Torrant sniffed, turning his attention back to the prisoners.

"Please," Hector said. "Do what you want with me, but let the children go."

Lord Torrant laughed, his pale eyes holding no mercy. "You think you can bargain for their lives, traitor? I know full well who you are." He grasped Hector's chin between his jewelled fingers, turning his head one way and then the other. "You appear somewhat battered and bruised, but you are well enough to stand trial before the Grand Magister."

"My lord, please, don't take them. I will do anything if you just—"

"Do not presume to tell me what to do," Lord Torrant snapped. Though he didn't shout, his words rang out with an air of unquestionable authority. He moved to regard Raif, Rose, and Dog, then looked at Commander Brodell. "Which one is it?"

"The girl, Lord Torrant," Brodell said. "One of my soldiers assured me she is the one who was hunted previously, by, uh, by Commander Sulemon. Before the man absconded from the Commune's service."

Lord Torrant visibly stiffened. "I see," he said. He knelt so he was face to face with Rose. For her part, the young girl remained unflinching, meeting his gaze with wide-eyed defiance. At her side, Raif still clutched her hand.

"You're to come with me, child," Lord Torrant said to Rose, eyes flitting towards Raif. "Is this your brother?" The girl nodded briskly. "Of course. Well, to make sure there's no temptation on your part ..." He nodded to a nearby soldier. Without hesitation, the man stepped forward and punched Raif in the face, knocking him to the muddy ground. Rose cried out and Dog yelped, though both remained rooted to the spot as though afraid to move.

Hector lunged, wanting to protect them all, but two more soldiers jolted to his side, holding him back. He grimaced and flailed, still too weak. "Damn it, Torrant," he cried. "What are you doing? They're only children!"

Lord Torrant ignored him, instead addressing the soldier. "Detain the boy. Take him to the carriage," he said, then turned attention back to Rose. "Do you understand, girl? If you try to use your powers against me or any of my men, there will be consequences for your brother."

Rose didn't turn her face away from him or blink. "Yes," she whispered.

"The dog, is it yours?" Lord Torrant asked, surprisingly gently.

Rose nodded in response.

"I will allow you to keep it, for now, but I will take it from you if you give me reason." Lord Torrant gave Rose a final hard stare, an eyebrow raised, before nodding at Commander Brodell.

"Take her, and the dog," Brodell said. "Quickly, now."

Hector struggled against the soldiers binding him. "No, you can't have them," he said. "Please, show some mercy."

Rose looked back over her shoulder, eyes glistening. She gave Hector a tiny nod. It said, *I trust you. You can save us.*

Hector was sure his heart would break then. "I'll find you! I'll find you," he called. "You piece of shit, Torrant. You'll pay for this, you disgusting—" One of the soldiers holding Hector delivered a swift blow to his stomach. He slumped over, gasping for breath.

"I don't think so," Lord Torrant said, giving Hector a satisfied smirk. "Pathetic. I would kill you myself, but you do not deserve a quick ending. No, you will be sent to Taskan and made an example of. A public execution for a Veritas pig."

"I will see him escorted there myself, my lord." Commander Brodell pounded his fist against his chest.

"Yes, very good, Brodell," Lord Torrant said. "Perhaps when you are finished in Taskan, you might like to …"

They walked away, and Hector lost interest in their words, trying to return his breathing to normal.

"No, please," he croaked, watching as Raif and Rose were forced inside a black carriage. "Please."

It was no use.

The carriage was closed, Lord Torrant returned to his horse, and they were on their way, leaving Hector's grasp once more.

When Commander Brodell returned and dragged him to his feet, it was all Hector could do to remain standing, his legs trembling with exhaustion and defeat. "There's no point in fighting anymore," Brodell said as he escorted Hector back to the wagon, pushing him inside. Hector slumped backwards, hitting the floor. "Accept your fate, man. Have the dignity in death that you never had in life." The look in his eyes was almost pitying as he said, "Here, you may as well be together for the final part of the journey." The soldier threw Cara's cage into the wagon before closing and locking it.

"Are you well, my love?" Hector reached for Cara's cage, placing it gently on the bench beside him.

I'll recover. I'm more worried about you, old man.

Hector sat with his head in his hands, unable to reassure her, as the wagon jolted into motion.

We can save them. He sensed Cara watching him through the bars of her cage and glanced up to meet her yellow eyes, bright even in the darkness of the wagon.

"Can we, girl?" Hector exhaled. "I don't know this time. I think all our chances might have run out. There aren't any more options."

Your powers will come back.

Hector snorted. "It's too late."

We'll kill them all.

Hector looked up to find his beloved staring at him with blazing yellow eyes; her gaze filled him with a final beacon of strength. He smiled, though it was weak and did nothing to soothe his aching heart. "What have we got to lose?" he said, lying back on the floor of the wagon and shutting his eyes. "We might just do that."

Sleep evaded Hector as his mind worked to form a plan. He had to believe it possible, just one more time. He would save the children.

We will save them together. There's always a way. With Cara at his side, he could achieve anything. He stroked a finger against her head through the cage bars, giving a grim nod.

"After that, the Commune can do what they want with me," he muttered.

With both *of us.*

"Yes, my love," Hector whispered, a tear rolling down his cheek. "Both of us."

CHAPTER 35
JONAH

As he recalled the last conversation with his mother, Jonah paced back and forth in his cabin aboard *Septima's Blessing*. After a tense few days, the confrontation had taken place the night before he was due to leave. "Did you bring her here knowing what she was?" His mother's eyes were full of disbelief, pain, outrage. "The Curse, Jonasaiah. To bring it back here, after all that has happened."

"Mother, she is not what you believe. You cannot think she would do what Ezzarah's rebels have done before. That she would hurt anyone," he said, shaking his head. "No, she would never."

"How can you know that, *a'laha*?" His mother tried to grasp his arm, but he shook her away, irritated by her words. Her face creased with sadness, eyes glistening with tears. "Do you not recall your own father?"

He looked at her, mouth agape. "How can you ask that of me?" he said, voice barely more than a whisper. "I know what Father did. His involvement with the uprising ... Mother, how could you—"

"You were only a child when he and his followers tried to use Ezzarah's Curse to overthrow *Samalah*. He was blinded by arrogance, like Ezzarah himself. The suffering and destruction they caused. The violence." She closed her eyes as though taken back to that time. When she spoke again, her voice trembled. "It almost destroyed our home. Our people."

"I know, *Su'mula*," Jonah snapped, irritated at the implication that he could ever forget. "But Evelyn is not—"

"You cannot be sure. You can never be sure. I never knew ... Your father, he ..." Her lip quivered as tears flowed down her face.

Ashamed to have caused his mother such pain, Jonah stepped forward to comfort her. "Mother, I am sorry. But please, you must believe me—Evelyn would never use her powers to hurt anyone."

"No, Jonah," his mother whispered, face hardening. "You took a risk. And what is more, you hid it from us all. From me."

He knew then what had hurt her most—his lack of honesty after so long away. Even now, he could not tell her everything. He thought of the unfinished note to Eirik tucked into his robes, felt sure it must be a beacon of betrayal glowing in the darkness of his childhood home.

"We are leaving in the morning, Mother. The island will be out of danger."

His mother nodded, dashing away her tears. "I suppose it will be many years before I see you again, *a'laha*."

Jonah met her gaze, guilt gnawing at his heart. He exhaled, softening his rage before he spoke again. "No, Mother. I will return to you once we have done what we need to do."

Her eyes shone up at him. "And what of the man? Does your heart not yearn to be with him once more?"

Jonah found that he could not respond, could not lie to his mother anymore.

She smiled weakly as she stood. "I must sleep now, Jonasaiah. I will not see you again before you leave." She kissed him on the forehead, and he caught a final whiff of her delicate, flowered perfume. "Do not forget where you belong, *a'laha*."

Perhaps it was those words that troubled him the most.

Where do I truly belong?

He no longer knew. Once it had been with his family, and believing only in the goodness of Veritarra. They'd been happy for a time. Then his father rose up, tried to change their sacred ways, acting under the curse of an angry and vengeful god. Jonah grew ashamed, afraid to see the looks on the faces around him when he walked through his village, for he knew well his resemblance to his father. It was clear his presence brought back unwelcome memories for those most impacted by the uprising.

He chose to flee, seeking somewhere new to call home, promising he would return before long—a man grown, full of certainty and confidence in his place, proving that he was not as his father had been.

Instead, he met Eirik; thirteen years passed in the blink of an eye. Their time together might as well have been his entire life so little could he remember of the person he was before. He knew in his heart they were still connected, drawn together by an invisible thread pulling and twisting until he could hardly bear the pain any longer.

Samalah told him he must forget all about Eirik, focus only on his mission if he was to succeed. But could there be another way? Could he convince Lord Torrant to turn his back on the Commune? To relinquish his powers, to choose their love? *After all, I changed my views. It is possible to change, to turn away from the Commune. I have to know. I have to be certain before I give up on him.*

He pulled the note out of his tunic, sat, and smoothed the crumpled paper on his lap. Quill in hand, he read over the words and finished what he had started so many days ago.

I write to you with a plan, one that I am not even sure you will agree with. One that may even cause you to call me a traitor, to hang me at the gates of Taskan as you have ordered so many hung before.

Though we cannot go back to what we were, I wonder whether we could be together and move forward, change Septima for the better? You do not need your powers to do that. We could work as one to bring an end to the Grand Magister's tyranny and corruption. ~~I have the means to take~~

~~away his powers, render him weak and vulnerable.~~ I have a plan. One we could enact together.

Is it possible? I must know. I must have an answer or forever live with an abominable ache in my heart.

If you are willing to speak, send a note back with the messenger, detailing the time and place of our meeting.

If I do not hear from you, I will know what you chose. I will have my answer.

Yours,

Jonah

Once finished, Jonah folded the note with care, retrieved a nearby candle, and sealed the letter with wax. *Eirik will not think much of that,* he thought, smiling despite everything.

A knock at his cabin door came as he was tucking the note away.

"Yes?" he said, looking up as Evelyn entered the cabin.

"I came to see if you were ... well," she said uneasily.

"I am." He stood before her eyes could linger on the quill, ink, and candle, all still beside his bed. "Shall we walk the deck?"

Outside, he was surprised to find the sun high in the sky.

"Do you think the plan will work?" Evelyn asked.

His heart skipped a beat. *How does she know?* "Work?" he said, looking ahead to avoid her gaze. "I-I'm not—"

"Veritarra's Gift," she said, hand on her pouch.

Relief flowed through him. *She does not know about the note.* "Oh, yes," he said, touching his own new pouch. "At least, I hope so." He inhaled and looked up at the sky, the sun warm on his face. "From what *Samalah* said, the new flowers are more potent, a further blessing from our dear Goddess. *Samalah* seemed sure that using all of it would be enough to render the Grand Magister powerless. The hardest part will be getting close to him."

"It will," Evelyn said, chewing her lip. "I'm sure we'll find a way. Veritarra gave us Her blessing, after all."

"Yes," Jonah said. "I am sure we will, too."

She was silent for a moment, the waves washing against the ship and the great gulls wheeling overhead the only sounds to be heard. It might have been peaceful had his very soul not been torn in two.

"I'll be by your side," she said suddenly. "We'll do it together. For everyone in Septima." She beamed up at him, so sure of herself it made his heart ache.

She cannot know of the note. She cannot know of the betrayal I have all but carried out. "We will," he said, voice straining against the tightness in his throat.

They stood together for a while, enjoying the salted breeze and warm sunlight. When they returned to Septima, the kingdom would be darkened by the winter months. They would be faced with the difficult reality of their mission.

Until they set foot on the shores of Septima once more, he would do his best to forget Eirik, forget the letter, forget his own selfish longing. He would stand united with Evelyn and hold the belief with her—that they had a chance of succeeding.

And so, as they sailed away from his homeland, surrounded by the brightness and joy that came with the heat of the Nomarran summer, he allowed his heart to fill with hope, no matter that he knew it would not last.

CHAPTER 36
HECTOR

The wagon jolted to a halt, and Hector lurched from the bench, thudding to the floor.

Something's very wrong. Cara sat upright in her cage, staring at the wagon door.

Hector sensed it, too—a tension in the air outside the wagon.

"Keep back! We are soldiers of the Commune. Any attack against us is an attack against the Grand Magister himself. Stand down or face the consequences!"

"Who would dare attack the Grand Magister's men?" Hector muttered, moving to peer out the grated window. A stab at his heart made him think of Veritas, of the missions they'd carried out against such soldiers in years past.

They're gone now, he thought, hands tightly gripping the iron grates of his prison, his knuckles whitening. *All gone.*

Concentrate, Cara urged him. *What can you see?*

It was growing dark outside as another day drew to a close. An ice-cold breeze blew across from Taskan Bay, some miles to the south. To the north, Hector could just make out the dark outline of the eastern border of Taskan Forest through them.

Commander Brodell directed his voice towards the trees. Some of his soldiers held lanterns; some had their swords drawn, poised for attack.

Cara hissed. *Stay down. Danger.*

He ducked down as an arrow shot out of the shadows. There was a wet choking sound from outside, the thud of a man slumping to the ground.

"You will pay for that, mark my words, trai—!"

A cry of attack filled the air, followed by the thunder of hoof-beats, the clash of swords. More arrows *whooshed* past the wagon; more men screamed in pain, then fell quiet. The attack seemed to come from all sides. Hector dared not move.

Your powers. Try your powers.

He grunted, not holding out much hope of success. Nevertheless, he reached his mind outside, roaming for the closest consciousness he could locate. To his surprise, he immediately connected with a soldier of the Commune, mind full of panic.

Ha! It worked!

Focus. Cara let out another hiss.

"Yes, sorry." He straightened up and pushed outwards with his powers again. This time, it was expected when he connected with the same soldier, and he snuffed the man's life out without a second thought, darting on to the next. His anger drove him to take lives where before he would have hesitated.

The time for hesitation is over, Cara assured him. *We have to save Raif and Rose.*

He groaned in response, his powers requiring more of his concentration than usual while he still recovered from his ordeal at Orion's hands. Another soldier's mind smothered, he moved on ... and found himself in familiar territory. He gasped and drew back.

It can't be. Hector glanced at Cara in her cage.

Executed, Brodell had said. Hung as traitors.

Do you think you made a mistake, Hector?

He pulled on his moustache, flustered. "A trick of my imagination, I'm sure. A burning hope I know cannot be true." He slumped down, exhausted, and waited for the attack to end.

"I think we've got them all," said a deep, gravelly voice, close to the wagon door.

"What about the wagon?" said another.

"Is it locked?" The chain rattled. Hector positioned himself to pounce on whoever opened the door. "Find a key. It must be on one of the soldiers. Hello, in there! We'll have you out soon, don't worry."

Hector remained silent; his trust had been broken too many times for him to let his guard down so easily.

"Nice boots on this one," someone said. "I'll have those."

"We can see to that once we've freed the prisoners," said the first man, sounding annoyed.

Hector experienced another jolt of recognition at the man's voice. *Don't get your hopes up.*

"Ah, here it is. Must be the leader." Someone spat on the ground. "Commune bastard."

Hector glanced at Cara, wanting to believe, afraid of being wrong. He remained poised for attack, waited for the door to open. He had to see the man's face before he let his guard down. The sound of the key in the padlock seemed to last for an eternity.

"Quickly; there could be more of them."

"I'm going quick as I can!"

"Sorry, we're nearly in there with you," the voice said to Hector.

"You sure it's not empty? Awfully quiet in there."

Hector's thighs burned as he squatted low, ready to lunge at the first sign of trouble.

The door creaked open. Hector blinked against the lantern held into the wagon. Despite his plan, he remained frozen. The figure was a dark silhouette hidden behind the flickering flame, yet the hair was long, the voice, now he reflected on it, all too familiar ...

"There's nothing to be scared of," he said. "The soldiers are all —" The man gasped. "Hector?"

Hector's heart lurched. He held his hands out to catch himself before his shuddering legs gave way. "Mak?" he croaked, hardly daring to accept what he saw before him.

Perhaps we're already dead, Cara quipped, though Hector felt her relief as palpably as his own.

"My friend!" Before he knew it, Hector was hauled out of the wagon by his arms and locked into an embrace. "Now we know how those soldiers dropped dead before our eyes! I should have known." Mak laughed, the sound full of triumph.

Overwhelmed by emotion, Hector stammered, "How—how is this … I was told you were hanged. The—the Commune. All executed."

"Ha, not likely," Mak said. "I won't let that piece of shit the Grand Magister get me so easily, you know that. Here, let me free Cara."

As he leaned over the cage, Hector studied his old friend. Despite his cheery tone, a change had come over Mak since they'd last seen each other. His eyes seemed duller, his cheeks mottled with bruises and shadowed by stubble. His long brown hair hung past his shoulders, uncut for some time. Still, he smiled with genuine happiness as he handed Cara to Hector and called out, "Everyone, come and see who it is!"

As he clutched his beloved companion, Hector was surrounded by familiar faces: Arturo, the archery master; Griff, the young errand boy, and his mother, Cass; Tavin, who had acted as Avanna's guardsman, and his ward, Bo. Each of them held a bow or sword, determination marking their faces with a fierceness he was sure they hadn't possessed before. They greeted Hector with a nod or smile. Within each face, he saw the truth of what they'd been through. They might have escaped execution, but they had lost much.

"No doubt you have much to tell me, old friend," Mak said, placing an arm around Hector's shoulders as though all that had transpired when they'd last seen each other had been forgotten. "For now, we must be away from here. We're not far from Taskan. There will be other soldiers patrolling these roads soon enough." He cleared his throat, turning to the others as they scavenged clothing and provisions from the Commune soldiers.

"Where are you camped?" Hector asked, placing Cara on the ground so she could stretch. She rubbed her face on his legs before trotting away into the trees. *Don't go far,* he thought, stomach clenching at the thought of losing her again.

"Into the forest," Mak said, leading Hector towards the dark trees, holding his lantern high to guide their way.

"Isn't it a risk?" Hector asked, glancing behind at the others who were deftly moving over the soldier's bodies. "So close to Lord Torrant's home. To Taskan."

"That's the point, my friend," Mak said, flashing him a grin. "They wouldn't expect anyone to be fool enough to lay in wait so close. You know me, Hector. I *am* that foolish. We can talk more when we're settled by the fire."

They walked for a time in silence, the night closing in around them, the sky above glittering with stars. It was too beautiful, too peaceful. Hector pulled his eyes away from it, heart clenching and eyes burning.

He watched his step as best he could, though he tripped more than once on hidden roots and underbrush, grasping at nearby tree trunks to prevent himself from falling to the ground. His nostrils filled with the smell of damp and rot; his boots slipped on a bed of mud and mouldering leaves. Finally, they emerged into a small clearing, where crude tents had been erected between trees. In the centre, a small fire had burnt down to embers.

"See if you can find some wood," Mak said, moving to prod what remained of the smouldering logs and sending orange sparks into the air. "I'll get some food ready."

As Hector searched, Cara bolted out of the forest to join him, a mouse dangling from her mouth. He sensed her intermingling pride and hunger; even with the burn on her leg, she hadn't lost her prowess.

"Go to the camp," he told her. "Eat, sleep. Regain your strength."

You should do the same.

"I will; just got to get some wood or I'll be eating uncooked food."

Nothing wrong with that, Cara thought. *Not good enough for you, old man?*

Before he could respond, she darted into the night—white against the darkness—and away from his view. He chuckled to himself as he bent over to retrieve some twigs.

Back at the camp, Hector began to rebuild the fire as Mak prepared two rabbit carcasses. "We hunted them earlier," he said. "Though, if the rumours are to be believed, we're lucky to find any game in these woods." He glanced around before leaning close. "Wolves roam this forest," he whispered. "Lord Torrant himself holds an annual hunt to keep their numbers in check."

Hector shuddered at Mak's words; wolves and Lord Torrant, both dangerous predators, without a doubt, though he knew which he would rather face.

A wolf cannot lie or cheat or manipulate, Cara pointed out, earlier indignation forgotten.

"That's true," Hector muttered.

"Hmm, what was that?" Mak said, arranging the rabbits on spits over the fire.

"Lord Torrant. I heard he'd attacked Veritas, the camp. I thought you were all dead," Hector said. "The children taken."

Mak's eyes dropped. "It's true, in part," he said. "We were able to escape only through sheer luck. Lord Torrant led a group of soldiers into the camp. He was ... ruthless. Rounded up the children, ordered the adults executed there and then. Without a leader, everything fell apart after Avanna, uh ... After you and the boy left." He absentmindedly rolled the shoulder that had been pierced by Raif's arrow, memories of their last conversation evidently reminding him of the injury.

Avanna. Hector would have to tell Mak of his sister's death, though he scarce knew the truth of what had come to pass. "I see," he said, waiting for his friend to ask the inevitable question.

"I … I am sorry about what happened." Mak cleared his throat. "Did you find her, Hector? Before the Commune got to you?"

Hector sighed. Despite all Avanna had done, the three of them had spent years together, saving those who would have been taken by the Commune, creating an alternative way of life where those with powers could flourish rather than live in fear. That was gone now, shattered by Avanna's selfish actions and the subsequent destruction of their camp.

"Hector?" Mak glanced up from turning the rabbits above the fire, the flames causing the shadows about his face to flicker and shift.

"I went to Nook Town, took the lad. After what you told us, we set out to catch up with your sister there," Hector said, remembering how naïvely full of hope they'd been.

Mak swallowed. "What happened?" he asked, taking a seat beside Hector as the air filled with the smell of cooking meat.

Hector let out a bitter laugh. "Where to start?"

By the time he was finished, the rest of the camp had returned. No one spoke for a few minutes. Mak remained subdued, head down, for Hector had repeated Orion's words about finding Rose with a dead woman, and the reality seemed suddenly all too clear —Avanna had been killed by the young girl she'd sought to control.

"So, where are they now?" asked Griff, breaking the quiet. His mother, Cass, elbowed him sharply in the side, but he continued nonetheless. "Raif and Rose. Hector said they were taken, too, but they weren't in that wagon. They must be—"

"Hush, boy, or you'll be getting more than an elbow from me," Cass said, giving Hector an apologetic smile behind her son's back.

"It's okay," Hector said. "I suppose it's best you know now. Lord Torrant has them. They were with me for a time, and then our wagons were stopped on the road a day or so ago, and there he was, demanding to take them. I would have stopped him, but my powers were … Orion, the church elder, did something to me, and I hadn't recovered yet. I was too weak." He hit his fists into the log upon which he sat, rough bark scraping against his knuckles.

Mak held his hands out to stop him. "We've all lost people we care about," he said, the words so quiet they could barely be heard above the crackling fire. He clasped Hector's shoulders, looked into his face with an expression full of grim determination. "But these children are still alive and might still be saved. What my sister did ..." He shook his head. "Was unforgivable. Now we must focus on what we can do. What's your plan?"

"My plan?" Hector asked, narrowing his eyes.

"Come now, Hector. There's always a plan." Mak jutted out his chin. "Surely you mean to rescue them? The man I once knew would have done so without hesitation."

Hector cleared his throat. "Well, yes, but I mean to do it alone. I can't put you all in danger. I won't. This is my fault and my mistake to—"

"No," Mak snapped, eyes darkening. "It's not your mistake. My sister led you to that place with her actions. If she hadn't, well, I can't say where we'd be for sure, but Lord Torrant wouldn't have those children. He might not have attacked our camp. You would never have returned to Nook Town."

"Mak, I cannot allow—"

"I'm helping you, Hector. It's what needs to be done. To make amends," Mak said. His face broke into a joyless smile, and he held his arms out wide. "Besides, what do you think we're doing here?"

"What do you mean?" Hector looked round at everyone. "You mean to ..."

"Take revenge," said Bo. "On the Commune. On Lord Torrant. For what they did, for all the people they killed." The young man had the wispy moustache and round cheeks of youth, but in that moment, Hector sensed he would kill any soldier he laid eyes on without a second thought.

Because that was what the Commune had driven them to.

"Well then, I see it's me who'll be joining your plans," he said, grinning.

Mak patted him on the back. "Just like old times, my friend."

The rabbits were prepared and handed around by Tavin. Hector gratefully received a leg and ate the steaming meat, puffing between chews, too hungry to wait for it to cool. At his feet, Cara had reappeared and carefully tucked herself into a neat ball, purring gently. For the first time in a long while, he allowed himself to relax.

"So," he said, wiping his greasy fingers on his trousers. "Where do we start? I'm sure you'll understand the children are my priority; I need to make my way back to Torrant's home without delay."

"And we'll be with you all the way. You have my word on that," Mak said. Murmurs of agreement spread through the group, and Hector was flooded with relief.

I told you, Cara thought. *There's always a way.* Hector leaned down and stroked her head.

"It simply means attacking Lord Torrant sooner than we'd planned," Mak continued. "It was always going to be a risk, but it's one we're willing to take. That man, he needs to be shown what we're made of. He ..." Mak waved his hand as his voice broke.

"We'll show him," Tavin said. They were the first words he'd spoken that night. Hector was surprised at the fury in his tone—pure and unabated. He looked to Hector as though able to read his mind and said, "My wife was among those executed. We'd all be dead if we hadn't been out hunting. But I should have been there to protect her. I should have saved her." The bearded man stood and stalked away into the trees, shoulders tensed, fists clenched. Hector watched him go, sensing the man's restless grief and anger like it was a burning fire within him.

"Avanna left the camp in disarray," Mak said, drawing Hector's attention back. "Her betrayal cut us deep, all of us. Veritas relied on her. Without her, the trade deals with the mountain tribes fell away. She was the one to form alliances. So adept at convincing people of her goodness. After she was gone, some people left the camp altogether, seeking shelter elsewhere. I tried my best. I arranged hunting parties to bring in food. We were out that day." He looked up at Hector, eyes glassy. "There's nothing left for us." He inhaled and sat up, regarding the group once more. "So, we'll take out as many as we can before they kill us. Lord Torrant first, and all the way up to the Grand Magister himself."

"Tomorrow, then?" Hector said.

"Tomorrow," Mak agreed.

At that, everyone agreed to set a watch and get some rest. In the morning, they would make their way to the Torrant Estate and begin their fight.

Hector laid down on the forest floor, wrapping his cloak around himself. Cara moved to nuzzle into his chest.

"We're going to do it, my love," he whispered.

I know we are. I knew it all along.

Hector looked up at the night sky through the canopy of trees. The moon glowed with an intense light, a great orb watching over them all. The sparks from the fire floated upwards, and he allowed his mind to drift with them.

I'm coming, Raif, Rose.

I'm coming for you.

Lord Torrant will pay.

It was the last thought in his mind before his eyes closed and sleep overcame his weary body. He had much to prepare for; tomorrow, they would begin their plan of revenge.

THE KING'S DECREE

THREE YEARS PRIOR TO THE EVENTS WITHIN THE COMMUNE'S CURSE SERIES

There was a sharp *knock, knock, knock* on the door. The King was roused from his drug-induced sleep, eyes throbbing in his skull. "Yes?" he called, dragging himself to his feet, rubbing his temples with trembling fingers.

A tall, slim man entered, face cast in shadow by his hood. Cosmo shuddered at the black robes of the Commune's servants, a response so visceral, he was barely aware he was doing it anymore. But the Grand Magister insisted upon them, assuring the King that each and every member of the Commune was loyal and trustworthy, not someone to be feared.

An acolyte of the realm, fighting for the good of Septima.

The King glared at the dark outline of the man's face. "Well?"

"Sorry to disturb you, Your Highness," the acolyte said, tone displaying neither any hint of apology nor respect towards his King. "He has sent for you."

Cosmo's stomach lurched, though his expression remained unflinching. "*He's* sent for *me*?" He scoffed. "I asked to see him three days ago, who does he think he is—"

"The Grand Magister is extremely busy, Your Highness," the man said, head tilting back to reveal a square jawline, lips pinched tight with distaste. "He has been examining new recruits, tirelessly working to build an army for the protection of Septima—as well you know."

The King couldn't find it in himself to be annoyed at the interruption. He leaned against the frame of his bed, weakening by the moment. "Very well," he said. "I need time to dress, eat and see to my—"

"There can be no delay, Your Highness," the acolyte said, cutting him off again. "He is awaiting your presence. Now."

This time, Cosmo's fury flared like a fire in his gut—a momentary surge of energy that revealed the king he might have been. "Interrupt me again and I will have your head on a spike at the gates of Taskan, loyal servant of the Grand Magister or not."

The man's dark eyes flashed with uncertainty. "Yes, Your Highness," he said, bowing his head so that his hood fell forward once more.

"Wait outside the door. Do not disturb me again. I will join you when I am ready." The acolyte left without another word, closing the door with a gentle *click* as Cosmo's legs gave way beneath him. He cursed his aching joints—those of a man thrice his age—and wondered not for the first time how different his life might have been had he taken his father's stance against the Commune.

But his father had died years ago, when he was just fifteen years of age. "What's done is done," he muttered. His royal power had slowly trickled through his fingers with the passing of time; there were limited options left to him. Now he needed the Commune to remain in control, though he dared not admit that to anyone. He let out a long sigh. Here he stood, a man wracked with weakness both physical and mental, and he hadn't even reached his thirtieth year.

How did I let this happen?

Oh, but he knew the answer to such a question all too well. The temptation of an ally as powerful as the Grand Magister had been enough to convince him that the Commune's path was the correct one.

Father should not have scorned me, treated me as though I was not worthy of the royal blood flowing through my veins, he thought, mind still tinged with bitterness after all this time. After his older brother Gairas died of a short-lived ailment, his father was left with no choice but to name him as heir. "Look at me now, father," he declared to the empty bedchamber. He held his head high, banishing the guilt and shame that lingered at the periphery of his mind. He'd done what was necessary to prove his worth to the Grand Magister. There was little point in wondering what might have been different, these thirteen years later.

Father's fate was inevitable. The old fool saw my true strength too late. With a shake of his head to dismiss the invading memories, he summoned his serving maid, Mira, to help him dress. He chose clothes to underline his authority, certain the Grand Magister had meant no slight in his abrupt summons. *I am too sensitive these days. Too eager to expect the worst.*

As the maid dressed him, Cosmo studied himself in the mirror. He tugged at his gold-embroidered purple waistcoat, straightening the sleeves of his cream shirt, and smiled at himself, satisfied with how the colours brightened his blue eyes. His trousers were chosen to match the waistcoat, cinched across his slim waist with a gold-buckled belt.

"The fur cloak, I think," he said, glancing at the bare trees, ice-coated grass, and empty flowerbeds in the gardens outside his window. "And my cream leather boots."

Finally, Mira handed him a wooden cane, gilded with gold and tipped with the sigil of the royal household—the head of a great owl, finely carved from the tusks of mammoths from the northern-most reaches of Septima, a remnant of his great-grandfather's time. It nestled in his hand comfortably, a decorative accessory he'd come to rely on of late.

"Your tincture, Your Highness," Mira said, holding out a small glass bottle filled with a black liquid. He gulped down the astringent medicine, wincing as it hit his tongue and scalded his throat.

"Thank you," he said, grateful for the maid's diligent but silent work. She bowed low, giving him a glimpse of her ample cleavage. He flicked his hand to dismiss her, the sight stirring nothing but frustration within him, and she left the room. Cosmo took a moment to prepare himself for the walk along Taskan Palace's long corridors and out to his carriage. The tincture worked its magic on his body quickly and his strength was renewed, for a while at least; it would not do to show any weakness in front of the Grand Magister.

Outside, he squinted against the low-hanging sun. The Grand Magister's acolyte appeared, seemingly from nowhere, and fell into step behind him, a shadow at his back. The sky was a sheet of clear grey, the air crisp and cool—it might have been described as pleasant, if every step didn't send a spike of pain through his entire body. As a child, he might have hoped for snow so he could while away the hours in the Palace gardens, competing with Gairas over who could build the highest snow-soldier, complete with wooden spear and shield. If it snowed now, he would only be concerned about the impact on his health. *When did I become so sheltered? So miserable?*

"Your Highness," his coachman Aleph said, bowing at his approach. At least his own servants retained a modicum of reverence towards him. Cosmo glared at the acolyte by his side—This *is how you should behave*—before taking Aleph's hand and stepping into his gold and white carriage. When the black-hooded acolyte tried to follow, Cosmo took great pleasure in holding up a hand to halt him.

"You'll ride with Aleph," he said. "Ensure he knows where to go."

For a moment, he thought the man might argue, his pursed lips twitching within the shadow of his hood. But then he exhaled and muttered, "Yes, Your Highness," before closing the carriage door.

Cosmo slumped back against the cushioned headrest and closed his eyes. The journey would be a short one, but the tincture's effects were, to his alarm, already waning, his fatigue taking over once more.

Must see the apothecary. The dose must be strengthened.

He hoped the Grand Magister wouldn't require too much of his time. He already desired to be back in the comfort of his bedchamber, away from prying and judgemental eyes.

THE KING WAS SHAKEN awake by the hooded acolyte. He held a quivering hand up against the daylight, letting out a low groan. *Oh, my head.* He rubbed his eyes, attempting to massage away the pulsing pain nestling behind them.

"We've arrived, Your Highness," the acolyte said. "Would you like me to escort you to—"

"No," Cosmo barked. "I know the way."

The acolyte gave a brief bow and flitted away. The King bristled. "Damned insolence," he growled, waiting for his coachman to assist him from the carriage. He made a mental note to bring the matter up with the Grand Magister—the acolyte should be punished. He was king, deserving of respect, deference, esteem. The Commune answered to *him.* It was time those black-robed bastards remembered it. Full of a renewed sense of determination and vigour, he took his coachman's hand and stepped into the courtyard of the Grand Magister's mansion at the centre of the Commune's compound in Taskan. "Thank you, Aleph," he said. "I shan't be long. Wait here."

"Yes, Your Highness."

Cosmo turned to the mansion, taking in the black bricked walls that always sent a stab of dread through his heart. Many noble families had followed suit after the formation of the Commune a century ago, building new homes in the same dark brick as a sign of allegiance to the organisation that promised protection and prosperity for their beloved kingdom. He knocked his cane against the cobble-stones and moved forward, pushing through the growing stiffness in his legs.

A hooded figure opened the door as he approached, proffering their head. As Cosmo entered the red-carpeted hallway, heavy incense caught in the back of his throat. He did his best not to choke, holding a kerchief up to his mouth and coughing delicately into the embroidered cloth. *Every time, you fool.* He dabbed at the tears gathering in the corners of his eyes. How he could forget the intensity of that smell was a mystery, but it happened time and again. It hung in the air, sickening in its richness. More than once he'd wondered what dark secrets it concealed, though he had never dared ask such a question. As king he would receive an answer, of that he had no doubt—it was simply that he had no wish to know it. He had learned long ago it was best to leave such curiosities untouched, buried deep and unacknowledged. It was the only way he could live with what he had allowed within his beloved kingdom.

Cosmo made his way down the hallway, footsteps and cane muffled by the thick red carpet, doing his best not to inhale too much of the strangling scent. The Grand Magister's private study was halfway down the corridor. At either side of the door were portraits of steely-faced men in red robes: the Grand Magister's father and grandfather, the founder of the Commune. He avoided gazing on them for too long, their flint-grey eyes boring into him as though able to read his innermost thoughts. *Ridiculous,* he chided himself. *Paintings of long-dead men.*

His hand hovered over the golden knob of the door, mentally steeling himself for the meeting. As he breathed deeply, attempting to still his racing heart, the Grand Magister's voice rang out from inside the room.

"Enter."

Cosmo flinched. *How dare he presume to tell me what to do?* Another part of his mind whispered, *Such are the strength of his powers; he knows of my approach.* He braced himself as he pushed into the room.

His eyes settled first on the fiercely crackling fire, before which sat two dark leather armchairs. The Grand Magister, Cosmo knew, often enjoyed pondering his plans here, staring into those bright flames as he plotted where next to spread his influence. Irritated by the thought, the king rapped his cane on the ground. "You requested my presence, Magister," he said coldly.

The Grand Magister remained seated as he turned, evidently unperturbed. "I am glad you were able to attend so quickly," he said. His hard grey eyes, so like those of the portraits outside his door, seemed to reach inside Cosmo's mind.

The King gulped, clenching his cane so hard the carved owl's beak bit into his palm. He cleared his throat and said, "Yes. Though you'll recall, Magister, that I requested a meeting with you some—"

"Oh, come now, Cosmo. Sit down before you exhaust yourself." The Grand Magister's voice was low, eyes narrowed. Once during a mock fight with his brother, Cosmo had been hit in the stomach with a wooden sword. In that moment he felt as he had then: deflated and breathless. He lurched towards the empty chair.

Fool.

He should have known better than to try and assert himself so abruptly. He had to be subtle, to allow the Grand Magister to explain why he'd been summoned and then lay out his own expectations... their relationship was one of give and take, it always had been. A game he must play to retain his authority. At least, that was what the king told himself when he lay awake in bed at night.

Embroiled as he was in his own self-chastisement, Cosmo was absurdly grateful for the wine offered by a black-robed acolyte who slipped out of the shadows behind his chair. He took a full glass of the rich, red liquid, gulping down its contents in one go.

"You are well, Your Highness?" the Grand Magister asked, the fire casting flickering shadows across his wrinkled face. Much like those haunting portraits, he wore red robes to distinguish himself from his servants, though his features were remarkably plain. It was his eyes, hard and steely and unfeeling, that told of the true power and authority he held over Septima.

Over me. The King placed down his empty glass. "As well as can be, Magister," he said. "I sent word to you some days ago. I've had troubling news from the Taskan courts that I need to—"

"Yes. You will forgive my... delay." The Grand Magister's thin lips twisted. "We had a number of new recruits. Children and adults alike. My energy has been focused on finding the strongest amongst them."

"A number, you say?" Cosmo tapped a finger against his empty glass and waited for the acolyte to replenish it. "This is good news. Though perhaps relevant to the gossip rippling through my courts." He sipped his wine before continuing. "Tell me, from where do these new recruits come?" Cosmo was pleased to see the Grand Magister's face drop—an unexpected question, it seemed. Emboldened, he went on. "I have heard troubling stories of villages being ransacked to the north and west of Septima, people taken, farms and homes burned to the ground. I confess, it somewhat alarmed me to learn—"

"Your Highness." The Grand Magister held up a hand, shaking his head. "I can assure you, my soldiers have only followed *your* orders. When last we met, we agreed on the strategy. Surely you recall?"

The King froze, glass halfway to his lips.

When last we met.

He closed his eyes and tried to remember their meeting some weeks before. All that came to mind was a blur of pain. His entire body had been wracked with pain, a flare up unlike any he'd experienced before. Cosmo took a long swig of his wine and said, "Of course." He chewed on his lip, feigning a recollection of a conversation that was a fog-filled hole in his memory. "The strategy, yes. These new recruits you mention, are they from these, these villages?"

The Grand Magister gave a fleeting smile. "They are, Your Highness," he said. "We have been able to locate further children with powers. A few adults too. They will be trained according to their abilities, assigned positions as needed. A successful endeavour and one that helps to secure the future of the Commune. The future of our kingdom. And yet…" He bowed his head as though what he meant to say pained him.

Cosmo frowned, patience growing thin. Our *kingdom?* There was some slight here he should be aware of, but he found it increasingly hard to focus his mind. *The damned tincture, too weak by far.* He held his glass out again; wine would have to suffice as a substitute for now, to take his thoughts away from his physical pain, to pinpoint his concentration. He realised the silence was dragging on. The Grand Magister's head remained down as though waiting for the king's permission to speak on. Cosmo scowled, irritated at the unnecessary delay. "And yet?"

The Grand Magister sat back in his chair, drawing himself to his full height. Cosmo jerked back unconsciously, some part of him acknowledging this wasn't an old man, weak and past his prime, after all. This was a *dangerous* man. And yet as the king watched the leader of the Commune, awaiting his next words, he noticed the sickly pallor of his skin, the tinge of yellow in the whites of his eyes, the thinning of his silver hair.

He weakens.

"And yet," the Grand Magister said, voice booming as though to counteract Cosmo's thoughts. "It is not enough. There are those who actively defy what we do."

The king deigned to meet his gaze—and what he saw there sent a chill through his heart. Dark as a storm cloud before it unleashes its full force, the Grand Magister's eyes fixed him to the spot. Cosmo licked his lips. "How can that be so? If our plans are succeeding, the villagers are meeting your requirements. Surely that means—"

The Grand Magister barked a laugh, harsh and cold. "Do not be a fool, Your Highness. Think of the vastness of the kingdom. How little the reach of the Commune has truly spread since its formation. Not to mention those *bastards* in Nook Town who continue to defy me."

He glared at Cosmo. "If you would permit me to send my soldiers there, we could—"

"No," Cosmo snapped. For a wonder, the Grand Magister blanched. Cosmo sat forward in his chair. "Nook Town is protected under the formation oath signed by your grandfather, my great-grandfather. That still means much to me." The king exhaled heavily. "The Church of Perisma in Nook Town is under my protection. Allowed to continue the worship of a god who was once revered across all of Septima. And they shall continue to do so."

"Perhaps the oath has been… *outgrown*," the Grand Magister said. "Over a hundred years have passed. Per the oath, we should be paid our dues. Those with powers *must* be born there, as they are everywhere else in Septima, yet there are none sent to us. Surely, they are being hidden from the Commune's guidance, under the protection of this false god whose worship the rest of us have long since—"

"The oath will remain in place," Cosmo snapped. "There will be no more said on the matter."

It is the least I can do for my father. Protect the worship of a god he still believed in. Who he believed would protect him, even to his dying breath.

The Grand Magister must have seen something in the king's eyes for he nodded and said, "Very well, Your Highness." He stood, picked up a stoker and began to prod at the fire, red robes pooling at his feet like dark blood. "We shall move on then. To the reason I summoned you." He looked up from his task. "I need your approval once more."

"My approval?" Cosmo gave a satisfied nod. *He knows he cannot act without my agreement.* "Indeed, Magister, though you appreciate that I must act in the good of my kingdom, not simply at your whims and desires."

The Grand Magister's gaze flitted towards him, darkening. "Whims and desires?" His knuckles tightened round the metal poker as he stabbed it into the burning logs. "Do not take me for one of your petty nobles, with their pathetic lives and shallow cares. Everything I do is for Septima. To protect our kingdom from those who would do it wrong. Or would you see another war, another uprising of the uncontrolled masses, like that before the Commune was formed?"

Cosmo tried to meet his eyes for as long as possible.

I am in charge here. I am king.

Yet even as his mind repeated those words, his body weakened beneath that hard stare. Finally, he looked down at his empty wine glass. "No, Magister," he said. "Of course not. That is why I support you, the Commune, all you do. But that is not to say—"

"I always knew you were a wiser man than your father. It's why I came to you when you were so young. I saw in you the knowledge and discernment to do what you must for the kingdom, no matter the cost."

"Yes, but I—"

"Your Highness, I'd like you to meet Captain Lence Agron."

A man stepped out from behind the Grand Magister's chair and Cosmos's heart skipped a beat, wondering how long he'd been in the room.

Am I so drunk? I must be more careful.

He placed his glass down and sat back in his armchair, studying the captain as though he'd been aware of his presence all along.

"Your Highness," said Captain Agron, bowing low. His hair was heavy and dark, hanging past his shoulders in thick curls. On the lapel of his black leather jacket was pinned a ruby the size of Cosmo's thumb, glimmering with reflected firelight. When Captain Agron lifted his head once more, he had no hesitation in meeting the king's eyes. Cosmo might have been affronted had he not been drawn into the man's black gaze, hypnotised by eyes like endless pools of darkness.

"The captain is a loyal servant, trusted ally and talented sailor," the Grand Magister said.

The words snapped Cosmo back to the moment. "Oh?" he said, tearing his eyes away from the captain. "And what is his... purpose?"

The Grand Magister returned to his seat, Captain Agron standing at his side. He steepled his hands, watching the king for a moment. "I have held growing concerns for some time now about the Nomarran population in Septima."

Cosmo's chest tightened. "The Nomarrans?"

"Yes, Your Highness. Their numbers grow. We see more arrivals from the Noman Islands every day and, with that, comes an increase in risk."

Cosmo frowned. "Risk? What possible risk could they—"

"Is it not obvious?" The Grand Magister shared a glance with Captain Agron.

The king looked between the two men, grasping for some modicum of understanding. Finally, mind a whir of confusion, he had no choice but to admit his ignorance. "I'm afraid, Magister, that I don't quite follow."

"With increased numbers comes an increase in the amount of that abominable *powder* they possess. The very weapon that threatens us all."

"Veritarra's Gift, Grand Magister," said Captain Agron.

Cosmo scoffed in disbelief. "Veritarra's Gift was instrumental in defeating the rebels in the Seven-Year War. It is not a weapon, but a—"

"I'm afraid, Highness, we have been rather naïve." The Grand Magister slapped his hands into his lap. "We should have seen the potential for rebellion, the knife poised above our heads, far sooner. I fear we must act before it's too late."

"Rebellion? Knife? What are you saying? The Nomarrans have been loyal allies these past hundred years." The king shook his head vehemently. "I can't see that they would pose any threat to Septima, a place that many from the Noman Islands call home."

The Grand Magister clicked his fingers, summoning the acolyte to refill Cosmo's glass. "Imagine if you are wrong and they have already started plotting our downfall. They showed their ability to bring down those with powers in the Seven-Year War. And think of the uprising in the Noman Islands some fifteen years ago. Did that not reveal their true contempt towards those with powers?"

Captain Agron nodded. "They call the powers a curse, do they not?"

"An old superstition," the king said. "Nothing more." And yet he felt his resolve weakening. He reached for the wine with a trembling hand.

What if he is right? What would happen to me? I have no strength to lead a war.

He put his glass back down, sloshing some of the crimson liquid onto his hand. "What would you recommend we do about this, this threat?"

A tiny smile played at the corner of the Grand Magister's lips. "I knew you would understand. That you would see the truth." He looked up at Captain Agron who moved to retrieve a scroll from a small table in the corner of the room. When the king took it from his hands, it took a moment to process what he was reading.

"What is this?" he asked. "A *decree...*"

"It is what must be done," the Grand Magister said firmly.

Cosmo's brow furrowed. "But it says the Nomarrans will be..." He gasped. "Rounded up! Their homes and livelihoods stripped away; their temples torn down. No, no, no." He ran his finger over the document. "*All Nomarrans are to be appointed new positions within the kingdom, as approved by the Commune.*" He swallowed. "Surely, Magister, this is... this is too much."

"Swift measures for swift reform. Isn't that right, Grand Magister?" Captain Agron said, beating his fist against his chest.

"Exactly, Captain Agron." The Grand Magister leaned forward. "I see your concerns, Your Highness. That you feel the measures proposed are too harsh. Yet think of the alternative." He sat back, clasping his hands across his stomach, head cocked as though talking to a simple child. "Think of what I have said. The potential these people hold in the palm of their hands."

Cosmo blinked down at the scroll in his hands. *Are they truly a danger, these people who provided my great-grandfather their aid? Who saved our beloved Septima?*

"It is the only way to ensure our power over Septima is maintained, Your Highness," the Grand Magister pushed.

Our *power over Septima...* Cosmo felt a sudden, sickening throb of pain through his body. A deep fog descended on his mind as though to remind him of his weakness. He was a young man, his body old before its time. He needed the Grand Magister to ensure his own rule, a symbiotic relationship from which there was no escape. "You'll be fair to them, the Nomarrans?" He looked up from the scroll. "Afford them the dignity and respect they deserve?"

The Grand Magister smiled, an unpleasant expression to look upon. "Of course, Your Highness. All they deserve. I am glad you see the necessity for these measures."

The king waved the scroll for Captain Agron to take.

"Captain Agron possesses great powers. He has a crew of men at his disposal. He will travel through Taskan, northwards to Castleton, where the Nomarran population is concentrated. He will see to it that the new decree is implemented. And, if required, he will use his ship and crew to chase down any who try to flee the kingdom without reporting to the Commune and handing over this *Veritarra's Gift.*" A sneering emphasis was placed on those last words, as though the Grand Magister could barely bring himself to say them.

All the while, Captain Agron stood at the Grand Magister's back, dark eyes locked onto the king. Cosmo felt their gaze but dared not meet them, instead focusing on the words spoken, nodding slowly.

What harm could it do?

Perhaps simply sending out this Captain Agron and his men would send a message: the Commune's laws, *his* laws, must be obeyed. Yes, this was the right decision; the certainty flowed through him, warm and comforting to his tired, aching body.

"Very well," he said. "Do what must be done."

The Grand Magister rubbed his hands together. "Excellent, Your Highness," he said. "Perhaps some more wine to celebrate? We are in control. We will show those who would fight against us what it means to betray your benevolent wisdom."

Cosmo held his glass up to be refilled. Had there been something he meant to bring up with the Grand Magister? If there had, it had slipped from his mind.

No matter. I have done what my kingdom needs. I act only for Septima's people, for what is best.

He beamed with pride, holding his wine aloft. "For Septima." And if he noticed in that moment that neither the Grand Magister nor Captain Agron were drinking anything, he scarcely had a mind to be concerned about it.

He was King Cosmo Septimus, after all. A sign of respect, he had no doubt. They deferred to him in all matters.

ACKNOWLEDGMENTS

Well, where to start? It feels like it's been a bit of a long, complicated road to get here, but I'm so excited to now be releasing this second book in The Commune's Curse series—even if it's not the way I thought it would be, back when Awakening (Book 1) released in May '22.

So, here goes. Thank you—

To my husband, Ross, for his ongoing support (AKA occupying our toddler so I can have time/space/the mental capacity to write).

To my dear friend, Cindy, who read the first draft of this book way back when it was first written, and gave me such helpful feedback—and for always giving support in my writing/allowing me to rant about the struggles of being an author.

To my fantastic beta readers: Lydia, Isa, Dominic, Matthew, David and Jennifer. Each of you gave me valuable insights, feedback, and thoughts that made *The Mad Man's Hope* that much stronger.

To Trudie, for the self-publishing advice. I'm certain I wouldn't have been able to work it all out without you!

To my developmental editor, Crystle Pishon, for the amazing edits and advice you gave me. Another step to make this book what it is now. You're awesome!

To my copy editor, Jennia D'Lima, who went above and beyond in polishing this book up, and giving some last minute insights to tighten it even further. It was wonderful working with you.

And to my readers: I sincerely appreciate you picking up this book and giving my series a chance. I hope you enjoy the journeys of Evelyn, Raif, Hector, and Jonah.

ABOUT THE AUTHOR

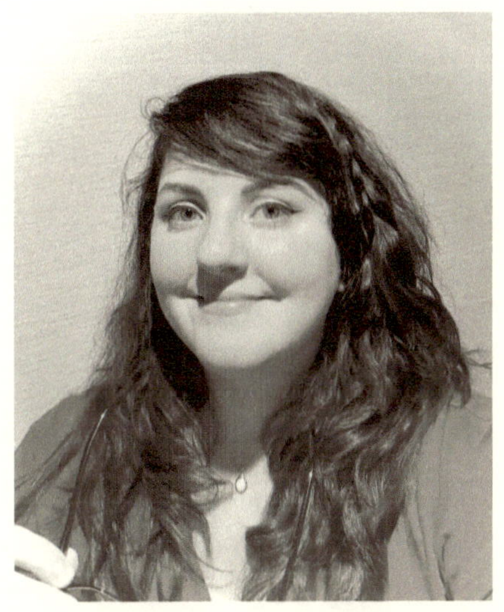

Lucy A. McLaren is a fantasy author and professional counsellor, passionate about writing stories that include a realistic representation and exploration of mental health issues. She is a lifelong fan of fantasy stories, and enjoys reading, writing, watching, and playing them (when she's not wrangling her toddler and husband). McLaren's debut novel, Awakening: The Commune's Curse Book 1, released from Santa Fe Writers Project in May 2022.